What Was I Thinking?

What Was I Thinking?

Camille Moore

To order additional copies of this book, contact:
Xlibris Corporation
1-888-795-4274
www.Xlibris.com
Orders@Xlibris.com
44235

Dedication

I want to thank everyone who supported me and gave me the words of encouragement needed to move forward and actually publish this book. Descaro, my loving, supportive, forgiving husband, I truly thank God everyday for you. You truly are a gift. My babes Diara and Nyere, I live to make you guys happy. Mommy, I couldn't have asked for a better mom, I love you so much. Grandma you helped make me who I am today, thank you. My Grandfather, Ralph Blacke, I miss you so much. Daddy, I love you. Most importantly, thank you God, for loving me and blessing me.

The Big Day

Staring in the mirror, I had to admit that I had never looked more beautiful. I was a little pale, but that was only because it was spring, so my skin hadn't had a chance to get that golden brown with a hint of red that it gets from the hot Philly summer sun. That was one thing I truly hated about winter. By January, I was always back to my natural yellow skin tone. Not that there was anything wrong with being high yellow, but caramel looked so much better on me.

I had let my hair grow just for this day. I had worn it short for years, except the times when I was in my long luxurious moods. When that occurred, I just ran out to get some twelve-inch Micro Yaky Permed hair and made an appointment at the salon. It was as simple as that. Believe me, I could wear some hair, but anyway back to the day and the reason I have my own long hair.

My dress was stunning not an old-fashion wedding gown like some women wear. It was me all the way. Sexy but elegant, fitted but not tight, simple, yet dazzling. The arms were sheer, and there were small pearls scattered throughout the sleeves. The dress had a boat neck and was sheer all across the top until it got to my bust line, where there was beautiful white satin. Yes, I said white. It fit every curve of my size-ten shape as it flared out at the bottom. I made sure to have a detachable train so I could get my groove on at the reception. My headpiece sat on top of the beautiful ribbon curls that were pinned in place ever so perfectly by my one and only Tamera. She was one of the best hairstylists I'd ever seen and my motto was always have the best. Why settle if you don't have to?

I didn't wear much make-up. It was never really my style, which was probably why my skin stayed so smooth. Since I turned nineteen, I have always worn a fake mole over my upper left lip. I just thought it was sexy. My mole is so much a part of me that I wanted to get it permanently tattooed, but my sister

Traci, convinced me not to since I might not always want it, so I never did. My full African American lips were often traced with a nice lip liner, depending on what I had on with the perfect shade of lipstick, Mac of course. It's funny, I was now proud to have these full lips, but I can remember how much I hated them growing up. Back then, full lips or as the boys called them, big lips, were, not an asset. But I bet some of the same boys who said I had big lips yesterday would kill to be all over these full lips today.

I batted my 109 lashes over my dark brown eyes and took one last look in the mirror at Anya Dennings. I hoped no one would make me cry during the ceremony because the glue would get wet and make my lashes lift, so no matter what happened, there would be absolutely no crying.

Traci stared at me through the mirror. "You look amazing," she said grabbing my hand.

"Are you sure about this?" I didn't even look at her. I just nodded, took a deep breath and turned from the mirror.

There was a knock on the door as it opened. "Okay girls. Line up. We're about ready!" We all quickly grabbed hands and my sister said a quick but meaningful prayer. She was good for that. After the prayer, she turned and hugged me real tight, she couldn't kiss me since I couldn't go down the aisle with lipstick on the cheek you know.

Everyone left the room and there I was with my perfection, my thoughts and God, the three things I didn't want to face at the moment. I'd ignore perfection and continue to be a slave to it and go out there and have the perfect wedding and live the perfect life as I had done for so long. I couldn't think because my brain might actually be working, and since God knows me so well anyway, he can deal with me later.

I was startled by another knock on the door. My coordinator came back in, told me how beautiful I looked, put my train over her arm and said, "You're up." I didn't have butterflies in my stomach like I did with my first husband; I just felt kind of nauseous. I reached over and downed one more glass of champagne, fixed my lipstick and headed for the rest of my life.

The traditional wedding march was not me, but this was Michael's wedding too, so I agreed to walk in to that horrible Dun Dun Dun Dun. Still makes me sick just thinking about it. The church we had selected was beautiful, but why did the hall have to be so long? I felt hot all over and had begun to sweat. As I got closer to those huge double doors, the music got louder and I felt every note of that organ grab my heart. I looked up and saw my grandfather standing there in his tux waiting for me. He was always there for me, and I loved him like he was my real dad. I put my arm through his as I faced the altar. It seemed like there were a million people at the church. I wanted to have a quiet small ceremony, but this was Michael's first wedding and he was so happy that he wanted to share it with everyone he knew. Being who he was, I guess he had a certain obligation to the people he'd known and worked with. Believe me, I know a lot about being obligated after all, I was there right. Twelve weeks ago five hundred invitations had gone out and we had received 423 affirmative responses, and from the looks of it, everyone had shown up dressed in their wedding best. What kind of crap is that?

I looked at all the blurred, smiling faces, and by the time I got to the thirteenth row, I was numb. I knew I was walking down the aisle, but I felt like I was hovering over my body watching the whole ceremony. A thousand things were running through my mind, and I still had not been able to so much as glance at Michael. I looked through him, and I hoped he couldn't tell. I thought I looked as if I was suppose to, if for no other reason, the pictures and the video. I know it sounds terrible, but I'm serious. It took forever, but I finally made it to the end of that aisle.

"Who gives this women to be wed?" the preacher said.

"I do," my grandfather said.

The preacher nodded, and Michael came down five steps to get his beautiful loving new half. He leaned over and whispered, "I love you" as we walked up the stairs. "I know," I said. "I know." He held my hand and gazed at me as if he had been wondering through a maze looking for happiness and fulfillment his whole life and at this very moment, realized I had the map.

"Michael and Anya have decided to recite their own vows," the pastor announced. What he should have said is "Michael wants the world to know how he feels about Anya and wants to recite the vows he's written, but Anya would prefer to just say the standard wedding vows and just fill in the I do's." Don't get me wrong. Michael was wonderful, almost too wonderful. What a complaint, huh? My point exactly. That's why I'm here.

Michael looked at me to say his vows, and I could see the love in his eyes, and though it spoke to my emotions, it couldn't reach my heart, which quite frankly, I was still trying to figure out if it belonged to someone else.

"Anya, today I feel as if the Lord has taken a piece of sunshine and put it inside of me and warmed me. The day I met you, my life changed, and it has not been the same since. I never believed in perfection until day after day you became a part of my life. Today, I take you as my wife as an outward statement of the love, respect and honor I have for you. I will take every day of my life to make sure that your life is without worry, pain, sadness, and fear. Anytime you feel those things, I will attempt to replace them with peace, wholeness, joy and security because I love you."

"Anya. Anya your turn" the pastor said.

I hesitated then I looked up at Michael, and I knew he loved us enough for both of us.

"Michael, from the day I met you, I knew there was something different about you, but who knew that I would be standing here committing my life to you? You have loved me in a way that has never caused me to mistrust you, and I needed that. I love you because you believe in me and you . . . ."

Before I could finish my sentence the church doors flew open and a voice cried out, "Wait, please wait." I could hear the tears in the man's voice and I wondered why my life could never run smooth. This is my life, welcome to it.

Everybody turned to see the idiot who actually believed it was legal to stop a wedding in real life. I probably would be crying and cheering the guy who burst through the doors if this were a movie, but it wasn't. It was my life and at that very moment, I wished it belonged to someone else.

"Anya," the voice pleaded, "what are you doing? You did this to me once. Please don't do it again. Wasn't one wrong man enough? You and I both know he's not the one you really love, the one you really want to spend the rest of your life with."

My Lord he looked good even frustrated and half crying, there was no getting around it. Julian was a chocolate fantasy come to life. Ok, but this was no time to think about that, I needed to stay focused on the catastrophe at hand.

"Man what are you doing? Anya who is this?" Michael asked.

I pleaded with my eyes for him to leave, but he remained.

"Julian, please don't do this. Just leave. It's not worth it. Why are you doing this?" My heart felt as if someone had snatched it out, along with my lungs too, because as Julian turned and walked away, I couldn't breathe.

We attempted to recover from the disruption, but Michael saw it all over my face. The pastor asked me to finish my vows, but I couldn't, so he filled in for me. "Anya, do you take Michael to be your husband, to love and cherish till death do you part?" I knew at that very moment I couldn't say no, but I couldn't quite get a yes out either. I just stood there, my tears like streams of fire trailing down my face. My heart was beating fast, and I wanted to pass out on that altar and wake up somewhere else, but unfortunately, my life isn't that good. I looked over at my sister, the tears burned my eyes to the point that she was a blur.

My sister, who had been my sister my entire life, betrayed me in front of everyone. "I love you and I love Michael, and you know I love Julian, but I told you to deal with Julian four months ago." OUCH!!! Then Kim, my best friend, stood next to my sister and just shook her head in disbelief. Uh I'm sorry, but weren't they supposed to automatically be on my side?

At that very moment, I realized that maybe the Lord hadn't completely healed me from the dysfunctional relationship I called marriage that I had forced myself to enjoy for five years. I was still clinging to love and the idea of it. Deep in my heart, I'd known since I was thirteen years old that Julian was who I'd loved. I think. He knew me better than any man and still loved me in spite of myself.

I said sorry, because I really was as I removed Michael's ring, picked up the train of my four-thousand dollar dress and ran to the dressing room. I felt like hell. I locked the door behind me as I stormed the dressing room. I locked everyone out and locked myself in with God. I know, a little late for that, but better late than never, right?

Like I said, welcome to my life. Before I go on, let me take a moment to bring you up to speed.

My First Big Mistake

I had met my first husband John, my last year of college, and he was wonderful, but aren't most men in the beginning? He was a few years older than I was, and I think that's probably what won me over. I was so tired of playing the dating game with the men my age. I can't even count the number of immature dogs I had dated between high school and college. Trust me half of them I try to forget. The only one worth keeping had been Julian, and I blew that big time.

John was different though I can still remember the day we met like it was yesterday. I was downtown paying a parking ticket, and I saw him out the corner of my eye. He was about five-eleven, maybe 220 pounds and as sexy as any man modeling a suit for Armani. His skin was dark chocolate, and when he smiled his perfect white teeth complemented that beautiful smile that needed no assistance in the first place.

I'm normally not an obvious flirt, but I couldn't help it. I had to do something to get this man's attention. I had already had everyone else's Mr. Wrong including my own, I had to take a chance, after all he might be the one.

As I walked away from the window, I pulled one of the oldest tricks in the book, praying he would fall for it. God knows I was praying. As he stood talking to the security guard, I dropped my receipt as I walked past him. I kept walking, but slowed to a stroll, giving him time to notice the paper, pick it up and catch me. It didn't work. I should have taken that as a sign, but nooooo, not me. I got outside wondering why this fool didn't pick up my paper and give it to me. I looked behind me, and he was still yapping with the security guard. I went back through the door, and as I opened it, I saw my receipt blow towards him. "Excuse me," I said. "I believe that's my receipt by your foot. I must have dropped it. Would you mind handing it to me?"

He arrogantly looked down by his foot, picked up the receipt and handed it to me.

"Thank you," I said with a fat attitude. Who did he think he was?

At that point, it didn't even matter. The challenge was on. I mean he looked good and all, but so did I.

I took a moment to fold the paper and put it in my purse. As I stood there, I let my left knee bend a little to open the split in my long black skirt, which I'd worn instead of my normal college gear. As I turned and headed for the door, I glanced back, cut my eyes and gave the smile, you know the one that says your turn.

"Oh" he said, "Let me get the door for you. Hey, I'll catch you later, Fred."

"Alright," Fred said. "You be careful with that one." He chuckled.

"Be careful with this one", I said, "How many do you have?"

"That's just Fred being Fred." He smirked

"Umm-Hum. Right"

"Really." he said.

"Hey, I'm just a girl with a lost receipt. You don't have to explain anything to me," I said flirtatiously. "Thanks again. You have a good day." I gave my sexy smile, turned and switched away.

"Hey, umm excuse me. I didn't get your name." Got em. If only I had known exactly what I was getting, I would curse the day I ever parked illegally to get some fish.

"Anya."

"Well, Miss Anya, I was wondering if maybe I could call you sometime."

"Umm, I guess that would be alright. Now you aren't married or don't have a girlfriend or anything else I need to be aware of do you?"

"No. The fact is I don't have a lot of time to date. My career keeps me pretty busy." I took out a piece of paper, wrote my home number on it and gave it to him.

"When should I call?" he asked.

"Whenever you like," I said, implying the sooner, the better.

When I got home, I checked my messages. Surprise, surprise, a call from the one and only John Thomas.

"Hi Anya," oooh, I just loved the way he said my name, with his sexy voice. "this is John Thomas. I met you today outside the courthouse. You said I could call whenever I like and I like right now, so please give me a call when you get in. I would like to see you again as soon as it can be arranged. My work number is 633-2100, and my home number is 741-8158"

"Umm, girl, who was that?" my roommate and best friend Kim asked as she stood in my door listening.

"Girl, don't trip. Just this fine chocolate bar I met today when I was downtown paying that parking ticket."

"How fine?"

"Too fine to put into words."

"Try."

"Girl get out of here."

"Ain't you gon' call Mr. Goodbar back?"

"Not yet. I've got to make him wait just a little bit. Dang. I don't wanna seem all desperate."

"But you are." She laughed.

"Shut up and get outta here." I playfully threw one of the pillows from my bed at her.

Later that night, I called Mr. Thomas back, but his voicemail picked up. "Hey, John, this is Anya. I got your message. Give me a call when you get in."

Fifteen minutes later my phone rang.

"Hello."

"Hi, Anya. Its John."

"Oh, hey. What's up?"

"I was in the shower when you called. What are you doing?"

"Nothing really. Just finishing up this paper I was working on for school."

"Oh, so you're still in school?"

"Yes. I'll be graduating in two months though with a degree in psychology, but I also studied interior design, and that's what I'm going to pursue. So what do you do, Mr. Your Career Keeps You So Occupied?"

"I'm a lawyer. I work for Smith and Associates. I'm the youngest black lawyer with the firm, so I make sure I handle my business."

"Umm, I'm impressed." In my mind, I was thinking I really was impressed. John was a real-live grownup with a real job.

"Anyway, I was wondering if you hadn't eaten yet if you'd like to grab something."

"At ten O'clock? I don't think so." I don't know what he was thinking calling me so late to go somewhere with him, like I knew him like that.

"Well how about this Friday?"

"Friday sounds good. About what time?"

"I'm thinking around eight, but I'll call you Friday while I'm at work to tell you how my day is going. That way I can be sure."

"Okay that sounds good. I'll talk to you then." I said before I hung up.

Well Friday came, and John called like he said he would. He got ten points for that alone. I was surprised he hadn't forgotten who I was by then. He even came at eight O'clock like he had planned. We went to an authentic Italian restaurant. I happen to love Italian food. We talked for hours and John made me laugh till I couldn't laugh anymore. It was great. He was very arrogant, but for some reason his arrogance and confidence turned me on even more.

We continued to date for the next several weeks and it was wonderful. He would say and do all the right things, and it didn't hurt that he was a successful black attorney. Even though he was spending a lot of time with me, he just seemed like a ho. I hate to say it, but I had that feeling. Of course I had no proof but I was no dummy. I knew I had a good thing, and I was holding on to it.

One night it finally happened, I got a little evidence. Kim and I were coming from the movies, and I saw John with some woman sitting at the bar of a café.
"Aren't you going to say something," Kim asked.
"No. I don't have time to be trippin. I have finals next week, and I can't afford any stress."

As Kim and I were walking down that street, I just couldn't let it go. Some kind of force was making me go back, so I did. I watched John for a moment through the glass, trying to figure out what I should say. I didn't want him to think I didn't trust him, but at the same time, I wanted to know who this woman was. As Kim got ready to walk in the door, I grabbed her arm and asked her to wait. I wanted to see if John's body language gave me any indication of who the woman was. She couldn't possibly be a client, not at ten o'clock at night and not sitting at a bar with that tighter than saran wrap sweater, that barely covered her breasts, which by the way were screaming to get out of that too-little bra.

Then it happened, John leaned in, put his arm around her waist and whispered something in her ear. Something extremely pleasant by the look of the smile it left of her face for the next three minutes. She picked up her glass, swallowed the last of her drink and motioned with her eyes that she was ready. I had all kinds of butterflies in my stomach as John got closer to the door. I wanted to run but I didn't. I took a deep breath, and as he got to the door, I opened it. Talkin' about buying somebody for a penny, I could have gotten him for free that night.

"Hi sweetheart," I said as I grabbed his hand and kissed him ever so softly on his lips. I looked down just in time to see him drop his other hand from the mystery woman. "What are you doing here?" I questioned. My expression said I could just slap the you-know-what-out of him, but I was refraining so as not to embarrass myself. Believe me, it took all my strength not to do it. All his stupid butt could do was stand there. Eventually he told me the woman was his friend, somebody he worked with, and they just decided to get a drink after work. As sorry and as tired as his excuse was, I let it go. I think it was to prove I was the one, the winner.

He introduced me to Jennifer, and I kindly told her I didn't buy any of the lawyer bull they were selling and if I ever caught her anywhere outside of work with John again, I wouldn't be as polite. She would curse the day she ever decided to go to law school, let alone take a job at Smith & Associates. She gave a little nervous grin and I smiled and told her to have a good night. As she walked down the street, John got ready to say something to her, but I pinched his arm and dared him to.

After one year and two months of arguments and stress, I finally decided it was time to get out. I really cared about John, but I couldn't take the lies and the mistrust. Although he ended things with Jennifer, after awhile there were many more women and so many different stories, that they may as well have all been named Jennifer. What difference does a name make? I seriously began feeling as if something were wrong with me. Why could I not keep him satisfied enough not to desire to be with other women? It's not even like he had an occasional slip-up here and there. This was a constant battle, and for some reason his smooth, sweet-talking self always managed to make me forgive him. I guess that's why Smith and Associates paid him so well. I love you, I'm sorry and jewelry could only make up for so much when there is no change in behavior. So I called it quits.

I was depressed at first. Maybe I just didn't want to be alone. Two days later I found myself debating whether I should call John. Thank God for roommates because if I lived alone, I probably would have called his sorry butt.

I was sitting in the living room listening to Anita Baker a couple of days after my breakup with John when Kim came in the door, asking if I was okay. "Enough. You haven't been to work since you and John broke up. You haven't even been off this couch, but it's Friday night and we going out for drinks." She said. "Forget that fool. There are too many more of em' out there. This from a girl it took four years to break up with a fool who had not only one but two kids while they were together, and neither of them were with her. In spite of that, I knew she was right. I had to get out of this funk before I had no job, no life and before I was too bitter to even get another man.

I got up off the couch, went to the kitchen, poured myself a glass of wine and dragged myself upstairs to run a hot bubble bath. I stayed in there almost two hours because even though Kim was right, getting up was still hard to do. I could hear Kim talking to me, but it was like everything she said was as foggy as the steam in the bathroom. Her banging on the door brought me back to reality.

"Come on girl get you butt out of there and let's go eat and have a couple shots of tequila." Tequila I thought.

"This ain't got nothing to do with me and John's breakup." I hollered to her, but she didn't hear. I reached next to the tub, picked up my phone, and called her line.

"Hello."

"Kim."

"Girl what do you want? Just get your butt out that tub and get dressed so we can go."

"Okay I will, but not until you tell me the real reason we're going out for some dang gone tequila shots."

"That's why I can't stand you. Just come on. I'll tell you in the car." She slammed down the phone.

As I was getting dressed, my phone rang. I wasn't going to answer it but I figured I couldn't hide forever. Big mistake. It was John crying those fake tears, with that I'm sorry, I miss you, I need you. Not this time. I had a drawerful of his sorrys and his love. I just hung up while he was still talking. The phone rang again six more times, and deep down I was glad John called, just not glad enough to go back.

I continued trying to get ready, but it was as if I had lost who I was. I could hardly put an outfit together. Nothing looked right, felt right or fit right, it was worse than being on my period. Finally after only six tries, I pulled it together and was physically ready to go, not emotionally, but physically.

In the car I finally found out the real reason we needed tequila. Kim had quit her job that day to go into business for herself. She was a florist, a good one, and unfortunately no one wanted to pay her what she was worth. She found out her loan had been approved for her to start her business. It had all happened so fast that now she was scared. I wasn't though. I knew she could do it.

I was glad I had gone out I needed some fresh air, and fresh air is exactly what I got, a nice chocolate breeze.

The Chocolate Breeze

As we were pulling up to the restaurant, five guys were standing by a car talking. One of them caught my attention in such a way that I am still embarrassed to this day. I mean the man was so fine, so chocolate, so delicious that my mouth literally fell open as I gazed at this chocolate temptation. For a minute I forgot who or what a John was. As we drove past, everything seemed to be moving in slow motion, and all I could say was "Dannnnng!" as I squinted and attempted to catch my breath. My window was down, and he heard me. I was embarrassed, but not for long. It seemed that my dramatic entrance into the parking lot drew him to me.

Kim and I were headed to the door when my chocolate breeze walked toward us and said, "Excuse me. Uhhh, can I talk to you for a minute?"

"I guess so," I said. He was kind of short, although not shorter than me, just about my height or a half an inch taller, five-six maybe. He was a little thugged out, but very well put together. His hair was cut nice and low and that goatee complemented his face. It was extremely sexy. His walk was even sexy. I was trying to pull it together but I must admit, he had me.

"Oh, you guess? The way you were just looking at me, I thought you knew."

"Cute, real cute." I said.

"Anyway, what's your name?"

"Anya," I answered, looking him over and thinking, dang this is one I have to have. There is no getting around it. there is no way I can pass this up.

"Umm Anya, I like that." he lifted his right eyebrow and looked me straight in my eyes, with this sexy half smile. "So Anya, How might I contact you so we can hook up sometime? That is if you don't have a man."

I had given him so much already. I had to pull back just a little. Smiling, I explained I had just gotten out of a serious relationship and that there was

18

a chance that we might work things out, so I thought it was too soon to really start dating again.

"Oh, is that right? Like that? Well listen, why don't I give you my number, just in case y'all don't hook back up then I can take you out to celebrate."

"Celebrate what?"

"You making a better choice this time around," he said grinning. I took his number, put it in my purse as I walked away.

"Girl, I can't help it. I've got to have him," I told Kim as we walked in the double doors. "I only thought God made angels that beautiful."

She stopped dead in her tracks. "You got to have everybody. That's your problem now. You just had to have John too, and look how that turned out. How soon we forget."

She was right, but I couldn't stop thinking about him all that night. After three shots of tequila and chicken fettuccini, I wanted to go home and call him, but Kim said it was too soon. Deep down I knew it was, but I didn't care. You have to understand, he was something else, a sexy little thug, I hadn't had one of those since high school. So of course, what did I do? I called him when I got home. It was a pager of course, but that was alright. I paged him and even used the little code #02 he wrote on the paper. Surprisingly he called back and really remembered who he had given the number.

I had never asked him his name and he didn't write it on the paper, so that was my excuse for calling.

"Quit frontin'. You know you called 'cause you wanted to talk to me, but it's Anthony."

Man he was arrogant, but I liked it. It was sexy, and that spirit was always my downfall.

"Ayyy, what you doing right now?" he asked.

"I'm sitting here talking to you. What do you think I'm doing at eleven o'clock, having a party?"

"I'm about to come get you," he said, like he knew me and I was really about to go somewhere by myself with this man I had met only a few hours ago.

"Uhh, I don't think so," I said in a tone that said are you crazy? I don't know you. But I guess I wasn't quite strong enough or either my stupid powers had taken over because eventually I said okay.

Twenty-five minutes later, my phone rang. "Hey, I'm outside your spot."

"Yes," I said, "and I'm inside, so if you want me to come outside where you are, you had better come ring my doorbell."

"Man, quit trippin' and come on."

"I'm not trippin'. I'm serious." It had been a long time since I had broken the thug out of a man, and I enjoyed the challenge.

"Aw here you go. Alright. What number is it again?"

That's right I thought, I am not one of your little hoochies, and you will respect me. I was really hoping he would too because I wanted this one so bad I could taste him. The doorbell rang, and I ran down the stairs of the town house Kim and I shared and opened the door. My God he looked even better than he did earlier. Where did this man come from?

Where exactly are you taking me?"

"I was thinking we could just go have a drink or something." It was the "or something" I was worried about.

"To tell you the truth, I had a few drinks at dinner, and I'm cool. I can make you a drink here if you want."

"That sounds cool."

So that's just what I did. I took his jacket and poured him a glass of wine. That turned out to be the wrong answer. He thought I was going to make him a real drink, I guess, but me and Kim weren't real drinkers, so all we had was wine. He offered to go to the store and get some Tanqurey, which happened to be his favorite drink. I began to think maybe this wasn't such I good idea, so I told him we'd try this again another night. Besides it was getting late. He was cool with that. He stayed another twenty minutes, and we just kind of talked about nothing. He asked if he could take me to the movies and dinner the next night so I said sure. At least that was closer to a date than him sitting on my couch at midnight. I walked him to the door and told him I looked forward to seeing him the next day. He sized me up with those eyes of his.

"Huh, yea me too." He said seductively. Umm the man gave me chills.

I went upstairs to get in bed, two seconds later here comes Kim. She felt that I shouldn't have let him come over so late because he was going to think I was a ho. I didn't get that feeling, and besides, I wasn't so who cared.

I deleted all the messages on my answering machine. John's beggin' butt. Oh, he was really out of the picture now. I had found just the thing to help me get over him. As I lay in the bed, I asked the Lord to heal my heart. John had done so much damage, and I just wanted the pain to be gone. I was kind of missing John when the phone rang, I almost didn't answer it for fear it was him again.

"Hello." It was Anthony, he wanted me to talk to him on his way home. I know he had just left and it was kind of corny. He was probably just trying to lay the groundwork to get some, but I was sprung.

The next morning I paged him, just to say hi. This time, I didn't punch my number in, I just left a voicemail, telling him that I was thinking about him and telling him I couldn't wait to see his chocolatety good self. He called back and said he was thinking about me too. He asked if I wanted to go to breakfast. Of course I said yes.

I got out the tub and lotioned down real good. I shaved the little stubble under my arms and my bikini line. I wasn't planning on giving him any. I just felt good that day. I ironed some jeans but put on a nice shirt and some cute shoes so I wouldn't look like I was trying hard to impress him. I threw on just a little eyeliner, added my ever-faithful mole and a little lip liner with a gloss topped off with a layer of lip glass. Ahhh, for the final touch, a few sprays of Issy Miyake. Its scent is light but it smells so good on me. Just as I was changing purses, the phone rang. It was Anthony. He said he was almost there and wanted to know if I was ready. I was, but I played it off so I didn't seem too eager.

About ten minutes later, the doorbell rang.

"You look cute," he said.

"Thanks. You saying a little something yourself." It wasn't just the tequila from the night before. Anthony was an eyeful. I ran back upstairs to grab my purse and my pager, and we were on our way.

He had a pretty nice car, a new dark blue 5.0, and of course he had all that loud music hooked up in his car, which I could not stand. He use to hate for me to get in his car because he knew all that bump in the trunk he paid for was going to waste when I sat down.

Anthony and I went out every single night for the next eight nights. He loved movies for some reason, and they were cool but did we have to go four times in one week? We would go eat every day after I got off work, and we would laugh and talk for hours and hours. Even when he would drop me off, we would sit in front of my place and talk for another hour or two. He made me feel so special, and when he wasn't with me, he was calling. He built up a trust I didn't have with John. I know it had only been a week, and that early in a relationship everyone is on their best behavior, but Anthony was different. I don't know what it was, but I liked it, I liked it a lot.

Kim kept saying I needed to slow down, that Anthony and I were spending way too much time together, but I couldn't. In just a week he had become a part of me. About a week and a half after I had met Anthony I was at my sister's house and she was asking how things were going with John being out of the picture. I explained that I really hadn't had time to miss him since I had been spending so much time with Anthony. She looked at me, and immediately she nailed me.

"Girl I know you did not give that boy some already."

I didn't say nothin'. What could I say, especially since I had? I looked at it like this: most people date once a week for about eight to ten weeks before they do it. Well I had gone out with Anthony every single night for eleven nights before I gave him some, so that's the same as two months, right? My sister just looked at me. I could tell she disapproved but she couldn't do anything but laugh at my logic. "Where did you get that crap, Hoeology 101?" she said, crackin' up. "Girl, what am I going to do with you? You didn't even give John none for almost six months."

"That's because I really liked John and with him being an attorney and making all that good money with his fine self, he was a prospective husband. I had to hold out. I didn't want him to think I was a ho." Besides, it's different with Anthony. I can just be myself. I don't have to be John Thomas's perfect girlfriend. If things don't work out with Anthony, it ain't going to be no big deal. We just kickin' it."

"Well you might as well tell me about it since you done already gave it up," she said smiling. I could hardly put it into words. I leaned back against the counter and just smiled. "It began very innocently. We were at his place after the show the night before last talking about my job and how much I wanted to start my own interior design business. Not that I didn't like working for my boss Asha, and she paid me well, but I just wanted my own. I knew I wasn't ready though, I still had a great deal to learn about the business, and I was grateful to be working with and learning from Asha. I had worked my way from assistant to one of her lead decorators in just a little over a year. This was a great accomplishment, and I was proud of it. I had always had an eye for decorating and only went to school to expand my gift. I was glad I had gone, too, because if I hadn't, there was no way Asha would have even interviewed me.

Anyway, we were talking about my job and my dreams, but he never really wanted to talk about his. All I knew was that Anthony had his own janitorial business, and I guess that's all I really wanted to know right then because before I knew it, we were kissing and not doing too much talking, then he began to undress me, and as much as I wanted to hold out, I couldn't. It was too right, and it wasn't the wine. He would whisper extremely erotic things in my ear, things I had never done but wanted to experience the way he said them. He was a straight freak, but I liked it. I tried to play it off, but my protests were so weak, we both had to laugh. Anthony knew how to seduce a woman, and seduced I was. I was slobbering at the mouth and trying to hold myself together just telling my sister about it.

"Girl, you better be careful," my sister said, looking at me out the corner of her eye with a half-disapproving smile.

"Oh, I'm cool, but girl I can't get over it. I ain't never had no sex that good in my life." A chill ran through me just thinking about him. Whew . . .

Well things were going pretty well with me and Anthony. We spent so much time together we became sickening to everyone around us, but who cared? We were in our own little world, and it was safe there, and we loved it. He began taking me to and from work and by the fourth week I was practically living with him. I don't know what happened or how it happened, but if it wasn't love, I was enjoying whatever it was.

Then the blow came, and I knew at that very moment, I had to be on God's hit list, if I wasn't, how could this be happening? I had been feeling kind of sluggish and passed out at work. Well, I'm sure with that in mind the next sentence will be no shock. Yes, I was pregnant, thirteen weeks. I couldn't believe what was happening. I only remembered missing one period. What was going on? I was so mad. I had never believed in abortion until that very day. I sat in the doctor's office in tears, begging her to tell me there was a mistake. She even retested me just to calm me down, but the stupid test still came back the same, positive. I wanted to scream. I wanted to wake and say, "I had the craziest dream," but I couldn't because it wasn't a dream. Once again, this was my life.

I didn't know if I should tell John. After all, we weren't together anymore, and if I didn't keep the baby he would be none the wiser. I guess I would have to tell Anthony and just hope he would understand. When Anthony picked me up from the doctor, he could see something wrong all over my face. It's like he knew me so well, but how could he? He didn't know me at all, did he?

"Baby, what's wrong?" He had this kind of worried look as if I really meant the world to him. "Is everything alright?" I just sat there numb, not saying anything as the cars drove past in slow motion. The air felt thick, I could hardly breathe. Everything felt so surreal. Anthony finally pulled the car over. "Okay you're scaring me. What did your doctor say?"

"Oh damn, Anthony, I'm pregnant," I said as I broke down in tears. I felt like running, but there was nowhere to go. I was trapped by the choices I had made.

"Are you sure?" he questioned. "I mean we used something every time. We've been so careful." Oh my God, I thought, this idiot thinks it's his.

"No Anthony, I'm three months."

"But, he began with confusion on his face. Then it was as if everything became clear to him.

"Oh it's not my baby huh?"

"No," I said very sarcastically, "it's not."

What happened next, surprised me. He had a look of relief but disappointment at the same time. He grabbed my hand and rubbed it. "Don't worry. We'll get through this, so quit talking to me like I'm the enemy, alright?" I wonder how long that was going to last.

"Anya, Anya, look at me." I didn't want to look at him. I felt so stupid and ashamed. I don't know why though. John and I had been together for more than a year. But isn't that how it always went, you get pregnant when the relationship is over?

"Anya, just trust me. It's gonna work out," he said as he grabbed my hand, looked to the left and pulled back into the flow of traffic.

"Just take me home, Anthony, please." I sighed.

"But Anya."

"No, Anthony," I cut him off. "I don't wanna talk or even look at you or myself right now, so please don't say anything. Just please take me home."

"Okay. I'm done."

I had decided that it would probably be better for me to stay at my house that night because I was experiencing a bunch of emotions and couldn't contain them. I definitely didn't want to continue to take them out on Anthony. I wanted to tell Kim but I knew if I did I would start to cry all over again, so I just acted normal when I walked in the door.

"I can't believe it. I thought you forgot where you lived," she said, laughing. "What happened? Did you kill the poor man or does your coochie need a break?" I wished that was the problem.

"Girl, shut up." I tried to laugh. "I just felt like coming home. I've been spending way too much time at Anthony's house, and I don't want to get too attached. I'm getting ready to go upstairs and soak in the tub. I'll talk to you later."

"Yeah, go soak that coochie," she said, snickering.

"Anya," she called as I walked away.

"Huh?"

"Is everything is okay?"

"Yeah girl couldn't be better."

"Then why are you home? You didn't even spend this much time at John's house and y'all were together over a year. You've been happier than I've ever seen you, and I'm suppose to really believe you just felt like being at home. I don't think so."

"Drop it Kim. Just let it go," I yelled, went into my room and locked my bedroom door, which is something I hardly ever do, but I knew she wouldn't drop it. I knew she was going to come in my room and grill me, and trust me, I was in no mood to be grilled. I hadn't opened my bathroom door and turned the water on good before I heard her at my bedroom door questioning why I had locked it? I put on Luther and closed my bathroom door. I wanted to shut everything and everyone out. The reality of my situation was settling in more and more by the minute. I blasted the radio in hopes of escaping, but I couldn't. I couldn't go anywhere that the baby inside of me wouldn't follow.

I sat in the tub for over an hour, continuing to run more hot water in the tub every time it would start to cool down, then my phone rang. I just knew it was Kim. I pressed talk, "Kim", I said, "I'm fine and I don't want to talk." To my surprise, it was Anthony. He just wanted to make sure I was okay and to see if I needed anything. I told him I was fine and I just needed to decide what I was going to do. Apparently he hadn't given that any consideration. He just automatically assumed I was going to keep the baby. He said he didn't really want me to be without him. He was on his way to come get me. I didn't put up a fight because at that point I had no fight left in me.

I got out of the tub, still wet, and I lay on the bed staring at the ceiling. What was I suppose to do? My head began to ache from thinking so hard. Finally without putting on a drop of lotion, I dried off, threw on some sweats and packed a bag. I called Anthony and told him not to mention the baby to Kim because I hadn't told her.

"Are you sure you're alright baby? You don't sound good at all." How was I suppose to sound? My life had just come to a screeching halt and could be changed forever. I was so irritated that he was so calm about all this, it made me even more depressed. Where did he come from, the land of perfect?

About twenty minutes later, there was a knock on my bedroom door. "Anya baby, open the door." Anthony, grabbed my bag and we went downstairs. Kim was laying on the couch acting like she was reading a magazine. She just looked at me and shook her head. "I thought you were staying home," she said. "Look I don't know what's going on, but somebody better tell me something." Anthony looked at me and I looked at Kim. "You want me to go wait in the car?" he said. I nodded and told him I would be out in a minute. I looked over at Kim and just blurted it out. "I'm pregnant." She hit the roof, which I knew she would then she went into this speech about safe sex and how I had only known Anthony for a month.

"Now, if you're finished," I finally said, "first of all, you are not my mother. Second Anthony and I do practice safe sex and are very careful." She cut me off, saying it wasn't too safe since I was pregnant.

"It's not Anthony's, stupid. It's John's." That news just dropped her to the floor. "You have got to be kidding me," she said, looking even more disgusted than I felt. It's not that she didn't like John, but the bottom line was he was a dog, and she was glad when I finally decided I deserved better.

"Well what are you going to do?"

"I don't know yet."

"So Anthony knows?" I nodded. "What did he say?" She looked at me kind of scared to hear.

"Girl you won't believe this." I looked over at her, smiling. "He said and I quote, 'We'll get through this.' You see, he doesn't want me to be without him. Girl, he called while I was in the tub and said he was coming to get me because he did not want me to be by myself, knowing you were here."

"Umm girl, you better hold on to that one"

"You see my bag packed, right?" I said and smiled through my tears.

She got off the floor, hugged me and assured me that everything would be okay and no matter what I decided she would always be there. I told her I was sorry I didn't tell her when I first got home but I didn't feel like talking about it because I would get all emotional again like I was doing right then. Of course she understood. She was my best friend and had been since we were in the first grade.

The next morning, I called my boss Asha and told her I would be in a little late, but she told me not to come in since it was Friday and she knew I wasn't feeling well the day before. "Get some rest and be fresh for Monday. I need to see you early, too, because I need you to go to New York to meet with the Ellises within the next two weeks. They want you to do the brownstone they just purchased. You're moving up, kid." I loved Asha. She was the best boss, and she was always happy for people when they were doing well. She had really been a blessing in my life. The decorating business is so competitive that I was glad to work with a creative team that wasn't cutthroat. Everyone helped one another, and we made a great team. It really was like family, which I enjoyed, because my dad was killed in a car accident on his way home from work when I was eight. I might as well say I lost both my parents in that accident because it seemed like my mom died with him. She was never the same. My sister, Traci and I went to go live with my grandparents when I was ten. My mother still suffers from depression. For some reason, she just can't snap out of it. She loved my dad just that much.

I remember getting out of bed when I heard the doorbell ring and coming down the stairs and sitting right in the middle of them. My mom opened the door to two police officers. One of the officers took off his hat and said, "Mrs. Dennings?" before he could go on, my mom began to shake. My sister stepped over me and ran to my mom. "No", my mom screamed, "No I don't want to hear it." It was like as long as she didn't hear the actual words, then he would come home. Needless to say, he never did, and neither did she.

People always say I look like my dad, but I have my mother's smile. I'd be more than happy to give it back to her though if she'd use it.

At the funeral. My mom was so sad, it was all over her face. She didn't cry loud or anything and fall all out. She just sat there in my grandmother's arms, the tears steadily falling from her eyes onto her suit. Even in grief, with no make up she was beautiful. She just stared at my dad in a trans, under some type of spell, still under it too. Some kind of love spell. It was so weird. When they got ready to close the casket, my mother stood up, and walked over to my dad. She stood there looking down at him, her tears dropping on his face, then she leaned over into the casket and laid her face on his. She put her arms around him and pulled his lifeless body into her and wept. She loved him so much. Finally my grandmother went over to her, "That's enough baby. It's time to let go. He's with the Lord now." Those words were of no comfort to her, all she knew is he wasn't where she needed him to be, there with her.

She had two nervous breakdowns in the seven months to follow and by the third one, my grandma said it would be best for us to come stay with her and grandpa for a while. Awhile for turned into my third year of college.

I hardly see or talk to my mom, it's like we remind her too much of my dad and I guess her heart just can't take it. So I just leave her alone and face the fact that both my parents did die in that car accident that night. I guess I just hate that me and my sister weren't enough for her to live for. I wish she could have loved me as much as she loved my dad. I still love her though and I'm always hoping that one day, she will just come back, until then, I just think about all the good times we all had together before they died. To this day, she still sees a therapist, which is a waste of money, because they haven't fixed her yet.

She works at this art gallery now and has a different life I guess. A life that doesn't include my sister and I. One day I went to ask her to come to grandma's house the night of my high-school Senior Prom, so she could be there while I got ready and see me off. She wouldn't even talk to me, she took one look at me and began crying uncontrollably. She asked me to leave, she said her heart just couldn't take it, two days later, she was back in the psychiatric ward. That happens every time me or Traci try and go see her. She never dated anyone else after he died. I know my dad would not want her to live like this. She once said that she got married for life and she was getting married once and only once. She said my dad was the only man she would ever be able to love and one day when I fell in love, I would understand. But I don't ever want to love anyone that much.

My Choice

Maybe New York was what I needed, I could schedule my meeting with the Ellises for Thursday or Friday and just stay over for the weekend to think and regroup. I hung up the phone and went in the kitchen to tell Anthony. He was excited for me, as he always was whenever I shared my work accomplishments with him. I couldn't believe I had only known him for a month. It seemed like forever. I guess I wasn't on God's hit list after all.

"Aren't you going to work today?" I asked him. He shook his head and said he was staying with me. I told him I was fine and that he didn't have to, but he said he didn't mind and besides, he was the boss so he could. We went into the living room and I plopped down on his tan leather couch next to him. He put my legs on his lap and began rubbing my feet. For a minute I almost forgot there was a crisis.

"Oh Anthony," I blurted out, "what am I going to do?"

"Shhh. Don't think about it right now." "I have to, or have you forgotten, I'm already like three months? If I'm gonna do that, I have to do it soon."

"Look at you, Anya you can't even say the word. That should tell you right there what to do." He seemed frustrated. "Look, are you hungry?" He stood. "I'm about to fix us something to eat. I know it's hard, but try to relax and not think about the baby for the next couple of hours." I watched him turn and walk into the kitchen, and before long I heard the click and clank of pots and utensils. No matter how loud the clatter, it wasn't loud enough to drown out my thoughts. I knew I needed to rest. I didn't sleep at all the night before, but I couldn't stop thinking about the baby and how it would change my life if I decided to keep it. I could see the change already. Look at me. I needed to be at work, but instead I was like a lazy person on the couch in the middle of the day.

After we ate, we got back in bed and Anthony just held me like he had all night. I felt safe. It didn't hurt that I loved his bed too. He had beautiful taste. I mean you could tell it was a man's apartment but it was so clean and organized. Nothing was out of place. I won't even talk about this huge pine sleigh bed that I was snuggled up in. It sat high off the floor, which surprised me, seeing as how Anthony ain't that tall, but he had matching steps and he had no problem using them to climb up into that big ole king size bed.

He slid his arm from beneath my neck, sat up and looked down at me. "Anya, you know whatever you decide, I'm behind you. I'm not going to leave you because you're pregnant. That happened before you even knew me, and I can't reverse time. All I can do is move forward with the things that come my way each day, and I'm glad you came my way that night. There's something about you that's just different from anyone else I've ever been with. I know it's only been a month and a lot of people would just cut their losses, but I want to be with you no matter what. I just wanted you to know that in case it might help you make your decision." He caressed my hand and leaned back into his chest and let out a sigh of despair.

I slept all that day, and when I woke up, I had made my decision. I was not ready to have a baby, to be a mother. My career was moving in the direction I wanted it to, and I was happy for the first time in a long while. I didn't want to have a baby before I got married. I had always said that, and there was no way I wanted to marry John, plus I wanted a fair chance with Anthony. A chance without any added pressures, relationships are hard enough. But could I actually go through with getting rid of the baby? I could feel the panic glazing my insides as my heart began to race. I couldn't stay in the bed. The longer I lay there, the more I thought about the baby and the worse I felt. I was restless and my brain wouldn't slow down to give my heart a chance to catch up with its own beat.

Anthony must have heard me tossing and turning. He slowly opened the door and peeked in. "Hey, sweetheart, I see you're finally awake. How are you feeling?"

"As good as someone in my present situation can feel, I guess."

"Do you want me to get you anything?"

"No," I said. If only I could have what I really wanted, which was not be in this present predicament. "I just need you to hold me and make it all go away. My head just keeps spinning, and I feel like it's the end of the world. Even though I know it's not, it sure does feel like it." Looking up at him and smelling him made me want to be more than held. He looked so good standing at the end of the bed, and the way he treated me attracted me to him even more.

He came around to my side of the bed, sat down and put my head on his lap. As he rubbed my head, his hand felt like velvet against my face. I know I was in the midst of drama but as I allowed myself to melt into his touch, I felt a little bit of peace come over me. I took a deep breath and tried to temporarily forget about everything and just live in that exact moment of rest. What did I do to deserve him? Anthony was too good to be true, which made me wonder how long this relationship would really last. I looked up at him and told him I didn't want to the keep the baby. He looked kind of surprised and asked me if I was sure. "Yes, I'm sure," I said before turning back over and continuing to allow myself to stay in that peaceful place with him.

Monday at work was the worst. When I got up, I didn't feel any different. Other than the fact that I knew in my mind I was pregnant, I didn't feel it until about 10:30 when I threw up on Asha's office floor. I was so embarrassed. I felt it coming, and I tried to catch it as it crawled up my throat, but when I turned to run to the bathroom, I didn't make it. Splat right at the entrance to her office and on my brown and pink Prada shoes and my favorite brown slacks. I was so irritated that was the moment that officially sealed the deal. There was no way I was going through another six months like this. I couldn't even work, and I had come too far, put in too many hours and worked my butt off to throw it all away just like that.

Asha jumped up from her desk and ran over to me. "Are you okay Anya? Maybe you should have stayed home again today."

"No, I'm okay maybe it was something I ate. I'm going to run home and change, and I'll be back." She wanted me to stay home and get better she said. I couldn't do that though. I had to do the Ellis job, and if she thought I was that sick, she would probably have given it to my co worker Aaron. Not that I had anything against Aaron, I loved him and he was a wonderful decorator, but this was business, and if anyone should have that account, it should and would be me.

I called Anthony to come pick me up to change, and I went in the bathroom to clean up a little while I waited. I looked in the mirror, and I hated myself. I hated that I allowed this to happen to me.

Anthony called from downstairs, and I buzzed Asha to let her know I was leaving and that I'd be back by two. When I got into the car I just began to cry. I could not believe this was happening to me. After I took a shower and changed, I told Anthony I had decided not to keep the baby for sure and that I was going to call my doctor to set up an appointment. He looked at me and sighed, asking again if I was sure. But I was sure, and there was nothing that would change my mind. I know it sounds selfish, but what would you do?

When I got back to work, Asha came into my office and asked me if I was sure I was up to going to New York. I assured her I was. Just as I suspected, she said, "Well you know honey, if you're not, I can send Aaron. I can't have you down there throwing up on people." Though she was laughing, I knew her well enough to know she wasn't joking. This was her way of saying don't blow it or it would be me and her, and it wouldn't be pretty.

"I can handle it," I said, looking her in the eyes with the utmost confidence. "Don't let me down, Anya, and more importantly, don't let yourself down." With that, she turned and walked out of my office, closing the door behind her. I hated when people made me feel like that. Like they were disappointed in me or like they didn't believe in me. But that would always just push me to accomplish a goal even the more.

As soon as she left out my office, I picked up the phone and called my doctor. I told the receptionist that I had decided to terminate my pregnancy and needed to know what I should do. She advised me I could come in that week because I was already three months, and they did not want me to get too much farther along. Luckily I spoke with Mrs. Ellis, and she wanted me to come to New York the following Tuesday. So I scheduled my appointment for that Thursday at two o'clock.

Living With The Decision

The whole ride to the clinic, I was so scared. What was I doing? All these thoughts were racing through my mind like what if I die? What if they mess up and I'm never able to have kids? Will God really forgive me. I was panicking when I felt Anthony reach over and put his hand on mine and ask me if I was sure about this. I couldn't even respond. I just stared out the window and tried not to think.

Well, this is it, I said to myself as we approached the building my doctor had sent me to. He didn't actually perform abortions, so his receptionist gave me all the information about the doctor they had made the appointment with. It was a clinic and this was all they did, take babies all day long. Oh God, what was I doing there? As we pulled into the parking lot, I began to sweat. I felt nervous and scared and even a little dizzy, but I knew what I had to do.

When we walked in the office, the room was full of women, all ages and races, from hood rats to professional women, it was just a mixture and we all had one thing in common: a seed we didn't want. What am I doing here? I kept asking myself over and over. I always talked about these women who laid down irresponsibly and who wanted to kill their responsibility, the little life growing inside them, but look at me. I was one of those very same women and suddenly, I understood, and I could no longer judge them without first judging myself. Life is ugly that way sometimes.

I had never been to an abortion clinic before. I always thought you just go to your regular doctor's office and no one was the wiser, but that's not the way it worked. Here, everyone knew your secret. We walked to the window, and I gave the receptionist my name. Here. Fill this out and bring it back to the window when you're done." She handed me a clipboard with some papers. She didn't even bother to look up. I sat next to Anthony and began to fill out the papers.

Maybe it was just me, but why were they different colors? The top page was white like most forms, but then there were two pink papers, a blue one and the last one was yellow. Did they do this intentionally to make you feel even worse? Why would they use baby colors? *These people are twisted*, I thought, but in spite of all that, I filled out the papers and took them back to the window. Again, without looking up, she grabbed the clipboard.

"Have a seat. Someone will be calling you shortly." I turned and walked back across the beige carpet, sat next to Anthony and waited for them to call my name, to announce to the whole room how I, too, was now one of the abortion statistics. After about fifteen minutes, the door opened, and I heard "Anya Dennings." I looked at Anthony as if I was never going to see him again, stood, turned and walked through the door.

First a counselor talked to me to make sure this was what I wanted to do. She explained the procedure and told me how to care for myself afterward. She kept asking me if I had any questions, and I kept telling her no, so I don't know why she kept asking. Even though they don't have a job if no one is getting abortions, it really seemed as if she was trying to talk me out of it. Needless to say, it didn't work. After she finished her spiel she had me sign one last paper, then she lead me down the hall where all these small dressing rooms had just a curtain up to them. She gave me a key and told me to get undressed, put my clothes in the locker that corresponded with the number on the key, put on a blue gown and pin the key to the gown then have a seat in one of the chairs up against the wall.

I took off my shoes first and wished I had brought some flats. I wasn't thinking. I knew I wasn't going to walk in heels after this, at least I didn't think I was. Next, I took off my skirt and blouse and folded them up, then I took off my bra and panties and put on the blue gown the counselor had given me. I sat on the little bench in the dressing room and slid my feet into the booties as I tried not to think about what I was getting ready to do. I took a deep breath, stood and gathered my belongings. I opened the curtain and walked over to the lockers, put my stuff in and turned the key to lock it. The key had a safety pin on it so that I could pin it to my gown like when I was little and I use to go swimming. I turned around and looked at the row of orange chairs against the wall and began to walk toward them. They were all lined up, and out of the ten chairs there, girls, ladies, women, whatever the case filled the first three, so I sat in the forth one. The nurse called us in one by one, and by the time I was called the chairs were filled again with more bodies. It was like we were on death row, I guess in a sense we were, if not us, the life inside of us.

The nurse came for me, and we walked into the itsy-bitsy stark-white room, and I thought at least it appeared to be very sterile. I know that's awful, but that really is all I was thinking about at that moment. I didn't want to begin to think about what I was getting ready to do. I wanted to stay numb. The anesthesiologist and the nurse tried to make small talk with me as I got up on the table and they began to prep me. I could tell they were trying to make me laugh because I probably looked scared. I know I was shaking, and I'm sure they could see it. This was no laughing matter to me though. How could they stand around joking when they kill babies all day? What a hypocrite I was. Would it have been better if they looked sad and depressed like it was really tormenting them to do this job? I don't know, but I know the laughter was not it.

The anesthesiologist told me to lay back and relax and take a deep breathe. I was deathly afraid of needles so the nurse held my hand while he put the IV in my arm. Just then the doctor came in and asked if we were about ready. As I lay on that table, looking up at the ceiling, I felt the tears filling up my eyes, and my heart began to beat a mile a minute. I could hear it in my head getting louder and louder. Then the doctor had me put my legs in these stirrups, and the anesthesiologist said he wanted me to count backward from ten. I could feel the cold fluid running through my veins, and all I could say was, "No! Stop! No wait I changed . . ." then everything went black.

I woke up a few hours later, but it seemed as if it had only been a few minutes. At first I couldn't remember where I was. I slowly looked around as I focused on the hospital beds around me. Instantly I remembered where I was, and I was devastated. I had actually killed the little life inside of me. I remembered telling them to stop. Why didn't they stop? I felt the tears burning my cheeks, and I tried to get up, but I felt really tired.

One of the nurses I guess assigned to watch the recovery room saw me and came over. "Here," she said, handing me a graham cracker and some juice. "Drink this, and eat these crackers, then you can get dressed whenever you're ready. She walked away and went over to the phone. I could see her talking. I heard, "Okay." then she placed the phone back on the receiver. A few minutes later, the counselor I spoke with earlier came in and walked down to the bed I was in.

"After you get dressed, I need to talk to you and have you sign some more papers," she said, smiling at me. I wanted to smack that stupid smile right off her face. "How are you feeling?" What a stupid question. What was I supposed to say to that? Something like "Great, couldn't be better. I think I'll try and get pregnant again in a few weeks so I can come back again because this was so much fun? I didn't say anything. I just glared at her until she broke the silence. She took a deep breath, and said "Okay then." Both her eyebrows rose up. "I'll see you in my office." She turned and walked away, and I lay there until I could no longer see her white coat swinging from side to side.

About ten minutes later, I got down off the bed, walked to the locker and got my clothes. I felt really drained as I went into the dressing room to change, and that's when it dawned on me, they didn't do it. I didn't have a pad on like the nurse said I would. That's why the counselor wanted to see me. That's why she was smiling at me. I felt scared and relieved all at once. I put on my clothes, threw the gown in the hamper and walked down the hall with those booties on. I signed a paper just saying that they didn't go through with the abortion based on what I had said right before the procedure. Even though I didn't go through with it, the nurse told me I couldn't drive and asked if my ride needed to be called. I explained Anthony was in the waiting room. They told me I would feel a little groggy for a couple of hours and to drink a lot of water so that I wouldn't get dehydrated from the anesthesia. I could tell the counselor was glad I hadn't gone through with the procedure, but not as glad as me. I stood, picked up my shoes, grabbed my purse and slowly walked out.

When I opened the door, Anthony looked up, and when he saw me, he came over and grabbed my hand and asked if I was okay. I smiled and looked at him and told him no, but I advised him I would be. On the way down the elevator, he grabbed my hand and kissed my cheek and just stared at me. I still couldn't get over how supportive he was being through all this. Was he getting ready to say what I thought he was? Before he could say anything, I blurted out, "I didn't do it."
"What do you mean you didn't do it? As long as you were back there, what were you doing?"

I didn't want to tell him like that but I really thought he was going to tell me he loved me or if not that, something that might send my emotions haywire, and before he did I wanted him to know I was still pregnant. How stupid was that?
"Are you mad?" I said, looking at him, and from that moment it was on.
"Mad at you?" He smiled "Why would I be mad at you, Anya? I love you girl."

My God. There it was, but how could he love me after a month? What kind of fool was I, to believe him? I realized in that moment I loved him too. I know it sounds crazy, but I did. I loved the way he talked. He wasn't proper or anything and could actually stand a few English classes, but his voice and his facial expressions were so sexy. I loved the smile he smiled and the walk he walked. It was like he glided across pavement. I loved the way he dressed, in fact, till that day, I had never seen the man in the same thing twice. Hell, he loved to shop more than I did, and believe me he was always coordinated from hat to shoes and every stitch of clothes in between. He made me laugh, and he treated me like I was a part of his world, not just a visitor. He made me feel important, like I really mattered to him. It was just me and him till the end, and I loved that feeling.

The elevator stopped, and the doors opened. As I walked through them, I felt as if I were walking into a new life. For a brief moment, I really believed that maybe everything was going to be alright, maybe even more than alright. I mean that is possible, right? A new life, a new man and a new little life to love . . . How could I have even considered abortion? If my grandmother knew, she would literally go upside my head with her fist. After all the years of Sunday school, church choir and everything else, you would think I would know better. Actually I did know better, but what does that really mean? I knew abortion was against what I had been taught all these years, and I knew God didn't want me to do that, but when I got pregnant, and it was actually happening to me. I was willing to go through with it because I knew God would forgive me. I know that's twisted and it's not right, but I'm just being real.

While we were walking to the car, Anthony stopped and turned me to him and told me he was serious when he said that he would stick with me through this and that he wouldn't leave me. He meant it too. The next four weeks were hell on me. I was tired all the time. I would drag myself to work because I really couldn't afford to slack up. I had a baby on the way. He made me feel so special. He didn't care that I was pregnant. We still went out all the time, and even when I began to show and his friends would talk about him for "running up behind me" as they would say, he didn't let it bother him. He kept loving me right on. I thought that us not having sex would eventually push him away, but he said he wasn't trippin,' that he could wait till after the baby was born. I just didn't feel right having sex with him, being pregnant by someone else. He always told me he had been in enough relationships to know they were based on more than sex and that ones that were based on that never really lasted once the sex was no longer exciting. I guess I'm glad he got that grand revelation before meeting me and using me up until my sex was no longer exciting.

Which reminded me, I eventually needed to tell John. I mean it was only right. At least that's what the correct logic told me. However, Anya logic was something altogether different. It went a little something like, what he don't know won't hurt. He had called several times since we'd broken up. Kim even said he came by the apartment a few times, but of course I was practically living with Anthony, so I never had the pleasure of receiving his unannounced visits. He did, however, show up at my job one day. but my assistant told him I wasn't in. I was in my office, but she knew the drill. Anthony told me I should have told John a long time ago, but I just didn't want to see him. Maybe it's because I knew if I saw him, I'd have to admit I really wasn't over him. I know it's sad. Can you believe it? After all the crap we'd been through, I still had some feelings for him. Maybe that's why I spent so much time with Anthony, because I knew if I didn't, maybe there was a chance I would forgive John and eventually let him back into my life. Pitiful, I know, but there is a little sad truth that rings through, loud and clear.

The next day at work I knew I couldn't put it off any longer, so I took a deep breath, psyched myself up a little and did the one thing I had been dreading. I finally broke down and called John's office.

"Good afternoon. Smith and Associates, how may I help you?"

"Um . . . hi. Is John Thomas available?"

"May I tell him whose calling?"

"Yes, Anya Dennings."

"And the nature of your call?" What is this, I was saying in my head, the damn FBI?

"It's personal." I said with an attitude.

"Just one moment please. I'll see if he's available." She knew exactly who I was. She had been the receptionist since I knew him. What was her problem? Maybe she finally got her chance to be one of his flavor samples. John really thought women were like ice cream, and he couldn't just go to Baskin Robbins and get his favorite. He had to get that little pink spoon and try every one. A few minutes later, I heard his voice on the other end.

"This is John," he said as if she hadn't told him who was on the other end of the line. Although, his voice sounded heavenly, suddenly I was slapped back to the real world and remembered why I broke up with the dog in the first place.

We both just kind of held the phone for a few seconds. I don't know why he wasn't saying anything, but I knew exactly why I wasn't. I guess it's because the words that I was going to spit out were going to tie me to this man forever. This was one soul tie I wished I could cut. Good Lord, even the thought of it was enough to almost make me hang up the phone. I knew though that on the other side of that phone he was quiet, waiting for me to say how I missed him and how this breakup was a mistake and that I wanted to see him, because that was John, God's gift to the female realm.

Finally I took a deep breath and told him why I had called. "Look, John, the only reason I'm calling you is because I have something really important to tell you." Just then I heard his intercom buzz. He asked me to hold on just one minute, and even though I agreed to, I hung up. Maybe that was a sign that he didn't need to know. I sat back in my chair knowing that my logic was not logical at all. What was I afraid of? I decided to leave a voicemail for him at his house, then my intercom rang. Of course it was my assistant. "Anya, John Thomas is on the phone. I told him you weren't in but he said he had just spoken to you. What's that all about?" I told her it was okay to put him through and that I would fill her in later. I hadn't told anyone at my job I was pregnant yet, not even Asha, and even though I was four months, I hid it very well. I knew this wasn't going to last too much longer though. I just hoped Asha wouldn't trip.

"Why did you hang up?" He sounded a little irritated, but I could care less.

"I don't know. I guess I just didn't want to have to tell you why I called."

After that I just came right out and told him I was pregnant. I didn't even give him a chance to react before I went into my whole speech about me not needing him and him not having to do anything for the baby and how I just thought he should know. I don't know how I expected him to react because I was so concerned with how I was dealing with all of this, I never really thought about it. He was happy though. He was all like, "Are you serious? We're going to have a baby," and getting all hyped up about it. I told him that I was the one having the baby, and since it was his I just thought he should know. He wanted to see me to talk, but I told him other than this baby there was nothing to talk about, and since we had several months before the baby was born, we had plenty of time to arrange a meeting. I told him I had to go and that I would be in touch then I hung up.

My God that was a load off. I couldn't believe he was happy about it. What was he tripping on? He use to always say how he never wanted to have kids before he got married because he wanted to always be in the same house with the mother of his children, sharing every part of their lives, not just weekends or summers, so why was he so juiced? I hoped he wasn't thinking this meant we were going to get back together, because it didn't. Even if for some reason down the line Anthony and I didn't work out, I knew there was no way I wanted the drama of trying to make a relationship work with John. I mean dang, didn't I realize a good thing when I had it? And wasn't he getting wayyyyyyyy too old to be a ho? Excuse my language, but wasn't he?

A few moments later my intercom buzzed. I knew it was going to be John on my line, but I really didn't want to talk about the baby anymore. I leaned over and pushed my intercom button and before Cindy could get a word out, I said, "Put him through to my voicemail please? Thanks."

"You got it." she replied.

I knew he would probably call back, but I'd said what I had to say, and that was it for the moment. Besides, I was at work, which meant I should probably get some done before the day was over. I was already mad because the table I had ordered for one of my clients was ready to be delivered, but the painters had painted the dining room the wrong shade of orange, which meant they now had to prime it and repaint it. Of course the floor couldn't be laid until this was done so we had to reschedule the appointment for the floors and they couldn't come out for another three weeks. It was all messed up and of course being the decorator, it was all my fault. Mrs. Ferello didn't want to hear any excuses. She wanted her dining room finished, and when she came home and saw those loud orange walls, she called me, and the proper princess I had worked so well with in the past let me have it as if I had intentionally come to her house myself with a bucket of paint and a paintbrush and did it. She and I both selected the color and the painters even gave me another sample to make sure it was what we wanted, so how then was my fault that they brought the wrong paint? It wasn't. They got the paperwork for Mrs. Ferello mixed up with another one of their customers. All I do is coordinate, not paint, but that's neither here nor there now. I had to call about this table then call the floor company and see if I could talk to the owner and bump up my date. It wasn't their fault, but all the business I gave them, they should come out on Sunday at midnight to lay the floor if necessary.

That day when I got off work Anthony sent his friend Mike to pick me up, which I didn't mind, but it was the second time he had done it without telling me. I didn't have a set time I got off, so I would usually call him about an hour before I was finishing up to let him know what time I would be ready, and since he was his own boss, it was never a problem. When I got in the car, I asked Mike where Anthony was, and he said Anthony called him and said he had to handle some business and asked him to pick me up. I called Anthony's cell phone and asked him what he was doing, and he told me that he had a few things he got caught up doing and that's why he had Mike pick me up. I was just like whatever. All I wanted to do was take a long, hot bath and go to bed. Maybe I needed to start driving myself to work again.

Over the next couple of weeks, I began to notice lots of little things that either I hadn't paid much attention to before or that Anthony just wasn't allowing me see. For a minute I thought he might have been messing around with someone else because sometimes his pager would just be going off all late, and then some nights, he started coming in like at two in the morning. I said to myself he might be gettin' some since I wasn't giving him any, but still if that was the case he just needed to be honest about it. After all, we did have an awkward relationship. Of course he denied seeing anyone, but I had my doubts. Then one night we were at the movies and it all became crystal.

We were watching the movie, and he kept looking around, and when I asked him what he was looking for, he said nothing. We were sitting on the left side of the theater about four rows from the back, kind of close to the wall, and I swear he must have turned around thirty times looking behind us nervously. After the show, we were walking to the car and he was still doing it. I couldn't figure it out. Finally I stopped and asked him if he was messin' with someone else. He hesitated for a minute and looked at me so disgusted, as if he couldn't even believe I had the nerve to ask him that, but what else was he looking for if it wasn't another woman?

"Well," I said "don't just stand there looking at my like I'm crazy. Answer me. Tell me who or what you been looking for all night."

"Is that what kind of man you think I am? As open as we are about everything, do you really believe if I had started kickin' it with someone else I wouldn't tell you?" I wanted to believe him, but past experiences made it hard for me to.

I was so dang emotional that I was about to cry, I would be so glad after I had this baby so I could go back to my regular self. He saw me getting ready to cry and put his arms around me to comfort me, and that was the beginning of the end. When I hugged him I felt something hard and stiff, and it wasn't in his pants. I stood back and tapped his chest. "What is this?" He just stood there looking stupid, talking about don't trip. Don't trip? I think I needed to trip seeing as how he had a bulletproof vest on and I didn't and I was with him. I should have known this was too good to be true. Why did this kind of stuff always happen to me?

I was irritated to the fullest extent of the law. I wanted to know what was going on, and I wanted to know right then. After I found out he sold drugs, it did all kind of fall into place: the wonderful fictitious company he had that allowed him to be at my beck and call, the cars, the clothes, the eating out all the time, the whole lifestyle he lived. How could I have not seen it? Maybe I didn't want to see it. I just sat in the car quiet on the way home. He kept trying to talk and explain, but we weren't in high school, and this was not cute.

While in high school, I'll be the first to admit I had dated a few D-Boys and had a few good friends who sold drugs, too, but I think back then, we didn't really understand the effect it was having on us and our communities. What we did see was the money and the things that money could buy, and I can't lie, I enjoyed it. But I tell you this, I will never forget this one time in the twelfth grade. I was mad at my boyfriend Julian so I went out with Tone of Kim's boyfriends' friends. He was cool too. I kind of liked him and ended up going out with him even after me and Julian made up. This one night we were sitting at a stoplight in his Blazer, and this car pulled up on the side of us and these two dudes jumped out. One stuck his arm through my window and the other came up from behind I guess and stuck his arm through Tone's window, and there they were, two guns pointing directly at us. I was so scared I couldn't breathe. All I knew, was I was getting ready to die and for what, I would probably never know. All of a sudden the guy on Tone's side pulled off his mask and said, "See man, you slippin'. We coulda got yo ass," and they all started laughing. I had almost peed my pants, and these fools were playing. I mean I was glad they were, but I didn't play like that.

I made up my mind that night that dating a drug dealer wasn't worth my life. The cars, the gifts, the restaurants, none of it was worth my life, and it's still not. Besides, I've lost a few close friends to that lifestyle, all so young, and it was sad. I had friends never finish high school, let alone go to college and really get a chance to see what life is all about, what their future held. Nobody values life anymore. Our generation was dying off almost as fast as we were producing illegitimate children, and it was sad. I couldn't even fathom how Anthony could still justify being as old as he was and selling drugs. More than that, I can't believe I was so far removed from the game and from the realities of life that I didn't see what had been right in front of me. I felt so stupid.

When we got back to the apartment, I got my keys and told him that I would be back to get the rest of my things later. "Oh, like that? Just like that you gon' straight bounce on a nigga? Look, Anya, I don't plan on doing this my whole life. This is all I've known since I was fourteen, and it's not as easy as it sounds to just stop. This is my life, this is my job."

I cut him off cause I didn't want to hear anymore. It was a cop-out to me. He could have gone to college five times over the way he blew money. We were the exact same age, our birthdays were three weeks apart. He was too old to still be selling anybody's drugs for a living. He was too old to be that stupid. I couldn't even look at him I was so mad. He was the best thing that had happened to me in a long time, and now it was over, just like that.

As I opened the door, Anthony ran over, reached over my shoulder and pushed it back closed.

"Anthony don't . . ." I couldn't turn around and look at him because I knew I would cry. I was an emotional wreck already with the baby, now this. I didn't know how much more I could take, but I was soon to find out.

"Anya," he said leaning his forehead on the back of my head, "please Anya, please don't leave. Just give me time." But that was what I didn't have. I didn't have time to have a stray bullet take the life of me and my child. I didn't have time to watch him get rich off someone else's pain. I didn't have time to pretend that love conquers all and that I was okay with all of this. I was a grown-up today and I needed someone else who was a grown-up, not someone who was still promising to grow up.

I put my hand on the doorknob and quickly turned it and ran out. I wasn't trying to be dramatic, but a clean break was the only way I knew to get out of a relationship. See not looking back is key. If only I was always able to follow my own good advice, I would be so much better off than I am today.

I was driving home, trying to figure out why it always turns out bad for me. Was it me? Was there some kind of curse over me that needed to be broken or what? Next all I heard was the sound of a horn blaring in my ears. I don't know how long I had been sitting at that green light, but apparently it was too long for the guy behind me who backed up and went around me through the yellow light. As I got ready to put my foot on the accelerator to go the light changed back to red. *Ooooooh girl, you gone*, I thought.

When I got home, Kim and her boyfriend were on the couch watching a movie.

"Hey, what's up y'all?" I said

"Hey, girl. What's up?" Kim looked up briefly from the television.

"Hey, Anya. What you doing here?" Marcus asked jokingly, but I was in no mood for jokes.

"Oh, my fault, Last time I balanced my checkbook, I thought I lived here, seeing as how I pay half the rent and half of everything else."

"What's wrong with yo' funky-attitude-having butt?" Kim said, putting the movie on pause.

"Hey," Marcus hollered, "I'm watching this too, you know."

"Sorry, baby." She got up from the couch and came over to me wanting to know if I wanted to go upstairs and talk, but I didn't. I was all talked out and it had gotten me nowhere thus far.

"Okay Sweetie, I'll let it go, but Anya, you know I'm here for you, like I always have been. Don't think you're in this alone. Okay?"

"I know Kim. I'm sorry. I'm just tired and frustrated." I grabbed her and hugged her, and as soon as I did, I just burst into tears. Maybe that was good though. Maybe I needed to cry and just let it all out. I backed away after a few moments. "Whew, girl I'm okay." I kind of smiled through my tears, "but trust me. It's been a long day. I just need to lie down."

"I feel you. Holler if you need me."

"Will do." I sucked up my tears and wiped my face with my fingers and continued my journey up the stairs.

"What was that all about?" I heard Marcus ask as I was walking up the stairs.

"Nothing for you to worry about, just rewind the movie."

"Well, is she gonna be alright? Do you want me to leave?"

"No, Marcus, you don't have to leave." I hollered down the stairs as I opened my room door. Shoot, I needed him to stay. That would keep Kim off my back.

It was, in fact, easier said than done to make a clean break. All that night at home, the bed I hadn't slept in, in more than two months felt out of place to me. I missed Anthony. I missed him holding me and talking to me at night and rubbing my feet and him period. Every time the phone rang, I refused to pick it up because I figured it would be him, and I was sure that if I allowed his voice to penetrate my heart, I'd go back. I looked around my room and tried to figure out where I would put the baby's bed, and I realized I truly needed to start thinking about a plan. You know how long would I work? How long would I stay off? How long could I afford to stay off? I guess I really did need to start budgeting, too, and stop spending so much money on shoes and purses and a bunch of nothing. I figured that this weekend I would go look for some baby stuff. It might help take my mind off Anthony.

Well, do I know myself, or what? I was right. I was only able to hold out for three days, I know that what Anthony was doing was wrong, but I couldn't help it. I loved him, didn't I? Or was it that I loved the way he loved me? Whatever the case, I called him back the third day, and he came and took me to lunch, and that night I was back home, his home, my home away from home. That night in bed, he whispered, "Anya, I promise I'll never let anything happen to you or the baby." I believed him too. I rolled back over and went to sleep. I felt safe with Anthony, go figure.

In the weeks to come, John tried hard to see me, so I finally gave in. I told Anthony though because I didn't want any secrets. I didn't want him to think there was more to the relationship than the child in my stomach, because there wasn't. I had Anthony drop me off at my house one day because John was suppose to meet me there. I was sitting on the couch watching videos when the doorbell rang. I walked over to the door and opened it. John looked good, and he smelled so good, I wanted to run but I couldn't. I was trapped. I wanted to be over him completely, but I wasn't, and I hated that I wasn't. He had brought me a box of long-stem roses. He said he just wanted to make peace and wanted us to be friends. Since when did red roses represent anything other than love? What was he thinking anyway? We weren't friends, and I knew he couldn't possibly think the hell he put me through the last year was love.

"Whatever," I said, rolling my eyes. I had to play hardball with John. There was no way I was going to let him know that I even had an ounce of affection left for him.

I told him he could come in and sit down as I tossed the roses on the table. "So what's up?" I said.

"Come on Anya you're carrying my child. We have to talk about it some time." He got up off the couch and walked over to me. I was standing up against the living room wall, being strong, you know. Why did he have to have that suit on? He knew it was my favorite because he looked so sexy in it and wore it so well, and that tie he had on we had gotten the last time we were in New York. I remembered tying that very same yellow-and-navy tie around his neck and looking into his eyes thinking how we would be together forever. Oh well. In spite of everything in the past, there was no denying the tie not only complemented the suit, it complemented his skin tone. He was so delicious. It still gives me chills. To be honest he could probably pull off a pink-and-green pinstriped suit with an aqua tie and aqua shoes.

John told me how much he had missed me, of course, and how he knew he was wrong, but that he was just scared of committing himself entirely because of some girl who slept with his best friend in college. He stepped back and took off his suit jacket. He walked into the dining room and hung it on the back of one of the chairs. He stood there for a moment with both hands resting on top of the chair. I could see his upper body inflate and deflate as he took a deep breath and blew it out in frustration. He turned toward me, and rubbed down his face. "Okay" he said sighing, "Whatever it takes."

That's when I looked at him. He was for real. I could see it. There was something different this time. What, I wasn't sure. Maybe it was the life inside of me.

"Anya, I know things weren't the best, but other than me messing up, we were great together, and you know it. I love you, and maybe this baby is God's way of telling us we need to stay together and make this work."

Oh yeah, that's it. Bring God into this now. Was he listening to God all those times he cheated too? "I can change, and you and my baby are enough to make me want to. I don't want to be without you, and you already know that, and I really don't want to be without my baby. I want to be there to share everything with you." He was actually crying. I couldn't believe it. This could not be happening. Why was I letting him hold my hands? I was falling for this. I couldn't do this to Anthony. I pulled my hands away and fell back against the wall. I was trying not to cry, but I couldn't help it. All my emotions just gushed out through my tears.

"Oh, now you can change. You can change because I'm carrying your child, but you couldn't change for just me alone? I wasn't worth changing for, I guess."

"Don't think of it like that, Anya. It's not that you weren't enough to change me. It's just that I didn't realize it until I had already lost you. Anya I've been trying to tell you this for over a month, but you never return my calls, and I know Kim told you I came by several times, but you're never here. I was beginning to wonder if you really still lived here. I even came to your job to try to take you to lunch one day, but as I was pulling up I saw you getting into the car with some dude. At that point, I gave up. I just didn't know what to think or what else I could do to get you to hear me out. So to tell you the truth, I'm glad you're pregnant because it will give me a chance to prove myself to you. Anya, I swear I'll never hurt you again. I promise."

He leaned over to kiss me, but I turned away. Did he really think it would be that easy? "Just hold on, John. Give me a minute to think."

Just then Kim walked in. She looked puzzled at first, then she said "sorry" to us and went straight upstairs. I sucked up my tears and told John he could not do this to me. Why did it take a baby for him to want to change? Why wasn't I enough by myself? I slid down the wall onto the floor, and he sat next to me and put his fingers through mine and said, "I know we can do this, baby. It's worth a try, don't you think? Do you really want to raise this baby alone?"

The fact of the matter was that I wasn't alone. I had Anthony, and he was more than willing to step in for John with no hesitation. Who was I kidding though? What kind of future did I have with a man who wore a bulletproof vest and sold drugs? I was scared, and I think the fear is what made me take John back. He was sitting on the left of me, and I looked over at him and gave a stupid chuckle. I reached over and ran the tips of my fingers under the straps of his suspenders and remembered how hesitant I was standing in the men's department at Bloomingdale's wondering why yellow, but for some reason it worked and it was still working.

I couldn't just go cold turkey, so I continued to see Anthony, and I started staying home a little more often. I let John back in slowly, giving me enough time to get out of the mess I had gotten myself into with Anthony. It was sad though because I think Anthony was looking more forward to this baby than I was, and he would always talk about how this was his baby it didn't matter if it wasn't his biologically. How could I ignore his lifestyle, and how could I let him raise my child? The bottom line was I couldn't. I know many who could, but I couldn't. His lifestyle went against everything I believed and had been taught my whole life.

Eventually he pulled my card when I was at his house one night. I was in the kitchen slicing chicken breast for a salad. I wasn't really talking because I had a lot on my mind. Then out of nowhere, he hollered from the living room, "So you back with dude huh?"

I was like what? What are you talking about? Oh my goodness, I played dumb to the fullest. Was it obvious? What had I been doing differently that would give him any indication that I was back with John? He didn't get mad though. He just said he didn't want me to play him, and if I wanted to be with John, or dude as he called him, I should just be honest about it. Even after he let me off the hook I lied. I told him that I had thought about it because John was the baby's dad but that I loved him so much that I couldn't imagine my life without him. Well he fell for it, but it really was true I guess or did I just want to have my cake and eat it too? "Good," he said jumping up off the couch, "cause I got something for you today."

I went into the living room with my salad and sat there on the couch waiting for him to come back. He went into the bedroom and came back with two huge bags.

"Okay wait, let me rephrase that. I got some stuff for my baby today." He smiled. "My other baby." He opened one of the bags and pulled out a bumper set for the crib that I had yet to buy. He was all excited. "Man, I saw this today, and I had to get it for the baby." He was so happy. "See," he said, showing me the picture on the front of the bag. "It can be for a boy or a girl."

It was cute, but I wasn't surprised. He had excellent taste in everything else. "Wait. Hold on, check this out." He slowly pulled out the matching mobile to hang over the crib. "And can't forget this." It was a teddy bear lamp, and the base of the lamp was a big cloud just like on the comforter with the bears sitting on the cloud like the mobile. "Okay, okay, last but not least, this one is for you. It's a body pillow. It's suppose to help you sleep better when you're pregnant."

I jumped up and hugged him and kissed him. "You are the best. What did I do to deserve you?"

"I don't know. You just lucky, I guess." He burst out laughing. He was so silly. I gave him a little push.

I sat back on the couch. He pushed the bags to the side and got down on the floor in front of me. He opened my legs and rested his head on my stomach. "When do we go back to the doctor?" He put his chin into my belly and looked up at me. He was beautiful. I rubbed the top of his head.

"Next Thursday," I replied.

"He said we would be able to hear the heartbeat this time, right?"

"Um-hmm"

"Are we gonna find out what we havin'? I kind of want to know, so I'll know how to hook that back room up."

"What?" I sat up.

He rested back on his feet. "Well I was thinking as much as you're here, I would hook that back room up for the baby."

"What are you going to do with your weights?"

"I don't know. I might just put 'em in the bedroom. It's big enough. Or." he looked at me. "I could get a bigger place if you want me to. I mean you practically live with me already. This way you don't have to worry about nothing. You definitely wouldn't have to worry about going back to work right away. You can stay off as long as you want with the baby."

I wasn't expecting that. It sounded like a nice fairytale, too, but I didn't want to live with a man I wasn't married to. I really wasn't about to give control of my financial well-being to anyone other than myself. I couldn't chance something going wrong and me being stuck because a man was taking care of me. Thanks. But no thanks.

"I don't know about that, babe," I said nervously. "You kinda caught me off guard. I don't think I'm ready to give up my apartment yet." That was my independence. I dare not tell him I didn't want to live with a man I wasn't married to. He was liable to ask me to marry him then how much more escalated this mess would be. I didn't know what to do at that point, but I knew I couldn't play this game forever, and if I did continue, it would make me no better than John.

It didn't take too much longer for me to have to make a decision, or should I say before the decision was made for me. I was at work a few weeks later and I was meeting John for lunch. I got my purse and headed out the door. I got downstairs, and I was getting into John's car as Anthony was pulling up, and I did the unthinkable. I acted as if I didn't even see him, knowing that he knew I did. I watched his smile and expression go from the joy off seeing me to frustration and dumbfoundedness. God, I felt like crap as I turned away, opened the door and jumped into John's car. I wanted to explain. I wanted to go back, but I couldn't. My stomach felt weak, and I couldn't catch my breath.

"Are you okay Sweetheart?" I just looked over at him and told him I wasn't but that I would be and that was the truth. "Is it the baby?" he asked. I lied and told him it was and assured him that it would be okay though. As we drove I kept replaying Anthony's face back in my head over and over, how could I be such a dog after everything Anthony had done for me. To make things worse, you wouldn't believe what John had planned for lunch.

He always liked to go to really expensive restaurants, even if it was just for a little lunch, so us coming to Lacroix at the Rittenhouse and having valet service was no big deal. We were sitting at the table, and I was so caught up in trying to think of what I would say to Anthony, I hadn't even noticed how good John was looking and how attentive he was being. After we ate, the waiter came over and offered us dessert, and I declined. The waiter looked over at John as if he was waiting on him to see if that was okay. That annoyed me, then John said "Baby, just have a little something, This place has some of the best desserts in the world." I knew all that but I still didn't want any. "Well just bring her some cheesecake to go."

That really annoyed me. "I said I didn't want anything. What are you, my daddy?" He looked at me kind of surprised and said, "Wait, let me . . ." but before he could say another word here came the plate with a silver cover, which made me even madder because it wasn't even to go. The waiter smiled and set it down in front of me, looked over at John and asked him if there would be anything else. "No, Thank you," he said, but I butted in and said, "Yes, there is one more thing. You can take this away because I said I didn't want any dessert." The waiter looked confused and told me to take that up with my boyfriend.

"He's not my boyfriend!" I yelled.

"What the hell is wrong with you? I know you're pregnant, but just because you are doesn't give you the right act like a . . . well you know."

"Go ahead and say it, a bitch. Is that what you were going to say? I don't even know why I'm here. What was I thinking?" I stood to walk away from the table when he grabbed my arm.

"Wait, this is why you're here. I just hoped it would have gone the way I planned it in my mind." He snatched the top off the plate and under it was a beautiful black velvet box. He picked it up, opened it and turned to me, looked me dead in my eyes and said, "I love you, Anya, and the last few months without you have been hell. I really believe this baby is a second chance for us. I want to spend the rest of my life with you, and I don't know where your head is right now but I want you to know how I feel, and I want you to take all the time you need."

I didn't even know what to say. Marry him? How could I marry him when I just hated him last month? Oh Lord, why did this have to be my life?

I couldn't say anything. The ring was a carat solitaire and would look so good on my finger, but I knew that wasn't the point, was it? I was beginning to wonder. I just looked at him, and before I knew it, I had said yes. I know, I couldn't believe it myself. What was I thinking? He was so happy, he grabbed me and kissed me, and the people at the next table clapped. I had never been so embarrassed in my life. He slid the ring onto my finger and told me how happy I had just made him. I felt like I was in some corny movie.

When I got back to work, I went into to Asha's office to share the great news with her. "You don't sound like a woman getting ready to marry the man she loves? Where's your excitement?" She looked up at me from her work. "Could it be that maybe you don't really want to marry him?"
"I don't know, Asha. I don't know what I'm doing"
"You know, honey. You don't have to marry him just because you're pregnant." How did she know? I hadn't told anyone. I felt so stupid. "Don't worry. It happens to the best of us. You think as long as I've been around I couldn't figure it out?"
I began to cry, I was so confused. She just held me and assured me everything would work itself out. "What are you going to do about Anthony?"
"Let's just say I don't have to worry about that anymore." She just kind of nodded and said she would leave it alone until I wanted to talk about it.

I attempted to call Anthony several times, but he didn't want to talk to me. His exact words were "I'm cool on you" and then he would just hang up. If I went to his place, he wouldn't answer the door, and I couldn't use my key because he had the locks changed. I wondered if that meant he no longer wanted me to move in. I'm making jokes, but it's really not funny. I guess it was for the best and eventually I just let it go.

The Marriage

Since I was pregnant and John really wanted to get married before the baby was born, we just went to my old church and had my pastor marry us in a quiet ceremony in his office. My grandparents, Kim, my sister, both John's parents and his best friend Joe were there. Afterward we all went out to dinner, then John and I went to the Bahamas for five days. We said we would have a big reception the following summer so that all our friends and family could share.

We had a wonderful time in the Bahamas, We laid on the beach and talked like we use to when we first started dating. He would rub my feet and my back and he would bathe me, and it was wonderful. For the first time since I had even agreed to marry him, I felt like I had done the right thing. Boy, I tell you about your feelings, they sure will lie. A little bit of me was scared though, scared that eventually one day I might no longer be enough.

Everything was going great to my surprise. I was still working, John didn't appear to be antsy with just one woman, one pregnant women at that, he was spending a lot of time at home since I had moved in. I was in my sixth month, and the baby was healthy. John was going to the doctor with me and making sure I had whatever it was he thought would make me happy. He even went to the bookstore and bought all these children's books, and at night he would read to my stomach. He so excited, and we were happier than we had ever been. We had even started to go back to church, and I know that was a big part of our oneness. Then something had to go wrong. It wouldn't be my life if it didn't.

I was standing in the kitchen making a salad to go with dinner when I began to feel these sharp cramping pains in my back. I thought they would pass, but as I stood there, they got worse. I grabbed the counter, picked up the cordless and called John. He had already left the office, so I called his cellular phone. He picked up.

"John Thomas."

"Baby it's me. I think I need to go to the doctor."

"What's wrong?" He got alarmed.

"I don't know, but I'm in a lot of pain, and I'm scared." I was shaking, and I began to sweat. John told me to hang up, that he was almost home and that he was going to call the doctor and to just lay down till he got there. I was too scared to move, so I slowly got down on my knees and lay on the kitchen floor. I wanted to stay on that kitchen floor, but it was marble and it was cold so I sort of got on my side and dragged myself to the hallway so I could lay on the carpet. All of a sudden it seemed as if the pains went away. John came through the door, and he had my midwife on the phone. She wanted to talk to me. John threw his coat and briefcase on the floor and sat down next to me on the floor and gave me the phone.

She asked me what the pains were like and exactly where they were and how long they had lasted. She also asked me if I had had any spotting or bleeding, which I hadn't. I told her that I had had about four of them in the thirty minutes I was on the floor and that I didn't know how long they had lasted because it felt like forever. I did explain to her that they had stopped. She told me to get in bed and put my feet up and to come in first thing in the morning unless the pains started again. In that event, she wanted me to go to the emergency room and call her service. I felt a little better because she didn't sound too worried, and I hung up the phone. I told John what she had said but he still looked scared.

"Are you sure we shouldn't just go to emergency?" he said. But I shook my head no. Afterall I was only in my seventh month, so it was too soon for the baby to come.

"Okay come on. Let's get you into bed." He began helping me up. "Never thought I'd be saying that to you and not be trying to get some." He gave me a nice comforting smile.

"You are so stupid." I pushed him on the arm, and we both started to laugh. "You getting me into bed is what got me like this in the first place." I was smiling up at him.

"Yeah, I know," he said, bending to help me up. "That's why my boy in there giving you the blues."

"Naw this is mommy's baby girl in here."

"Whatever. We'll see when he gets here." John wanted a boy so bad, but I wanted a girl more than anything. Even though I wasn't ready to be a mother at first, I had to admit I was excited about my baby.

"Whew, girl, you gettin' big. Naw, I'm just playing," he said, snickering as he pulled me up.

When I stood, there was blood running down my legs, and I screamed. John tried to calm me down, but it wasn't working.

"Baby, just lean here against the wall and let me get your coat." He went over to the closet, grabbed my coat then he grabbed his coat, off the floor. He put my coat around me and picked me up and carried me to the car. He called Laura, my midwife, and told her we were on our way to the hospital and that I was bleeding. In the car I was cramping more and more, and I began crying because it hurt so bad.

"John, I'm scared. Am I going to die?"

He looked over at me. "What? How are you going to die? Our life is just beginning, and the baby is going to be fine."

I wanted to believe him, but I couldn't because he couldn't feel what I was feeling. I was in so much pain, I just wanted to die right there on the spot, just to make the pain go away. I closed my eyes real tight and begged God to make the pain stop, but he didn't.

When we got to emergency, John pulled up, jumped out of the car and ran through the doors. About two minutes later an orderly came out with a wheelchair. I was scared to move. Something didn't feel right. It felt like the baby was coming out. They rushed me in, and no need to go through all the horrible details. When I woke up, John was holding my hand, and I could tell by the look on his face that I had lost the baby. Maybe that's when I lost him too. I just lay there staring at the ceiling. I couldn't even cry. I wanted him to say something, but he didn't. He wouldn't even look over at me. Sometimes, silence can be louder than a bomb being detonated, so I just continued to lay there in that loud silence.

A while later, the door slowly opened. It was my sister and Kim with flowers and balloons, but who celebrates your baby dying? I know they meant well though and were just trying to cheer me up. They both looked a little nervous. My sister kind of half smiled as she walked over to the bed, leaned over and kissed my forehead.

"How are you?"

How did she think I was? I mean really come on. "As well as I can be after losing a baby, I guess."

"I'm sorry, Anya. I just don't know what to say. I just wanted to be here for you."

"Well, it's good to know someone does." I looked over in John's direction. He still had not said one word to me.

He stood from the chair he had been paralyzed in. "Uhhh, I'mma be at the house. Kim and Traci can sit here with you. The doctor said they're going to keep you overnight for observation, so I'll just see you in the morning."

"You just gon' leave like that?" I was amazed, but why? I should have known better than to think that John Thomas would ever be concerned about anyone but himself.

"Ain't nothing I can do, Anya. The baby is gone." He didn't bother to kiss me or anything. He just walked out the door.

"Damn, what's wrong with that fool?" Kim said. "Is he crazy?"

"I know this may sound a little harsh right now, Anya," My sister said, "but maybe it's for the best. Maybe it's a sign you need to leave that fool."

"Naw, he'll be okay. He's just upset about the baby. You know how much he was looking forward to this." But so was I. I felt like crying, but I wasn't hardly about to cry about a man in front of Traci and Kim. Uh uh no way forget that.

The next few months were the hardest. Things were already bad, but they continued to get worse as John put more and more distance between us. I was losing my mind. I know we had both lost something, but I was the one who had the baby growing inside of me. He seemed to have wanted and needed more comforting and more attention than I did. He never tried to help me heal. He just moved on and buried himself in his work, so I did the same thing.

It was never the same after I lost the baby. We tried to get pregnant again, but for some reason I couldn't. I remember sitting in the nursery we had set up for the baby, and I just rocked in the chair and recalled how much time John and I had spent in that very room, laughing, painting, putting up borders, making love. And in one instant, it was all gone. All the love, all the excitement, just gone. I can still hear the laughter bouncing off the walls. We never even set foot in the room after I lost the baby. The door was always closed until oneday. I slid out of the chair onto my knees and begged God for another chance. I knew the only thing that was going to bring John back was me getting pregnant again.

After sobbing until my eyes were dry, I stood and realized it was really not about me having a baby. I stood over the crib that I had finally picked out. It was beautiful, white washed and hand carved. I ran my fingers across the rail and began to untie the ribbons that held the bumper on. I slowly pulled the sheets off and folded them neatly into a small square. As I removed the mobile, I wound it up and listened to the soft lullaby as I walked over to the closet to get the box it had come in. The lullaby slowly played, and though it wasn't sad, it made me sad, and I was sort of glad when it played out. I lifted the lid and slid the mobile down into the box and closed it back up. I set it on the floor next to the sheets, then I went down the stairs of this house void of joy and full of anger and made my way into the kitchen to get a screwdriver. I made my way back up the lonely staircase into the room that once held our laughter. As I re-entered, I went straight over to the bed and searched for the perfect spot to take the first screw out. After about thirty-five minutes, I was done. It's funny how it took us hours to put the thing together and how quickly it came apart, kind of like our marriage. I leaned the bed and the mattress up against the wall next to the changing table. I stood in the middle of the room and took one last look around at all the faces of the bears painted on the walls. They were all smiling, even the one who was lying on the cloud asleep, even his dreams were happy. I kind of smiled to myself as I closed the door behind me because I still had hope, not hope in a baby or marriage, but hope in me. There was only one thing left to do, which was calling the Salvation Army to pick up the baby's items, someone might as well get use out of them; However, I wasn't quite ready to make the call.

It wasn't long before the vows John had made were out the door. He was back to his old tricks, literally. He began working late, but of course he was never at the office when I called and often he wouldn't get my page or my favorite, he didn't hear his phone. Whatever. I don't know why I stayed as long as I did. A part of me really did love John, and I really took those vows seriously. I thought that he really had changed, and the first two times I caught him, he begged and pleaded for me not to leave him. He swore nothing was going on, but I'm not stupid. I guess in a way, even though I knew deep down he was lying, I wanted to believe him, so I wouldn't feel so stupid for staying with him.

Both times he cheated, our relationship was great for about three months following him getting busted. He would come home at a reasonable hour, we would go out dancing and to dinner, and we would make the best love in the world. It would be great. It was almost worth the pain it would cause me in the beginning when I would first catch him, just for the months to follow. A person can only take so much before it breaks them. Some women do it for years, but years wasn't something I was willing to throw away. Life is too short.

The third time should be called the charm because I could not believe the lengths this man went through to cheat. It was unbelievable. He had to go to New York for the day on business and said he would probably just stay over and catch an early flight out the next morning. Well this was no big deal. I didn't think much of it because this was something he did when he had to go up to New York for cases. The next morning I was sitting at the table drinking some coffee and eating a piece of toast, debating if I was going to work out before I headed into the office. John came down the stairs into the kitchen with his garment bag over his arm, gave me a piece of paper with his flight information on it, kissed me on my forehead, said he loved me and that he would call me if he decided to stay over. I looked up at him and told him to have a safe trip and that I loved him. He looked back over his shoulder and told me he would miss me with a boyish smile. That smile I had grown to love I just as easily grew to hate sometimes. I just sat there for a moment sipping my coffee watching this stranger I once knew. Who once knew me and I thought loved me. How did it come to this? I wondered. Eventually, I stopped trying to figure it out and forced myself to get up and work out so I could get ready for work.

I went upstairs and threw on a sports bra and some shorts, and walked down the hall toward our little workout room. I put a CD in and blasted it. I always needed music to work out to. It motivated me and made the time go by faster. I stood on the sides of the treadmill while I set the speed, put in my weight, and my time. I pressed start and began my five-minute walk before getting into my twenty minute run. I could feel the sweat pouring down the sides of my face, and I could hear my breaths in my head, but that didn't prevent me from trying to sing along with Stevie Wonder. I was so glad when I was able to walk that last five minutes out. Running just refreshed me, and even though I hated the initial startup, once I was on, I was in the zone, no thoughts, just the run and the music in my ears. When I was done, I always felt as if I had really accomplished something. I guess I did though. The runs afforded me the right to still eat pasta and cheesecake.

I walked back down the hall and turned the shower all the way to hot. I closed the door so the bathroom would get real steamy. I loved a really steamy bathroom. There was something mystical or magical about it. It reminded me of those steaming hot brooks you see in movies. I shed my sweaty attire, opened the shower door and stepped into my steaming hot brook. While in the shower, I had a funny feeling something wasn't right. I didn't know exactly what it was, but it was in the pit of my stomach? A nervousness, but there was nothing for me to be nervous about? Although I didn't know what that feeling was right then, I knew time would reveal it.

Later that day, Kim called me at work to see if I wanted to go to lunch, but I was swamped, especially since I didn't get in till after ten. I asked her if she wanted to go to dinner since John was gone and I knew more than likely he would probably just stay over in New York. There was this new Italian restaurant that had just opened, and I had been wanting to try it, but John and I just hadn't made the time to go. So Kim and I decided to meet there because I love Italian food, almost more than life, especially if it's good. I called and made reservations and told Kim to meet me at eight o'clock.

On my way to the restaurant, my cell phone rang. It was John letting me know that he had just gotten out of his meeting and that he was just going to get a hotel room and catch an early flight out.

"Okay, I'll see you in the morning," I said.

"I love you," he said.

"I love you too."

Everyone was right. That food was kickin'. Oh my goodness, the Alfredo sauce on the fettuccine was on hit, and the chicken was so moist, juicy and tender, it was ridiculous. I'm not going to even get on the bread. Kim and I got so full we could hardly talk. The restaurant was nice, too, and the service was great. Everyone was all smiles, but it usually is like that when a place first opens, hopefully it will stay that way. Kim and I both sat there laughing as she caught me up on her current love affair. It was good to see her happy. I was kind of worried that when I moved out she would be sad, and of course we both were but she was doing great, and she had turned my room into a home office so I guess she didn't miss me when she brought paperwork home from the flower shop. We probably had about six apple martinis between the two of us, but no amount of Grey Goose could prepare me for what happened next.

Kim got up to go to the bathroom, and she came back so fast I was like "Dang, girl, you are the quickest pee on the East." She was all excited like, "No, I didn't go yet, just listen. Oh . . ." she said, looking at me like my dog had just died. Then she grabbed my hand and told me to just come with her. I could not believe that crap. We walked toward the back of the restaurant where there was this section that was a little dimmer and you could sense the romance in the change of ambience. It wasn't just the lights, there was a fireplace and a live violinist and most of the tables back there were for two, extremely intimate. Kim motioned for me to look to the left, my heart fell to the bottom of my stomach, and I felt sick. John was sitting there with some girl, and I have to say girl because she couldn't have been more than twenty, if that. He was leaned toward her holding her hand and talking and laughing the way he use to do with me. Their chairs were right next to each other, and he whispered something in her ear, which caused her to blush and kiss him softly on the lips.

She was pretty, too, brown skin with a long black silky weave, I'll give it to her, her hair was bangin'. Her beautiful smile was smiling all up in my husband's face. I'm not sure if she had on a dress or if she had on a skirt and a shirt but I could see she had one of her legs under the table wrapped around his like two high school kids who couldn't stay off each other. The boots she had on were killin' em' too. Dang where did he find this girl? I almost wanted to go over there and snatch her by that weave and swing her around like in the cartoons and then fling her into a corner. But that wasn't an option. I was tired of competing for something that was suppose to already belong to me. Not that I felt that I couldn't compete, I mean truthfully, she was no prettier than me, and I am a stylish dresser myself. That's why I had to give her props on the boots and the hair. She was just younger that was all. Regardless, the point still remained that I shouldn't have to compete.

I looked at Kim with tears of rage, hurt and jealousy burning my eyes. Who did John think he was playing me like that?

"Are you going to say something?" Kim looked at me.

"Oh yes. We are going to make our presence known. Come on." I grabbed her, pulling her into the bathroom. I had to pull myself together. I was not about to embarrass myself or give that girl the satisfaction of knowing she got to me, even though between me and you, she did.

"Okay Kim, this is the plan." I told her what we were going to do, and she agreed, I wasn't about to make a scene and let John know how much pain he was causing me.

We both went to the bathroom, washed our hands and went back our table. We ordered another drink then asked that a bottle of champagne be sent over to John and his little girlfriend. I told the waiter to make sure John knew it was from our table and to give him a message for me.

The waiter looked at me and said, "Yes? What would you like me to tell him?"

"Tell him I said congratulations on the New York case and on his new life."

"Anything else?"

"No. I'm sure that will be sufficient." I laughed. I had to, to keep from crying. Kim gave me a high-five and said she knew I didn't want to hear it but she was glad it happened, now maybe I would leave John because he wasn't any good and probably never would be. She was right, too. I did hate to hear it, but at the same time, I knew she was right.

"You sure you okay?" she asked.

"No," I said sighing, "but I will be." I let out a half laugh. "Hell, sometimes you gotta laugh to keep from crying, and this is definitely one of those times."

We watched as the waiter went over to the table. They were having such a good time, I hated to interrupt. I saw John explaining he hadn't ordered any champagne.

After talking with the waiter, John got up and asked the waiter to point out who sent the champagne. I saw them both come to the edge of the entryway and as the waiter pointed in my direction, I stood and blew him a kiss. You could see the look of stupidity all over his face as Kim and I got up and grabbed our purses to leave. He came over to the table, but before he could even get the lie out, I put my hand over his mouth and told him as much as I loved him, this was it. I couldn't do it anymore. I turned, and though I felt a little weak, I couldn't let it show. I wanted to look back just to see the stupid look I'd have to deal with, but I thought it would be better if I kept walking through the door. Maybe I was afraid if I turned around he might not be standing there.

When I got in the car I called his cell phone and told him not to bother coming home. I also called a twenty-four hour locksmith and asked him to meet me at my house so I could change the locks. Kim followed me, because she didn't want me to be alone, but I told her I was fine. She didn't believe me so she stayed. Truth be told, I really was glad she did, no matter how hard I tried to be.

Kim stayed downstairs with the locksmith while I was upstairs packing a suitcase for John. He was lucky I was nice and not spiteful because I really could have pulled a waiting to exhale and who would blame me? I went into the garage and pulled down the big plastic bags we kept the suitcases in. I opened the biggest one, which had others inside, so I took those out, slid them back into the plastic bag and went upstairs with the biggest one. I wanted John to know I did not plan on him coming back for anything. I tossed the suitcase on the bed and let it flop open. I opened his drawer and began to grab things. I filled the suitcase with boxers, dress socks and undershirts. I wanted to put all mismatch stuff in there but I wasn't going to stoop to that level. I walked over to the closet and took out several dress shirts and folded them neatly along with the ties and matching suspenders. I removed six suits from the hangers and placed then nicely in the suitcase, trying not to get them too wrinkled. I would have put then in his garment bag, but he had it with him. I pulled a duffle bag off the closet shelf and put three pairs of shoes in it. He always kept his shoes in the boxes they came in so they wouldn't get scuffed up. That's why I only gave him three pair, that's all that would fit.

When my task was finally complete, I zipped the suitcase and set it on its wheels. I grabbed the duffle bag, threw it over my shoulder and headed for the door. I dragged everything out into the hallway and down the stairs and set it right outside the front door just in case he came by after taking his little girlfriend home. I wanted him to pull up and know I was serious this time, there was no get back at this point. I could tell the locksmith wanted to say something, but opted to do the smart thing and keep his thoughts to himself.

"Are you about done?" I looked over at him from the entryway.

"Yes ma'am, about two more minutes."

"Thanks." I stood there waiting for him to be finished, still not able to fully grasp what had just happened.

I wasn't surprised, but yet I was. It's like when you know something deep down inside, but you don't really want to admit it because then it will cause you to have to make certain decisions that apparently I wanted to avoid making. Maybe I was afraid to be alone, but why, I had been before, and it didn't bother me. Maybe I just didn't want to admit the marriage failed, or that I wasn't enough to keep him at home. No matter because either way it went, I was a fool regardless, but I'd be an even bigger fool if I stayed.

I went in the kitchen and made another apple martini then another and another, and Kim and I sat in the living room talking about old times, laughing, and then I had a thought. I needed to call Anthony. I reached over and picked up the phone.

"Who are you calling?" Kim asked.

"An old friend," I sang out with a more than devilish charm.

"No way. You better not be calling Anthony!" she exploded. But why couldn't I call Anthony? At this point I had been in this miserable marriage for over five years and never once did I cheat on John, even after I found out he had been cheating on me. Hell, I deserved this. I turned and looked at Kim and told her how unfair this was. I began to cry, and it started off as tears of pain and bitterness but miraculously, the cry of frustration turned into a laughter of freedom that came from the very pit of my stomach. No, I wasn't just drunk, okay maybe a little because the reality of the night was enough to keep me sober no matter how much I drank but instead I was realizing I was free to start over and eventually have a chance of being happy again. I think, if happiness is even a realistic possibility.

We both jumped when we heard keys at the door. We looked at each other and just sat there as if frozen in time. Like we were doing something we had no business doing and our parents had just come home early. I didn't even hear John's car pull up.

"What are you going to do?" Kim whispered as she looked at me.

"Call a lawyer in the morning," I said and just began to crack up.

When John realized his key no longer worked, he began to ring the doorbell and bang on the door. "Come on, Anya, open the door and quit trippin'."

No this fool did not tell me to quit trippin' when he was the one at the restaurant with some hooch while he was suppose to be out of town on business. I acted like he wasn't even there. Then the phone rang. I picked it up. It was

John, calling from his cell phone, begging me to let him in. He was crying and whining, but those tears were no different than the last ones, and I had a whole collection of sorrys, I could just pick one out of the box where I had stored them over the years. I took great pleasure in saying, "Sorry, John? Sorry you did it or sorry you got caught? Not this time," and hanging up the phone.

"Anya!" He stood at the front door. "Anya! open the door. This is my house." I went up to the door and calmly told him that we would see what our lawyers could work out. But until then, we would temporarily call it my house and he could stay wherever he was really going to stay before he got busted.

"Anya, don't make me kick this door down."

"Be my guest, John. Nine-one-one is only a three-punch process. Now you can leave quietly and go stay the night at your little girlfriend's, that is if she doesn't still live with Mommy and Daddy. You can stay on the property and sleep in your car or you can keep banging on my door and be escorted from the property, which I don't think will go over too well. That kind of thing doesn't look good for law partners, you know? So tell me, sweetie, which will it be?"

"Anya please, why are you doing this to us? Let me in, and we can talk about it. Anya, I love you. Please. I'm sorry. Maybe we need to go to counseling."

"Oh now you wanna go to counseling? I've been saying let's go to counseling since we lost the baby. I said let's go to counseling the last two times you cheated. What's so different now? Why do you want to go to counseling now? Is it because you know I'm serious this time? Is it that obvious that I'm finally tired of your bull and most of all, I'm tired of you?"

"Anya, come on. Don't do this. Please."

"Oh, John, I didn't do this, you did. That's your problem now. Nothing is ever your fault. Your law school logic can always help you justify your crimes instead of taking responsibility, admitting guilt and taking your punishment like the crook you are. You have robbed me for too many years of my life, but not another day. Now get your sorry self off my steps and away from my door." Slowly backing away from the door, I felt confidence run through me, confidence of letting go. I walked back to the living room and sat down. Kim looked at me, smiling.

"I'm proud of you. I know that was hard for you."

"Yes, yes it was, but I'm proud of me too." My grand speech didn't stop John from ringing that doorbell though. He went on for another thirty minutes or so before we finally heard him get in his car and pull off.

The next morning I sat up in the bed and suddenly it hit me, everything that had gone down the night before really happened. Wow, I couldn't believe it. I went and took a shower and put on some clothes. It's a trip though. I didn't feel any different. I didn't feel as if my life was over or as if I couldn't go on. I always saw women in the movies fall apart at separation time. Maybe it was different for me because no matter what, in my heart I knew I would be better off without John in the long run. I'm sure it would take some getting use to, but sometimes change is good, right? At that point, all I could think of was shopping. Huh, maybe I was a little depressed, just a little, but I knew once I took Kim home to change I would be one step closer to Mall Boulevard, and I would feel much better. I could feel my spirits lifting just thinking about stepping through those doors, breathing that store air, especially the leather, as your walk through the shoe and the handbag departments. Just the thought of it made me smile. I could imagine it was probably what heaven would be like, one big Via Spiga, Gucci sale after the next. Just kidding. I knew heaven would be a million times better, but shopping was my little piece of heaven on earth. After the previous night, I definitely needed some new shoes to walk out on John. Maybe even a matching bag to put a brick in and hit him over his head if he even attempted to think he was getting out of this one.

When we opened the garage to pull out, who did we see but John sitting on the front step. I just looked over at him with pity, closed the garage door and pulled off.

"Wait, Anya. Wait, he yelled, running over to the car, but I just kept driving like he wasn't even there, because he wasn't. He wasn't a part of me anymore. The chain was broken, and I was finally free, and surprisingly it wasn't as hard to let go as I thought it would be.

Maybe part of the reason I stayed so long was because I didn't want to be another statistic that ended in divorce, and maybe I married him because I didn't want to be part of the unwed, baby daddy statistic either. Lord knows I didn't want to be part of the best friend I-told-you-so statistic. I was on my way to officially becoming two of those three statistics, and you know what, so what? So I made a mistake. Hopefully I'd learn from it and move forward. No sense in dwelling, right? Looking back, isn't it just as bad being the statistic who everyone feels sorry for because their husband is screwing half the city?

The Divorce

The divorce wasn't as bad as I thought it would be. John was acting all crazy because he thought I wanted the little bit of money he had, but that wasn't me. I didn't need his money. I did very well for myself as an interior designer and once we got married, I no longer had to pay rent, a car note or utilities because John made enough money to pay everything, so other than shopping, my check had gone straight into my savings for my entire marriage, I was phat. I even told my lawyer I didn't want the house, unless of course John didn't want it, and if that was the case, I would agree to buy him out for his half. Even then, I would still be getting over.

John contested the divorce. I could not believe this man. He refused to sign the papers. I thought we had everything squared away. My attorney and I were to meet with John and his attorney at John's law firm. Everything was fine until he stood in the meeting, came to my side of the table and dropped to his knees, begging me for another chance.

"I love you, Anya. I know I messed up. I know I was wrong, but please, I love you. I need you in my life. Please don't do this, Anya I know we can make it work. I don't know what I was thinking. I was just young and stupid."

How much could he have grown in three months though? I wasn't having it. I stood and I was sharp too. I wore my new Gucci shoes that I had bought to walk out on him in. I saved them just for that day.

"Give me a break. Love keeps your dick in your pants. Love makes you tell the truth. Love can't wait to get home to tell your wife about your day. Love is something I gave you, but I got a bunch of lies and hurt in return, so you can get up off your knees because the critics give this performance two thumbs down."

I grabbed my matching purse and told my lawyer I couldn't deal with this kind of drama, and with great pleasure I walked out. I wanted to feel sorry for him. Sorry that he didn't see that he still had a lot of growing up to do and that no matter how much money he had, it wasn't a license to cheat on me. I couldn't feel sorry for him though. My heart had grown cold toward him, and I knew I should not have allowed that to happen, but I did. I didn't hate him, but I hated what he had done to me, and to be honest, other than being sorry he got caught, I didn't believe he was sorry at all.

I decided that none of it was worth it, I called a realtor and told her I needed to see some houses. The more I thought about it, I didn't even want John to know where I lived. He had been calling all the time, coming by the house and just sitting out there for hours. I didn't feel threatened or anything, just annoyed. I guess he thought he was going to wear me down, but it didn't work. The more I was without him, the more confident I was that I was making the right choice.

It didn't take the realtor long before she found me the cutest condo in Chestnut Hill and I moved in. I did take the living room furniture and the bedroom furniture and all the kitchen appliances because after all I had picked them out. I didn't take the dining room table because it was way too big for my condo, but if it hadn't been, trust me, I would have. You know I took the big screen out the family room, the TV out the bedroom and the computer because we had bought a new one. He was okay with all this. I guess he thought if he was nice enough or if he begged long enough, I would change my mind, but I never did. It was over.

He finally signed the papers, and we sold the house. After all that he didn't even want to stay there, even after I agreed to move out. He moved closer to his law firm. Eventually I had to start paying my own car note. I had bought a new BMW the year before but that was life. Some days I would miss him and think about him and almost break down and call, but then I would have a flashback of the humiliation and hurt I felt in the restaurant that night, and I would quickly come to my senses.

The divorce was official in May, but by then we had been separated for five months. I was married and divorced at age twenty-eight, who'd of thought?

The next several months I decided not to date but to really focus on me and my wants and desires. I attempted to figure out what was wrong with me, why I attracted the wrong men, for the wrong reasons, all the time. Why did John feel he could treat me the way he did? Maybe it was me and maybe it wasn't, but I didn't want to take any chances, so the only person I dated for the next few months was God. That was the safest relationship I could get. I really began to understand the need for fellowship with the Lord. I was always striving to finish highschool, then striving to get into college and get my degree, striving to look my best, striving to keep my man and keep him happy. Striving to be happy myself, striving to excel in my career, but when it was all said and done, I was empty, happy in some aspects of my life but so unhappy in others. My grandmother always tried to talk to my sister and I about God and how living without him was pointless, and believe me at that point in my life, I was really beginning to wonder. Was my life just about me getting a degree, having a great career so that I could make a lot of money to buy material things and then dying? Was that it? I couldn't even include the marriage and the kids because we see how well that worked out.

No, that wasn't it, and the more I began to pray and read the word of God, I began to feel purpose. It wasn't just going to church as it had been when growing up. I was no longer going because I had to or out of routine. To be honest, I hadn't been in quite some time. Not that I didn't enjoy church when I started going back, but I had a new desire for life in my spirit. It was different for me. I began to feel the presence of the Lord in my life, and I can't explain it, but I was different. My desires began to change, and I began to realize that everything was not always about me and about how I felt or the way circumstances affected me. It was really about what God wanted for my life and the people I might be able to touch and help during my brief stay in this realm we call earth. I made a decision and a commitment to God because I really wanted to live right. I was tired of just winging it in a life of sin with no purpose. Who knows, maybe if I got myself together, the Lord might bless me with the right man and maybe it would work.

Over the next few months, I felt good about myself in every aspect. Don't get me wrong. There was still a part of me that desired a man in my life, but it just wasn't worth the uncertainties. I just wanted to wait and really allow God to heal me because I was still a little bitter about the way John did me, you know, just a little. I even found out later that my Anthony wasn't all he was cracked up to be either. Just an undercover ho who had covered his tracks extremely well.

A New Beginning

It had been a little over a year since John and I had split up. I decided to go to New York for New Year's to celebrate. Yes, all by myself. I was learning to be happy with me. As I stood in Times Square with thousands of other people, I looked up at the ball dropping and listened to the screams and said to myself, *What am I doing?* As I made my way through the crowd, people were grabbing me and everyone else they could get their hands on. Hugging and kissing absolute strangers, all while yelling "Happy New Years! Happy New Year!" Not even New Years was enough to make me want to kiss complete strangers. I was so glad to finally get back to my hotel. I was completely frozen. You would think I didn't have a big coat, hat, scarf and gloves. Underneath all that, I had on a pair of corduroy pants and a thick Gap sweater. What was the problem? I had a chill on the crowded elevator.

"Looks like you could use some warming up," a voice said from behind me.

I turned in his direction, but I didn't look up into his face. "Yes, and I will as soon as I get to my room." I could tell he was flirting, but I was cool. I stood there and waited for the twelfth floor to light up.

"Good night," he said as I stepped out of the elevator.

"Good night. Happy New Year." I smiled as the doors were closing. He was kind of cute, but not cute enough to get me back into the dating game.

I walked down the hall toward my room. I pulled my key card out of my pocket and slid it down into the slot on the door. I waited for the light to flash green, turned the handle and entered the room. I was so glad to be in that room. I could not believe how cold it was outside. It had to be about twenty degrees if not colder, and we had been standing outside like dummies waiting to watch a ball drop.

I took off my coat and hung it up in the closet. I shook the melted snow, which was now just cold water, out of my hat and scarf, and threw them on the table along with my gloves. I was scared to touch my face for fear it would crack and fall onto the floor into a million pieces then what would I do, walk around with no face? I think not. I took off my clothes and laid them over the back of a chair and put on my robe. The room was nice and toasty so I pulled the covers back and laid on top of the sheet, grabbed the remote and turned on the TV. Of course there was nothing on TV, so I was forced to order a pay-per-view movie that I could barely hear over all the laughter and the drunken people outside my balcony on the streets below. I ordered room service and eventually fell asleep.

The next day I spent the afternoon just walking around lower Manhattan and doing a little New Year's Day shopping. I felt happy, why I didn't know, but I did. What was I trying to prove to myself coming to New York alone? I decided to just go back home. Who went to New York alone unless it was to work? I should have at least brought one of my girls. I was trippin'. No matter, I did get two pair of bad boots. That alone was worth the trip.

I was at the desk, checking out of the hotel and there was a guy a little ways down getting his messages. He looked at me, smiled and said hello. I spoke, signed my credit card receipt, picked up my bag and headed for the door.

"Excuse me," a voice said hesitantly. "Umm . . . hi . . . umm . . . I'm sorry, but I don't normally do this, but I just couldn't let you walk out that door and risk not seeing you again."

Okay, was I suppose to fall for that crap?

"I mean you are a very beautiful woman, and I would really love to take you out to dinner sometime."

I looked up at him in disbelief. "You're serious, aren't you?"

We both just broke out laughing. He stuck his hand out and introduced himself as if I didn't know who he was. He was in film and had had two big ones in the last few years. Everyone knew who Michael Harrison was, but I played it cool, like I wasn't even trippin' he was a star and stuff. I grabbed his hand and shook it.

"Anya," I said. "Anya Dennings."

He looked me straight in my eyes. "Beautiful name. Almost as beautiful as you."

Did he think he was shooting a movie? Dang he was corny.

"So how about it?" he said with his smiling eyes.

"How about what?"

"Dinner, lunch, breakfast, whatever you'll allow me to take you to."

"I don't think that's such a good idea. Besides, I was just heading back to Philadelphia."

"Oh, come on. At least let me call you. I'll be in New York on location for the next three months. I'm sure I can find time to come to Philadelphia to take you to dinner."

I don't know why but I gave him my business card and told him to give me a call and we would work something out. The whole drive back, I was wondering exactly why Michael Harrison wanted to take me out. There are a million women swooning over him across America, and he wanted to disrupt my life.

I couldn't believe it. New Year's day had fallen on a Friday, so I had initially planned to stay in New York till Sunday and just go to work Monday. Since I came back early and I hadn't been in since Tuesday, I decided to swing by the office and pick up the swatches and layout for an account I was working on. While I was there I decided to check my voicemail. I couldn't believe it. Michael had called already.

"Hi, Anya. I know you probably won't get this message until Monday, but I wanted you to know I was serious and that I could not stop thinking about you."

Okay God, is this some kind of joke? Is he that desperate? I didn't know what to think. He left his cell phone number and his room number. I was tripping out. Michael Harrison was jockin' me big time. I sat back in my chair and smiled while I looked up at the ceiling, spinning in my chair. Was this really happening?

Yes, it was. That night I called the hotel and left a message at his room just letting him know that I had gotten his voicemail, I would call him in the upcoming week and that he better not jock me so hard, I could get the wrong idea. I wanted to tell someone because this was too unreal but I thought I'd better keep this one to myself for a minute, at least until I saw where it was going. But why would he be willing to come to Philly to take me out? What's up with that? New York is full of beautiful women, and I was sure he could have his pick.

When I got to work Monday I had a voicemail from Michael asking me what I meant when I said I would get the wrong idea. He said he normally wouldn't do this but there was just something about me. I personally thought it was the freshness of no man on me. It was the essence of happiness and the fragrance of confidence that the Lord had given me over the past few months, and I guess I was wearing it well.

After a week of voicemail tag, he finally caught me in the office and asked me why I wouldn't just give him my home number so when he got in from shooting he could call me and not my voicemail. I told him because he hadn't asked for it. He did, however, ask me if I would mind coming to New York that weekend to have the dinner he'd been waiting on. At first, I wasn't too sure, especially with it snowing and stuff, and on top of that, he said he was going to come take me to dinner. What did I look like running off to New York behind some man I didn't even know? Where do men get off thinking that women are so desperate for a date that they would come to another state? In spite of this wonderful speech, I said what the heck, why not and told him okay.

That Friday, I was suppose to leave, and I could tell from Michael's conversations that week that he was really looking forward to me coming, but why? The man didn't even know me. Everything just felt too right, and it scared me. I had packed the night before so that when I got home, I could just grab my bag and a cab and catch my flight, but all that afternoon I had butterflies in my stomach. I kept telling myself it was cool. It was nothing but dinner. It's not like he was asking me for some kind of commitment. After all, I went to New York all the time and had lunch and dinner with perfect strangers for my job, so I would just act like I was going on business. Besides, he did make a lot of money, and I was sure at some point, he would need an interior designer to do some work for him, so why not be his friend? It could make for good business later and maybe even get me a few Hollywood referrals. You never know, I could be one of the most sought-after designers from the east coast to the west coast if I played my cards right.

I stood at my window, looking at the wet ground, thinking how cold I had become, how emotionally uninvolved I was. Here this fine man, paid wanted to take me out to dinner, and I could rationalize myself out of this date, and on top of that, I was trying to think how it would be beneficial in the long run business wise. What had John done to me? I thought I was fine. I had taken the last year to really spend some quality time with the Lord, I felt good about myself and my life, so why couldn't I move forward? Was I afraid of being hurt again? I couldn't be, I was so over John it wasn't even funny.

As I stood at that window, I felt like crying, but I couldn't figure out why. I felt so overwhelmed with emotion, all this because a man wanted to take me out to a simple dinner. *Get it together Anya*, I told myself over and over, but I couldn't. I walked over to my desk and picked up the phone to call Michael and let him know I wasn't coming. I left a message on his cell phone just saying that I was sorry but I wasn't going to be able to make it and that I would talk to him later. I felt bad about it but decided I just wasn't ready for all this dating stuff again. Maybe God still needed to do a little more healing in me in places that I thought were already healed.

I continued to work that day as usual but I couldn't help thinking about Michael and of course I couldn't even run it past anyone because I hadn't told anyone and I was kind of glad I didn't. I couldn't get any work done. Every idea I had that day was horrible. Nothing seemed to go together on any of my layouts, and I was becoming more and more frustrated as the day progressed. I grabbed my purse and looked at the clock. If I left right then I could still make it home in time to catch my flight. What was so hard about this just go Anya and quit trippin'.

I got to the airport and just stood at the gate right through to the final boarding. I couldn't do it. I picked up my garment bag, took a deep breath and walked down the corridor right out to the front of the airport and got a cab. As I rode to my house, I just stared out the foggy window. I sat back in the seat trying to recall the day I first met John, and as I replayed it in my mind, I wished I didn't have to have every man that looked so good to me back then. That's why I was in this mess I was in. Before I knew it, the driver pulled up in front of my place and I paid him and thanked him, for what I don't know. It's not like he helped my situation any. In the movies, don't cabdrivers always give people advice based on their facial expressions when they enter the cab? Well this one didn't. He didn't even ask me what was wrong. I shouldn't have tipped him.

When I got in the house, I dropped my bag and went in the kitchen to make some hot chocolate. I waited while the water boiled, wondering what Michael was thinking about me. I checked my messages, but there wasn't one from him. I guess I was kind of hoping there would be. I got a mug down from the cabinet and poured the boiling water into it. Then I got the package of hot chocolate and poured it into the cup and grabbed the Redi Whip from the fridge and sprayed it on top. I went upstairs and ran some water in an attempt to soak my craziness away. That was always my answer to everything, a long, hot bath. I lit some candles and put on Rasaan Patterson. I almost fell asleep in the tub. I was so relaxed that when the phone rang, it startled me.

"Hello" I said in my I don't-wanna-be-bothered voice.
"Hey Anya, What happened? Is everything alright?"
Okay for one he was asking me way too many questions not to even know me.
"Oh hi, Michael. Yeah, everything is okay." I quickly sat up in the tub.
"So what happened? Why aren't you coming?"
"I don't know, Michael. I just couldn't come," I said, agitated that he even felt I owed him a detailed explanation.
"Well I have two days off next week, Wednesday and Thursday. What if I come there and take you out and you show me around a little? I've never been to Philly before."

"Michael, I just don't think it would be a good idea. I'm just not in a dating mood right now."

"Oh, I see." I could hear in his voice that he thought I was just blowin' him off, but I wasn't. I really wasn't. "Alright then, Anya. It was nice meeting you. Maybe you can give me a call when and if you decide you're in a dating mood. I enjoyed your conversation, and I definitely enjoyed meeting you. Well . . ." He kind of paused. "Well, I guess that's it huh? Well, have a nice life and take care." he hung up the phone.

Now what? He must have thought I was a real bitch, and really I wasn't. I felt so bad, but I hadn't even done anything. A couple of hours later, the phone rang. It was Michael. He was so sweet. He called back to apologize for being rude when he hung up, then he blew me out of the water with his next question. He asked me if I wasn't going out with him because he was white. I couldn't even believe he asked me that. Now I have to say I, as a black woman have never been attracted to white men. I wasn't really even attracted to light skin men. I just always preferred Hershey's chocolate, but Michael was different. He was so sexy, and I really didn't think about him being white. He was one of those men where color didn't really matter, almost like Robert DiNero. I don't care what nationality you are, if you're a woman, you love Robert DiNero. Michael was the same way, only young. He wasn't tall, but wasn't short either. He was just the right height for me anyway, about five-eleven. He had the most beautiful smile, which I'm a sucker for anyway. His eyes danced when he smiled too. His hair was dark brown, and he wore a full beard and moustache for the film he was shooting. His build was slender but his body was tight. He might not have a six pack, but it was definitely a four. He was kind of a pretty boy with a touch of rugged sex appeal. I think the scar on his left cheek helped him pull that look off. He was too sexy for words. I can't explain it, but if you've ever seen him in a movie, you know exactly what I'm talking about.

I told him it had nothing to do with him being white. If that was the case, I would never have given him my card to call me and then turned around and given him my home number too.

"Okay, then what is it, if you don't mind me asking?"

Actually I did mind. I minded very much, but I told him anyway. I sat there for three hours and told him all about John and my jacked-up marriage and my year off from dating. I explained that I just wasn't ready to get back out there again. He wanted a chance to prove that there were good men in the world, and he said he just wanted to get to know me, no strings attached, no pressure, just friends going out, hanging out and having fun. It's not like we lived in the same city and could spend a lot of time getting attached. After I thought about it, this might be ideal, talking to him over the phone, seeing him a couple of times a month, no way to get all caught up and attached. This just might work. It's not that I didn't believe there were good men left. I knew there were, I just didn't want to have to go through any more to get to one of the good ones, you know?

After I poured my soul out, I felt better. It was like a burden was lifted off my heart. We began to talk on the phone at least once a day to fill each other in on what had taken place that day. His stories were often way more exciting than mine, but he still wanted to hear them, and I liked that. John had stopped listening a long time ago, that is if he ever really was listening. John was so wrapped up in him and his world, and I really believe I just made for nice decoration. Oh what a beautiful arm piece I made at his office parties and dinners. I was so stupid, and it's not that I would even mind being an arm piece for someone who loved me for more than just that.

I remember one night John's law office was having it's annual anniversary banquet. This was before we were married and we'd only been dating a month. I was all excited, so I took off work early. I had looked for the perfect dress for almost two months. I know Kim was sick of me dragging her in and out of stores all weekend for weeks on end, but she went anyway, until I found it, the perfect dress. I might still have it in the back of my closet somewhere. Anyway, I left work and went straight to the shop to get my hair done. When I got home, I jumped in the tub, lotioned down real good, did my makeup, took my shoes out of the box and slid 'em on. Finally, I slid into that dress and looked in the mirror. I was on if I do say so myself, and I do. I sprayed a few squirts of perfume, and as I was putting my lipstick in my purse, I heard the doorbell. "Kim, can you grab that? It's probably John. Tell him I'll be down in one minute."

A few minutes later, I headed down the stairs, trying to walk all sexy, you know.

"Baby, you look amazing, but listen, I picked something up for you today. I know you already have a dress, and you're all ready, but when I saw this today, I just knew it would be perfect."

"What's wrong with what I have on? Didn't you just say I look amazing? That was you that said that, right?"

"Anya, you do look amazing. It's just that I think this would be better for the party. Please, Anya, for me. I just want everything to be perfect. You know I want to try and make partner by the time I'm thirty."

I just stood there for a moment in shock before I agreed. I looked over at Kim. I could tell she was disappointed in me, but what was I suppose to do? I just wanted everything to go right for the party. He handed me the dress, and as I turned to walk up the stairs, he said, "Oh Anya. Here." He handed me a Nordstrom's shopping bag with a pair of shoes and a purse.

Kim followed me upstairs. "What are you doing?" she said under her breath, "After everything we went through to get this dress? You're wearing this dress. Ain't nothing wrong with what you got on. You look good. Tell him you're wearing what you bought or you ain't going."

"Kim, quit trippin'. It's just a dress."

"Oh my fault, I thought it was the perfect dress." She grabbed my arm, turning me around to look at her.

"Yeah, me too, but I guess it depends on whose eyes you're looking through," I said, taking my dress off.

"Girl, what are you letting him do to you? You are not the Anya I know. Anya, if he's this controlling now, just imagine how he'll be down the line."

"Kim, please just drop it. If I don't wear the dress we won't have a good time tonight because he'll be trippin', so I'll wear the dress he wants, we'll have a good time and I'll wear my dress another time. It's not a big deal." But it was a big deal, a big fat funky deal that I got dealt the bad hand in. I went in the bathroom and changed my lipstick, I put on the new dress and shoes, and changed purses.

"Anya," John hollered up the stairs, "we're gonna be late."

"I'm almost ready," I hollered. "I guess he thinks it only takes five minutes to change. Men."

"Naw, don't say men, say John, 'cause I ain't never seen no man come to take a woman out and make her change when he get there," Kim snapped. She hollered down the stairs, "You need to chill because she was ready until you came in here talking about she needed to change her clothes." She was pissed. I eventually made it back down the stairs.

"Hey, now that's what I'm talking about. My baby know she lookin' good." The funny part about it was I knew I looked good before and part of me looking so good was my self-confidence, which he totally shot down for the night. So there we went, the young successful attorney and his personal black Barbie. I couldn't believe I was really going out like that.

But, that's neither here nor there now, back to Michael. He was so crazy, he would have me crackin' up, and I had missed that. Being able to just laugh at nothing and feel carefree about so much was great. It was more than great. It was a part of me that I had even forgotten existed. I guess I just needed someone to bring it back out of me. It felt good not to be so serious all the time.

After three weeks of all this phone calling, I got a box delivered to my job. It was on my desk when I came back from meeting with a client. I could tell it was probably roses. I was right. What else would be in a long white box with a big red ribbon? Two dozen of the most exquisite red and yellow roses you ever wanted to see lay beneath the lid. When I opened the box, it looked like each one had been handpicked for perfection. The card was from Michael, of course, and it said that to his understanding, yellow was for friendship and red was for love, and he wanted me to know how much he loved becoming my friend. It was beautiful. I felt sixteen okay maybe seventeen because that's when I got my first box of roses from my ex-boyfriend Julian. Standing looking at them, I had the same overwhelming sense of joy in my stomach the he-really-likes-me feeling, and it felt good. I immediately picked up the phone and left a voice mail on Michael's cell phone telling him how swept away I was and that I thought I might be ready for that dinner.

My assistant came in my office, just being nosy. I guess she had been elected by the office to come find out who the flowers were from. I didn't give up too much information though. I let her read the card. She was sprung. "Umm," she said, looking at me, "Who are these from? Who is Michael and how friendly have you become with him?"

I just laughed and told her if it turned into more than a friendship, she would be the first to know. I could tell that wasn't good enough, but that's all the info I was givin' up at the time.

I had to go to New York in two weeks to meet with a client, so I thought then would be perfect to see Michael. Besides, it would give me time to get myself mentally prepared. I had to go for work anyway. I couldn't just not go. It wasn't an option. Plus, it wouldn't be like I was chasing him since I would already be there, and with all the phone conversations we'd had, we were no longer complete strangers.

Although I felt good about it, I know we had only been talking on the phone, but it just felt right, I felt like he really knew me and that I knew him and that I could just be myself. I didn't have to be what I thought he wanted me to be. He was happy with just me. No, he appeared to be ecstatic with just me. I finally called him and told him I was coming in two weeks. He said he was happy. He didn't really want to wait that long, but it was better than nothing. He was right. What was I holding out for? I decided that I would surprise him that weekend. I asked my assistant to book me a flight out that Friday afternoon. I figured I would check into the hotel and hope he didn't shoot too late, and I would surprise him and we'd go out to dinner or maybe Saturday we could do something.

I got there Friday evening and checked into the hotel. Michael was in the presidential suite so I got a room on the floor below. I know I didn't need to be spending that type of money on a hotel room, but what the heck? I was going so I might as well go in style, but trust me, I decided if this became a habit, all future visits would be on him. I called his room just to see if by chance he was there, but he wasn't. I called his phone but I got his voice mail. I left a message telling him to call me on my cell phone when he got in because I was probably going to be out that evening. Okay, I took a bath and laid out two options of attire, a sexy dress just in case we did go out, although it was so cold, I really didn't want to see outside again. Also a casual pair of cords and a turtleneck sweater in case I just went to his room. I laid across the bed waiting for him to call and ended up falling asleep. When I woke up, it was 9:45P.M. Well I said to myself, *I guess it was going to be a late one.* I decided to just order room service.

I was sitting there eating a cheeseburger and some fries and a salad, looking for a good movie to buy when my cell phone rang. I picked it up and said hello.

"Hi, sweetheart. How was your day?"

I don't know why but Michael's voice gave me instant assurance that I had done the right thing by coming. I told him it was okay and asked about his day. He said it was long and that he was just getting in and all he wanted to do was take a shower and go to sleep because he had an early shoot the next morning. "Oh, I hate you're so tired. Maybe I should let you go get some rest."

"Now you know I'm never too tired for you. I have to take you when I can get you. He said laughing. "What are you eating? You sure make it sound good whatever it is."

"I'm just eating a burger and fries."

"That sounds good. Maybe I'll call room service and get me a burger."

"Maybe you should. Why don't you go ahead and order your food and take your shower and call me back while you're eating or after you get finished."

"Are you trying to get rid of me?" he said, laughing "You're right though. I'll call you in an hour. Where are you?" I just laughed and told him I was around and would be waiting for his call.

"Yeah, okay, I got your around."

After we hung up, I got dressed and called room service and questioned if Mr. Harrison had already called his cheeseburger and fries in, because if not I was calling it in. The gentleman advised me that it had been called in and should be up in about fifteen minutes. Of course, I went up to his floor in twelve minutes and hoped I hadn't missed the delivery. I leaned on the wall in the hall for about five minutes, but it seemed like twenty-five. I felt like a groupie. I was kind of nervous. My heart had begun to pound in my chest. Maybe this wasn't such a good idea after all. Just as I had given up, I heard the elevator bell, then the sound of wheels coming in my direction. I wanted to run, but it was too late. I was face to face with the bellman. "Hi," I said nervously. "You can leave that with me." He, of course, refused. Initially that is. I don't know if it was my twenty dollars, my flirtatious smile or a combination of the two that persuaded him, but he grabbed the money and told me to have a nice night.

I stood at the door and took a deep breath, feeling a little nervous about the whole surprise thing. I was hoping he would think this was a good surprise, no actually I was hoping for more than that. Hopefully he wouldn't think I was too forward. I stepped forward and knocked on the door. I heard that familiar voice say, "It's open. Just leave it on the table. The tip is there for you."

"Okay," I called in the direction his voice was coming from as I closed the door behind me. "Is there anything else I can do for you?"

I think that was the moment he caught my voice. He came flying out of the bedroom with just a towel wrapped around his waist. Umm, not too bad, I was thinking. His chest was just as nice, if not nicer in person than on the big screen. What was I doing there? I wasn't going to fall back into my same pattern though. I was going to take it slow and just see what happened.

"Oh man, I thought I was losing it. I knew that was your voice. Aw man, I don't know what to say." He paused and looked a little overwhelmed, but I could tell he was glad I was there. I was relieved. It was almost like when you're in school and you like someone who is really popular and you think they would never like you and then you find out they do and you can't believe it. Okay well that's the expression he gave. He lit up and walked toward me and kind of hesitated before he grabbed me and hugged me. "Oh, I can't believe this. This really is a surprise. I needed this after the day I had. Oh, you just don't know." He literally was coming undone in disbelief, but it made me feel good to know I could still do this to a man. I could get use to this.

He finally let me go. He held on to the side of his towel as he went toward the room and told me to hold on while he threw something on. I took a moment to look around the room to try and get a feel for him. I guess it would probably have been better if this was his home as opposed to a hotel, then I could probably get a true sense of who Golden Globe golden boy Michael Harrison was. When he came out of the bedroom, I felt even more comfortable knowing that he felt comfortable with me just poppin' up. He had on a pair of green and navy plaid lounge pants and a navy fleece pullover. He looked so cute. I couldn't believe it. I was actually attracted to this man. Hmm sometimes, I shock myself. I don't know if I was more shocked that he was white or that he was Michael Harrison. Either way, I was shocked. I told him to just relax as if I weren't there and eat like he knew he needed to so he could get some rest. But he said he was too excited to even think about resting. We sat at the table and talked while he ate. I watched him as he took one big bite after the next out of that gigantic cheeseburger. I wasn't even able to finish the one I had earlier, but he seemed to have no problem, what-so-ever. He was so funny. I couldn't believe it. I sat there just watching him talk and smile that sexy boyish smile. I think I was in awe, but I'm not sure because I was too busy being in awe. After he ate, he went and washed his face and hands, which he desperately needed after that messy burger. Moments later, he reappeared and motioned for me to follow him into the living room. We found our way to the couch, and he asked me if I'd flown or driven, and I told him I had flown.

"Do you mind if I take my shoes off?" I looked over at him.
"Why would I mind?" He looked a little puzzled. I removed my shoes and placed them neatly next to the couch. I turned and sat with one foot underneath me while the other remained straddled alongside the couch. I leaned my head onto my hand, which was resting on the back of the couch.

He asked me if I had found out if I had landed the client from lunch Wednesday, and I told him that I hadn't heard from them yet. I was just psyched that he cared or that he remembered. I felt so relaxed as we sat there and made small talk continuing, down the path of getting to know each other. I pulled my foot from beneath me and began to massage it because it was falling asleep. "Here" he motioned for me to give him my foot, "let me do that." I told him he didn't have to rub my feet, and he said he knew, but that he wanted to, so I put the other one up in his lap and let him, and I enjoyed every minute of it. I could get use to this. I hadn't had my feet rubbed since Anthony and I had broken up. I was usually the one doing the rubbing, rubbing John's back, his neck, his temples. I had forgotten it could be like this.

I told him I wasn't going to stay late, since he said he had an early shoot I wanted him to get some rest. Of course he didn't want to let me leave, but I told him I was staying till Sunday and if I only saw him for a couple hours the whole weekend it would be okay, especially since we hadn't planned any of this. He finally agreed to surrender me at 12:45A.M. He wanted to walk me down but I told him it wasn't necessary. At the door he leaned in, kissed my forehead and made me promise to think of him that night. How could I not? I still couldn't believe I was there. He opened the door, and I kissed him on his cheek and passed through the door.
"See ya," I said.
I could tell he was still watching me as I walked down the hall because I hadn't heard the door close. I wanted to turn around so bad it was killing me.

"Anya?" Yes. It was my chance to look back. I paused and slowly turned back, looking over my shoulder. I didn't say anything. I just looked and smiled. "I'm glad you came."

"Yeah, me too." I giggled, turned back around and continued my journey down the deserted hall.

I was in a whole 'nother world on the way back to my room. I actually couldn't wait to see him the next day and hoped that he wouldn't have to shoot late again. I pushed the elevator button and smiled at myself, glad that I had come, and wondering why I had waited so long. When I got back down to my room, Kim had left a message on my cell phone wondering where I was. I hadn't told anyone but my assistant where I was going, and she wasn't quite sure of the reason, but she had her suspicions. I could tell because she was trying to pump me for information all day. I called Kim back and told her I had forgotten to tell her I had to come to New York that weekend on business. I usually always let Kim know when and where I was going and for how long, but I was keeping this secret just a little while longer. She is my best friend, and she would probably be glad to know I was dating again, but I just didn't want anyone to know, just in case it didn't work out. All I do know is I thought about Michael until I fell asleep that night.

When I woke up, I felt refreshed. I called room service and ordered some juice, a bagel and some fruit. I opened the curtains and looked out over New York City and figured it was me, my checkbook, my debit card and all the Manhattan shops until Michael returned. I ran through the shower and threw some slacks and a sweater on. There was a knock at the door, and when I went to open it, there was a note slid under the door. I picked it up and opened it. It was so cute. There was a sunshine drawn in the upper right corner and the note simply read, *I'll be thinking of you today. Please think of me. Call me when you wake up. I'll try to make it a short day.* Awwww, Michael was reeling me in, and I was taking the bait. I had a tingling sensation run through me. I jumped up and did a little happy dance over to the phone. What was it about him that I liked so much? I grabbed my cell phone and called him. Voice ail. Of course. My message? Simple as his note. "Good morning. Thank you for my note. It was very thoughtful. I'll be thinking of you too." That was that. I sat down to the table, opened the little package of cream cheese and spread it over my raisin-and-cinnamon bagel. I took one bite and drank half the glass of juice. I was hungry until I read that note. I guess I was too excited to eat or maybe just too full of hope, hope of what this might actually grow to be. I know it was a little too soon to be getting all psyched up, but I couldn't help it.

As I walked down the busy New York streets, the cold didn't even bother me, I was warm on the inside. Not to mention, the warm feeling inside I get from shopping. I felt better than I had in long time. I wanted to pick something up for Michael, but I didn't know if I should. Was it too soon for that? I'm so mad because I have no one to bounce this off. I'm in the men's department at Sak's and I see a salesclerk, so I just asked him. I tell him the whole story of course omitting the part about it being Michael Harrison, and he thought I should get Michael a little something and just play it off and say I was out shopping and I thought of him working hard all day and I would have felt bad not getting him something too. I told him about the night before and he suggested one of those wrap-around towels that men put on when they get out the shower. We both laughed but I thought that was a good idea, so I bought a really thick soft white one and had Michael's initials monogrammed on the left corner in red. It was perfect. I had it gift wrapped in a plain shiny white paper with a big red ribbon.

My hands were full of bags and at two o'clock I decided to stop at a café in Rockefeller Center and grab a bite. I sat down at a small table next to the window, pulled out my phone and called Michael. Of course I got his voicemail, but I told him I was out shopping and was just checking in to see how his schedule was looking and to let him know I was having lunch and then heading back to the hotel where I would remain until he got in. After I ate, I got a cab back to the hotel. I kept staring at Michael's gift, wondering if I should have gotten it. Why did I always question myself?

I decided to do a little work to help pass the time. I took out some layouts and my sketchpad and pencil and plugged up my laptop. I really had all intentions on working, but no matter what I did, my mind would wonder back to Michael. It really was quite annoying. I decided I could at least look through a few art magazines, you don't need a lot of focus for that. After about two hours, the phone rang, and it was Michael. He said they were wrapping up and that he would probably be finished in another hour or so. I told him that was fine and that I was going to call downstairs and see if I could get a massage. He told me to wait and he could have someone come up to his suite and give us both one. I told him okay. I hoped he didn't think because I was going to be naked in his room getting a massage that he was getting any. He didn't seem to be like that, but you never know. I ran a bubble bath and lotioned down real good, put my hair up in a clip and put on this sweat suit that I had gotten at The Gap earlier. I kind of had a feeling I was going to need something loungey after seeing him all kicked back the night before. I don't know why, but I felt really comfortable around him, like I didn't have to be the glamour girl I always try to be. When he called, it was 7:30 P.M., and he said he was on his way to the hotel and that the masseur was coming at 8:30 P.M. I was like cool. When it was time to go upstairs, I just put on a little lip liner and some clear gloss, I wanted to put my mole on, but I knew it would get wiped off so what would be the point? I grabbed my key and was out.

When Michael came to the door, he told me how cute I looked, and I was glad, at least he knew I wasn't trying to impress him. I thought he was going to get a massage, too, but he said it would probably just put him to sleep so he was going to take a shower and look over the script for the scene they were shooting the following day. I told him that I could wait for my massage, but he insisted that I get one, so I did. Shoot he didn't know, when it came to a massage, a free one too, you didn't have to tell me twice. I went into the other room like lightning and changed into a robe. I came back and hopped on the table. Oh, this was on. I could feel the masseuse working the knots out of my upper back. I hadn't had a massage in over a month. this was great. I lived for massages and pedicures. It felt good to be stretched out and kneaded like dough. I was relaxed but I couldn't stop thinking about Michael the whole time I lay there. One thing I realized was I wasn't scared. I wasn't scared of being hurt. I kind of trusted him, and even that didn't scare me. Maybe I was going to be okay after all.

That girl hooked me up. I'm the one who ended up falling asleep on the table. When I got up, I was so relaxed, I didn't want to do anything but lay there. I dragged myself off the table and went in the room where Michael was. He was standing by the window walking back and forth, mumbling to himself. I just leaned on the door and watched him, that is, until he caught me.

"Oh, you're finished. I was waiting to see if you wanted to go get something to eat." I told him I was way too relaxed to go back out into the cold and the hustle and bustle of the New York City streets. He said it was no big deal, we could order whatever I was in the mood for, light the fireplace and relax. After I went back and put on my clothes, we did just that. He even ordered Italian food from who knew where, it must be nice to have that kind of pull.

"You're just too tired from all that shopping today. Did you get anything good, or did you just try on a million pairs of shoes, a thousand pairs of pants and say you couldn't find anything you liked." I looked over at him smiling. "Ha Ha you are sooo funny. Actually I bought quite a few things. Now that I think about it, do you think I can leave some stuff here until I come back? I forgot I only brought my garment bag. I'll bring an empty suitcase with me next time. I just hadn't planned on doing any shopping, but I had to do something to amuse myself while you worked." He told me he would be glad if I left some stuff there, then at least he knew I would be back. It wasn't like that though. I was looking forward to coming back. He just didn't know how much.

"I see you did all that shopping and didn't even think of me. You could have at least brought me an empty bag," he said, pouting. I slid over next to him and told that I had bought him something, but he thought I was just playing, but I told him I really had. I explained that I had gotten him a little something, but didn't know if I should be giving him gifts because it was too soon for all that. I told him about the whole salesclerk conversation, and he started crackin up.

"Aww you went through all that stress for me? Aren't you just a sweetheart. Okay so where is it? What did you get me? You might as well give it up now." He thought this was so hilarious. I had left the gift in the room because I wasn't going to give it to him. He was like a kid though so I got up and went down to my room and got it.

When I got back upstairs, he acted shocked, as if he thought I was just playing. He really didn't think I had gotten him something. I walked over and sat on the floor next to him, and I was still a little nervous about buying him a gift so soon but handed it over anyway. You would think it was Christmas and he was six years old the way he lit into that box. It pleased my heart though because I loved making people happy, and apparently I had made him very happy. He looked down into the bag and grabbed the box. He sat down and put it in his lap. "Oooooooh, professional-looking bow." He smiled. "I'm impressed." He pulled the mini envelope from the box, opened it and read my little note out loud. He cleared his throat, "Michael, how could I not think of you today or any day since I've known you."

"Anya, you just keep surprising me. Now, for the goods." He took the top off the box and held up the towel and was juiced but that wasn't the clincher because he hadn't seen his initials yet. He stood and wrapped it around his waist and fastened the Velcro, brushed his hands over it and looked down. That's when his eyes lit up. His smile covered his entire face, and happiness radiated from his eyes, and I knew the gift was a good idea. "Whew, I get initials and everything. I knew I was special. I knew you liked me," he said laughingly. He pulled me up off the floor, hugged and thanked me. I could tell it really made his day. He walked all around the room modeling it, stopping and posing. He was so silly, but I enjoyed it and was glad I was there.

When it was time for me to go, of course he asked me to stay, but I wasn't with all that. I had explained to him before that since I had renewed my relationship with the Lord, that I was celibate. He had said before that it didn't bother him and that he respected my decision and my reasons. He was a Christian too, although he admitted he never even entertained the idea of giving up sex until marriage. He said it was just too hard to stop once you got started. I felt him though, because it was hard for me at first, too, especially the first three months, but after I got use to not having it, there would only be certain times I wished I could get some, but for the most part I was okay. I just refused to allow myself to get that intimate and give that part of myself to any man again other than my husband. It took too much out of me emotionally to get out of those relationships, and sometimes you can be out for a long time and you might run into the person and have a quickening in your pants, a flashback, and the next thing you know you're in his bed. Well I had had enough of temporary emotional attachments that still left me empty, pleasing my flesh while my spirit died.

Michael had told me that he didn't mean stay and sleep with him. He said he was just saying I could stay up there if I wanted, in the other bedroom or anywhere I wanted. I believed him, but I didn't, so I thought it would be better for me to just go back to my room and keep temptation down and life simple. After all, my life hadn't been this smooth in a long time. Why mess it up and complicate things? Once again, he walked me to the door, kissed me on the forehead and told me to have a good sleep.

When I got to my room, my hotel phone was ringing, which was odd because who would be calling? I picked up only to find Mike on the other end. I can still hear his voice, so sincere, so seductive.

"I miss you already." I could hear the smile in his voice. As bad as I wanted to go back, I didn't. I had come too far. God had done too much in my heart to blow it.

"I miss you too," I said, laughing. "As much as you can miss someone you just left less than five minutes ago." He was trying to reel me in but the only problem was, I didn't want to be reeled in. I wanted to keep my safe distance, but it was hard because he was so sweet and made me feel so wanted. I sat there holding the phone thinking that this was about to get complicated.

I tossed and turned all night. I guess I really was scared. I was scared of what I was feeling. Where did it come from? I was so sure I could handle my feelings just a few hours ago. I tried to go to sleep, but every time I closed my eyes, I thought about being with Michael. It was way too soon for me to even be thinking like that. I hadn't even known him long enough to care if things didn't work out, so why did I? Why did I always put this kind of pressure on myself? Why couldn't I just enjoy it for what it was right then, a friendship? Who said friendship had to end in love?

The next morning I felt like crap. I didn't get any sleep. I got up and decided to leave early. I couldn't do this, I couldn't let anyone back in. I wanted to, but

I couldn't. I didn't know how. I sat on the edge of the bed crying, but I couldn't figure out why. I think they were tears of fear. I wrote Michael a letter and slid it under his door before catching a cab back to the airport. I felt so bad. What the hell was wrong with me? He was definitely going to think I was some kind of basket case. In this particular case he would be correct.

He called that night, a little upset. He said he didn't understand. He thought everything was good that weekend and that I enjoyed myself. I didn't pick up the phone. I just listened to the voicemail after the phone had rang.

How pathetic was I? I was hiding out from his phone calls. I needed to be slapped. I tried to pray, but I couldn't hear God clearly or maybe I wasn't really listening. Maybe I was just talking and never giving God a chance to get a word in edgewise.

I thought I was off the hook but surprisingly, on Monday I received roses from Michael. The card simply read, *Call me when you're ready. I'll wait.* Well how long can you wait after reading that? See what I mean? He was just so perfect, but men have always been perfect in the beginning. I called him, and he amazingly answered his phone.

"Why are you so perfect?" I blurted out.

"Because I understand you and I like you and I really believe you only find the perfect one once in a lifetime and for some reason, I believe you're her. So what's a little time out of my whole life taking the time to find out if I'm right? From the moment I saw you in the hotel lobby, I can't say I was in love, but I felt like I wanted to love you. There was just something about you that drew me in, and it won't let me go. Believe me, do you really think if I didn't think there was something there I would be pursuing you in this manner? Not to be vain, but I have women throwing themselves at me left and right, but the chemistry I feel when I see you and when I hear your voice can't be compared to anything I've ever felt."

For the next several months we both traveled back and forth seeing each other. I was glad his movie ran behind schedule because it kept him in New York longer, which kept him closer and allowed us to see each other almost every week. Things were going pretty well if I do say so myself, and if you can believe this, I trusted him more being in a whole 'nother state than I did with John in the same house. Michael never questioned if I was seeing anyone else, and I really believed that he knew I wasn't, it was hard enough for him to get in to my heart, so I don't think he was worried. I never asked him if he was seeing anyone or trying to get some from somebody else because he sure wasn't getting any from me. I'm not sure if he was, I didn't feel like he was and I didn't think he was, or maybe, I really didn't want to know. Either way, I didn't ask.

The picture was finally done early June, and to celebrate Michael wanted to take a vacation and wanted me to come. I was a little hesitant at first but agreed to go. It's funny, I never asked him about sleeping arrangements but hope he gets up separate rooms.

I was really excited about my trip. I had never been to Jamaica before, so you know I had to shop, shop and shop some more. We were going to an all-inclusive couples resort, but I was hoping he wouldn't want to just stay at the resort, because I really wanted to get out and see the island. We were going to be there for six nights and seven days, and I wanted to be prepared for whatever, hence all the shopping. I tried to pack light, but it just wasn't happening, I definitely had to have a different swimsuit for each day, and I bought a few pair of linen pants and some halter tops. I did bring a few sundresses and a couple of club dresses even though I wasn't really a clubber. When it was all said and done, I had a garment bag and two suitcases. One suitcase just had shoes. I was able to talk myself out of taking real purses, I settled on three small ones, just big enough to fit ID, lipstick and my camera.

The day finally came. My alarm clock went off at 5:00 A.M. I was not at all pleased about that part of the trip. I hate getting up that early. I had arranged for a car to pick me up at seven o'clock to take me to the airport. My flight didn't leave until 10:20, but I liked to be there early so I wouldn't have to rush. I had laid out my clothes the night before and set my bags by the front door. I jumped in the shower and got dressed. I knew it would be hot in Jamaica but cool on the plane so I put on a baby-blue-and-white DKNY capri sweat suit with some footies and a pair of blue-and-white DKNY tennis shoes. I had on a white tank top under my jacket, so as soon I hit Jamaica, that jacket would be history and it would be my flesh receiving the benefits of the golden hot rays of the sun.

I opted not to wear any lashes. I figured it would be so hot there the glue might melt, which of course meant no mole either. I could see it running down my lip, on a bead of Jamaican sweat. I was so excited, I couldn't wait. I ran downstairs to the kitchen and threw a few scoops of Gevallia Hazlenut into the Brew and Go as if I needed caffeine as excited as I was. I went over to the pantry to get a doughnut out as the doorbell rang. This is it, I thought, and I began to chant on the way to the door. "I'm going to Jamaica. I'm going to Jamaica." I'm going to Jamaica. I opened the door.

"Good morning mam." The driver said. "Are these your bags here?" He looked down at the floor.

"Yes, they sure are." I continued to chant softly on my way back to the kitchen. "I'm going to Jamaica." I put on my little matching DKNY mini backpack, grabbed my coffee and my doughnut, stuck my phone in my pocket and grabbed my keys from the hook on the fridge. I set the house alarm, closed the front door, locked it and made my way down the walkway to the car.

I couldn't wait to see Michael. Visions of us walking along the beach and having candle lit dinners flooded my thoughts on the ride to the airport. I was hoping we would have some real movie moments. Don't act like I'm the only one who daydreams about those kind of romantic times and hoped that one day I'd find myself in one, really experiencing what I'd only dreamed of.

"Taking a little vacation, I see." The driver looked at me through the rearview mirror.
"Yes. A much needed one at that."
"So where you headed, if you don't mind me asking?"
"Jamaica!!!!" I sang out in my best Jamaican accent.
"Cool. Alone?" He looked puzzled. As if I couldn't go on a trip alone if I wanted.
"Nah, I'm meeting my boyfriend there." Wow I couldn't believe I'd just said that. Was Michael in fact my boyfriend? I wasn't really sure about that one, but as far as the driver knew, he was.
"Well I'm sure you'll have a good time."
"Oh, I plan on it." I could not seem to remove the silly grin I was wearing.
We pulled up to the airport, and I checked my bags curbside to avoid the line on the inside. "Have a safe trip," the driver said as he put my last bag on the dolly for the skycap.

"Thanks. Enjoy the rest of your day." I tipped him and turned and walked to the skycap and handed him my passport. He handed back and advised me my flight would be leaving out of Gate 18. I stopped at the bookstore on the way to the gate and browsed a little. I bought two magazines, two candy bars, some gum and a bottle of water. I walked down to the gate and sat and waited for boarding to begin. I should have known Michael was going to book me in first class, but I would have been fine flying coach, after all I'd been flying it all those years. I must say I was curious to see what all the hype of first class was about. "Now boarding first class and pre-board passengers on Flight 1463 to Montego Bay, Jamaica." Wow, I thought, *that's me, first class. I might like not having to squeeze past fifty people to get to my seat.*

I walked down the corridor after handing the attendant my boarding pass. I stepped in the doorway of the plane, and bam, there I was in row two. I made my way over to the window seat and noticed the soft full leather seat difference. It was definitely way more comfortable than coach. I guess I could see doing this for long flights, but I couldn't see paying more for short ones. No way. I had even more room than I expected because there was no one sitting next to me.

When the captain gave the okay for electronic devices, I pulled out my DVD player and watched a movie. I even listened to a few CDs, but nothing could make the time go by any faster. I wished I would have stayed awake all night. That way I would be sleepy and I could close my eyes, go to sleep and wake up in Jamaica. This was a downside of having no one sitting next to me, there was no one there to make idle conversation with when you needed them. Now, of course, if I wanted to get some sleep I would have some motor mouth sitting right next to me blabbing my ear off. Finally, after almost four hours I heard it. "Ladies and gentlemen, welcome to beautiful Jamaica!" I couldn't believe it. I was actually there.

I stepped off the plane and walked down the hall, heading for baggage claim. As soon as I passed through the unrestricted area, there was a man standing with a sign that read Dennings. I walked over to him and stopped.

"Ms Dennings?" He attempted to pronounce my name but had a very heavy but sexy accent. If I didn't already know he was saying my name, I probably would not have understood him.

"The one and only," I responded, all smiles, still excited to be there.

"All right. Let's get your bags, and we'll be on our way." He turned and walked toward the baggage claim.

While riding through the city, I just looked around in amazement. This was a long ride. Thank the Lord for air conditioning. It took about an hour and a half to get to the resort, so I took a lot of pictures, but I wished I had brought my video camera. It was so beautifully hot. Of course I had immediately come out of my jacket when we got to the car. Some parts looked poor, but the island was amazing. The women must not believe in pants because I did not see one woman in them. They all had on skirts or dresses, maybe because it was so hot. Whoever was making halter tops there, was making a killing. Even the pregnant women had on halters. I wanted to stop so many times on that ride to the resort, but I figured I would wait till I got to Michael. I never thought about coming to Jamaica with a white man. I wondered if they trip like that out there. Maybe I wouldn't be seeing a lot of the island after all. I didn't want to feel self-conscious. I never really tripped on Michael's skin, but maybe other people would.

The car drove up a long, winding road. There was water everywhere. The resort sat right on the beach. It was gorgeous. I had never seen true blue water before. Shoot even when you buy bottled water it's clear, not blue, but this water was seriously blue like a Crayola color, mixed to an aqua sapphire perfection. As we drove into the resort, it was different than what I had pictured. I was thinking big luxury hotel in Jamaica or something, but I couldn't have been more wrong. It was like a village from a movie. The architecture had a new old-school Victorian feel. It was amazing. As we drove through, I looked at the side-by-side two-story villas, one after the other with balconies that overlooked the small little town they had created.

We pulled to the front, and I admired the lush greenery that surrounded us. The grass was so green and the trees looked more like tall perfectly placed plants. Flowers? Beautiful. Not that I had not seen beautiful flowers in Philly, but this was different. It was so peaceful and seemed to be a world away. I was probably just trippin', but the sky even appeared bluer. The driver came around and let me out. I stepped from the car, looked up into the sky and slowly gave the grounds one more look before heading for the doors. Maybe I thought if I left and came back, it would no longer be there, that's how beautiful it was. The bellman took my bags out of the trunk and followed as I walked in through the front doors, admiring the beauty of the artwork on the walls. It was so simple and so not over the top, I think that's what I could appreciate about it. One of the paintings was actually more of a mural painted directly onto the wall behind the small wooden reception desk. It was simply beautiful, just a large palm tree surrounded by mountains. The floors were a cream ceramic, but they were polished to perfection. It wasn't marble, but if I looked, I could probably see myself. The big green plants placed throughout the room were even shiny. I just stood there for a minute casing the room before I went up to the desk and checked in.

"Is this your first time with us?" the desk clerk asked.

"Yes."

"You will definitely be back. I can tell." She smiled. Was I that obvious? She told me where the pool and sauna were located. She gave information regarding meals and gave me my key.

"Please do not hesitate to let us know if there is anything you need."

"Thank you." I took the key from her and followed the bellman to the room. I knew Michael was there already. His plane was due to arrive four hours before mine.

The bellman showed me to my room alright, with his fine self. He removed the key from my hand and unlocked the door. He motioned for me to go in first as he held the door. The room was amazing, so calm. Again, the simplicity of it made me want to just relax. It took the pressure off. The only thing I didn't like was that the floor was ceramic tile like the lobby. I liked carpet, because I liked to walk around barefoot, but that was my only complaint, which wasn't really a complaint because the floor was warm and it was extremely clean, so I guessed I would survive.

There was a king-size bed with a night table on each side. There was a small doorway that lead into a pretty nice-size living room with a floral couch that was so fluffy I wanted to sit on it right then, but I figured I'd hold out until the bellman left. The table was right at the balcony door. It was like a patio table. The base was iron, and the top was glass, and there were four iron chairs with striped burgundy-and-beige pillows. On top of the glass, there was a huge floral gift basket with a card from Michael. He was so thoughtful it was sickening sometimes. I was going to have to get on my job. He was always trying to outdo me, but I liked that. It was nice to be pampered for a change. I walked out onto the balcony. I wanted to scream. The view was breathtaking. I almost forgot the bellman was still there. He had placed my bags by the door and patiently waited for me to view the room.

"Everything to your satisfaction?"

"Beyond. Thank you."

"Is there anything else I can do for you?"

He was a cutie. Good thing I was a good girl. I normally wouldn't even care for dreads but his were so neat and shiny, not all fat and nasty like some men wear them. Let's not get on that bangin' body. They need to get a new uniform, 'cause those little khaki shorts showed off his beautifully sculpted legs. Oh I know he be at the gym. I could see the print of his chest under his shirt and it wasn't even a tight. It was a regular white button-down with short sleeves. My word, his arms were amazing.

"Uh no. Thank you though." I walked over to him and placed a tip in his hand.

"Oh, I can't accept that ma'am. Thank you, but we don't accept tips." He backed up, refusing the money.

"Oh, you don't?" I was puzzled, hotel, bellman, tip. Right? Maybe it was a Jamaican custom I didn't know about. No matter, I put the money back in my purse.

"You never have to worry about tipping here, okay, remember that. Are you here alone? He smiled as he placed my key in my hand. His teeth were perfectly straight and so white, he must live in Crest white strips. He was waiting for a reply with those pretty brown eyes burning a hole through me with lust.

"Uh," I stuttered, "actually, I'm meeting someone here."

"Okay, I understand. Still, be sure to let me know should you find yourself in need of anything."

"Anything like what?"

"Anything."

"Anything?" I repeated.

"Anything." Okay, he has to leave right now with his sexy talking self. He wasn't about to have me out there caught up in some twisted affair. Besides, I wondered how many women he gave anything to.

All flirting aside, I couldn't wait to see my man though. I went next door and knocked softly but there was no answer. I waited a few moments before knocking again. Still there was no answer. Michael knew what time my plane was arriving and even with a good guess, he could estimate the time from the airport and me checking in, so why wasn't he in his room waiting, like I would be for him? I went back to my room, took off my tennis shoes and got out my little matching DKNY flip-flops. I figured he couldn't be too far so I decided to see if I could track him down, plus I wanted to get a sneak peek at the grounds. I didn't get to see much of anything since I went to the pool area first, Michael was along the pool sitting at a table eating a sandwich. I crept up behind him and kissed the back of his neck. "Hey." I pulled the chair out across from him and sat down. "I figured I'd find you if I looked out here."

"Oooh," he said, looking up, "I'm so glad you did. How was your flight?"

"Great, and yours."

"Good. You hungry?"

"Starvin".

I sat down and picked at his chips while I waited for the waiter to come back. "This place is amazing. How did you find it?"

"My mom told me about it. I've never been here before." That made me feel special. At least I knew this wasn't the norm for him: meet a girl, woo her, then take her to a resort in Jamaica, make her fall in love because it's so romantic, it's hard not to and then move on. We ate then went back to his room to look at the activity schedule. We decided to go snorkeling the next morning because they had a tour at ten. We just hung out the rest of that day, walking around the little city there, going to the shops and buying stuff we didn't need from the various artist displaying their works on the corners.

The resort had some fabulous restaurants. We went to all five while we were there but you know my favorite was the Italian one. I know it was Jamaica and all and not that the jerk bar and traditional Jamaican foods weren't good, but I just love my pasta and was glad they were able to accommodate me.

We went snorkeling, which was cool. I had my little underwater camera and took pictures of the fish. The only thing I couldn't get the hang of was the windsurfing. I kept falling over and by the end of that lesson, I just wanted to soak my tired body. But I can say we got our money's worth on this trip because we did it all except scuba diving. I was too afraid to put all that gear on and go down deep into the sea. I don't care how blue the water is or how many spotters they have, no way. I am way too claustrophobic for all that.

We had a great time. We were gone for a week, and I was so sad when it was coming to an end, I could have stayed there forever. After all the walks on the beach, looking at the bluest water you ever wanted to see and the dancing, non dancing in Michael's case, festival they had Friday night, all the activities, the eating, the shopping, the spa and the hot tub, can you believe that we still hadn't even kissed, other than a little peck on the lips. That came to an end the last night we were there. We were in the garden lying in a hammock, just talking and looking at the sky, holding hands as the gentle winds rocked us. Michael held my hand to his lips and told me that he couldn't remember ever being this happy in a relationship and that he loved my security. He said I never questioned him, which showed him that I trusted him, and because of who he was and what he did, his relationships never got past the trust portion. He said he usually ended up ending things because he couldn't deal with the stress. I explained to him that I didn't question him because he hadn't made me any kind of promises or commitments that I was expecting him to live up to. He said he knew that but that I never pressured him about a commitment either, and that was rare. He pulled me in closer to him and whispered in my ear, "I never want to lose you or this feeling." Now that probably would have scared me right back on a plane a month or two before, but not then, I had come too far, and it was going too good. I had to keep taking a chance and see where it would end up.

I looked up at him and told him that he'd never given me any reason to question his motives, and as long as he didn't and as long as he never hurt me or lied to me, he would never lose me. He caressed my face with his left hand, and before I knew it, he had leaned in and kissed me very softly but very passionately and then he leaned back and said not to worry, he would always treat me as if he was still trying to win my heart. I hated so much that this was going to be our last night together. I just knew he was going for it, trying to get some but he didn't. I liked that about him.

The next morning I packed up and got ready for my long ride back to the airport. We rode back together even though my plane was leaving forty-five minutes after his. We cuddled in the car on the way to the airport, and I almost wanted to cry. I really wasn't ready for it to be over, but it was. From Jamaica, Michael flew to New York, and I flew back to Philly. I hated to be away from him. It was almost killing me I missed him so much. I started getting a little scared. I didn't want to be consumed. That is where I always messed up. I couldn't be consumed.

When I got back, Kim and my sister came over. They had had enough. They wanted to know who this man was I had been seeing and what was the big secret. First my sister started in on me wanting to know they couldn't meet him and why they didn't even know his name. Then Kim asked if I was messin' with John again and felt so stupid that I was too ashamed to tell them. Then she looked at me for a minute. "Naw that ain't no John smile you been floatin' around here with. Come on. What's up?" I stood and told both of them that all I was going to say was that his name was Mike, I met him on New Year's when I went to New York and he had been wooing me every since. He treated me better than I'd ever been treated and more than anything, he had become my friend.

"So you mean to tell me, y'all ain't getting y'all freak on?" Kim said in disbelief.
"Nope. Not even so much as a little feel. As a matter of fact, we just had our first real kiss in Jamaica this week."
"Girl you lyin,'" my sister said. "Are you sure he ain't gay?"
I assured her he wasn't, but that he respected the fact that I had decided not to have sex anymore until I got married.
"Huh, yeah, I still can't get over that one. John really did mess you up," Kim joked.
"Ha ha ha funny," I said without so much as a smile.
"I'm just playing," but everyone knew there were no jokes left in me for John. "I'll give it to you, though, I wish I could do it, but I can't. Sex is way too good. I think you just forgot how good." Kim just gave a devious little smile, so I let it go. Nothing was going to make me flash back to the misery of John and ruin what I was feeling with Michael.

After they finished grilling me, I ran upstairs, grabbed the phone and plopped down on the bed to call Michael. It felt so good to hear his voice. I missed him so much. He let me know that he was headed back to Los Angeles in three days since the movie was done, but he promised he would come see me every weekend because he was taking a few months off unless a script came up that he couldn't refuse. And he did just that. He would fly in every Thursday night and leave on Sunday, but I was still keeping him under wraps. I didn't let him stay at my house because I didn't want Kim or someone just poppin' over there, and he said he understood, so he stayed at The Crowne Plaza each time he came.

It was going on eight months since we had met that January and I don't know why, but this one weekend he came, I decided that I was going to give him some. I knew it wasn't right, and I really wanted God to understand, and I'm sure he understood, but he didn't condone it nor was he giving me permission to do it, so I was pretty much on my own on that one and operating all in the flesh, but I was just ready to go to the next step with Michael and of course biblically speaking, that would be marriage, but I think we all know I was not ready to head down that road again.

It was a Friday night, and it was late because I had a late dinner with a client and wanted to go home and shower and change before going to see Michael, who of course couldn't understand why but he said okay he would just see me when I got there. I put some prep time into myself. I took a hot shower, shaved my legs and everywhere else hair really shouldn't be and made sure I had no underarm stubble. I arched my eyebrows and oiled myself down really well. I had gotten a pedicure and a manicure on Wednesday, which was my normal day, but I usually only went every two weeks. Though I had gone just the week before, due to the special occasion, I went again. I had gone to Victoria's Secret and got a little something but opted to go with this other little item I had bought the month before and just hadn't worn yet. I was a real lingerie freak. I couldn't help it. I had been since high school. I bought the sexiest lingerie I could find, and it didn't really have anything to do with a man. It was for me. It always made me feel confident knowing that under my clothes was pure sexiness. In my opinion bras and thongs and garters when required should always be a matching set. That's just how looking in Victoria's Secret all these years had trained me to think, and I'm glad it did. I curled my weave and lined my lips with a Chestnut liner by Mac and filled it with Icon lipstick topped off with a little lip glass. I put my mole on over my top left lip, put my eyelashes on and my honey contacts. Oh, it was about to be on. I called Michael and let him know I was on my way. He thought we were going to a play but I had a different plan.

When I pulled up to the hotel, surprisingly I wasn't even nervous, although I'm sure the two martinis I had may have helped calm my nerves. I got out of the car and walked toward the hotel. It seemed particularly quiet for a Friday night and extremely still. All I could hear was the sound of my boots on the pavement. As I walked through the lobby I wondered if the people were wondering if I was a hooker seeing as how I had on these thigh high patent leather boots in August. I was working 'em though. Those boots wrapped my legs like a stocking. My hair was flowin', and I could feel it bouncing with every step. I felt like I was walkin' down a runway. I was perfection on earth that night. I could feel it all over me. I had on a short patent-leather raincoat that tied in the front, and as I walked, I pulled the belt to make sure it was secure, seeing as how all I had on under it was the bra, thong, and garter attached to my boots. I was dancing to a different song that night, but the beauty of it was although the music was only in my head, I seemed to wear it, and everyone wanted to join in on this dance.

"Good evening." The desk clerk smiled. I glanced over at him, returning his smile,
"Yes, it is. Yes, it is." I sashayed my all-too-fine self to the elevator and pushed the button. As I waited, I could feel people staring at me, probably wondering who had hired this escort and how I could be in this line of work and hold my head as high as I was holding it. You know we always judge before knowing the facts. Shoot I found myself doing it at times, and I knew that's what everyone was doing to me, except of course the ones who wondered how much I charged and if I had a card because you know professional call girls are just that and usually do have a card. But you know what? The funny thing was, it didn't even bother me, not that night, because I knew the truth. I knew exactly who I was and what I wanted and forget what they thought. Maybe this one lady needed to pull the freak on her man and he wouldn't have been staring at me so hard. I just glanced over and gave them both a corporate "hello" as if I had on a suit and was on my way to work. When the elevator doors opened, I stood there and waited for three people to come out. I stepped in, waited for the other couple to get in then I pressed the button for Michael's floor. It seemed like the longest ride ever. The elevator stopped on the seventh floor where the couple got off. I hoped for no more interruptions. The only thing I wanted to erupt at that point was me with Michael. The doors opened a few floors later. I was glad there was no one in the hall as I walked toward his suite. All the confidence I had previously contained was now gone. My legs wavered like rubber beneath me as I got closer and closer to the door. It wasn't too late, I thought. I could still turn around and go back. I could call Michael and make up some excuse about not making the fictitious play. That would give me time to go home and put some clothes on and be the lady he had known thus far, but for some foolish reason, I didn't and the next thing you know I was at the door lifting my hand.

This one moment, well hopefully it will be longer than a moment, but regardless, this would change everything. After that night, nothing would be the same. Good or bad, who's to know in advance, but was I ready to chance this relationship-altering change? Did I really want to give myself to yet another man who although had great potential may or may not be my husband? Did I want to do this to myself yet again? I guessed so because my hand was no longer frozen at the door, but instead made contact. As Michael opened the door, I leaned on the wall of the doorframe, tilted my head down looking over the rim of my sunglasses, allowing my eyes to seduce him. Starting at his feet they made their way up every inch of his body, stopping to behold his beautiful, angelic face. Licking my lips like the sex-starved maniac I had become in the last twenty-four hours, I finally allowed words to come forth from my mouth. Never breaking eye contact, "Hey, sexy" rolled off my tongue. My hand slowly went to the belt that covered all my lust, and in one motion it was released as I gave one nice tug, revealing the true intentions of my visit, as well as the matching red bra and thong set that I must thank Mr. Lauren for. From the look on Michael's face it had done just what it was intended to do, and I don't mean reduce unsightly panty lines. Michael was clearly taken abreast, but he was also confused. Was this going to be a look-but-don't touch episode? What was going on? I stepped past him into the room and waited for him to close the door behind me. It took a moment though I think he may have still been in shock, but eventually he managed to close it. As he turned around toward me, I met him with a hug, not a church hug, oh no this was far from that. I gave him the hug where every part of my body found a matching part to align itself with his. Placing my hand on the back of his neck, I rubbed lightly and pulled back just enough to see his face. I was extremely glad to see him, and from the closeness of him, I could feel he was happy to see me too. At least I thought he was. I guess his flesh was saying one thing, but his brain was saying something totally different, something I didn't care to hear.

"What are you doing?" He stood there in shock as if he couldn't move. This wasn't the reaction I had hoped for, and suddenly I wondered the exact same thing. "Don't get me wrong. You look wonderful," he stuttered, trying not to look at my nakedness, "and I had been dying to see just how wonderful under your clothes, but where is this all coming from?"

I thought, maybe he is gay. But that was my way of petting my ego. Most men wouldn't even care where it was coming from. They would be so happy to be getting some, and surely if there were any reservations, they definitely wouldn't be brought up until after they came. Sorry, but you know I'm telling the truth. All I could say was that I thought I was ready to go to the next level in our relationship. I explained how much I wanted to share the most intimate parts of myself with him and that I thought he would be just as happy receiving me as I was giving me. How off was I? He had the nerve to remind me that based on what I had been preaching to him all these months, the next level would be marriage, not sex. I could not believe this. I just looked at him kind of puzzled. I wanted to die.

"What? So I can't have none? Is that what you're saying?" Yes, I know that was a little ghetto, but for real though. I just stood there looking at him like I wanted to slap the . . . well you know what I wanted to do. He walked over to me, took both my hands, held them up to his lips and kissed them.

"Honey, it's not that I don't want you. Believe me, I want you," he said stepping back, looking me over, smiling. "You messin' my head all up, coming in here looking as good as you look, and throwin' a little freaky twist onto it, but at the same time, I know how you feel about having sex before you get married again, and I respect that, and I really hope you don't think this is something I'm expecting from you or that you have to do this to keep me happy. Anya, I've never met anyone like you before. You don't have to worry. I'm not going anywhere, and I'm not looking for anything else. There is nothing you need to prove to me Okay?" I shook my head. "One of the things I find most attractive about you is your passion to respect yourself and your body and keep yourself happy, no matter what anyone else says or thinks or does. Don't change that. Don't compromise." He lifted my chin and softly kissed my lips.

I stood there feeling so stupid. I pulled my hands away and walked into the bedroom. I opened the drawer, grabbing the first T-shirt I saw and put it on over my little thong and bra. I took off the boots and set them against the wall and went into the bathroom to regroup. I swear if this were a house I'd escape through the window and drive off in my car, but unfortunately, it wasn't. There wasn't even a window, and if there was, it would be a long way down. I guess I wasn't embarrassed enough to die. The longer I stood in there and thought about it, I got more and more upset with myself. Then I had the nerve to get mad at God for letting me make a fool out of myself. I did not want to go back out there. I was so embarrassed, even though I knew Mike wasn't trippin', but I was. I wondered if he would still look at me the same and still respect me the same. How could I be so stupid? I paced in the bathroom, talking to myself. I did have to admit though I was glad he was willing to respect me. At the same time though, this was a huge blow to my ego. I had never been turned down for sex before. This was definitely a first, and to be honest I hoped it was a last. Shoot women aren't built to be turned down. So now here I go again, attempting to comfort my ego. Maybe Michael was intimidated by me, maybe it was a white thing. I didn't know, but I tried to think of anything to make it not be about him not being attracted to me. I knew deep down, that wasn't the case at all. But really, how could a young, single guy turn down this? I looked in the mirror. I was trippin'.

I had been in the bathroom about twenty minutes when he knocked softly at the door and asked if I was okay.

"Yeah, I'm cool."

"Good, then get your little hot tail out here and act like you're still happy to see me."

That kind of made me laugh, and I figured I couldn't stay in the bathroom all night anyway, so I came out. When I opened the door, he was standing right there smiling at me. "You are so cute. You went through all this trouble for me. I can't wait till we get married, so you can surprise me with little things like this all the time."

Married? Married? That kept playing back in my mind. I don't even know what he said after that, and frankly I didn't care, but I know he did not say marry. I hadn't thought about marriage. I didn't even comment. I just let that one run on off somewhere by itself to find a woman who would be glad to hear something like that. He hugged me, kissed my cheek and said, "Well, I guess we're not going to a play, huh?" He thought that was so funny, he fell out onto the bed laughing. Me, I was not amused. "Well, since you don't have any clothes on, I guess we can't go out anywhere," he said, holding his side still laughing, his face turning red as a Crayola. Was this some kind of white humor I was not privy to? "I'm sorry, baby, I'm just teasing you. He grabbed me and pulled me down on the bed. I guess he could still see the embarrassment I was wearing. "Come on now, you got to admit that it was funny." I was looking for anything remotely funny in this scenario and I was coming up with nothing. "You were going to mess up your hair for me? I am definitely moving up in the world." Okay, maybe, just maybe that one was a little funny because he knew how I was about my hair. Lying back on the bed I stared at the ceiling while he stared at me.

"Thanks," he said.

"For what? I didn't get a chance to give you anything to thank me for." I chuckled.

"Thank you for trusting me enough to give you to me. You don't know what that means to me, I just hope you don't think you have to do this because we're so far apart because you don't." He sat up, looking down at me. "I want you to know that." He leaned down and kissed my ear and whispered how glad he was that he had met me and how I had changed his life. My insides were smiling, but they were a little nervous too. I hadn't really seen the seriousness of this relationship sneaking up on me, but it was there and I wasn't sure if I really wanted it to be.

All of a sudden he jumped up, grabbed my hand and pulled me off the bed. "Come on. Let's go to your house and get you some clothes and go out. Let's go to a jazz club. I feel like hearing some jazz."

I was with that. I put my ho boots and my raincoat back on. I turned to Michael and asked him if it bothered him to be seen with me like that. Of course he said no, that he didn't care what anyone else thought, because he knew me. But I could just see us on the cover of some cheesy tabloid at the check-out counter: "Michael Harrison caught in Philadelphia hotel with hooker." God, he was wonderful. I didn't really believe these men existed, that is except for maybe my high school sweetheart Julian, but, that was another time. It almost seemed like it was another life.

We went to this dark little jazz club that my assistant had taken me to before, and Michael, of course, was trying to be incognito, but there is always someone who recognizes him. I didn't really mind sharing him with the world, but it is a little nerve-racking sometimes that we couldn't just have a little quiet time without being stared at or interrupted, but I never let Michael know because I didn't want him to think I was tripping or that I was jealous. Besides, all the women he could have, he wanted me, and that had become very obvious over the last several months. So I would just smile when people would come over and ask for autographs. Some women, if you can call them that were so rude and disrespectful. Whenever we were together and they did more than just a little flirting, Michael would always check them, and I loved him for that.

We had a good time that night, and on the way back to the hotel we put the top down on the Benz he always rented when he came, and I took off my shoes and put my feet up on the dashboard, reclined my seat and looked up into the night. It didn't seem to be as many stars as it was when I was little, but it was enough for me to see the beauty of the night and be reminded how great God is, that he created all of this and still had time to make Michael. It might sound corny, but that's what I was thinking. He reached over and grabbed my hand, kissed it and rubbed it along his face. The hair on his face tickled my hand and made me giggle. I heard him take a deep breath and sigh. It was a sigh of happiness, and I knew it because at that very moment, for some reason I was able to breathe it in, and when I felt it run through my body, it was comforting. I relaxed in his happiness, and I closed my eyes and allowed the night winds to kiss my face, and his happiness turned to mine. It was beyond reality. At least any reality I had experienced thus far in my life.

As the warm night air continued to massaged my face, I attempted to hold on to this good feeling. My eyes were closed, my mind relaxed, and for the first time in my life, I didn't have one single thought. I simply enjoyed the moment for just what it was, stolen time from the universe of perfection. Just then, a song came on the radio that I hadn't heard in forever. "Awwwww that's my song. Hurry up, pull over." I looked anxiously around. "Oh, right over there, in that parking lot. Hurry before it goes off." Michael raced to the empty parking lot of a grocery store.

"What's wrong?"

"Nothing." I turned the music up and jumped out of the car. "Hurry." I ran around to his door and opened it. "Get out." He stood, and I took his left hand, put it in mine and held it close to my face, then I put my arm around his neck, and we floated away somewhere as we danced. I sang softly in his ear, with my non-singing self. But he didn't seem to mind. If I close my eyes, I can still smell the sweetness of that night. I wish I could be there right now, right in those few moments and just live them over and over. Eventually the song ended, quickly if you ask me. At the end of it, Michael tried to dip me, but I wasn't prepared so I fell.

"Anya, once again I'll say, I've never met anyone like you. You are crazy, but I love it."

He helped me up and hugged me, then I reached in the car and turned the radio down. I walked around to my side of the car and got in. "So, you ready or are we waiting for another one of your favorite songs? You know, I could stay here all night." He closed his door then kind of hesitantly leaned over and kissed me. "You are something else."

"So they tell me," I said jokingly.

"No, really you are."

When we got back to the hotel, I didn't want to leave, and I could tell he didn't want me to either. He asked me to stay and said he would sleep on the sofa bed, but I told him that I trusted him enough to sleep in his bed with him. It was almost three o'clock in the morning, and he didn't want me driving back home. Sometimes if it got really late he would send me home in a car, but for some reason, this night he asked me to stay. It must have been the image in his mind of me when I unveiled myself earlier.

We got in the bed, and we were both tired. I knew I was going to be out in like 2.5 seconds, or so I thought. Michael put his arm around my waist and pulled me to him.

"I just want to hold you and make you feel secure," he said. I turned and looked at him and said, "That's why I love you. It's just different with you. You're different." I couldn't believe I let those words spill out of my mouth.

The words seemed to have quickly found a place in his heart. "You got me," he said. "You have instantly filled a place in me that has been empty for so long. Do you know how hard it is to date being who I am? You don't know if a woman wants you for who you are or if she wants you because of who you are in the industry or because you have money or because she wants to use you to get into the business. Anya, you are so real. You never cared that I was Michael Harrison the star, but just that I was Michael, good old Mike just be good to me and we will get along Harrison." As he leaned over to kiss me, I could feel his heart racing. I felt his fear, as if it was his first kiss ever. He kissed me so softly, his lips were so warm, how could I not open my mouth to receive him. I could feel him hesitate, then he slid his tongue into my mouth and began to massage my tongue. The kiss never got hard and erotic. Instead it stayed warm and fresh like a back east summer rain. Don't get me wrong though. It was extremely intense and passionate, but he had was a respect for my body. He wasn't forcing himself on me, as men had done in the past. He was patiently waiting and only taking what I would yield.

As he continued to touch me, he suddenly stopped. "Anya, you don't have to do this. As bad as I want to peel those red underwear off, I would be just as content continuing to look at them overlaying your silky carmel body. I can wait. I don't want you compromising who you are to please me. I'm fine with just holding you and smelling your hair and feeling the warmth of your body next to mine, to enclose you in me so that you feel the love I have for you." When I looked into his eyes, I was assured of his sincerity. My guard was completely down, and at that very moment I let out a sigh of contentment. He was right. I did feel safe. I appreciated the fact that he was willing to deny himself. I could feel how hard he was, and he wasn't letting his penis think for him as a lot of men do, and I was sold.

I looked into those hazel eyes, and I took his hand, placed it back on my thigh, and I continued to yield. Every part of my body melted under his touch, and it was beautiful. The strength of his hands on my back and the warmth of his mouth kissing every part of me was so erotic. Just thinking about it makes me quiver. I enclosed him with my legs and allowed him to make passionate love to me. Gentle, warm love, not triple X sex, but genuine love. Not that there was anything wrong with triple X sex, but this wasn't the time and frankly on this very night, this was way better than even the best sex I had had. The great thing about it though, was I didn't feel dirty like I had sometimes in the past after having sex. In fact I can honestly say that there had only been one man from my past that I felt this free with, but that was the past and until that very moment, I never knew it was possible to feel that way with anyone but Julian. It was amazing. Not even my own husband made me feel like that. Don't get me wrong. I enjoyed sex in the past, but most times when it was over, I felt a little icky and a little ashamed, but I didn't feel that way with Michael. I felt beautiful and loved, and most of all, I felt respected. I didn't feel like I needed to give him some to make him like me more or to keep him. It was just different.

As I lay there, I couldn't stop thinking about that kiss, about how it made me quiver, how delicious it actually was. Something about it was just different and made me quiver again right there and made me want him again, even more. So I tried to think of something else to take my mind off the possibilities to still be explored, especially with him right there. I didn't want him to think I was a freak. True enough I was, but he didn't need to know just how much, at least not at that moment.

"Are you sleep?" I asked a little while later

"Nope. Just thinking."

"About what?"

"About how I found you."

"Awww, that was so corny," I said, laughing.

"Yeah, I know, but I was though," he said. I could feel him smiling in the dark.

"Sorry I ruined your perfect image of me."

"Don't be. I think I'm enjoying the new image even better."

Sorry, I couldn't hold out. The more I thought about Michael, the more I wanted him, and shoot he was right there. Look, it had been almost two years since I had had some. I guess that's why you have to keep yourself out of tempting situations, but it was too late. I was too far gone. I began to nibble his ears, then I kissed his neck, making my way up to his face. I slid up on top of him, leaned into him and began to trace his lips with the tip of my tongue. I kissed him with all the stored-up passion I had been holding in for the last several months. I put my hands in his above his head and whispered in his ear, "Just one more time, just one more time. Then I promise, I'll let you sleep." I could feel his smile on the side of my face.

"Anything for you." We both laughed, and it was on.

The next morning, I woke up and I couldn't believe it. I felt great. I looked over at Michael. He was so beautiful, even when he slept. I could have lay there all morning just staring at him, but duty called. I had to meet a client at one so I had to get home, shower and change. Since Michael was still asleep and I didn't want to wake him, I washed up and crept out. I was at home in the tub when the phone rang. I forgot to bring the phone in the bathroom with me, so I jumped out of the tub to catch it, in case it was Michael.

"Hello," I answered. On the other end was Michael "Oh I feel so used," he said laughing. He is so crazy. I explained to him that he was sleeping so well that I didn't want to wake him. I told him I had a client at one and that we could hook up for an early dinner. He was okay with that.

"I love you," he said when we got ready to hang up, and it caught me off guard.

"Yes, I know. I love you too." I almost didn't say it, but I felt like I was supposed to. What was I getting myself into? I mean I did love him but saying it out loud made it real and I don't know if I was ready for reality to enter into this relationship. It had been doing so well as the perfect fantasy. Oh well, I didn't have time to really think about it, which was good, because you know how I get when I think too much. Instead, I got dressed and headed out to my meeting.

The Proposal

Michael continued to come in every weekend for the next three weeks, and things were good, no they were great, yet somehow, this was the beginning of the end. One morning we were in the bed talking, and he just broke out with, "We can't keep doing this."

In my mind I was like I knew it. The real him was about to come out. I sat up and looked at him. "Doing what?"

"I know that you really don't want to be having sex before you get married even though I wouldn't know by the way you keep putting it on me but . . ."

I cut him off. "Stop trippin', Michael. The Lord knows my heart, and I know that doesn't make it right but what am I supposed to do?" He put his hand over my mouth.

"I know your heart too." He reached under his pillow and handed me this red velvet box. I was in shock. I had a feeling what it was, so I really didn't want to open it.

"Open it," he said. I took a deep breath and did as he requested.

"Oh my God." it was gorgeous.

"Well what do you think?" he said, looking a little worried.

"I think it's about two and a half carats of flawlessness. The clarity is exceptional."

"Stop playing." He cut me off all serious, but who was playing? "You are always using your jokes as your defense. It's okay to be serious and show your real emotions sometimes, Anya. I want you to be my wife. I love you, and the feeling that you give me when I'm with you, I long for it when I'm away from you. Over the last eight months, I've fallen more in love with you with each passing minute. I can't imagine my life and you not being in it, so I'm asking for the greatest commitment and wanting to give you the greatest commitment. I want you to know what you mean to me and how much a part of me you have become." He slid off the side of the bed, got down on one knee and took the ring out the box. He took my left hand and asked me if I would be his wife as he slid the ring on my finger.

How could I say no? I wanted to say yes but at the same time part of me didn't. I mean he was wonderful, he was so good to me, he was extremely sexy, the sex, was off the hook and he offered financial security. Who could ask for more?

We got along, he made me happy, he made me laugh, and he understood me. Most of all he loved even the ugly parts of me, the parts that God was still fixing and healing on the inside. But dang, marriage? I didn't know if I ever even wanted to get married again after John's sorry butt, but when I looked down into Michael's eyes, I was sold. This man lived to make me happy, and I knew it.

I stood, pulled him up from his knees and kissed him. "Yes, Yea, I'll marry you, Michael Harrison. I would love to marry you. Why not?" He grabbed me, picked me up and swung me around.

"I knew it, I knew it. I wasn't sure at first if you would say yes, but I was praying the whole way here. One more thing. I bought a new BMW so I can stop renting cars every weekend. It's going to be delivered to your house Tuesday. I hope that's okay. I thought it would be since you have a two car garage." And it was. It was just happening so fast. The rest of the morning he just darted around the suite like cupid had not only stuck him but stayed and gave him continuous injections of love. It was cute though. Just thinking about it makes me get tickled on the inside. It's a trip though because what if I had said no? Would we have broken up? I sat up against a pillow watching TV while he was in the shower. I looked down at the humungous rock on my finger and realized this relationship was getting more real by the minute. I just hoped I was ready for it.

Later that afternoon at lunch Michael's cell phone rang. He talked in codes, and after he hung up, I asked who it was but he told me it was a surprise.
"Michael, I don't think I can take any more surprises today. I'm feeling a bit overwhelmed as it is."

"Trust me. You're gonna love this surprise." In my mind I thought that remained to be seen. I continued eating my salad, and we talked about a little of this and a little of that, but I couldn't focus. All I could think about was what might be waiting for and if I would be able to handle it. Wasn't an unexpected proposal enough for one trip? At three o'clock, I found myself pulling up to the Jaguar dealership. When we got out, he handed me another box, only this one held a platinum Jaguar key ring. "This is for you to put your key on." He looked over and smiled. Okay life was way too good. It was the most beautiful car I had ever seen in my life. It was a frosted silver with a big ole red bow on it. It had just been delivered, and when I sat in it, the leather felt like butter. It had to be a sin to love a car that much, but it was beautiful. He was so sweet. I had told Michael almost six months ago that when I bought another house I was going to buy my Jag because I had really been wanting one, but I didn't want that kind of car note until I knew how much my new mortgage would be. Even though I wasn't married and didn't have any kids, I wanted a big fat house. I deserved and could afford it. I worked hard, and I made good money, good investments and good financial decisions, and eventually I was going to start my own interior design firm, maybe sooner than I thought. I had brought my current company a lot of revenue over the last six months and though my boss had been very good to me, I wanted to be the boss and run my own business. It was no secret, and Asha was very supportive of me starting my own company although she admitted how much she would not only miss the revenue I generated, but, that she would miss me too.

I couldn't believe Michael. He was just heaven on earth. Every since I had met him, it had always been about him trying to please me. After I was able to tear myself out of my car, I grabbed him and hugged him, and I thanked him, not for the car although it was nice, well more than nice. I thanked him for being what every man should be. And this day, my friend, was the beginning of the end. Why couldn't we just stay boyfriend and girlfriend? Why did he have to take it to the next level? After all, it was the nineties and soon to be the year 2000. God would have forgiven us for living in sin, I'm sure of it. I know that's not right to say, but that's how I kind of felt. I mean, I didn't really want to live in sin, but I knew marriage would ruin everything.

As bad as I wanted to drive my Jag home, I told Michael that I wanted to spend the rest of the day with him and that I could pick it up later or they could deliver it to me at home Monday. "Are you sure Anya? We can take it now and just drop it off at your house, or we can take my rental back" That worked for me. Man, I was driving down the street in my brand new, let's not forget paid for Jag. Paid for with someone else's money. Dang, life was good this year. It had been worth all the bootleg relationships to get to Michael. I wished I had my Stevie Wonder's greatest hits to slide into the CD player. Aw, man, I was trippin'. I guess it was time for me to tell Kim and my sister. They were gonna be pissed I kept this from them so long, but oh well.

Sunday I was taking Michael to the airport, which I normally didn't do, but sense we had taken his rental back I had too. On the drive I wondered how this all happened? When we pulled up at the terminal, I was so sad. It was different this time. I always missed him when he left, but this time I wanted to go with him. I didn't want to be away from him.

"Hey, what's up?" I guess he sensed my spaciness.

"Nothing. I'm just going to miss you is all."

"Aww, my baby is going to miss me. Now who's the corny, in-love one?" He blushed.

"Ha very funny." I rolled my eyes, but I kind of felt like I was about to cry.

"Man, I would have bought you a ring and a car a long time ago if I knew it would bring this kind of emotion."

We both laughed, then we kissed good-bye. "I love you." He beamed.

"I love you more."

"I'll call you when I get in."

"No no never. Don't ever leave me. I can't survive without you." I dramatically threw my head back, put my hand to my forehead and closed my eyes. Then I peeked out my right eye to see what he was doing. "Okay, I'm just playing. Call me tonight." I laughed. "That was good though, huh?"

"Oh yeah, baby. Academy Award all the way, but I don't think we wanna share those skills with the rest of the world. We'll keep that just between us." I watched him through the rearview mirror as he went around to the trunk to get his bag.

"Hey, hey, watch the car. I don't wanna see any fingerprints," I said jokingly.

"Yeah, okay," he said, looking over his sunglasses.

As I watched him walking through the doors, I jumped out of the car. "Hey," I shouted. He turned around. "I love you." He grinned from ear to ear. When I saw that grin, I was happy. I jumped back in the car and drove off. A few seconds later my phone rang.

"Yes?" I answered.

"I love you too. I'll call you later."

Yes, you might as well say it. I was trippin'. I felt like I was in high school again or something.

After I dropped Michael off, I called Kim and told her to meet me at my sister's because I had something to tell them. I called my sister. "What's up, girl?" I said. "What are you doin'? Me and Kim are about to come over." I knew she wouldn't care. She was always happy when I came over.

I hadn't been over that much lately because I had been spending so much time with work, and when I wasn't at work, on the weekends I was with Michael. When I pulled up in front of the house, Kim was already there, and I was kind of glad because I didn't want them to see the car just yet. I jumped out and walked in the door without knocking. They were in the kitchen, and my sister was making daiquiris. "Pour me one," I said, entering her perfectly coordinated kitchen.

I don't know why my sister never went into interior design with me. There was no doubt she had the knack. She could design the mess out of a house, apartment, studio, you name it. I had seen her do it for herself as well as her friends. When I went to visit her in college she probably had the only dorm that could have appeared in *Home and Garden*.

We were sitting out on the deck catchin' up, sipping our daiquiris when my sister noticed it.

"Wait a minute. Wait just one minute," she screamed. She got up, came over and snatched my hand for a closer look.

"Dang, Traci, leave my arm in the socket please," I complained

"Where did you get this? Better yet, when did you get this, and maybe I should be asking, what is it for? It could not possibly be an engagement ring because we haven't even met the man you been so-called dating for that last we don't even know how long."

Okay she was pissed. I knew that there would be some discussion but I didn't think she would really be mad.

"Okay" Kim chimed in. "Spill it. Who is this dude, and is this an engagement ring? I know you could not have gotten this serious with someone and not even let me in just a little. I can't believe you. We haven't even met him or anything. How would you feel if I did that to you? You're suppose to be my best friend." I would have been more than happy to fill them in, but they wouldn't shut up long enough for me to get one word out of my mouth, let alone an entire sentence or thought for that matter.

"Sorry. I told you guys before I just wasn't ready to let him from under wraps, and I thought y'all understood."

"Well we did," Kim said, "until you came over here with that phat ring talking about marriage."

Mind you though I hadn't once said anything about marriage right.

"This isn't another Anthony, is it? Another drug dealer you're making excuses for?" my sister said. She could really irk me sometimes. I mean give me some credit. I guess she could see from the irritation on my face that wasn't it. "Okay, if that's not it, then what's the big secret?"

I screamed and got up and went to the kitchen to pour me another Daiquiri. Of course they followed me.

"Look I just wasn't telling anyone about him because of who he is, okay. At least until I saw where it was headed, and believe me I didn't know it was headed here. It just kind of snuck up on me."

"What is he, in the mafia or something?" Kim asked. "And how does marriage just sneak up on you? That's a new one."

"Okay, I tell you what. Let's do a small dinner thing next weekend so y'all can meet him, and I mean small just us, Kevin and Vic."

Kevin had been my sister's boyfriend forever and a day. Why they weren't married, to this day, I still don't know. Vic of course was Kim's latest flavor, which had changed frequently the last several months, which was so unlike her, but I was just letting her have her moment. Every time I would try to talk to her about it, she would get really defensive and come with the whole "I'm still young speech." I didn't know where all this was coming from. She had never been like that before, but I thought eventually it would pass, so I didn't press the issue. Besides, Vic had been around for a little over two months so maybe there was hope.

They agreed to the dinner, at my sister's, because she could cook. They also agreed to get off my back until then. Well everything was going smooth and I even filled them in a little more about Michael and how he had proposed and of course about the first time we did it, in detail, but I still didn't let them know it was Michael Harrison. We all took turned filling one another in since lately we hadn't spent as much time together as we normally did. Everything was cool until me and Kim were leaving. My sister was walking us out, and they saw my Jag in the driveway. I had gotten so worked up that I had almost forgotten about my little engagement gift.

"Girl I know this ain't yours," Kim said, walking over to the car and looking in disbelief.

"Now wait a minute, when did you buy this? I thought you said you were going to hold off on buying it until you got your house?"

I started smiling, "well I got it yesterday, but I didn't exactly buy it. Michael got it for me. It's sort of an engagement gift, although he had told me if I would have said no he would still have given it to me because he had specially ordered it just for me." My name was even written on my floor mats. It was so cute.

"Wasn't that big ring enough?" my sister said, laughing. "You must have really put it on him. I guess all that time of celibacy wore him out when you finally let go. A Jag and a two carat ring after only eight months. Girl, he is sprung."

I admitted he was sprung but so was I.

I got in the car, pulled out the driveway and waved. My sister just shook her head in disbelief. My cell phone rang a few minutes later. It was my sister. "Alright, spill it. Who is this man and where is he getting all this money?" but I wasn't telling. I told her she would just have to wait until next weekend and that all her questions would be answered at that time, and I hung the phone up. My phone rang right back.

"Okay wait, just tell me this, do I know him?"

"Good-bye, Traci," I sang as I hung the phone up. Can you believe she called right back.

"Anya, you know you wrong, right? I'm your sister. How you gon' keep something like this from me? It's cool though. I'm going to remember the day my only sister held out on me."

"Okay, I'll make sure I remember it too, just in case you forget." I cracked up into the phone.

"Ooh, Anya, you wrong. Okay, I'll wait and meet your little funky fiancé next week, but this better be good. Bye, girl."

That week at work, I worked my butt off. I didn't even have time to remember that I had actually agreed to marry this man. But there would be time for all that soon enough. Michael called to tell me he loved me and that he missed me. I missed him, too, and as much as I missed him and as good as I felt, I still couldn't believe I was going to marry him. I felt good though, better than I had in a long time. It's amazing what good sex can do for you, not to mention a big diamond and a Jag. At least that's what I kept trying to tell myself, but it wasn't the sex or the car or the ring. It was Michael. It was wonderful, but there was something missing. I wasn't sure exactly what it was, but whatever it was, it wasn't enough to make me not marry him. I'd be crazy not to. Whatever was missing I was sure we'd get it eventually. He was extremely attractive, successful, well educated and he treated me so good, who was I kidding? He treated me much better than good. He worshiped the very essence of who I was, he loved who I was, and he loved God. So what was the problem? Okay there wasn't one.

I was sitting there stressing out and forgot I had to meet a client. I jumped up, darted to the elevator, got in the car and raced to the restaurant. As much as I eat out I should be huge. Praise God for treadmills and Stairmasters. I pulled up to the valet and rushed in. I was only about five minutes late, but that's a long time when you're waiting and it really doesn't look professional. I saw Mrs. Millbrook and I went over to her table and sat down.

"I am so sorry I'm late, Mrs. Millbrook. I really lost track of time." She was really sweet though. She assured me it was no problem, but I still didn't like to be late.

It was so nice living in the fantasy world while it lasted, but once again welcome back to the reality of my life. I was running some ideas past my client for the master bedroom at her summer home in the Hamptons and showing her some layouts, when it happened. I saw this wonderful vision of chocolate out the corner of my eye gliding past my table. Chocolate has always been hard for me to resist, but why couldn't I just like candy, cake and ice cream like most chocolate lovers? Why did it have to be men? I just don't understand. I could tell he glanced at me and then looked again, but I kept my head down. I could feel him staring at me. Finally I looked over in the direction he went, and I stopped immediately mid-conversation.

"Is everything alright?" Mrs. Millbrook asked.

"Oh," I caught myself, "I'm sorry. Yes, yes everything is fine," I said, attempting to regroup. I reached down into my portfolio and pulled out some wallpaper and paint samples.

"Anya, do you know the gentleman over at that table? He has not taken his eyes off you since he walked in."

"Actually, I do know him. I just haven't seen him in a long time." I knew him all too well. It was Julian. Once again welcome to my life.

And The Twain Should Meet

My goodness did he look good. My question was what was he doing in town? Was it simply to ruin my life? I wasn't really sure, but you know me, I had to find out. After finishing up my meeting, I stood and sashayed toward the door as if I was really going to leave without seeing him.

"Anya." That voice sliced through my body, but I acted as if I wasn't fazed. I turned around.

"Oh, hi Julian. It is so good to see you. What are you doing here?"

Well it turns out his little brother had gotten married the previous weekend and he decided to make a week of it instead of going right back to Chicago, which was where he ended up settling.

I had dated him all through high school along with a few others, but he was the only one I took seriously. He really was my best friend during those times. I had known him since I was in the first grade, and you know how it is when you get together when you're little. We did that boyfriend girlfriend thing all through elementary and junior high, but how serious can you be in elementary? It didn't get deep for us until around the tenth grade, well as deep as you could get back then at fifteen. I could trust Julian with everything, including my heart. He was nothing but good to me, a little too good. It was just too perfect, and I was so young that after my first year of college, I wanted a little freedom. He was even understanding about that. He's two years older and he didn't go away to college because I begged him not to leave me, and then what did I do? I turned around and pulled some crap like that. He ended up getting a degree in engineering and eventually moved to Chicago for some great job opportunity. Goodie for him.

I was the one who broke it off with him, so why was I the bitter one? Nope, not what you're thinking either. He wasn't married and living all happily ever after. He was still very much available. I had even thought about calling him once or twice after my divorce, but I just couldn't. I felt too stupid. Here I was, had the perfect man already but just had to see what else was out there. And believe me, no one else had ever compared to Julian until Michael came along. Shoot, me and Julian were happy before he had money. It was so cute the little things he would do just so that I would know how important I was to him. Like one Valentine's Day, he took me to this really nice restaurant, even though he didn't have a lot of money, so I was happy with that, but when the waiter brought the dessert tray around. Julian reached into his inside pocket and pulled out a long red box and placed it in front of me while I was choosing my desert. I opened it, and he had taken two pieces of string and placed them side by side and gotten some rhinestones and glued them down the middle of the strings making a bracelet. He took the bracelet out off the box and tied it on my wrist and told me one day it would be a real diamond bracelet and that he was sorry he couldn't afford one then. The moment was so beautiful. I still have that bracelet in my jewelry box. I'm about to cry, just thinking about it.

That was just Julian. He did that kind of stuff all the time, but I was just so sure that I was missing out on something. There had to be more. Didn't there? Anyway, that's neither here nor there.

I reached up and put my arms around his neck and hugged him. Ohhh he felt so good. I had missed him so much. My security blanket.

"Well, I see you're still keeping yourself in shape, girl."

"I try," I said. It was really awkward. I didn't know what to say, then suddenly I remembered my ring so I tried to keep my left hand down so he wouldn't notice it in case he hadn't.

"Ok" he said "So where are we going tonight?"

I just stood there looking kind of puzzled. "Um, going?"

"Yes. Can't two old friends go hang out for a bit while I'm in town? That is unless there's someone who wouldn't want you to be hanging out with a man that you're madly in love with," he said, giving an extremely confident grin. Confident enough for me to know he was serious. That was my opportunity to tell him about Michael, but what did I do? Got all defensive and grown.

"What? I'm grown. I do what I want when I want." I couldn't say ain't no rings on these fingers, because that would be a lie now wouldn't it?

"Cool. I'll pick you up around eight. We can go eat and then whatever else." He smiled. He went in his pocket got out a piece of paper and said, "Here. Write down your phone number and your address, and I'll call you when I'm on my way." All I could do was stand there and nod. I had missed him so much and had tried for so many years to put him out of my mind and my life and now here he was. Was this a sign that I shouldn't be marrying Michael? No, I was just trippin' as usual. I really thought I had gotten my you know what together, and if I had then what was I doing even playing with Julian? His super powers had always been more than I could handle.

I couldn't even get out the door good before I had turned around and gone back. I just wanted to watch him. I stood behind the wall peeking in just to look at him a little while longer. I watched him chew his food and swallow, and even that was sexy to me. I watched him talk to some guy and gesture, I watched him laugh, how alive it was, the way it made his eyes sparkle. Or was it just that I was really still in love with the man? One thing I did know was that I could not allow myself to be sucked in to his world, nor could I allow him to enter mine. Just then the host came over and questioned if I needed help with something. It startled me, and I jumped back to reality and stumbled out the door.

In my car, I thought about how I would feel if Michael went out with an ex, and I knew it would bother me, especially if he felt about her the way I felt about Julian. I was so confused, or maybe I was just scared. I didn't want to pray about it, for fear of what God might actually say, so I just tried to stay busy for the next few weeks so God would not have a chance to deal with me.

That night Julian did call, and he came and picked me up. I wasn't really hungry, so I opted to skip dinner. I wanted to tell him about Michael, but I couldn't. I had reluctantly left my engagement ring at home in the box. I know, I know that ain't right, but what was I suppose to do? Just flaunt it all in his face?

We were sitting on the ledge next to this water fall we use to sit at when we in high school. We use to go there all the time and just talk for hours about his family, my family, and how our life was going to be. It's so funny that when you make all these wonderful dreams, you really believe that life is going to turn out just like you plan it. Back then, no one could have ever told me that I would not have married Julian and lived happily ever after. I never imagined being married to anyone but him, but there I was, married and divorced and engaged again and still not to him. I was more screwed up than a little bit. It was time for some self examination. Maybe it wasn't always the men in my life, maybe it wasn't their fault. Maybe something was wrong with me. How could that be though? I was so together for a young woman my age, wasn't I?

"Anya, Anya?" Julian said.
"Huh?" I looked over at him. "Where are you at? You're just staring off into never never land."
I couldn't bring myself to tell him. "I don't know," I said, "It just seems funny sitting here with you after all this time."

He scooted closer to me and put his arm around my back. I dropped my head on his shoulder and just kind of sat there, not knowing what to say or do. "I missed you, Anya. I still think about you every day. I still think the reason I can't have a real relationship is because I'm holding out, hoping that one day it'll happen. You know, when you got married, I couldn't believe it, and you didn't even tell me, I had to find out from my brother. Do you know how much that hurt? How stupid I felt? But here I am again, because I know without a doubt you're the only woman I've ever and will ever love."

I felt frozen. I couldn't respond, so I just sat there trying not to think about Michael and trying not to listen to Julian, but every word he spoke was squeezing my heart, and I almost couldn't breathe. I jumped up.

"What's wrong?" he said.

"Oh, Julian, you'll never understand me and believe me when I say I don't deserve you. You deserve so much more than what I can give you."

"What are you talking about, Anya? You be trippin', girl." But I wasn't trippin'. I knew all too well what I was talking about.

Julian came up behind me, put his arms around my waist and began to rock me from side to side. The night was so clear and so pretty, and the breeze made the water from the fountain blow a slight mist, which felt good because it was so warm out. I relaxed back into his chest and closed my eyes.

"You really don't know me, Julian. You just know the me you knew and loved years ago, and I'm just not the same person." He turned me around and looked in my eyes. He kept one arm around my waist and took his other hand and placed it on the side of my face. "Let me love the new you. I know we're not exactly the same as we were when we were younger, but the root person is still the same. Give me a chance to decide for myself if I would still love the new you." He kissed me softly on my lips, and I could feel myself getting ready to cry, so I held him real tight, buried my face in his chest and wondered why this had to be my life. Why did I ever even go to New York? Or should I say why did I have to meet my client that day at that restaurant? Lord, I was so confused. I mean because if I hadn't run into Julian I would just be moving forward with no doubts, right?

That night I couldn't sleep so I got down on my knees and tried to pray, but I couldn't. I was too restless. I couldn't be still. It was only eleven o'clock west coast time so I decided to call Michael.

"Hi, sweetheart," he said, picking up the phone.

"You and that Caller ID get on my nerves," I said, laughing.

"What's up?"

"Nothing. I just needed to hear your voice, that's all." And that was in fact all I had needed to reassure myself that I could do this and that it was the right thing to do.

"What are you still doing up?"

"I just couldn't sleep is all."

"Not having second thoughts about marrying me, are you?" I could hear a touch of worry in his voice.

"Huh no, never that," I assured him.

"Well, it's not like I won't be there tomorrow," he said, laughing.

I knew that but I guess in a way I did kind of forget. I was use to him coming on Thursdays but he had a meeting Friday and decided to just fly in Saturday.

"Baby, it's late. Get some sleep. I don't want you to be all tired when I see you tomorrow. I do not wanna see big black circles under cracked red eyes."

"Thank you so much for that vivid picture. I'm going to rush and go to bed now." I laughed.

The next morning Julian called me as I was getting ready to go to the gym and I had already made up in my mind the night before that I was going to tell him about Michael and about the wedding and everything. But when I heard his voice, I just couldn't. He was so sweet and so understanding about the way I did him before, how could I do it again? I was so confused and so frustrated. He wanted to see me because his plane was leaving the next morning, so I figure cool, we'd hook up, laugh, talk and reminisce just like the night before then he'd go back to Chicago and we'd talk a few times on the phone, and it would eventually fade out. I'd stop returning calls and so would he and that would be that. Besides, he had a life there, and I had one here. So sure we could hook up before Mike got in town and that would be that. It was time to close this chapter in my life.

Well we didn't waste much time. We went to lunch after I came from the gym and showered. It was like old times, but better because now we had money. He told me about Chicago and how well his business was going but how he missed being in Philly because all his family was there. But at least he wasn't that far away like Michael who was on the west coast, but that's a different story altogether. We sat there for more than two hours just talking, then my phone rang. It was my sister.

"Okay, what time are we doing this dinner thing tonight?" Crap, I had totally forgotten about dinner. "Don't kill me. I forgot. Can we please please please change it to tomorrow?" I begged. "I'll explain everything later."

I could tell my sister was upset. "Yeah, whatever. You sure are becoming Ms Secretive lately," she said and hung up. I called her back and told her I would be over in about an hour to explain. She just said whatever in an unbelieving voice and hung up.

Julian wanted to know what that was all about, like I was really going to tell him. I just told him that we were suppose to get together at my sister's for dinner that night and that I had forgotten and now she was mad. "Well, I don't want to hold you if you need to be doing something else," he said. But how could I not be held? It's not like I could see him any old time, after all he'd be gone the next day.

After we ate, we headed out to the parking lot. He walked me to my car and told me how good it was to see me, and I expressed the same feeling. Then it was over. He kissed me, and I felt sixteen again. For a moment, or maybe even longer, I couldn't remember that eight years had passed between us and that we were no longer together. All I knew was how right it felt right then. That very moment, was all that mattered. I couldn't live in that moment forever and eventually, it passed, and I was in my car on my way to my sister's house.

When I walked in the door, my sister could read my face. "What's wrong?" she said. But the question was what was right? I told her that Julian was in town and when she called I was at lunch with him.

"What?" she screamed. "What are you thinking about? You know you're not strong enough or engaged enough to resist that. What are you thinking, and does your little fiancé know that you hooked up with your ex for lunch?"

"Of course not. Do you think I'm stupid?" It was killing her not to answer that but she knew if she did, I would probably kill her.

"Well, did you at least tell Julian about you and Michael?" I just kind of looked away and began walking to the kitchen, praying she had some Pepsi.

"You know you're playing with fire, and when this all blows up in your face like I know it's going to, I'll be here, but hopefully, you'll be alive. I hope you know what you're doing, because I don't know how much more of you Julian is going to put up with. I know y'all have this special bond and all that, but you're really pushing it."

I knew I was, but what was I suppose to do? I didn't always do the right thing like my perfect sister. She could never understand. She had never cheated on Kevin. Not that she should, but dang I always thought everyone made mistakes, well everyone but her is how the saying should go.

"Well how long is Julian going to be here?"

"He's leaving tomorrow."

"So why can't we have dinner tonight? Are you seeing him again? And where is this fiancé of yours while all this is going on?"

"Oh, no I'm not seeing Julian anymore ever," I said, trying to convince myself as well as her. "And Julian is not the reason I changed dinner. Michael usually comes to town every Thursday and leaves Sunday or Monday, but he had a meeting last night so he left this morning. His plane gets in at six fifteen, so I know he's not going to be up for dinner and socializing. He's really anxious to meet you guys because he always use to ask why he hasn't met any of my friends and he thinks it's because I'm ashamed of him because he's white."

"He's what?" My sister dropped her glass and stared at me.

"You heard me."

"You playin'." Not the number one chocolate lover in America, probably in the world. "Does Kim know this?" I shook my head no. "I can't wait to see the look on her face. No wonder you ain't brought him around. Girl, you trippin', don't you know when you get married for money it don't last."

"I'm not marrying him for the money," I said, throwing my ice at her.

"Well if he white and you only like those sexy chocolate drops, what is it then?"

"It just happened. I didn't plan on liking him. I just started, and once I started, I couldn't stop, and just 'cause he's white, I'm suppose to say, oops, sorry feelings. I must turn you off. You can't be wasted on a white man?"

"Don't get so defensive. I'm just messin' with you, but you must admit this is some shocking news. And where the heck does he live that he has to fly in every week?"

"Girl, California of all places."

"Wait a minute, so when y'all get married, where y'all gon' live? I hope you don't think you runnin' off to California."

"Naw. We'll live in both places, but I guess primarily here. We haven't discussed anything in detail yet. After all, we just got engaged last week."

"Seems like you would have talked about something like that before y'all even thought about marriage."

"I know, Traci, but it all happened so fast. We haven't even set a date or anything yet. I'm scared though, Traci. I'm scared I'm doing the wrong thing."

"You ought to be. Girl, all I know is you married the wrong man once. Do you really wanna do it again? Don't get me wrong. I'm not saying Michael is the wrong man. I'm just saying, make sure this time. Nobody can know for sure but you, especially, if you really know that he loves you. Don't do that to him.

Don't mess this man's life up if you don't really love him. I mean, dang, Anya, you always got some drama going on."

"I know I know." I jumped up and paced in a small circle.

"Well, Anya, I don't know what to tell you. I haven't heard Julian's name in so long, but I know you love him. At least you use to. I wonder if you're not just in love with what you two use to have. I mean you guys are grown now. I'm sure you two will always love each other, but I think if it were meant for you all to be together, you would have stayed together or at least gotten back together by now. The problem is you guys never let go. Everyone always holds a special place in their hearts for their first love, and because he never did anything to hurt you, you still have this fairy-tale relationship playing in your mind."

"I don't think it's a fairy tale, he can't have changed that much, and besides, I kind of think I owe him another chance after the way I did him."

"Owing him is not love, Anya."

"I know. I just don't know what to think. I love Michael too. He's great. Who am I kidding? He's more than great, and it's no accident I met him, right?" She got up and hugged me.

"Anya, you want me to do something that only you can do. You have to make this decision, no one else but you. But don't worry, sweetie, I know you. You'll make the right one. I just want you to be happy this time."

"I know." I sighed and plopped down in a chair. "Either way, somebody is going to get hurt, right?"

"I mean yes, that's true if that's the way you wanna look at it, but make sure it's not you for a change. That's part of your problem. You always worrying about hurting somebody's feelings. It's okay to put yourself first sometimes. Girl, I wouldn't take a million dollars to be in your shoes right now." Then she stared deep in thought and put her finger to her lips. "Oh wait a minute, who am I kidding, yes I would. Why would I turn down a million dollars all these bills we got?" She snickered.

As funny as it wasn't, I said, "I'd give a million dollars not be in my shoes right now. Maybe we can work something out." I laughed.

"Oooh, girl, you ain't right. I bet you don't be saying that when you driving that Jag around town."

"Huh yeah, you right." I smiled.

"By the way, I notice you ain't got that big rock on. Don't you think you better be sportin' it when you pick him up from the airport?" She shook her head.

"Aww man, you're right. I'm not use to it yet. I forgot I didn't put it on because I was meeting Julian. I better go so I have time to swing by the house before I go to the airport. I'll call you later. Oh, did you need me to do anything for dinner tomorrow?"

"uhh yeah, just pick up some dessert."

"What you want me to get?"

"Anything but chocolate." She looked up, trying not to laugh.

"Everybody's a comedian. Oh I better run and call *ComicView* and get you booked. You can just kiss my booty." I turned my butt toward her and slapped my booty cheek."

"Naw, I'm gon' leave that for Michael . . . , no Julian . . . , no Michael . . . no Ju . . . no Mic. Hah, let me know how it turns out."

Oh, she was on a roll. There was no stopping her. My best bet was to leave while we were still sisters. I began heading for the door. I called out to her, "I'll just pick up an apple pie and some ice cream. Is that cool?"

"Yeah, that's straight?"

"Do you know what you're cookin' yet?"

"Whatever it is, just make sure you and your little fiancé show up to eat it."

"Oh, we'll be here. You just make sure y'all know how to act when we get here," I hollered as I walked out the door and closed it.

I went to the house so I could get my ring. I figured I'd check my voicemail while I was there. I had a message from Julian. I was surprised but at the same time I guess I shouldn't have been. "Anya, ain't nothing changed. I miss you already man. I need to see you tonight before I leave tomorrow. Call me as soon as you get this message. Don't play me. Call yo' man. Alright?" I rushed and erased that mess. What was I doing? I just should have been upfront with Julian the day before. I just couldn't. I didn't want to hurt him again. I was in no position to be marrying anybody with my backward self.

I arrived early at the airport, so I decided to park and go in and wait at the gate for Michael. I pulled in the garage, got a ticket, threw it on the dashboard and parked. I went into the airport to look at the monitor to find his gate. Flight 1429 arriving at gate B12 was on time. I still had a good fifteen minutes before his flight was even due to land. I went to Cinnabon and got him a cinnabon and a bottle of water. He loved those cavity-giving pound-adding things. I walked over to his gate, sat in a chair and waited.

I saw the plane coming toward the gate. I hoped he wouldn't be able to feel my guilt. I know I hadn't really done anything, but at the same time I had. I was supposed to be committed, not dating. Now I had no problem dating anybody else all this time, now suddenly a ring was on my finger, and whoosh here come the problems. I would go so far as to say if Michael had never asked me to marry him, I bet you I would have never run into Julian. I wonder what would have happened if I would have run into him the weekend before Mike proposed. Would I have still said yes? Here I was thinking again.

Michael was the third person off the plane. He was carrying his garment bag over his arm and rolling a small suitcase. Umm, I loved to watch him walk. He was so sexy. I could tell he was surprised when he looked up and saw me standing there waiting. Smiling. "I'm getting all these new benefits being a fiancé and all," he said.

He stood his bag up, put his arm around my waist and kissed me. "I could really get use to this. Now don't start spoiling me unless you're going to keep doing it." He smelled so good. I had really missed him. I wheeled his suitcase, and he carried his garment bag so he could put his arm around my waist. As we were walking, a young lady walked up and asked him for his autograph. She was so excited.

"Would you mind taking a picture with me and my friend?" she said, kind of bouncing up and down. He looked over at me. I nodded.

"Here, I'll take it for you," I said, taking the camera from her. She motioned for her friend to come over. You could tell her friend was kind of shy. They both got on either side of him.

"Okay, you guys, smile." I snapped the picture. "Wait, don't move. One more just to make sure. Okay, all done."

"Thank you." She looked at both of us.

"Not a problem," he said. "It was my pleasure." He was such a little charmer. I had to admit though, sometimes it was awkward being with him. Just like that day while walking through the airport. People would look, some would point, others would wave. I just didn't like having a spotlight on twenty-four seven. This would truly take some getting use to.

When we got to the car, I popped the trunk.

"Why are you in my car? I know you're not tired of driving the car you've been dying to get already."

"Naw, I've been driving it, but I just like to change up my luxury sometime, you know." I laughed. I was still getting use to the fact that I even had an option when I got to the garage. I can't lie, I was loving that. I didn't even drive my little 325i anymore. It pretty much stayed parked. I guess eventually I'd sell it since Kim and Traci both had nice cars. It wasn't like they were hurtin' in that department.

"Okay, I'm just making sure. Do you want me to drive?"

"No, I'm cool. You just relax. I know you get tired of making that flight every week. I got this." We got into the car, and he leaned over and kissed me. "Did you miss me?"

"Like you wouldn't believe," I answered.

"Good, 'cause I missed you also."

"Oh, I forgot to tell you we were suppose to go to my sister's house for dinner tonight, but that was before I knew you were coming today instead of Thursday, so I changed it to tomorrow. I figured you would probably just wanna chill tonight. Is that okay? My sister's tomorrow?"

"That's more than okay. You know I've been dying to meet anyone you know."

"Yes, I guess I've kept you under wraps long enough. It's ok to share you a little bit."

"Does this mean I can stay at your house now?" Whoa I wasn't expecting that. "I mean we are engaged now, we've already had sex, and I'm having dinner at your sister's house tomorrow. What else is there?"

"Huh yeah, I guess you're right," I said with a half smile.

"Is something wrong?"

"Naw, I'm straight."

"Okay you're straight. What's that all about?"

"Nothing, baby, really. I guess I just hadn't thought about it, that's all. I'm fine. It just made me think about something me and my sister were talking about today. Can I ask you something?"

"Now come on. You know you can ask me anything."

"Okay, I'm glad that we decided to get married because I love you and that's great." I glanced over in his direction, trying to act like I was focusing on the road. "I was just wondering, do you expect me to move to California when we get married?" I turned the CD player down because I wanted him to feel how serious I was.

"To be honest, baby, I didn't give it much thought. I just assumed once we got married, you would move to California."

I cut him off. "But I don't want to move to California. I like it here."

"Okay well don't stress out about it. Don't worry. We can work that out. Although, Anya, I have to say I think you", he paused, "no I take that back, I know you would love Southern California. What is there not to love?"

"Oh, let's see, for starters the traffic, um okay I got one, what about the fact that my family is here, my church is here and wait, wait silly me, my job, no my career is here. Michael, I know you have money and all that, but don't think I'm going to give up who I am because I'm marrying you."

"Wait. Hold on, just hold on a minute. Who said anything about you giving up who you are? What is that all about? As a matter of fact what is this conversation really about? I mean where is all this coming from? It sounds like you think I'm the enemy. It seems to me that you're looking for reasons for it not to work. I think when you love someone, you look for ways to make it work. I mean what is it? Are you getting scared? Do you not want to marry me?"

I was so stupid. What was I doing? Why was I doing this to him? An even better question was why was I doing this to myself?

"You're really beginning to scare me." He sat up in his seat as if the position change would somehow clear things up and give him a better understanding as to what was going on.

"Yes, I know. I'm beginning to scare myself."

"Anya, I'm a little nervous too. I'm making a commitment to share my life with you, and that alone is enough to scare anyone, but you sound like you wanna back out. Anya, I know your first marriage wasn't everything it should have been, but you don't have to be afraid with me. I'm not him. Okay?" I simply nodded as if I were in agreement. "I love you way too much to turn back now."

"But why? To be honest, you don't really even know me."

"What?" he shouted in disbelief. "What do you mean I don't know you? What do you think we've been doing the last several months? I don't know you," he mumbled under his breath. "I'm not saying that I know everything about you, but that's what building a life is all about, learning something new each day about the person you love, be it good or bad. But you know what? I'm not about to do this. How 'bout this? How about you drop me off at the hotel and go home and get yourself together. I don't know what has happened between now and last week, but I don't want to say anything else right now 'cause I'm too upset. I mean you're way off on something else right now." He was just going off. I had never seen him get upset in real life. His face was turning red and everything. I know one thing. I didn't want this happening too often.

"Michael." He cut me off. "No, Anya, I don't want to talk about it anymore right now. I think we should just talk about it a little later after you've had a minute to think about what you really want and if I'm it."

"Man, whatever." I was a little irritated. Maybe I had a lot more to say and maybe I wanted to say it right then. "Yeah, it probably is best if you stay at the hotel. I'm tired anyway, and I guess you are too.

He had to be. I was use to him spoiling me and being so perfect. I guess I just expected . . . well, I don't know what I expected, but this definitely wasn't it.

"Yeah, maybe that would be best." That is not what he was supposed to say. He wasn't suppose to agree with me.

It was the longest ride ever. I didn't want to glance over at him because I could feel him staring at me in disbelief and disappointment. You know that look, when your mother or somebody catches you doing something wrong, and you really want to try to explain, and try and fix it, but your pride won't let you? I kept wanting to say something, but I didn't want him to think I was just going to be giving in to him when we disagreed on something. But I really wasn't even sure exactly what I was disagreeing with him about. After all, he did say we would work it out, but what did that mean? I guess I should have waited to find out, huh?

After what felt like an eternity, we pulled up to the hotel. I kissed him on the cheek, but I'm sure he could tell I didn't want to.

"Well, I guess I'll see you in the morning," I said softly.

"Man, like that. Okay whatever, just pop the trunk." The valet came over to the car and opened Michael's door, then he came around to my door. "Oh, I'm not staying. Thank you."

"Let me get that for you, Mr. Harrison." He reached in the trunk and got the bags. I watched Michael walk toward the doors of the hotel. I just knew he was going to turn around at any moment. Well I guess I watch too many movies because he walked right through the doors and right out of my sight. I sat there for a minute, contemplating what I was doing and why. Was this our first fight? I wasn't really sure, but I knew I wanted it to be our last whatever it was.

As I drove home, I couldn't stop thinking about whether I should call Julian back. I really wanted to. No, I mean I really, really, really wanted to soooooooo bad, but I knew deep down, I shouldn't. Well so much for shouldn't. I picked up my cell phone and called him. I know, I know, I should have been calling Michael to apologize for being a complete idiot, but I could always do that later. Maybe I subconsciously started that disagreement with Michael just so I could have an excuse to get away from him so I could see Julian. Either way, Julian wanted me to swing by his hotel for a drink on my way home, needless to say, I did.

I called Michael and I told him that I was going to go out for a drink with Kim because I was feeling a little stressed out. I know I'm terrible. You don't have to tell me. I'm fully aware.

"Am I what's stressing you out?" He sounded hurt.

"No, baby, it's not you. It's me, but I'm okay. I love you, and I'll see you tomorrow." Okay isn't that the oldest one in the book? it's not you, it's me. Uhh, I needed to be slapped.

"I don't get it Anya. I fly all the way out here for this? Just last night you couldn't wait to see me. Now you can't wait to get away from me. What's going on?"

"It's nothing, baby. I just need a minute. Please try and understand, okay?" I know I sounded a little nervous because I wasn't really sure what he was thinking or what he was going to say. I was just hoping it wasn't something like, "Come back so we can talk."

"Yeah, Okay, whatever, man. Isn't that what you told me earlier? I love you," he said in a very condescending tone, and before I could say anything else, he hung up. Well at least he was going to bed, so I didn't have to worry about him calling me back.

I should have gone home and changed. I think I might have been too sexy for Julian to believe I wasn't trying to come get down. I just had on some jeans, but I had on this low cut halter with a major push-up bra on. I had on these bad high heel sandals, and I smelled way too good. I had really gotten all cute and perfumed up for Michael, but I guess there was no sense in it going to waste. Right? I pulled down the visor and fixed my hair, put on a fresh coat of lipstick, grabbed my purse from the backseat, and I was good to go. I stepped out of the car, remembered my ring, took it off and stuck it in the ashtray. I got out of the car, pressed the alarm, and at that very moment I got nervous. Nervous about what this could mean. I never quite mastered the art of quitting while I was ahead.

When I walked in the bar, Julian was sitting there with his fine self. I thought about running before he saw me, if I knew what was good for me.

"Hey." I slid on the stool next to his.

"Hey yourself, umm umm umm you look good. What you trying to do up in here?" I played like I didn't know what he meant, but I knew exactly what he meant and exactly what I was doing.

"What you drinkin' tonight, Ms. Dennings?"

"Apple martini."

"I just had to see you before I leave tomorrow. I missed you girl" He looked me up and down, from hair to pedicure, then looked me straight in my eyes. You can't say you don't miss me, Anya." He pulled me up into him and hugged me. "So what we gon' do about this?"

"What can we do? My life is here, and your life is in Chicago, so that's that." I pulled away.

"Just like that?" He sat back down

"Yes, just like that." I sat down and took a sip of my drink, trying not to look at him.

"Girl, you know you need to quit frontin'. It's not healthy." He smiled.

"I don't need to front, Julian. The past is the past, and some things are just better left there. Apparently you've been doing just fine without me anyway, so why try to complicate your life now?"

"Maybe I like complicated." He leaned in and kissed me. I tried to pull away. Okay maybe I didn't, but it was too late. He tasted even better than the night before. Maybe I wasn't as ready as I thought for marriage.

"Looks like you like it complicated too."

"Naw. In spite of what you may think, I'm trying to simplify my life."

"I couldn't tell by that kiss."

"Alright, that's enough. Come on" I hopped off the stool, grabbed his hand and pulled him. "Let me whup on you a little at the pool table so I can go home and go to bed."

"Now you know you ain't got to go home to go to bed."

"Boy, do you think about anything but sex? Rack 'em up and let's get this show on the road." We walked over to the table. The bar area was surprisingly empty for a Saturday night. There were only about twelve people there total, including the bartender. He took a sip of his drink and set it on the table next to the pool table.

"Hey remember that time we played strip pool when you were house sitting for Tanya?"

"Aw, man, do I. How could I forget? I think that's probably why I went ahead and learned how to play, you can't be losing at strip pool, not when every ball you sink represents a piece of clothes."

"Yeah," he said, "especially when you didn't hardly have any on to begin with. That sure was a quick game. Man, those were the days."

"Yes, they were. Seeing you brings back so many memories." I stared at him with pure lust.

"Not that our memories aren't great, but we don't have to have just those memories. We can make so many more if you would give in and do what you know you really want to." He leaned over and broke the balls. "I tell you what, let's make a little wager. You win, you go home no questions asked, no begging, no nothing. I'll go back to Chicago, and I'll send you a Christmas and a birthday card each year until we're old and gray."

"And if you win?" I looked up before I took my shot.

"If I win, you stay with me tonight. You admit that you're still as much in love with me today as you were seven years ago, and you give us another chance."

"I don't know about this."

"You said you was gon' whup me. Don't be no punk. If you're confident you're going to win, you don't have anything to worry about. Right?"

I couldn't stand him. He knew me well enough to know I wasn't hardly about to walk away from a challenge.

He walked over and pinned me up against the pool table. "So we on?" He smelled my neck. "Ummm, I missed your scent, Anya. Some days I close my eyes, and I can still smell you. You know back then it wasn't all about perfume. All you could afford was Victoria's Secret Pear Glace. Remember?"

"How could I forget? I'm surprised you remember."

"How could I forget? I smelled it enough." We both smiled as we reminisced on that.

"Oh Julian, if only it were as simple as a game of pool." I shook my head and slid away from him.

"You always have liked to make things harder than they have to be. Okay, well go ahead and take your shot, punk."

"You talkin' all that trash. You know what? You're on, but I ain't worried, because I got this in the bag." I bent over and sunk the blue two ball right in the side pocket, then there went the green six. I was on a roll. I walked around the table to take my third shot. Dang, I missed it. "Oh, don't trip, I just thought I'd give you a chance to play."

"Oh, trust me, I don't mind watching you bend over that table like that. I could do this all night and when I win, I'll be doin' you all night."

Needless to say the flirting and trash talking went on throughout the whole game.

"Oh, I almost forgot to ask, how was the wedding?" I asked.

"Oh, it was real nice. Kenneth's wild butt, is a trip. Nobody ever thought he would get married, but Stephanie came into the picture and changed all that. I'm glad though. She's good for my brother. She's really settled him, and we all know it was time."

"Yeah, he always was something else. Remember that time those two girls were in front of y'all house fighting over him, and your mother turned the water hose on them because they wouldn't get out the driveway?"

"Oh yeah, I had forgotten all about that. That fool was always in some mess with some women. I use to try to tell 'em players don't get caught. At least not as much as he did." We both cracked up. It was funny to see though. I guess I really did miss Julian.

We both ordered another drink. I told him two had to be my limit so I could drive home. I had to admit though, I was having a ball. "I don't know why you keep insisting on going home. You can drink as much as you want and stay right here. You're grown you don't have to report home to nobody." He was trying his best. But after being there, I didn't think I would want to be with him. Besides, all he kept talking about was gettin' some, and quite frankly, it was beginning to get on my nerves. I mean dang he was a grown, not to mention fine black man with a fat checking account. You couldn't tell me he wasn't getting some on a regular basis, but the way he was acting, you wouldn't know it.

"That's it." He grabbed my stick out of my hand. "We not gon' be able to keep playin'."

"Why" I said laughing, "cause I'm winning?

"No, it's not that. You just messin me all up. I can't keep watching you bend across that table like that. Please come upstairs with me."

"I can't, Julian."

"You can't or you won't or you don't want to? I mean come on, Anya. Give me a solid explanation, and quit talking in circles. You owe me at least that much."

But truthfully, I didn't owe him anything. "I just can't, Julian, that's all."

"Why?" He grabbed my arm.

"Because things are different now, that's all." I pulled my arm back. "How different could they be?"

"Huhhh." I put my fingers to my temples and began to rub in a circular motion. I could feel the stress building. "Let's just quit while we're ahead." I walked over and kissed him gently on his cheek. "I'll always love you, Julian, but our time has passed. It was so good seeing you. It brought back so many memories, good ones that I will cherish forever. I love you." I grabbed my purse and walked out. The question is should I have?

I was listening to click-clack of my heels on the pavement walking to the car. Julian ran out behind me. "Anya, Anya, hold up, man."

"Julian sweetie, just let it go already. Please, just let it go. I don't even know why I came here tonight"

"What do you mean? You know exactly why you came here tonight. You came here because you know you still love me. I know it's been a long time, but would it hurt to try and see where it goes? Do you know how much I loved you back then and still love you? What are you afraid of?"

"I don't know," I said. "I'm afraid of me."

"Well, you're the one who hurt me, and I'm not afraid of you. I'm still here. I know that what we had is over, but what about what we could have?"

Well it was over. I blew it. I knew if I looked in his eyes I would be consumed by his fire. I let out an exasperating sigh of surrender as I looked up into his eyes.

"I'm afraid of hurting you again. You think you know me, but you don't. Some days I look in the mirror, and I don't even know myself."

"I'm willing to take that chance." He pulled me into him and kissed me long and hard. I couldn't push him away. This kiss meant business, and I didn't wanna risk losing him, just in case. I know, just in case what? Well, I wasn't exactly sure, but at that point, I was lost in yesterday and bringing it into today. I knew deep in my heart I needed to resist, but all I could do was kiss him back just as passionately as he was kissing me. Even if I was supposed to be with Julian, I knew this wasn't the right way of going about it, but if I told him the truth it might mess everything up. I wanted him to know he could trust me, even though I didn't trust me. He tasted so good, much better than I remembered.

I let out a small moan. "You taste so good."

"What?" He chuckled.

"Did I really say that out loud?"

"Yes, I think you did, but you know I'm into that anyway. Talk a little more. Tell me how you really feel."

"Well, there won't be any of that tonight." I took a step back and grabbed his hand. "But you know, Julian, I missed you so much, and I still think about you all the time. I just could never bring myself to call you. I wanted to several times, but after what I had done and after so much time passed, I just said forget it. It just wasn't meant to be." I looked down, because I really hated to show this much emotion, but it seemed like the older I got, the less I could control my feelings.

"So," he said, looking at me, "where do we go from here?"

"Don't ask me. I guess we'll just have to wait and see where it goes. I've already let you in too much as it is."

"So do you still have to leave?" He looked at me with the saddest most begging face I'd ever seen.

"Yes, I still have to leave. I don't want to, but I need to." I nervously danced from side to side because I had no idea what I was doing.

"Okay then, I guess it's okay for me to call you when I get home tomorrow."

I thought about Michael and me being at Traci's tomorrow for dinner.

"Umm, I'll call you Monday. I'm going to be at Traci's for dinner tomorrow."

"What's the occasion, if you don't mind me asking?"

"Nothing. We're just getting together because we hardly see each other anymore, you know with everybody being all grown up now." I laughed. "You know how that is."

"Believe me," he said, nodding "I know all too well. That's why I've been thinking about coming back this way. I miss my family, and my parents are getting older."

"What?" I was surprised. "Are you really thinking about moving back here?"

"Yeah, really I am, and if I have you to look forward to, there's no doubt I'm coming back home."

"Wow," I kind of stuttered, "that would be great." Here we go with all this reality coming in and messin' up my perfect fantasies.

"But anyway, like you said, we'll see how it goes. I didn't want to mention it to you before because I didn't want you to feel like I was pressuring you. How is Traci anyway?" he said, changing the subject. I was pretty relieved he did.

"Oh, she's good."

"Man, I still cannot believe her and Kevin ain't married yet as long as they've been together. That just don't make no sense. Man, what they waitin' on?" He shook his head.

"I know, we all say the same thing, but you know my sister, she ain't changed, Ms. Independent. I think Kevin's probably scared to propose again after that first time." He took a couple of steps back and bent over laughing. "I know. I heard about that. Man, yo' sister is cold. Huh, I'm surprised they stayed together."

"Me too, because Kevin really wants to be married and have kids but Traci's so selfish sometimes it's hard to tell what she be thinking."

"She must love that fool though. They're still together."

"Yeah, but like I said, who knows what that girl be thinking? Anyway, let me get out of here. I'll talk to you Monday, or if it's not too late when I get home, I'll call you tomorrow night." I leaned up against him, kissed him and smiled. "Delicious," I said and we both laughed.

"Girl, you still ain't got the sense God gave you."

"And you are so glad I don't"

"Where you in such a hurry to get to?"

"Nowhere. I'm just tired and wanna go to bed, that's all. I've have had a full week, not to mention the emotional stress of seeing you." I laughed.

"Come on, Anya, stay in that perfectly good bed up in my room. I can pop the cork on a bottle of champagne, give you a massage, and we can sit up and talk like we use to. It'll be like old times, except the champagne will be better and the sex no doubt," he paused and smirked, "will definitely be better." We tried to keep straight faces but we both broke, thinking about our first time. It was hilarious thinking back on it. My God, we were both two clueless virgins. I have to say, it had gotten better over the years, but eventually we broke up. He probably just wanted to show me all his new tricks, but who cares? Relationships are built on so much more than good sex. Okay Okay I told myself, *just get into the car and drive off like the good girl you wanna be.* Practice makes perfect, so I had to practice being good, right? It wasn't just gonna come over night.

"Julian my sweet, I'll have to pass this time. As tempting as your offer is, I must pass. I bid you a fair good night."

"You mean an unfair night because this ain't hardly fair," he joked. "Next time?"

"Maybe." My lips spoke, but my eyes and the hug I gave him definitely said yes. I turned the alarm off on my car.

"Damn, girl, you do it like that? The interior design business must be way more lucrative than I thought. A Jag yesterday, a Beamer with new plates today. What's up with all that?" I forgot all about the fact that I was in Michael's car.

"Uh, don't trip. Sometimes that's how I get down. Just kidding. This belongs to a friend of mine."

"Must be a good friend." He looked suspicious, and I knew what he was trying to imply but I didn't even want to go there or anywhere near wherever there was.

"Yeah, kind of." I got in the car and rolled down the window. "So I'll call you Monday."

"Umm huh, we'll see." He leaned in and kissed me then he took a step back and waved I waved, then I drove off.

As I was driving home, I thought about Michael and how confused I was. What was wrong with me? Why couldn't I make good decisions and stick to them? Better yet, why couldn't there be two of me, one for Michael and one for Julian so I could have the best of both worlds? I felt sick to my stomach, but more than that, I was sick of myself. I wanted so bad to be normal. Look at my sister. Her and Kevin had been together for years and she just wanted him. Why she didn't want to get married I didn't know, but at least she could have one man and be happy with him without a bunch of drama. Maybe some people had to work at monogamy, and for some it just came natural. I was definitely one who obviously had to work at it.

I pulled up into the driveway, pressed the garage opener and pulled in. I sat there for a minute as the door closed, wishing I hadn't lied to Michael, I felt so guilty and rightfully so. I had no business going to see Julian. After listening to three more songs on the CD that was playing, I got out of the car and went into the house. I threw my purse and my keys on the kitchen table, undid my shoes and kicked them off. I reached into the cabinet, pulled down a champagne glass and stuck it in the chiller. I danced my way over to the CD player and decided I needed to hear a little Mary J. 'cause ain't nothing like Mary to get you through a man problem. I looked through my CDs, but I didn't see it. I stood there and thought for a minute before I ran upstairs and got it out of my computer room. I came back downstairs and put it on. I danced my way back to the kitchen, got a bottle of Moet out of the fridge, got my glass out the chiller and poured a glass. I went out onto the deck and sat in one of the wicker chairs, pulling another chair up to stick my feet in and I tried to figure out what I should do.

I knew one thing. I wanted to be happy, but at that point, I didn't even know what it would take to make me happy. All this time I had been ecstatic with Michael, I thought I was happy, but I couldn't have been if Julian could come in and make me question the very relationship that I was so happy to be in just two days prior. How flaky was I? What if I had already been married when I ran into Julian? Would I have cheated? Would I have even gone to see Julian that night. I kept sipping, and the questions kept rolling around in my head. I closed my eyes, put my head back and sang along with Mary. Whatever was meant to be would be.

I got up when my glass was empty and went back in the house. I walked over, turned off Mary and grabbed her out of the CD player, turned out the lights and grabbed the bottle of Moet out of the freezer and went upstairs. As I walked up the stairs, the thoughts came back, racing through my mind like cars at the Indy 500. I was trying to think of a way to tell Michael that I could not marry him. I went into my room, put Mary back on and began to undress. I put on a pair of Calvin Klein girl boxers and a half shirt and sat up in the bed sipping, when I should have been praying. I don't know why I insisted on doing things the hard way.

I was so deep in thought that the phone ringing scared the crap out of me. I was mad. I spilled my champagne all down the front of my shirt when I jumped. I looked over at the caller ID and saw it was Michael. I was a little surprised, but not really.

"Hello."

"Hey, what's going on?"

"Nada."

"You okay?"

"Umm hmm," I said. I know he was worried with those one-word answers. I know I would be.

"I was trying to hold out, hoping you would call, but you didn't, so I figured I'd call you since it was getting kind of late. I thought you would call when you got in, to at least let me know you made it home safely. You do when I'm halfway across the country, why not when I'm right here?"

"I was just giving you some space, that's all," I said quietly."

"Were you giving me some space or taking some space for yourself? Anya, I don't need any space. I look forward to seeing you all week, and I thought you did the same."

"Michael?"

"Yeah baby?" he answered curiously.

"Why do you love me?"

"Baby, how much did you and Kim drink?"

"I had two martinis because I had to drive home, but I sat up here and drank like a half a bottle of champagne. That's not the point though. I just need to know why you love me."

"Yeah" I heard him smile. "You have had a few."

"Michael, for real, why do you want to marry me? Out of all the women in the world, why me?"

"Girl, you are crazy'. What is this all about? I think the question really is are you sure you want to marry me?"

Before I knew what to say, "I'm sure" flew out of my mouth, and I couldn't get it back. But I don't think I wanted it back. I did want to be with this man and nobody else. "Baby, I know I'm spoiled, and I know I make you crazy sometimes, but I love you, and I think I just got scared. At some point in the last few days, I wasn't sure if I wanted to get married. I knew that I loved you, but I didn't know if it was enough to spend the rest of my life with you. I wanted to make sure we weren't just caught up in the moment and the idea of getting married. When I say 'I do' again I want it to be forever. I don't want to get divorced anywhere down the line. Michael, I'm a different person when I'm with you. You make me a better person. You taught me how to enjoy life again when I had shut down. I am so glad that I met you." This was definitely not the alcohol speaking. Maybe the alcohol gave me the nerve to get it all out, but this was really how I felt, and I was glad I now knew it.

"Wow is all I can say. I love you too. And yes, yes there is nothing in the world I want more than to spend the rest of my life with you."

"Good. Well, will you do me a favor?

"Depends on the favor," he said seriously before he chuckled, "Just kidding. Anything for you."

I mustered up the cutest, most irresistible tone I could dream up. "I know you're tired and I know it's late and I know I should have had you drop me off so you would have your car, but would you please, please, please have a car bring you over? I would come get you but I'm a little on the tipsy side." Drunk didn't sound ladylike. He wasn't saying anything, so I thought I'd better throw a few more pleases in there. "Please, please, please?"

"Anya, please not another please, okay?" I responded with an okay. "I never thought I could say this to you, but no." I was in total shock. He did not just tell me no after I spilled my heart out, but he did. That's exactly what he said, but I had to be certain. "No." There it was again. "I am not getting up, packing another bag, putting on some clothes, calling for a car or a cab to come there. No." He was serious too.

Pouting, I said, "But I said please. I'll put on your favorite dress and let you take advantage of me." I began to whisper into the phone things I would let him do to me.

The next words out of his mouth were, "I'm on my way. You better not fall asleep before I get there."

I had gotten some keys made for him earlier in the week because I knew this was coming eventually. I just didn't realize how soon. I knew that with us getting engaged he would eventually not want to stay at the hotel. I sat there for a few minutes more, then I got up, went over to the closet and pulled out my black wrap dress. It was just a plain dress to me, but he loved it. He thought it was so sexy. I laid it across the bed and took out my black frou-frou Victoria's Secret house shoes. I figured I'd better take a shower to wash the scent of Julian's cologne from my face, neck and hands. I ran downstairs and got a Ziploc freezer bag. I came back upstairs and took the shirt I had had on earlier and put it in the bag. I took one last whiff, before I sealed the bag up and tucked it in the back of the closet.

I showered off Julian, trying to wash away my guilt, and dried off. I lotioned down and put on one of Victoria's water bras, because this dress was a little low cut. I took out a matching thong, slid it up, then checked myself out in the mirror. I brushed through my hair and sprayed on a little Bath and Body Cumber Melon and put on a tiny bit of lip glass and a mole. Yes, all of this at almost midnight to sit in the house. To me this was a small thing to do for a man who's as good to me as Michael. I walked over to the bed and slid on my dress. I put just a touch of Cumber Melon powder in my house shoes and rub it in. I went to my jewelry box to get my ring. I was irritated when I realized it was in the car. Just then, I heard the doorbell ring. "Crap." I still had to run to the car and get my ring out.

I ran down the stairs quietly and opened the door to the garage. The doorbell rang again. I opened the car door, looked in the ashtray, got my ring out and slid it on my finger. I tipped back into the house and softly closed the door before heading to let Michael in. "Hi Sweetie."

"I thought you might have been sleep you took so long to come to the door."

"Never. I was just getting this dress on for you."

"Ummmmm, and I'm so glad you did," he said, picking me up and closing the door behind him.

"Aren't you going to get your bags?" I laughed. He was trippin'. He had closed the door and left his bags on the walkway. While he was getting his bags, I went in the kitchen, got a lighter and lit some candles, then I turned on a little Najee and dimmed the lights. I allowed my mind to drift. I wondered what Julian was doing and what I was going to do with him. Can you be in love with two people? Some people say you can, and if that's true, I know I am. The question is what do you do when that happens? "Hey, what are you thinking about?" Michael walked over to me. I was glad he did. I hated to even think about the situation I was in, and I was tired of dealing with myself.

"You," I said, looking over at him. He was so sexy. I just stood there for a moment staring at that freshly cut goatee. "Can I get a kiss now, a real one?" He put his face close to mine.

"That depends." He looked surprised, as if to say I know you're playing after I just got up out the bed and came all the way over here in the middle of the night. "What's the password?"

He lifted me up, and I wrapped my legs around him. "I love you," he whispered in my ear. Is that good enough?" That was more than good enough. He kissed me. "I was looking forward to that the whole ride here."

"Well, I am so glad that I could accommodate you, Mr. Harrison. The truth is I've been waiting for you to get here so I could give you a ride." I batted my eyelashes at him.

"You know how much I love for you to call me Mr. Harrison. You better slow down. I at least want to see you model that dress before I take it off." I hopped down, put my hands on my hips, and walked back and forth from the living room to the kitchen, wiggling my hips from side to side as smooth as butter. I guess it wasn't really a walk, more of a glide, and each step I took toward him said I want you, right here, right now on this imaginary runway I was prancing down. He began to clap. "Let's hear it for the lovely Anya soon-to-be Harrison, modeling a lovely show-stopping black dress that she's not going to have on very long for the distinguished, handsome Michael Harrison."

We both laughed then I looked at how happy we were, and it was really, for real no longer a decision. Now am I trying to convince you or me? I mean yes, I truly loved Julian, but maybe it just wasn't meant to be, but I knew one thing, this right here, Michael. This was definitely meant to be, and I was glad I hadn't messed it up. He took me by my hand, and we danced in the living room. He rubbed my lower back as we danced, and it relaxed me even more. Every now and then during the song, he would hold me away from him and stare at me. Then he would pull me back into him and hold me tight.

"Just imagine," I whispered. "This will be us one day, sneaking a dance in our living room while the music plays softly after we've put our children to bed."

"I know, Anya, I'm so glad you said that. I can't wait to be a daddy."

"I just hope I can make you a daddy, Michael. I guess I hadn't thought about it, what if I can't." I got scared.

"Shhh," he whispered in my ear. "Just dance. Don't even think like that. It just wasn't time before. Trust me. Not to worry. It will happen. Do you really think God wouldn't bless us with children?" He was always so confident that things would turn out just the way he planned and maybe that had been his life's reality, but unfortunately, it hadn't been mine. But right then, it wasn't even important. All that mattered was he knew everything about me and still loved my crazy mixed-up self. Well everything except for Julian. I continued to dance and he continued to rub my back, and life was good again.

We eventually made it upstairs and the great thing about it, he didn't even want to have sex. He just wanted to be there with me. I reminded him that I promised we could do anything he wanted. He assured me that, he was doing exactly what he wanted, to be there with me. He lit the two candles on each of my nightstands and turned out the lights. Then pulled me to him, untied my dress and slid it from my body. He draped it across the chair I had in the corner of the room. I stepped out of my shoes, sat on the bed and watched him undress. He slid out of his jeans then slowly pulled his shirt over his head and tossed it on the floor. We pulled the covers back and nestled down in the bed.

"Don't think you're getting away. After I rest up tonight, it's over for you in the morning."

"Not before church."

"Why? Is it a different sin after church? Is there some fornication rule I'm not aware of?"

Ouch, God. I thought. He was right though. What was I doing? All those months of celibacy and really trying to live right and yet, I continued to tempt myself. I wanted to become closer to the Lord, but everything went out the window because I allowed my flesh to get too close to Michael. I couldn't even blame him either because he was willing to wait. It was all me. I really did want to live right. It was just so hard. It was easy when I wasn't dating of course. It was even easy the first few months I dated Michael, but with each visit, it became harder and harder. Why was sex the only way I thought I was able to show a man how much I cared for him? One thing though, I was so glad I did not give Julian some the night before or I would really be feeling stupid right about now.

I had come so far, and I had such a new way of looking at myself. I didn't want to see myself the same way I did this time last year. I wanted to continue to move forward in my life, not backward. The thing about it is once you let a little sin back in, it just overtakes you. I was back having sex with Michael like it was nothing. I turned to Michael and snuggled up to him.

"You know, you're right. Maybe we should stop having sex until we get married."

"Okay" he stuttered. "Whatever you want. I had to open my big mouth. I didn't mind waiting before, but how do you expect me to stop after you already gave it to me, repeatedly? I mean do you really think we can do that?"

"I know it'll be hard, but don't worry, we can do it."

"Yes, I know. That's what I'm trying to say. We can do it."

"Ha ha very funny."

"No for real, Anya man, that's messed up."

"You'll thank me later." I laughed.

"Doubt it," he mumbled under his breath.

"Oh, baby, we can do this." I jumped on top of him. "Remember, you're Michael Harrison. Let you tell it, you can do anything."

"Then get off me man, or we'll be doing it all night with your fine self."

"Sorry." I slid down off him. "Well you know what this means?" He looked over at me as if he didn't want to play guessing games. "We gotta hurry up and set a date."

"I know, that's real." We laughed but his sounded a little fake. "Okay when I get home from church tomorrow I'll stop and get the pie and ice cream on my way home, then we'll pull out our calendars before we go to Traci's."

"Cool," he said. "See you in the morning, sweetheart." He kissed me and we went to sleep.

The next morning while getting ready for church, I noticed Michael just watching me as I ran back and forth from the bedroom to the bathroom to the closet in an attempt to be on time. I really hated to miss praise and worship. I had really come a long way. I remembered when I wanted to get to church just in time to hear the preacher preach and leave out the door as soon as he was done. That's why I use to always sit in the back so it would be easy to tip on out. I didn't know what I was missing back then. I didn't understand what it was to really have a relationship with the Lord, and don't get me wrong, I'm far from having it all together, and I have so far to go, but one thing I know is I thank God for his grace and his mercy. Without them I wouldn't be here today. One thing I've learned in this walk with God is take is one day at a time. "Why don't you ever ask me to go to church with you?" He sat up in the bed.

"What? What are you talking about?" I glanced over at him from the closet.

"You heard me. Why don't you ever invite me to come with you to church? I mean I'm a Christian just like you. I love the Lord probably as much as you, and don't women usually want their husbands, boyfriends or fiancés to come to church with them?"

It's not that I didn't want him to come. It's just that, well he was not just any guy. He was Michael Harrison, and I just didn't want to deal with all that. I know that's selfish, but what if it didn't work out? The fewer people who knew we were dating, the better it would be. Plus, my sister and Kevin went to the same church I did and that would have meant explaining it to them too. I tried to tell Michael all this but he said he just couldn't understand what the big deal was.

Eventually he lay back in the bed and let it go, but at the same time made it extremely clear he would be going with me the following week. I didn't have a problem with that. Besides, if we could get through the dinner at Traci's house, we could pretty much handle anything. I finished getting ready for church and headed out the door. Not without kissing him on the forehead and telling him I loved him. Wow, how did we in fact get there from a chance meeting in a hotel lobby?

As I stood in church with my hands lifted up to the Lord, I almost wanted to cry. Not because I was sad about life. I was kind of sad that I only asked God for his help after I would make my own mess, but I did. I stood right there and asked God to just help me to live a life that was pleasing to him and to help me and Michael not have sex anymore until after we got married. I knew that was going to be hard. I almost felt like going downtown in the morning and just getting married. At least we would be legal in the eyes of the God, and we could continue to get our freak on. I know, what a reason, right? So I guess I had no choice but to make an honest attempt to deny myself as best I could.

After that prayer, I continued to worship the Lord and thank him for just being God in my life. I lost myself in worship just thinking about the awesomeness of God. It felt so good to love him because I had truly been neglecting my relationship with the Lord as we often do when things are going well, but he puts up with me anyway. How? I'll never know. Why? I still can't quite grasp, but he does love me, and I'm so glad he does.

On my way home from church I stopped at Bakers Square and got an apple pie, then I ran in the grocery store an picked up some vanilla ice cream. After all, what is apple pie without the a la mode? I drove to the house thinking about how Michael had been the only man in my house since I moved in. It felt a little strange, but a good strange. I was looking forward to getting there and him being there. I guess even in the midst of all my independence, there was still a part of me that wanted to be married and wanted to be loved, and in love and I really thought that this time it might work.

As I walked through the door I smelled coffee brewing, and Michael was sitting at the kitchen table eating a bagel, reading the paper. Yip, I thought. I could really get use to this. His face lit up as I walked in. "How was church?"

"It was so good. Pastor was on today" I walked over, picked up the other half of his bagel and took a bite.

"Hey, get out of my stuff, greedy." He jumped up, grabbed me and began to tickle me. I hated to be tickled, but I tolerated it when it came to him because he seemed to enjoy it so much.

"Okay games over," I stated. Let's get down to business. Go get your planner while I put the ice cream in the freezer."

When he got back downstairs, we both pulled out our planners and attempted to set a wedding date. Neither of us really wanted to wait. If Michael had it his way, we would get married the next day, but realistically, we both knew how long it took to plan a wedding. Lord knows I was not getting married in the winter, so we had no choice but to wait until spring. We decided on May. The only thing was trying to figure out where this grand event was to take place. Most of the people he knew and probably would invite had money, so if they wanted to be there, they would come so it made more sense to have it at my church. It wasn't the kind I dreamed of, plus it wasn't real big or real pretty. Then it came to me. I scooted my chair next to his.

"I think I have a solution."

"I'm almost afraid to hear it if it takes you buttering me up like I know you're about to do."

"I don't need to butter you up. I just want to be close to you." I laughed. "Okay for real though. Listen to this before you say no."

"Now I know it has to be over the top." He shook his head. "Come on. Spit it out."

"I was just thinking, how about we get married in New York, after all that's where we met." Throwing that in couldn't hurt because he loved sentimental stuff. "I was thinking the Waldorf Astoria. What do you think?"

"Anya, I think whatever you want is fine with me. You just have to see if it's available. I guess that would be good. We could have the wedding and reception all right there, which would be convenient and guests could stay right at the hotel. This may just work. Which means I better keep working because I can see you just gon' spend all my little money, huh?"

I got up and straddled him. "Only if you let me," I whispered in his ear. I began slowly kissing him on his neck, working my way to his lips.

"I already said yes. Whatever you want now get up off me before you get something started, Ms. No Sex 'til We Get Married."

"You're right. I wasn't thinking. Sorry." Dang, I wasn't even twenty-four hours into celibacy again and I was about to die. I had forgotten the vow I had made to God just hours prior. I was so awful.

Meet The Family

Sitting in front of my sister's house, I wasn't sure if I was ready for this.

"What's up baby? Let's go." Michael tugged at my arm.

I took a deep breath and turned to him. "Let me just tell you, Kim and Traci are crazy. They have absolutely no sense. They will more than likely give you a really hard time, but don't trip. It's just that they don't know you and."

He put his hand over my mouth. "Stop stallin' and come on."

Okay, he was way too excited for me. After all, I hadn't met anyone from his family or circle of friends, and I was fine with that. Why couldn't he be more like me? What was the big deal? Why couldn't we stay in our little world and be happy?

He got out of the car, came around to my door and opened it. I finally got out and slammed the door. I didn't even know why we were doing this. I was mumbling all kinds of trash under my breath. He held my hand as we walked toward the door. With each step I got more and more nervous, but I didn't really know why. Suddenly I stopped. "Come on, let's not go in. Let's just go."

From the looks of it, that wasn't an option. Maybe I could bribe him with sex. It always worked in the movies. As I thought about it, ninety percent of the time it works in real life too.

"I don't understand what the big deal is," he said, dragging me up on the stairs. "Is it me being white? I really am beginning to think that's what you're so nervous about."

But that wasn't it, I don't think. I think it was part of me totally surrendering and though I hated it, it scared me a little.

"No" I looked at him defensively. "My sister knows you're white, she doesn't care. She just wants me to be happy."

"Then what is it?"

"Nothing. It's nothin'. I'm cool."

"You sure?" I nodded.

"Okay if you say so. Here goes," He rang the doorbell, and we both waited in anticipation at the door. Kim would be the one to open the door.

"Don't say nothin'. Just let us in." I said. I could see it all in her face she wanted to say something so bad, but just what, I wasn't sure.

"Oh hell no I won't. I know Michael Harrison ain't the dude you been runnin' around with the last few months. I just know he ain't." She literally fell out on the floor. "Okay Okay I'm sorry." She stood up. "I'm so sorry, Michael. I'm just in shock. Anya knows better than to be springing this kind of stuff on somebody, especially me." She stuck out her hand. "I'm Kim. Nice to meet you." She hugged him and welcomed him all the while giving me the evil eye. I knew I would get it later. There was no getting around it. Before I knew it, she had, slid her arm through Michael's and escorted him to the bar where my sister and Kim's boyfriend, Vic, were sitting. Kevin of course was behind the bar mixing drinks, this being his usual position at any of our functions because he made the best drinks.

"Look what I found," Kim boasted. Traci and Vic turned around, and Kevin looked up. My sister almost choked on her drink. "Aw hell no. You messin with Michael Harrison?" my sister hollered.

"I'm beginning to wonder if this is a good or bad thing," Michael said, looking confused. I wondered what was up with the cussin. I mean was it that serious? Because none of us really cussed. My grandmother always said it wasn't ladylike and though I had a serious trash mouth in high school and college, as we had gotten older I began to see her point.

"Relax, Michael. We just trippin' that she was able to keep you under wraps this long." Traci snickered. "But I'll tell you one thing, I ain't mad."

Kim cut in, "Okay, this explains that big fat ring and that car. Yeah boy. It's all coming together now. I just can't believe as long as we've been best friends, you didn't think you could trust me not to tell anyone."

Traci looked over at me, cutting Kim off. "Well I guess you obviously need no introduction, Michael, but this is my boyfriend Kevin and Kim's friend Vic."

"Hello, everyone. Nice to finally meet you," Michael said.

"What can I get for you, Michael?" Kevin asked.

"A soda is good, whatever kind you may have. Thanks."

"Okay well I'm so going to need more than a soda to get through this evening I'm sure. Hit me with an apple martini, Kev. You know the drill, getta shakin'." I smiled.

"So you think you wanna marry my little sister," Traci said.

"No, I'm sure I'm going to marry your little sister," Michael replied, taking a seat at the bar.

"Are you sure you want to get married?" Traci asked.

"Not just get married. I want to marry Anya more than anything I've ever wanted."

"And I'm pretty sure you're use to getting what you want." Traci gave him a stern look.

"Why do you think you want to marry her? I mean you haven't even known her a year."

"What?" He gave a nervous chuckle. Are you serious?"

"Hey how about we play some Taboo?" I tried to change the subject. "I didn't bring him here to be interrogated, Traci." I know she was my sister and she was just looking out for me, but that's exactly why I didn't want to bring Michael over. "It's okay baby. Don't get yourself all upset."

He turned and looked at my sister right in her eyes. "Because I love her." He paused. "Because the day I met her, I came more alive then I've ever been." He pulled me between his legs and professed his love to the entire room. "I love this woman. I don't know what kind of power she has over me, but I could never and don't even want to try to imagine my life without her now that I have her."

"Oh my God, he is so sweet." I said as I turned and gave him a quick kiss on the lips.

"He is so whipped," Vic said, and him and Kevin gave each other a pound and began to laugh. But whatever the case I knew Michael loved me.

"Alright already, break that mess up. I didn't realize your answer would be that sickening, but I forgot, you are an actor. This just better not be an act.

"Back off, Traci." Kevin gave her the you're-going-too-far look.

"Sorry, Michael, it's just that she's the only sister I have, so I hope you understand and don't take it personal. I don't want you to think just because you're a star and everything, I trust you anymore than the next man. As a matter of fact, it makes me a little more leery, because what are the odds of Hollywood marriages lasting? Just make sure this one does."

He looked me in my eyes. "There is no way it couldn't."

"Alright. For the last time, break this corny mess up and get Taboo on the stage and yall in love butts off." Kevin came from behind the bar to get the game out.

We played the guys against the girls, which we often did. Every blue moon if me and John's old tired but came over alone we would play couples with Traci and Kevin. That's a trip. Their relationship had outlasted my first true love and my marriage. How did that happen? Maybe my sister did have it right all along. Other than the fact that shakin' was a sin. Oh okay yeah, I almost forgot. After about fifteen minutes of playing, I was actually glad I had finally gotten bringing Michael to meet them over with. One thing I was glad about was the fact that Michael being white didn't seem to be an issue. I guess deep down inside, I was a little worried what they would say or how they might react. Of course, it wasn't the same as if he was black because face it, white people and black people are different, but it was cool, and I was glad.

Michael was up, and I know he wasn't on my team but he got the guys to guess five words, and you know that's good in Taboo. So of course I had to support my man in this new environment. Right? I was like "Go, baby. You the bomb. You the bomb." As he was walking back to sit down, I jumped up, grabbed him and proceeded to do a little victory dance.

"Um hello," Kim hollered. "Did you forget he's on the opposite team? I know he yo' man and all, but love ain't deeper than Taboo. You better pull it back in."

"I know, but he's so cute. Go, baby."

"Look like he ain't the only one whipped," Kim said, falling over onto Traci laughing as they gave each other a high five. But they were right. What was I thinking? I loved my man, but this was Taboo.

Of course the girls ended up winning because no one anywhere was a match for the three of us when it comes to Taboo. I hadn't had so much fun in I don't know how long.

"Let's eat," Kevin called out a few hours later. "I'm starving."

I think we all were at that point. I couldn't wait to see what my sister had cooked. She was always so secretive about everything with her ritzy self. I hoped and prayed as I got up that she had made some kind of pasta, but to my surprise, she had made grilled halibut in a Grand Marnier and butter sauce, which was just as good. My sister sure could throw down, I wished I had inherited that gift from my grandmother, but I didn't. I mean I could cook, but Traci would just get all into it with all her fancy-looking meals. Shoot I'm surprise she let me buy dessert. She usually made everything from scratch. Who had the time? I know I didn't and as busy as she was, how did she?

Me, Kim and Traci went into the kitchen to bring the food out. Traci of course had already set the dining room table earlier that day. She had been looking forward to this all week. She had the perfect house for entertaining, but her and Kevin didn't do much of it Nothing was ever out of place in that big ole' house. I think deep down that maybe that was part of the reason why she didn't have kids. There would be just too many little fingerprints to clean. Kevin's was enough. It would mean putting away all the beautiful vases and art work she had meticulously collected and placed in their rightful spaces for years. I'm telling you the girl had a designer eye. She'd even taken out her best china for the day. I have to say best because this woman had three, yes, three full sets of china. Who needs three sets of china? What she used was beautiful though, and it was set on these beautiful place mats. I'm a decorator and sometimes even I wonder where she finds some of this stuff. Of course the champagne flutes with the gold trim complemented her gold trimmed plates, bowls and silverware. Of course there was no tablecloth because that would cover the beautiful hand-cut glass table, which was stabilized by an amazing marble base. You'd have to see her house to believe it. My sister always seemed to have it so together. It just made me wonder why she wouldn't marry Kevin. Sometimes I wondered if she was afraid he'd die like Daddy.

I was putting the ice buckets on the table, one on each end with a bottle of champagne in each when I caught my sister looking at me smiling.

"What?" I questioned.

"You look happy, Anya. I haven't seen a real smile on your face in a long time. I had almost forgotten what it looked like. I'm so happy for you." She smiled, turned and went into the kitchen.

"I'm telling you, girl, you just needed some, that's all." Kim bumped her hip against mine. She really needed prayer. That girl was crazy. But no matter what, she was my girl.

After we finished setting all the food out, we called for the guys to go wash up and come to the table. We all stood around the table, Kevin at the head, Traci at the other end and Michael and I on one side with Kim and Vic opposite us. Kevin blessed the food, and we sat down and all you heard for at least the first ten minutes straight was serving spoons hitting plates, polite gestures of "pass me this" or "pass me that" and praises to my sister after taking the first initial bite.

Kevin looked over at Traci. "Baby, you really outdid yourself with this dinner." That was a real compliment because he had it like that all the time.

"Yeah," Vic chimed in. "I haven't had anything this good since . . ." He paused and attempted to remember, "well I don't know, but what I do know is this is good."

"Thank you, gentlemen." She smiled. But this was the kind of stuff Traci lived for, family. And we were in the process of adding a new addition. That's all she needed.

"So when is the big day?" Vic asked.

"We're looking at May. The date will depend on if the Waldorf Astoria has anything available for your highness here," Michael said.

"You love your highness though, right?" I leaned over in his face with my fish breath. He kissed me on my nose.

"Yes, sweetheart. Yes, I do."

"Oh, I know I'm going to be sick now." Kim made a gagging noise and began laughing.

"Shut up, Kim. You get on my nerves. I can't stand you," I said.

"I'm just still trippin'. You're about to marry Michael Harrison."

"Yes, me too." I smiled at him.

"Okay but how will you know when he's just acting?" She laughed again. She was full of jokes. I had to admit though she was starting to get on my nerves a little bit.

"So Michael, tell us," Kim asked, "do you have any new movies you're working on right now?"

"Actually," he said, wiping his mouth with his napkin and taking a drink of water, "we just wrapped a movie we've been shooting in New York. That's how I met Anya. It's due out next spring. Everyone wanted to know what it was about. Michael's movie quickly turned into the focal point of the conversation as everyone got the inside scoop on his new action film. We laughed and talked, and before long, he was no longer Michael Harrison, he was just my fiancé, Mike, and I got the feeling that's the way he wanted it. He just wanted to be a part of my life and my family, not because of who he was in the public's eye, but because of who he was to me. I think he was just happy to be there with us, and other than when he first got there, he didn't seem to be nervous at all, and if he was, he sure hid it well. Of course I knew this meant I would eventually have to meet his parents who lived in California. His mother was an artist and former Broadway actress, who owned a gallery and his dad was a playwright.

Kevin stood, and popped the cork on a bottle of champagne and walked around and filled everyone's glass. As he got back to his seat, he requested everyone stand. "I'd like to make a toast. To Anya and Michael, I hope that you two will be happy together and that you won't have to move away because we would miss you too much. I love you, Anya, as if you were my real sister, and I just hope that the Lord blesses you in your new life. Also, I hope that one day in the near future, Traci, you will also give into love and marry me and give me some babies." Kim and I kind of looked at each other a little stunned, but we of course were on Kev's side. It was way past time. "Cheers," he said, and we all raised our glasses in the air. My sister gave Kevin a look that could have very well killed him, but she smiled through the look, lifted her glass and said cheers along with everyone else. I knew my sister though, and I felt sorry for Kevin, because he was gonna get it that night after everyone left.

After dinner, things sort of wound down. I really think it was because of Kevin's comment. I think my sister wanted us to go so she could get him. We all stayed and helped clean up even though she said we didn't have to, but that wasn't us. My grandmother said never be the first one to leave a dinner and always offer a hand in the kitchen. I could tell Traci was mad as the minutes went on and it was killing her not to say anything.

I went in the kitchen with one of the serving platters and it came. "What was Kevin's little comment suppose to mean?" she asked me. I was so not ready for that, especially since I probably wasn't about to say anything she wanted to hear. "Well, Traci, the man has been waiting forever. Neither of you is getting any younger. I mean I'm sure he doesn't want to be fifty years old trying to toss a ball around with his son. I mean what are you afraid of? Y'all are so perfect together." I saw the tears in her eyes.

"Okay listen. You have to promise not to tell anyone, Anya." Just then Kim's loud butt walked through the door. "What's going on in here?" We both looked up with blank expressions as if we had a secret but were trying to act like we didn't. It's not like we could play it off. I'm sure Kim saw the tears that had welled up in Traci's eyes. "Spill it," Kim said. "What are you trying to keep from me? Last I knew, I was still y'all sister. Maybe not by blood, but in heart for life."

And though she was right, it wasn't my place to include her in this. It had to be Traci's call. Traci looked stressed as she took a deep breath. "Remember when I was in the hospital my third year of college."

We both nodded because we remembered all too well. My sister was so sick I was scared she would die. She had a cyst on one of her ovaries that had ruptured, and she waited till after finals to go to the doctor. She said that she had been having some cramping and minor discomfort in her lower left side, but she didn't really think it was anything other than nerves from studying, not eating right and not sleeping enough during finals week. It turns out the day after finals she got a real high fever and had to go to the emergency room and that's how she found out she had the cyst. Well the bad part is that the fluid from it rupturing had set up an infection in her body so she had gotten real sick. She was in the hospital for over two weeks, and when she came home, she was still pretty weak. I had never seen my sister helpless before, and it scared me. She had always been strong for me. I guess because of everything with my mom. Even though we had my grandmother, Traci had always taken on the role of mothering me.

"I never told you guys but they removed one of my tubes because of the infection. It was damaged. That would have been bearable," she said, looking away to catch her tears in a napkin, "but I also found out the tube I could keep was blocked."

"Damn," Kim said quietly.

"Why didn't you tell me?" I asked, putting my arms around her and hugging her tight.

She pushed me away. "We don't have time for this now, not with them being in the other room."

"I know, but Traci Kevin doesn't care. He still wants to marry you."

"How could he care when he doesn't know?" She quickly wiped her face and went out of the room, giving us no chance to respond. Kim and I just stood there and looked at each other. Kevin not knowing was pretty messed up. I'm sure there was something that could be done though. Wasn't there? Sometimes my sister was too strong for her own good. How could she even think about dealing with this on her own? I wanted to talk to Kevin about it, but I knew she would be mad. What could I do? I just stood there as I saw a part of my sister come to life that I had never seen before, a piece of imperfection.

I had always looked up to her because her life just seemed so perfect, but at the same time, did not being able to have children make a woman any less perfect? If Vic wasn't there, we would have definitely been dealing with things that night, but he wasn't family and technically Michael wasn't either, but he soon would be. After a few moments, I walked out of the kitchen, leaving Kim behind. I think she was too afraid to say anything at that point. She was probably still in shock. I know I was. How could Traci keep this from Kevin and us, all this time?

I went into the game room where Kevin and Vic were setting up for a game of pool. I walked over to Michael and whispered in his ear I was ready to go, and when Kim came out of the kitchen, I gave her the look, which told her it was time for her and Vic to leave as well. Of course Vic wasn't ready to go because they were getting ready to play pool but eventually Kim talked him into it. I'm sure she bribed him with sex. That's pretty much how she usually got what she wanted from men.

Traci was really quiet. I went over and hugged her and told her I would call her the next day. I knew she really didn't want me to because she knew why I would be calling, but she nodded and hugged me back. I walked over and kissed

Kevin on his cheek and told him I would see him later. Michael stood and told everyone it was nice meeting them all and that he hoped to see them all again soon. He thanked my sister for dinner and told her next time he would cook for them. I grabbed my purse, and we left out along with Kim and Vic.

On the drive home I wasn't talking much because I was really worried about Traci. I wanted to tell Michael, but I wasn't sure if I should, so I didn't. When I was married to John I use to talk to him about a lot of stuff but he really didn't care so I eventually stopped sharing things that I felt were important because he always found a way to diminish them. I knew Michael wouldn't do that, but maybe I would be betraying Traci's trust if I told him. On the other hand, it's not like she said not to say anything, right?

"Why are you so quiet?"
"Just thinking."
"About what? Me, I hope." I smiled when he said that.
"Now normally, about 99.9 percent of the time, my days are spent thinking of you, but this point one percent, I happen to be thinking about Traci. She told me something tonight that I wasn't aware of, and it's kind of bothering me, that's all."
"Is it anything you wanna talk about that I might be able to help you with?"
I shook my head and replied, "Not right now. It's kind of personal, and she may not want you to know."
"Don't worry, sweetie. I understand, but if there's anything I can do, just say the word."
"Will do." I turned the music up, reclined my seat and tried to lose myself in the music, but I couldn't, I was so worried about Traci. I reached in the backseat, grabbed my purse and got my phone out. I called her but the phone just rang. I knew she was there but I guess she knew why I was calling and didn't want to hear what I might have to say. Not in a bad way. She probably had just begun to realize it was time to deal with things and tell Kevin. These were probably the two things she dreaded most.

That night in bed Michael just held me real tight. He was so happy he finally met someone I knew. I could tell because he talked about it for at least an hour if not more in the darkness of the room that night. I could tell we would make a good couple because . . . well, I wasn't sure, but I could. I was happy and so was he, and we did that for each other. That was more than I ever thought possible after dealing with John for so long.

Letting Go

Letting go, that's funny how could I let go of something that was as much a part of me as I was myself? Was it really possible to leave the past in the past? If so why couldn't more people seem to do it? Was there a certain process or procedure? Was there a manual I needed to pick up? How does this leave the past in the past actually work? Can somebody please tell me?

Oh I had my speech all ready, you know the one I was going to give Julian when he called the following Monday like I knew he would. I began putting the words together in my head while I lay beside Michael watching him smile in his sleep. By the time I got out of the shower, I believed I had the perfect wording and sentence structure. I continued to go over it in my head while getting dressed. I even made a revision or two while putting on my shoes and getting my purse. I was certain it was the right thing to do as I kissed Michael's soft lips before leaving out of the bedroom to go to work. As I stood in line at Starbucks waiting to order my caramel frappaccino, I put the finishing touches on it in my mind. I rehearsed it one last time in the car on my way to the office, and I was confident that it was perfect, the perfect ending to a beautiful song. Even the songs we love the most have to end eventually. Julian I'm afraid was a song at its end. The final note was to be sung, and there was no repeat button. It was a live concert, unrecorded, and once the song was over, it was just that, over. So what happened?

I walked into my office, closing the door behind me. I set my briefcase and my purse down on my desk and pressed the speaker button on the phone to check my voicemail to hear what was in store for the day, other than my speech that is. There it was, a voicemail, a stupid voicemail, words over digital tracking stored at the phone company in some timeless, never-ending log of calls. "Hey, girl, I would have called you at home but I didn't know how early you had to get up today so I figured I would leave you a voicemail at your place of employment so that when you got to work you would have at least one non-work-related message from a man who loves you more than anything. I miss you more than you know. Hit me on my cell when you get this message. I love you, girl, and don't you forget it. We can, no we will, make this work. It's me and you all the way like it used to be, like it should always be." What was I suppose to do? Did I still give the speech? Wasn't I in love with Michael? Or was I still in love with Julian? I knew I would always hold a special place in my heart for him but I didn't think that qualified as being in love.

I couldn't deal with that right then. I needed a moment to collect myself. I finished checking the rest of my messages. Thank the Lord there were only three. I had enough work to do as it was. It was definitely not the day to add anything additional. It was going to be a smooth day other than the fact my client Jessica Martin called and left a message saying that now the marble table was actually delivered and sitting in her dining room, she didn't like it. This was one client I wished I had never won over. I didn't care how many virtual layouts we did, how many stores we visited, how many books we looked through, this one always wanted to make changes after stuff got delivered or after fixtures had been hung or walls painted. The woman had too much time on her hands, and her husband put too much money in them. Mrs. Martin for some reason unbeknownst to me thought most rules in life didn't apply to her and she made around three major room changes at least two to three times a year. She had been one of my best clients for the last four years, and true enough I made good money off her, but I was so ready to hand her off to someone else, especially since her last child was going away to college in the fall, she was really going to have even more time on her hands.

I Really Did Try. Really

That afternoon before I left work, I knew I had to call Julian. I couldn't put it off any longer because once I got home Michael would be there. Truth be told, I was praying Julian didn't call while Michael was there, and if he did, I really prayed Michael definitely would not answer the phone. I mean why would he? No one would be calling for him, but of course I didn't want to say don't answer my phone while I'm gone because then he would think I was trying to hide something, which I was, so I definitely couldn't go that route.

I picked up the phone and dialed the number. I was kind of hoping I would get his voicemail so I could just leave a message, but as only my luck would have it, after the third ring, he picked up.
"Hello."
"Hey," I said. "What's up?"
"Naw, what's up with you?" I been waiting on you to call me all day. Did you get my message I left you at work?

I explained I had gotten his message but I had been swamped with work all day from the moment I walked in and this was the first chance I had to really sit down and call. Of course that was a lie. I could have called earlier. I sure made time to call Mike twice that day. I felt so guilty. I had this man who loved me at least I was pretty sure he did and I was pretty sure I loved him, too, but I was so committed to someone else. I couldn't just leave Michael. There was no way I was doing that. Julian survived me leaving him before, and we were really together then. I was pretty sure he'd survive again.

"Julian, I need to say something, and it's hard for me to say, but I have to, so just listen for a minute without interrupting me so I can get it out okay?" I could feel my palms getting moist, and my voice felt weak, but I was determined to forge ahead with my speech as planned.

"No, Anya, I can't let you do that because I know what you think you're about to say, and I'm not with it. I love you, Anya. Don't punk out on me. I can hear it in your voice. I know you Anya," I wondered if he knew me so well why didn't he know I was already in a relationship. Why didn't his Anya sensors pick up on that? "Julian, believe me. I love you. I do. I probably love you more now than I did before, because I've grown up enough to understand love a little better now, and I probably will always love you, but I can't do this. I can't go back. I have to keep moving forward."

"So you're saying you can't move forward me with? What's holding you back? I wanna move forward too. I just wanna move with you."

"Nothing's holding me back. I just can't. The timing isn't right."

"Now you know that don't make no kind of sense what-so-ever. When two people love each other, they usually look for ways to make it work, not reasons why it won't. Anya, I don't feel like playing games. We're getting too old for me to still have to chase you."

But I wasn't asking for him to chase me. Or was I?

"You know what?" He sounded agitated and disgusted. "Maybe you right. Maybe it would be more trouble than it's worth. One person can't make a relationship. It takes two, and clearly I'm the only one down. I don't have time for this." He just hung up the phone, and that was that. Maybe it was for the best.

I began to clear off my desk and pack my stuff up. I called Michael to see if he wanted me to pick something up for dinner but he said he had cooked. That was cool but he wouldn't tell me what he made. Whatever. As long as it wasn't me over the stove, I could care less what it was. I put my briefcase under my desk because I knew I wasn't going to be doing any work once I got home. I kind of wanted to call Julian back, but I thought I'd leave well enough alone. I didn't want him to hate me though or think I turned into some psychotic lunatic. Or worse than any of those, I didn't want him to think that I didn't love him, because I did. I grabbed my purse, hit the lights and closed the door behind me.

The whole ride home, I couldn't stop thinking about Julian. Why was life so complicated? At least why was my life so complicated? I know people meet people every day, fall in love and that's that. What I wouldn't give for simplicity. At least that's what I always told myself, but maybe I actually liked to live my complicated, drama-filled life because no matter how hard I tried or if I had brief periods of simplicity in my life, it always ended up complicated once again at some point. Was that normal? I mean look at my sister, how perfect her life had been. We had the same parents, we went to the same schools, even had some of the same teachers. We went to the same church and even had some of the same friends. We even went to the same college, so what did she learn that I didn't? Other than her recent outburst at dinner the day before, my sister lived a fairly dull, fairly simple life.

Maybe that was it. Maybe the drama was exciting. Maybe I lived for it, but I was tired of it, and I didn't want to be in the predicament I had found myself in. I had to just relax and ride it out. Eventually I would not so much forget about Julian, but instead, the feeling would pass and Michael and I would live happily ever after. Yeah, I had to laugh at that one myself. Was there even such a place or such a thing as happily ever after? Not based on my life's experiences. At one time, I thought so, but I wasn't sure what I thought anymore. I mean would Traci have a happily ever after? Would Kevin be mad at her? Would they adopt? Could she get artificially inseminated? Then I thought that was it, she could probably get artificially inseminated.

I pulled out my cell and called Traci. "Hey, girl, what's up? she said, answering the phone.

"Hey, I'm glad you answered. You know what I was thinking? I'm not sure about this, but I think you can get artificially inseminated and still have a baby, even if your tube is blocked. I mean it will probably cost a little money but I think they can do that."

She was really quiet, and with Traci it's hard to know if that's bad or good thing. "Hmm. I never thought about that. Do you really think they can do that and bypass my tube?" She had a slight lift in her voice, like there might be hope after all. I was relieved because I had no idea how she would respond. "Okay let me call you back, I'm going to see if I can go online and get some information about it. If that's true . . ." she paused, "well never mind, let's just say if I can, that would be cool."

"Okay. Make sure you call me later." I really hoped that would work out. She sounded so relieved and kind of happy.

Well now for something I was looking forward to all day, spending some time with my baby before he left the next day. It was a trip coming home and having someone there. It felt awkward, but it was a good awkward. I put my key in the door and turned it. As I opened the door, I was greeted by the aroma of garlic and butter. Umm, I thought. Is this what it might be like? Not the food, but the feeling I had inside as I walked through the house in anticipation of seeing my man, soon to be my husband. I was excited about that, too, because then I would also include the anticipation of getting some when I got home.

Then, there he was, setting the table, I can't help it, I'm a romantic at heart. This was so special to me.

He looked over at me and smiled. "Good evening, my love. How was your day?" The truth was, the very moment I was living in right then was the best part of my day.

"It was good. I see you kept yourself busy and found your way around the kitchen."

"I wanted to surprise you, let you know I wasn't just all looks. He laughed."

I smiled to myself as I walked over and put my arms around him, hugging him from behind. I rested my head on the back of his shoulder. I breathed him in, filling my lungs with the very essence of who he was, and I exhaled and relaxed, hugging him even tighter. I never wanted to lose that feeling of satisfaction. Dang, if only we were already married, I'd be getting some right then, right on the kitchen floor.

"I missed you today." I swung around and kissed him.

"I know. I can tell by the way you're looking at me." He smiled and kissed me back. "I missed you too. It seem like it took you forever to get home."

"Now you know how I use to feel waiting for you at the hotel to finish shooting for the day. But you know, it's always worth the wait."

"Yeah, it most definitely is. The food won't be ready for about another twenty minutes."

"That's okay, I'll just sit here and watch you and keep you company. What are you cooking anyway?"

"You'll see." He looked over at me as if he had just swallowed a canary.

We talked more about the wedding while he cooked. I was on a mission to find a coordinator. There was no way I was going to try planning a wedding this big by myself. Michael had made it very clear he would basically be inviting the whole world. Plus, with work, I did enough planning and coordinating dates, times, furniture, painters you name it, I coordinated it, so there was no way I could begin squeezing in the planning of a wedding. I was called out of my thoughts by Michael's voice. "Anya, I need to tell you something." He looked up from his plate. "I've been on the phone with my agent and Joseph Fox," who was a well-known director. "They both really want me to do his new film, and I'm really thinking about it. That's what that meeting was about this past week."

Okay, what did all this mean? Whenever someone gets all serious, and have to prepare to tell you something instead of just telling you, it's usually followed by devastating or life changing news. In this case, the news wasn't too bad. He wanted to do this movie which meant he would be spending a lot more time back in Southern California shooting the film, and of course a lot less time with me. Although this was good news for him, it meant that my wedding plans would be scheduled around the shooting of this film, it also meant I was going to really miss him a whole lot. It was bad enough having a long-distance relationship, but now it was going to feel like one.

Okay, I didn't panic. I was cool with him doing the film, I think. Besides, what was I going to do? Be a brat and tell him he couldn't do the movie because we were getting married. Nah, I didn't think so. I wanted to be a supportive wife, not a nag. Maybe I could visit him a little, even with the way my work schedule was. I know it sounded real good coming out of our mouths, but was this the end to the fairytale that had become our lives for the past several months? Could we really pull off seeing each other once a month, if that? This brought me back to where our primary residence would be? I knew the kind of money he was sitting on, we could realistically live in both places, but I didn't want to. I wanted to live in Philly, and Philly alone. I didn't want one of those Hollywood marriages where I never see my husband and before you know I'm finding comfort with someone else and he's finding comfort on the set, and boom here comes the divorce. I didn't want that to happen to us, but how did I avoid it? Maybe I just shouldn't marry a star. All these thoughts continued to run through my mind until Michael spoke.

"I probably won't be out for the next few weeks." And so it begins. I guess he saw the look of disappointment on my face. Even though I had just thought the very same thing, it was reality coming from his lips. "Don't worry. I just need to get everything squared away with this deal. Plus, if I'm going to take this role, I have some serious training ahead of me. From what I understand it's going to be quite physically challenging." But he was in shape. Any fool could see that, but what did I know about the demands of a movie, maybe he really would need to train harder than he already did, which was hard to imagine as much as he worked out with his trainer, but again as I said, maybe he did. "I'm really going to have to focus on trying to get into this character too. It would be so much easier if you would just move to California, Anya." And there it was. "Move to California, Anya." I guess there was no longer a question of primary residence in his mind, but there was still one in mind. I wasn't trying to be difficult, but just as he had built a life there, I'd done the same. "I know you love your work, and I know you love Philly, but if you just gave California a chance, I know you would love it there too. And as for your work, there's no question of a career. You're good at what you do, and with all the people I know and the people they know, we would definitely keep you busy." I just sat there motionless because I knew good and well, there was no way I was moving there or anywhere else for that matter. "Okay. Look, Anya." He appeared slightly tense. "You don't have to answer now, but please, for me, please think about it." he pleaded with his beautiful almond shaped eyes. Think about it. Think about what? I didn't hear a question.

So dinner continued, but the atmosphere had definitely changed, and before long, it was time to say good-bye. Not that I was mad or anything. I just didn't see this working out. I loved Michael, and I wanted to be with him, but I guess I didn't love him enough to compromise for the unknown. Whatever the case, the next morning on the way to the airport, I was thinking, but I was trying not to be quiet. It just wasn't working, I just kept hearing those words repeat in my head. "It would be so much easier if you would just move to California." Like I was the problem, if, in fact, there was a problem. I don't know. Maybe I was just trippin', but I dropped him off on my way to work, and I kissed him as if I was never going to see him again because that's how it felt. Something had definitely changed, and I wasn't sure if that was good or not. It was too soon to tell. I rolled down the window as he walked away. "I love you." He turned, smiling at me as if he were relieved. "I love you too, Mrs. Harrison." I smiled too, when I heard that, relieved.

Those first two weeks were torture. I didn't think Michael being away would affect me the way it had, but it did. I couldn't stay focused, I thought about him constantly, and I missed him so much, to the point that I hurt physically on the inside of my heart. I needed to ease my pain, and the only antidote was seeing him. I had such a longing in me to see him, but I couldn't, not with the workload I had been carrying. There was no way. The flight was too long to just go for a day. It wouldn't make sense. Even though we talked every day, it didn't help. I still missed him. Time was at a standstill. I wasn't worried though that we were drifting apart or anything like that. I was just scared. I didn't realize what it would take to be married to a celebrity before I said yes, especially not one who worked and loved his work as much as Michael does and I just didn't know if I was up for it. I had gotten spoiled having him around so much. I didn't know if I was cut out for this long-distance bit.

Supposedly when you love someone, you're willing to go the extra distance, you do things that are out of your normal character, but shouldn't you also use good old-fashion common sense? I mean if I know I want a normal marriage, well, normal in my eyes, where I come home from work and see my husband on a daily basis. Why would I marry someone who I may only see once or twice a month if he's off who knows where on location or something? Does that make sense to you? I mean the newness of this perfect relationship would eventually wear off, and the realities of marriage would set in, and I'd ask myself, because

I know me, I'd say, "Self, why are you doing this when there is a perfectly good man out there who loves you and has a normal life just like you?" Then myself would start having regrets. I'd start thinking about that perfectly normal man who just went to work and came home every day to his beautiful wife. That man who wanted nothing more than a nice home, a few good friends, two kids, a dog and a vacation with his beautiful wife and their two kids twice a year. Before long, it wouldn't be enough, the big house, the cars, the money and the busyness of our lives. It wouldn't be enough to prevent me from longing for the simple life I passed up.

This got me to thinking, which can usually mean trouble, but it did. I thought maybe I was making a mistake, maybe I hadn't really thought this through. Maybe I was making a mistake, a big one, that I needed to fix before it was too late. Maybe, just maybe I wasn't suppose to be with Mike. Not that I didn't love him, because I did, I really did, very much so, but in all actuality, when the reality of life sets in, and it would, love is not always a good enough reason to be with someone, let alone marry them and ruin their life. There has to be more than love to bind a marriage together, and it's not that Michael and I had so many differences, but the few we had were major.

That's when I fell off. Going into that fourth week, I was in Target in the card section, because I have this weakness for cards, I love 'em. I sent Michael at least four to five cards a week if not more. Well this one particular day, with all these thoughts continually bombarding my head, there was a brief moment where my brain lacked the necessary oxygen needed to function properly due to the fact that it had been overexerted from dealing with the racing thoughts of being with Michael. A brief moment of stupidity was all it ever really took to alter your life.

While continuing to scan the love section for new cards I had yet to purchase for Michael, it hit me. The words jumped right off the card onto the surface of my eyeballs. "If only love could be explained." Curiosity got the better of me. I had to indulge my heart to find out what about love needed explaining and if the inside of this card really explained it.

> My heart didn't do what I told it to
> Instead it stayed with you
> Though many years have passed us by
> My heart has stayed with you
> I wanted to move on
> I wanted not to look back
> But I was pulled back to my heart

The same heart I had left with you
I still can't explain it
No explanation other than the fact that
Love cannot be explained
It is what it is
And it's with you I found it

Don't buy it, Anya. Don't complicate things, I thought, but I had to of course because if I didn't . . . well, I don't know what would have happened if I didn't. All the more reason that I knew I had to. So into the basket that card went along with the ones I had selected for Michael and off to the checkout stand I went.

I couldn't wait to get home, as I came in the back door, I kicked off my shoes, I grabbed a glass and filled it with ice and went into the other room. I sat at my desk in my little home office and pulled all the cards out of the bag as well as my Pepsi and Doritos. As I poured the Pepsi, I watched it cover the ice. I shook it a little so it would hurry and get cold then I watched the fizz and bubbles fly up out of the glass, out of control, just like me. As much as I tried to control my emotions, I still was sitting at my desk ready to fill out that card for Julian and fill it out is exactly what I did. I put a Dorito in my mouth and brushed my hand off on the Target bag so I wouldn't get the card dirty, and I opened up and wrote: *I know I'm complicated and hard to love, but I'm glad through it all, you do still love me. Don't give up on me just yet because I haven't given up on me. Julian, I love you. Things just aren't as simple for me as they appear to be. Love you till the day I die, Anya.*

I reached in my desk drawer and pulled out my old phone book. After addressing the card and sealing it I felt nervous. Why was I sending this man this card? What could I possibly hope to accomplish? I signed Michael's three cards and sealed them, then I stamped all four cards and dropped them in my purse so I could mail them in the morning.

Was I wrong? Probably so, but who could tell at that point? I just wasn't ready to let go all the way. I tried, maybe not hard enough, but I did try and didn't that count for something? I just couldn't let go, not now. Not just yet. Not till I knew for sure I was really going to marry Michael. I had to be sure I was making the right choice because the next time I got married, it was going to be forever.

Well, of course that card is what triggered the inner confusion that transpired over the next few months. Being in touch with Julian only made it harder for me to determine who I really loved. Maybe it wouldn't have been so bad if Michael hadn't decided to do that movie because then I would have seen more of him and less of Julian. As chance would have it, he did. Maybe this was a sign. If Julian could come in and make me doubt my love for Mike and just because Mike had not been there by my side every moment the last few months, then maybe I wasn't really in love with him. I definitely couldn't be trusted to be away from him, and if that was the case, our marriage was doomed to fail, no matter how great he was. Yet, I continued to plan the marriage of doom. Sometimes I seriously wondered not if but exactly how many times I was dropped on my head as a baby.

At the same time, I couldn't really say I was cheating. I mean all me and Julian did was talk on the phone. I might see him once a month, okay maybe twice, but we didn't have sex, so it wasn't really cheating. Okay well if you counted kissing and planning a future with him, then yes technically that would be considered cheating. I couldn't believe I was trying to rationalize the mess I found myself in. No matter how I tried though I couldn't. The truth was what it was, the truth. I couldn't believe I was this cruel and selfish that I would . . . not lie, but omit the truth from the two men I claimed to love. How do you make a decision when your heart won't let you? I know that's an excuse, because I do have common sense, at least I use to but I really think if you tend not to use it frequently enough, you lose it, hence the dilemma I found myself in.

I couldn't believe it was Christmas already. The months seemed to just be rolling by nonstop. I wondered how Christmas would play out. I should really say I worried how Christmas was going to play out. I knew I was expected to be in two places at once, but how? I had really let this go too far. How could I spend the holiday with the one I loved when there were two? Did I go to a special science lab and request a clone be made? And if in fact I could do that, was there a way to feed it all my memories and all my personality quirks, everything that made me me? Which me would I send to be with who? Wouldn't the real me have to go be with Michael? After all, I was marrying him in five months. No, maybe I should send the real me off with Julian to his family's house because he should have a chance to see as much of the real me as possible. After all, the real me was marrying Michael, and he would have me for the rest of my life, so it would only be fair. Okay, that settled it. That was what I'd do, I'd go overseas somewhere and get cloned, and we'd come back. The people at the airport would think we were twins. I'd let the clone entertain Michael, and I'd go off with Julian. Perfect. If only that were possible and if it were, who could afford that kind of crap? Not me.

Soon I would find out that that would be the least of my worries. Michael wanted me to come to California and spend Christmas with his family. What?

There was no way. See it was starting already. I couldn't remember a Christmas without my family, and I wasn't about to start making those kind of memories. I mean really. Did he really think I wanted to spend Christmas in a place that didn't even have snow? How could you even have Christmas with no snow? Was that even possible? Was is really even considered Christmas without snow? What did they sing, "I'm dreaming of a sunny Christmas?" Not. I knew this relationship was going to end up changing my life, and so far I was not excited about any of the changes. I liked my life just as it was. I didn't need a change, at least not a major one. It didn't dawn on me before I fell in love with the man that us being from two totally different worlds could cause a little conflict from time to time, but who knew it was going from chance meeting to marriage? Maybe he needed to find someone who really didn't like her current life all that much and needed a Michael Harrison to come and rescue her. I didn't need rescuing. I was just fine where I was.

It was the second week of December, and all I had bought was one gift, and that was for Kim. She was so easy to shop for since we had the same taste in clothes, shoes and jewelry. I never had a problem picking out a gift for her. I would just say, Do I want this for myself? and if I answered yes then I knew she would want it also. Sometimes it was hard though because I wouldn't want to come up off the gift because I liked it so much. That year, I bought her these bad Via Spiega boots. I couldn't wait to see her face when she opened the box. That's another reason I couldn't have Christmas in California. I had to be there to see Kim's face. It just wouldn't be the same later, or over the phone. It wouldn't even be the same on video.

I still had to get gifts for Kevin and Traci, my grandparents and let's not forget the people I worked with. Of course Michael's gift had to be the bomb, but I still had no idea what to get him. What do you get a man who has everything, literally? I had been trying to figure it out for the last month, but still nothing. However, I did know exactly what I was getting Julian. I know that's bad, huh? But I knew him. I knew what he liked and the types of things that made him happy. With Michael it was still kind of early so it was harder, especially since he never mentioned anything he wanted or needed. That's probably because everything he wanted he just went out and got. Must be nice. Of course when I asked him what he wanted he just said, "Whatever you want to get me is fine" or "Surprise me. You're good at surprises." So there I was two weeks before Christmas with no gift and no idea what I was getting him. Great.

I was determined to be finished that week, no matter what. There was no way I wanted to be in the stores with all the last-minute shoppers even though I was one myself. I was probably just going to get American Express gift cards for the people I worked with except for Asha. I had to get her a real gift, but what? I decided to get her a spa certificate. After all, I knew she could use that. That's what I got Traci and Kevin too. I got them a spa package for couples at some fancy place in New York. I had to get on the internet and find one. I also put a gift certificate in there for this restaurant Traci loved. She always went there whenever she went to New York on those little shopping trips. I had to call one of her little shopping buddies to find out the name of it. I went there with her one time, but Lord knows I didn't remember. They'd be on their own for transportation and hotel, but I knew they'd like the gift. I just had to figure out my grandparents and Michael and I'd be done.

The Holiday

For some reason Michael could not understand that I had to be home for Christmas, why, I don't know. I explained it over and over and over, and I wasn't going to explain it anymore. We weren't married yet, and I knew I had to give a little, but it was going to take time. He couldn't expect me to stop doing something that I had done for years overnight. I didn't see him offering to come see me for Christmas and leave his family. What's up with that? I came up with the perfect solution, well, as perfect as the situation could get, and though it wasn't perfect to him, he compromised, which was what I was doing as well so he'd better quit trippin.'

I figured I would fly to California and spend a week with him right on up through Christmas Eve then Christmas morning I would fly back to Philly. That way I could be there with him and my new family then come home and be with my real family. Now during the last month or so I had spent a little time with Julian, but like I said we mostly talked on the phone, so I knew he would be expecting me to fit him in to some portion of my day because he was going to be in town seeing his family for the holiday. I don't know how people can go for months and years in relationships with more than one person at the same time. It was draining me mentally and emotionally. I really believe the only thing saving me was the fact that I was lucky enough to have both my men living out of state. Did I say lucky? What was I thinking? I had to get my head right. This wasn't cool, and I knew it. It was scandalous and foul, but what was I going to do? Just what I planned, get my but on a plane to see my fiancé.

On the plane I tried to go to sleep and not be anxious but I couldn't help it. I was. I was anxious to see Michael because I really had missed him. I was nervous too, nervous that he might sense that something was a little off. I hoped he wouldn't pick up on anything like . . . oh Julian for instance. I squirmed a lot in my seat. The gentleman next to me asked if I were nervous, and if it was my first time flying. I looked over at the husky man with his salt-and-pepper hair and advised him I had flown plenty but that I was just kind of anxious to see my fiancé. That triggered a lengthy conversation, which I appreciated because it did help the time go by. Besides, I needed to stop squirming so I wouldn't mess up my clothes. I usually dress really casual and comfortable when I fly but I really wanted to be cute. After all, I had a Hollywood honey, and I couldn't afford to look anything less than perfect on my first trip to his neck of the woods. After we deplaned, I went to the restroom and fixed my hair and my lipstick, brushed and straightened my clothes then I headed for baggage claim.

Michael said he was sending a limo to pick me up at the airport. I've traveled a little in my day, but I've never had a limo pick me up from the airport, anywhere. Even when we went to Jamaica, it wasn't a limo, it was car, so I was excited about feeling like a star or maybe not a star but important. As I got closer to the baggage area I saw a gentleman holding a little sign that read A. Dennings. I motioned to him, and we walked over to get my bag. I just brought one big suitcase. I figured anything I didn't have I would definitely go purchase. I had never been shopping in LA before so I was looking for any excuse. When my bag came around, I pointed it out and he grabbed it.

"That's it?" He looked shocked.

"That's it."

"I like you. I'll pick you up from the airport anytime."

We both laughed and made small talk on the way to the car. When we got outside, I took a deep breath and sucked in the essence of no snow in December. That was a trip. It wasn't hot like television would have you to believe. It was about sixty-eight degrees, but I guess that is hot compared to the twenty-degree weather I had just left. I looked around at all the busy people, hugging, laughing, some crying, and I thought, that was the future of my holidays. Going to visit so happy to see everyone and then crying when I left. How awful that must feel, not being around your family sharing things all the time. I was so close to my sister, I didn't know if I could live so far away from her. True enough I didn't see her every day or anything like that, but I knew she was just a twenty-minute drive away.

We arrived at the door of the limo, and I reeled my thoughts back in. Mr. Jon, the limousine driver, opened the door, and I slid in and was pleasantly surprised by the welcome I received from my sexy leading man in the back of that limo. Mr. Jon hadn't even closed the door good before Michael slid across that seat and drowned me in his kiss.

"I missed you. Oh, Anya, I missed you so much." He was almost breathless.

"Oh my goodness what are you doing here? This was the best surprise ever." And it truly was. I looked around the limo at the rose petals that were all over the floor. There was champagne on ice, and best of all, that beautiful smile I had missed so much. Michael handed me a single rose, and I didn't want to get anything started you know, but I had to kiss him again, he tasted so good the first time.

"I couldn't wait to see you, so I figured I'd hide out in the car and wait." He grabbed me again and kissed me long and hard.

"Alright, you 'bout to set it off up in here." I looked at him with a look that said, you know I want to, but you know we can't. He leaned back against the seat.

"I know. I just missed you so much, I can't help myself."

"Yeah, I know the feeling." I smiled, fanning myself jokingly as if he was making me just that hot.

"Well, I know you want to go to the house and freshen up, but my mother is dying to meet you, so I promised my parents we would come by just for a minute on the way to the house and then we would meet them for lunch tomorrow when my dad is free."

"Hmmm. Great." I gave a nervous giggle. I knew I had to meet his parents when I came, but now that I was there, I wasn't ready. I wasn't usually self-conscious when it came to meeting people, but I did want them to like me. After all, I was marrying their son; therefore, I would have a great deal of contact with these people for the rest of their lives or mine, should fate have it that way. None-the-less, I felt the butterflies dancing around in my stomach. I was glad I had dressed cute and not too sexy and definitely glad I didn't have on sweats. I freshened my lipstick once again and fixed my braids back up neatly in the chopsticks that I was sportin'. I was attempting to let it grow out for the wedding. It was so hard growing a short cut out, so braids were my solution. My hair grew fast though so it wasn't too much torture, but I'll tell you, as soon as this wedding was over and we came back from our honeymoon, I was straight getting this mess cut right back off.

About forty minutes later, we pulled up to a black iron gate with a big gold H in the middle. I don't know how L.A. people dealt with this traffic. It was ridiculous. Michael rolled down his window and punched in a code, and the big black bars slowly began to open.

"So this is how the other half lives, huh?" I was in awe of the house, if you could call it a house. I guess it was really called an estate. It was huge.

"Get use to it." He looked over and smiled. "You are the other half, my other half." Although I was hearing him, I was still in amazement of the house and we were still outside. I could only imagine the inside.

"Just your parents live here?"

"And my grandmother, my dad's mom. My dad moved her here when my grandfather died two years ago. He had a heart attack, and Daddy didn't want her to live alone. She put up a bit of a fight in the beginning, but over time he talked her into it, and it's not like she's losing her independence as big as this house is."

"That is so sad. I'm sorry to hear about your grandfather. I think it's so sad when people are old and they lose their spouse. I mean it's sad at any age to lose the one you love, but it just seems even more sad when you're older and you have all those years together. How can you imagine your life without that person?"

"Yeah." He was looking off into nowhere. "I guess you're right. My grandfather really loved my grandmother too. I can tell she still misses him a lot. That's why I'm glad she's here with my parents."

"Yeah, that's probably for the best." Sometimes I was way too sentimental, but when I looked over at Michael, I knew I was making the right choice. I did want to grow old with him and raise children with him and dance in the living room with him. I wanted to go to our son's football games or chess matches or whatever the case might be. I wanted to see my daughter cheer at games or flip from balance beams, and I did want to simply grow old with him. It might sound corny, but I believed in romance. I didn't think it died with the forties and fifties. I believed it was very much alive, maybe not in everyone, but it was alive in me, and I loved that about myself. I loved love.

The car came to a stop in front of the huge double doors. "You ready?" He glanced over at me, staring at him, pulling me from my thoughts.

I took a deep breath and let out a sigh. "As I'll ever be."

The car door opened, and Mr. Jon took my hand and helped me out. I stood there still captivated by the beautiful landscaping as I waited for Michael to exit the car. We held hands and walked toward the door, but before we could get to it, it opened. A beautiful brunette woman came walking out, smiling. It wasn't a fake smile either. It was nice and warm. She was beautiful, too, very vibrant and young looking, almost too young. It made me wonder if this was in fact Michael's mother. Turns out, it was. She was a classic mom. She seemed so perfect, not one hair of her short bob was out of place. She was sporting a pair of Ralph Lauren slacks with a Polo T-shirt with matching slides. She could only have been a size five if that, but she didn't look sickly skinny like some women do. She was the perfect size for her height, I guess. "She's beautiful, Michael. The picture you have doesn't do her justice," She spoke to him about me as if I weren't standing there. She offered a big smile then walked up to me and opened her arms to embrace me. Her perfume was so strong it almost choked me, but I sucked it up and hugged her back. "Nice to finally meet you." I smiled at her after she finished hugging me and drowning me in that awful perfume.

"Oh, Anya." This excitement came over her. "We have so much to do. I mean the wedding is less than five months away. I have been dying to get you here." She grabbed my hand and began leading me into the house.

"Mom, we're not staying. I know Anya is probably tired, and I want to let her relax. There will be time for all this tomorrow." But there was no use in stopping a mom who has her own agenda. It's pointless.

"Nonsense." She looked back over her shoulder at him. "I have lunch all ready for you guys. Are you hungry, dear?" She looked at me. "I broiled some chicken and made a salad and baked fresh bread." I looked over at Michael who was giving me the eye to say no, but I didn't have the heart after she had gone through so much trouble. It just wouldn't have been right.

"Actually, Mrs. Harrison, I'm quite hungry. It was a long flight."

"What? What is this Mrs. Harrison stuff? Call me Mom or Jacqueline or Jackie. You're part of this family, you know." She gazed at me with a serious I-mean-it look.

"Okay, Jackie." I didn't feel right calling her Mom, after all, I barely knew the woman.

We sat down to the table in her huge kitchen. It was surprisingly sleek and modern. All the appliances were stainless steel, and the counters and floors were the exact same black marble. It was so shiny. Usually black makes a kitchen look smaller but this kitchen was so big, there was no way it could look small. It overlooked part of the yard because half of the walls were glass windows, and there were three glass doors. It was nice and bright too. I hated houses that got no sun. They were so depressing. Lilies must have been her favorite flower because they were by the front door in the entryway on a table against the wall and they were also on another small table in the hallway that led to the kitchen as well as a centerpiece on the kitchen table and on the side of the island sink.

We ate and talked about my career; her career, which had recently began winding down; as well as Michael as a child and things like that. Of course the wedding was discussed. I had brought four invitations with me that I had narrowed it down to so that Michael could tell me which he liked best, but they were in my suitcase. I needed him to make a decision so I could order them and we could get them out by the end of January. This would give people time to make their travel arrangements. His mom wanted to see them, but she said it was okay she would just wait until she got hers, although, I could tell she really kind of wanted to give her input. So naturally I turned, to Michael, batted my lashes and asked him to get my suitcase so I could get the invitations out.

"You're kidding me, right?"

"Come on, just get it, please?"

"Okay I think you two are hitting it off a little too well. You're suppose to be ready to go so you can get me alone."

His mom looked up from her plate. "Boy, go and get that suitcase. You have your whole life to spend time alone with her, now move it."

He came back in with the suitcase, and I pulled out my wedding envelope. Jackie and I went back and forth once we narrowed the invitation down to two. Michael said whatever I wanted was fine, he just wanted to get married.

"Oh, by the way," I said, looking over at him, "the church called me back yesterday. We're in."

"Yes. I knew we would get it though."

Remember we were going to get married at the Waldorf Astoria? Well, my grandmother said I had to get married in a church and she didn't know how those Hollywood people did it, but we were doing it the old-fashion way. Of course I wasn't going to argue with my grandmother, after all she had done for me so I had been trying to find a nice church that was close to the Waldorf because we were still going to have the reception there. Now that we had the church, I had to see if my Pastor was willing to come to New York to perform the ceremony. The other major thing was figuring out how we would get our marriage counseling in with Michael's schedule. We had to have it because although my Pastor was the bomb, there was no way he was marrying anyone, not even Michael Harrison without completing the premarital counseling workshop. No classes. No ceremony, it was as simple as that.

This was all happening so fast. It seemed like just yesterday Michael proposed. Now I was sitting in Woodland Hills with his mother picking out the wedding invitation that would invite the world to witness the beginning of the rest of our lives.

"I will say I have to agree with your grandmother. I think you guys should be married in a church, not in a hotel banquet room. This is a sacred ceremony of your commitment to one another before God, so the church is the more appropriate place."

"Yes, I know. That's exactly what my grandmother said, and you know you can't argue with a grandmother."

"Or a mother," Mike chimed in. "That's exactly why we're sitting here right now instead of at my house, soon to be our house."

His mom smiled and threw her napkin at him. He smiled then laughed. I gave a fake laugh and thought. Here we go with that living situation again.

"So, Anya, when do you think you'll be moving out this way? Are you going to wait until after the wedding?"

I took a deep breath, trying to hide my annoyance. "You know, I'm not exactly sure I'm going to moving out here or if Michael is going to be moving back there."

She began to laugh until she looked at my face.

"Oh, you can't be serious." Then she looked at Michael. "Can she?"

"We're still working the details out."

"What is there to work out? Your life and career are here. You're an actor. How many actors do you know who live in Philadelphia?"

"Not now, mom."

"No, Michael, it's okay." I turned to address his mother. "Jackie, my life and my career are in Philly, so why do I have to be the one to give up my home, my family and my career? I mean I may not make millions a film but my work is just as important as Michael's. It's my career, it's what I love, and I have the same passion for it as he has for his acting."

"I'm not saying you don't. It just seems to make more sense for you to come here. I didn't mean to upset you. The bottom line is it's a decision that the two of you will have to make. I don't know why I just assumed you would want to come here. It's such a nice place to live, no snow, no freezing temperatures." She reached over and placed her hand over mine. "I really didn't mean anything by it, you know?" I knew that she didn't. I guess I was just a little defensive about the whole thing. I enjoyed being Anya Dennings. I enjoyed who I was. I didn't want to become Michael Harrison's wife and cease having my own identity. That might be okay for some women, but not me.

We continued to talk a little more, quickly changing the subject to a less tense topic before we wound things up. I could tell Jackie didn't want us to leave, but I was pretty tired, I had been up since six o'clock east coast time to catch my nine-thirty flight, and I could feel the energy draining from my body. It was almost six California time, which meant it was almost nine back home, and all I wanted was to take a long, hot bath and relax with my man. So we said our good-byes and made our way out through the same door we had come in several hours prior.

On the way to Michael's house I told him how glad I was that I met his mom and how relieved I felt to finally get it over with. She was so nice to me, and she really made me feel at ease so I guess I was worried for nothing. I think I was probably more nervous about being black than anything else. I was hoping that it wasn't a big deal to her and apparently it wasn't. I had never dated anyone white before, so I really had no idea what to expect. I knew my family would be shocked, but I knew they weren't going to trip. I really wasn't sure about his. Well that was one down and one to go. I wasn't really worried about meeting his dad though. Men generally warm up to me. Huh, that was half my problem now, just a little too warm.

When we pulled up to Michael's, it made me think twice about moving to Cali. I mean, I could get used to this. He didn't have a huge mansion like his parent's home but nevertheless, it was still huge. It had to be at least eight thousand square feet, if not more, with six bedrooms and seven and a half bathrooms. Each bedroom had its own bathroom, and there was not a room in the enormous house that wasn't furnished. I loved it though. It was so open. When I walked through the front door and stood in the front entryway I could look upstairs and see the beautiful art work on the hallway walls. I loved houses where I could stand upstairs and look over into the rooms below. I just stood there thinking, *girl, don't be stupid. This could all be yours, and you wouldn't even have to be the one to clean it.* Because you know, somehow having to clean a big house makes having it less glamorous.

"There is no way you decorated this place," I said. I mean I knew he had good taste but as he gave me a tour of the house, it was just too perfect. Only a decorator had those kind of skills.

"Oh what, you think I don't have good enough taste to decorate my own house?"

I stopped in the middle of the sunroom that was at the back of the house, looked around and replied, "There is no way you decorated this house, no way."

He laughed. "You're right. Too bad I didn't know you then because now I know you're going to be changing stuff around, getting rid of stuff and getting new stuff, but I don't mind, at least not yet. The only room that's off limits to change is my game room. That's my sanctuary."

"Well before I commit, I'll have to see it first."

"You can see it all you want, and you can dislike it all you want, but the game room stays as the game room is. You got that?"

"Whew, you better slow down. You're turning me on, trying to stand up for yourself against something you know you can't resist." I walked over to him and traced the outside of his ear with my tongue. He grabbed my hand, and we began to walk down the hall.

"I don't think so. That ain't gonna get it. You'll have to pull out a lot more than that to change anything in this room." We got to the doorway and he pushed the door back. "Feast your eyes on this."

As I looked around, there was nothing that needed to be changed. The carpet was so thick and the pile was so high I took my shoes off so I could feel my feet sink down into it. There was of course a pool table, which I noticed people with big houses always had even if they couldn't play a lick of pool. "Wait, wait one minute. I know you don't have no air hockey up in here? Don't play," I said. Glancing around the room. I walked toward the air hockey table. "I will get down on some air hockey. Oh yes, I will be whuppin' on you tomorrow when I have the energy." I looked over at him.

"That'll be the day, dude. Don't let me have to make you eat your words. Remember where I come from. I'm white, and I'm a man. There is no way you can beat me in air hockey."
"Whatever. It's on tomorrow. That's all I gotta say, and dude is for surfers, not air hockiers."
"Yeah, I got your whatever and your hockiers. That ain't even a word, man. All I know is we'll see what you'll be saying when I'm through with you."

I continued to look around the room at the different helmets and football posters he had hanging on the wall. But there was no doubt that he was a Raiders fan. I don't think they have this much paraphernalia for sell at the Raiders store. I guess Michael watched the games on that fat plasma TV while sitting in one of those movie recliners, which were soft-as-butter black leather. They were oversized and had the Raiders emblem on the back of each one in gray. There were two rows of chairs with five chairs in each row. This was too much, people with money are so ridiculously spoiled, but I ain't mad, 'cause I was about to be one of 'em. Of course no man's game room would be complete with out an X-box and a Play Station 2. I guess they never outgrow video games, no matter what the age. Michael had a fully stocked bar in the corner, I guess for company, because he didn't really drink that much.

I finally finished touring the inside of the house and figured the outside would have to wait until the next day because it was dark and I was tired. I went back to the master bedroom and began to run water in the cobalt-blue jacuzzi tub. I walked back into the room and got my bubble bath from my case and poured a nice amount under the stream of flowing water. Before long the whole room smelled of Pearberry, too bad it's been discontinued. I pulled out the pajamas I had ordered from Victoria's Secret. I ordered real pajamas, nothing sexy. I didn't want to get anything started. It was a pair of simple silk pajama bottoms with a long-sleeve button-up shirt in baby blue. It was perfect, I matched everything so well. His sheets were a sky-blue satin and a navy velvet comforter covered the king-size bed. I laid my pajamas on the bed and went into the bathroom. I stepped into the large oval tub and leaned back in total relaxation. I had turned out the light and turned on the heat lamp. I wanted to light a candle, but they all appeared to be for decoration, so I didn't. I wasn't in there five minutes before my soon-to-be better half came in and sat down on the marble floor next to the tub, handing me a glass of champagne. He lifted his glass.

"To us, and our new beginning," he said.
"To us." I leaned forward and kissed his cheek. He proceeded to get undressed and got into the glass shower on the opposite side of the tub. Okay was this suppose to be a test? I grabbed my face towel, submerged it in water and folded it in quarters. I took one last look at Michael's naked flesh before laying back and covering my eyes with the warm towel.

After about an hour, if not longer, I forced myself from the bubbles that had been soothing me, got out and dried off. Michael had already gotten out of the shower and was already in bed watching TV. I removed my lotion from the dresser where I had placed it and went back in the bathroom and put lotion on. I returned to the bedroom wrapped in my towel and slid my pajama bottoms on. I then walked over to Michael's side of the bed, sat down and requested he lotion my back. His hand felt so nice as it massaged the lotion into my skin. Before long I could feel both his hands kneading my back and massaging my shoulders and neck. It felt great. I sat there and enjoyed every minute of it before going to put my top on.

I wrapped my braids up in a scarf then slid into the bed next to him and laid my head on his chest. I remembered him asking me if I thought I could be happy with him for the rest of my life, and that's all I remembered, I don't even know if I responded. The next thing I knew, it was morning. I slept so well, when I woke up, he was still asleep, I wondered what time it was. I walked over to the dresser and looked at my watch, 9:20, which meant it was only 6:20 there. I went to the bathroom, brushed my teeth and washed my face. I went back to the room, got back into bed and turned on the TV. There was nothing really on, so I flipped back and forth between local news stations. I tried to find TBN or The Word network or something to see if anyone was preaching. I did find Life In The Word, so I listened to Joyce Meyers preach on controlling your emotions. I think we all know I needed to hear that, well, not just hear it. I needed to do it, but how? I began to get restless. I walked over to the window and looked out over this overpowering yard or green grass without one spec of snow, and it made me know I would be homesick if I moved there. It was beautiful, I must admit. The sun was shining, and Michael had birds of paradise surrounding his pool, which was landscaped with rock and a gushing waterfall. There was no way those flowers would be alive in Philly right then. Even though the flowers couldn't survive the weather, I could. I thought I would die in this California sun though. I thought if I moved, Anya Dennings as I knew her, would die, and I had to do whatever it took to preserve her. I slid the window open and inhaled the fresh LA smog, and loved it.

"Good morning." Michael startled me.
"Hey. I was wondering when you would wake up. I was bored."
"Well, I'm awake now. What do you want to do that you're up so early?"
"Nothing. I just couldn't sleep anymore."
"Okay well let's get dressed and go eat."
"Sounds good to me."

After we were dressed, we went out to his six-car garage and got into his Mercedes SL500. As we pulled from the driveway, I began to get a little nervous. I mean who was I to be up there with Michael Harrison in his world?

Oh my Lord, the cars on the freeway drove like ten thousand miles an hour. Where were they all in a rush to get to? We exited on Le Brea and drove around a little bit before pulling up to the restaurant. "You'll love the food here." I probably would, too, but I wanted to go to Roscoe's Chicken and Waffles. I heard about it all the time, now I was finally close enough to go, and we didn't. I didn't want to say anything, because I figured Michael wanted to show me the places he wanted me to see like I do him when he's in Philly, so I figured if not on this trip, I'd make it to Roscoe's on the next one.

The next few days were great. We shopped 'til we dropped, which of course was one of my favorite parts of the visit. I had never been to Beverly Hills before, let alone shopped on Rodeo Drive, but I wanted to do it, just once, just to see what all the hype was about. It's funny, some dreams are better left as dreams. They were stores and boutiques like any other nice store or shop, the only difference was the prices. I mean to tell you the truth I wouldn't wear some of that stuff for free, but I guess people buy it because it's some kind of status thing. All you need is one star to start buying your clothes, and all of a sudden a T-shirt that would have sold for twenty-five bucks starts selling for one hundred twenty-five. It's ridiculous. Some of the stores didn't even have prices on the items, and that's how I knew I had no business being there. I needed to know how much I was spending and on what before I got to the register. Shoot I might get up there and decide it's not worth what they were asking. Nevertheless, just once I had to know what it was like to go into a store and not have to worry about money, and believe me, even once I married Michael, I would never again spend the ridiculous amount of money I spent on clothes, shoes and purses that day. I kind of felt bad about all the people who could have benefited from just one purse I bought true enough, it was a Ferragamo, but still, it was crazy. I was watching a television evangelist, James Robison and over there in Africa you can build a house for a homeless family for three thousand dollars, or you can put in a well for a village to have fresh water for thirty-two hundred, so how could I justify spending so much money that weekend? Exactly, I couldn't.

So in the end, I found out the shopping trip was a pretty overrated experience, so I guess I really rather would be spending that money to feed the hungry, cloth the naked and house the homeless. I guess some people have so much money they can do all those things and still buy a five-thousand-dollar bag or a thirty-five-hundred-dollar pair of boots or even a one hundred twenty dollar pair of panties or a thong in my case. My sister would be so disappointed in me, shoot, I was a little disappointed in myself. I had to use some self-control, especially if I was going to have this kind of money to throw around. It's not like I was broke and starving or that I wasn't use to nice things, but I definitely was not use to this. Ain't no sense in me frontin'.

I caught myself getting a little arrogant though, walking down the streets of Beverly Hills hand and hand with Michael Harrison, wondering how many people wished they could be me at that moment, and how great it felt to be me. So I guess I'd have to watch that too, cause Lord knows I didn't want to become some stuck-up butt hole that no one could stand to be around.

Well, Christmas Eve finally rolled around, and we went to Mike's parent's of course. Their family usually got together on Christmas Eve, but their family wasn't that big either, so it was a fairly quiet evening for the most part. After we ate dinner, which consisted of stuffed capons, steamed vegetables, cranberry sauce, rice, gravy and fresh-baked bread, we went into the sitting room, which was where the Christmas tree was located and all took a seat. I sat in the chair closest to the tree, and Michael sat on the arm of the chair before Jackie gave him the mom eye and he slid onto the floor next to me.

"There's a million chairs in here. You don't have to sit on the floor." Michael's mom looked over at him.

"Don't worry," his dad said, chuckling. "She already said yes. Give her some room." His dad had a hearty, full laugh. Full like a person laughs when they don't have a care in the world. You could even see the joy in his slim face.

He and Michael looked just alike, at least I could see the future of his look. Thank goodness, they weren't bad.

His mom and dad were sitting on the couch across from us, and his aunt on his dad's side was there with her husband and two of their children, both girls. One was grown, second year in college and the other was a senior in high school. They lived about forty minutes away, and of course Michael's grandmother was there too. They had this tradition of opening one gift Christmas Eve, so I decided to open my gift from his parents since Michael and I could open ours the next morning before I left. I was dying to know what on earth it could be considering they had only met me fours days ago. It was a small box, so I thought it might be some kind of jewelry, but at the same time, why would they buy me jewelry having just met me? Maybe they looked at it like I was going to be a part of the family so they wanted me to feel like it. Who knows? It really didn't matter. I smiled as Michael's dad walked over and handed me the oblong box. I accepted it graciously and said thank you. I began removing the bow and sliding the paper. I did it kind of neat and slow because I didn't want to appear anxious, like I wasn't use to having anything. Once I opened the box though it was all over. I screamed as if I wasn't use to having anything, because truthfully, I sure wasn't use to having a diamond Rolex. Why would they buy me a thirty-thousand dollar watch? All I got his mother was a silk scarf, and I bought his dad a golf club since Michael was always talking about how much his dad loved golf. And of course I didn't even pick out the club Michael did because I didn't know squat about golf other than yelling fore before you hit the ball. I know I know, Tiger Woods, but even though Tiger Woods started this major trend of black men in golf, I hadn't found myself dating one yet so therefore as I stated before, I didn't know squat about golf.

"Ahhh," I exclaimed. "Why did you guys do that? I love it, but it's way too much. I can't accept this." I turned to his parents feeling so embarrassed they had bought me this expensive watch.

"Nonsense," his dad said. "We couldn't have everyone else here getting great gifts and send our soon to be daughter-in-law home with a piece-of-crap gift. How would that make us look? And more importantly, how would that make you feel?"

He took the watch out of the box and motioned for me to lift my arm, and I did. Tears filled my eyes as he slid the watch I already had on up my arm just enough to lay that Rolex over my arm. "Oh yes." He gave a nod of satisfaction as he turned and looked over his shoulder at Jackie and smiled. "It's perfect." They both smiled and looked at each another as if to say, "yes, we did good." "Besides, we never thought this day would come, so we want to make sure we

172 | Camille Moore

have enough gifts to bribe you in case you change your mind," his dad said and let out another of his hearty laughs. He really did crack himself up quite frequently. I walked over and hugged each of Michael's parents as I tried not to let my tears fall. I gave Michael the evil eye as I walked back toward him mouthing, "Why didn't you tell me?" I sat back down, took my watch off, put it back in the box and closed it up. I had been so worried about meeting them and them accepting me, but they were cool and really down to earth, not all phony and uppity. I really enjoyed being around them, hopefully that wouldn't change.

That night back at Michael's we laid on the couch in front of the fireplace, drank wine, listened to music and talked. I was feeling a little sad that I was leaving the next morning and kind of wanted to stay, but I knew I couldn't.

"I missed you." I looked over at him.

"I missed you too." I just kind of stared at his profile. "No for real, I really missed you, like you wouldn't know."

"I really missed you too, like you couldn't imagine." He laughed.

"I'm serious."

"I'm serious too."

"Yeah alright." I gave a playful, disbelieving laugh. I leaned over and set my glass on the floor and sat up. I grabbed his glass from his hand, stood and began pulling him up. "Come on, let's open our stuff. I don't want to wait 'til the morning, and technically it is Christmas already, seeing as how it's one in the morning."

"Whatever you want." That's all I needed to hear. I ran upstairs to the bedroom to get his gift from my suitcase. When I came back, he was sitting on the floor next to the tree, which was fake and perfectly decorated by a professional tree decorating company. You know that would definitely be changing after we got married, right? What is Christmas without the smell of pine throughout the house? These people and their fake Christmas. I know it was really all about the birth of Jesus Christ, but at the same time I still loved the feeling that time of year always brought, the sharing, the giving, the singing, family, the whole nine. I loved Christmas. I loved it so much that I listened to Christmas music all year round, whenever I felt like it. I kissed Michael on the forehead and sat down in front of him Indian style. "Here, you go first," he said, setting my gifts down on the floor. I was feeling bad again because I only got him one thing and even that was a struggle because I couldn't think of anything to get in the first place.

I decided to once again open the smallest box first. I thought it was probably jewelry. I began to wonder if it was a rich-people tradition or something. It was a blue Tiffany's box. I pulled the white bow loose and lifted the lid. It was a Tiffany's key ring with a folded note that read. *You probably think I'm going to say something corny about the key to my heart, but actually this is a key ring for the key to my house.* I laughed out loud as I read it.

"Lift the cotton," he said. There were two keys in the bottom of the box. "Now look in the lid." I flipped the lid over. "That's the code to the front gate and the code to the house alarm, so don't lose that box."

I reached over and hugged him. "Thanks," I said, a little disappointed. Was that really a gift? I think it would be if we were just boyfriend and girlfriend, but we were engaged to be married, and this house was about to be mine anyway. Nonetheless, I appreciated the gesture of trust that came in that box. I opened the next box, which were boots and the third box was a purse. I guess he really did know me. I had tried on those boots the other day at Gucci but refused to pay that kind of money, even if it was his money. I figured eventually they would go out of style and I did not have a problem wearing last season's style, at half the price, sometimes at even seventy percent of the original price.

"I knew you wanted them," he said. He just didn't know how bad. Was this what my life was going to be like? Not wanting for anything? Spending large sums of money on material things? I didn't want to turn into that, at least I didn't think I did, did I? I wanted to remain the same ole me. The same ole me with these Gucci boots that were killin' 'em. I took my house shoes off and slid my bare foot into that boot and stood up, looking it over. That wasn't good enough, I needed to put the other one on too. I walked back and forth across the hardwood floors as if I was on my personal runway, struttin' like only a supermodel can. "Ahhh I love em!" I walked back over and got my purse out the box and gripped it in my hand, because it was a small handbag, not a big purse. "I'm doin' it. I'm doin' it." I made up a little song as I danced about the tree.

"Well I'm so glad I could make you happy."

He continued to watch me act a complete fool behind some boots. Oh well, he might as well know the real me, all parts of me, even the ridiculously silly side, which I don't think he had a problem with, 'cause he was just as silly.

"Okay okay, as much as I'm really enjoying this, it's your turn." I was excited, too, because I knew he would like it. He lived for mushy romantic but I couldn't fault him. I did too. That was one of the things I loved most about Michael. It seemed as though we lived in a world that was against romance, everything was about sex, money, sex, cars, sex, diamonds and then more sex. Me though I loved romance, even if it wasn't in style, even if it was primarily dead in our generation. It was very much alive in my heart and always had been, and I really hoped it always would be. I was a sucker for corny unrealistic movies, and I loved Lifetime movies that made me cry. I was a romantic, singing in the rain, making love on the beach, I loved love but up until that point, it never really loved me and now I had a little too much love.

Anyway back to Michael's moment. He picked up the eggshell envelope that had his name handwritten in calligraphy. Inside was lined in gold that was made especially by the printer for me, or should I say for Michael. He slid the card out and read aloud: "What do you give a man who has everything? The only thing I could think of was the heart of the woman he loves, but he already possesses that. So then what?" He picked up the box.

"Should I be scared to open this?" He glanced over at me.

"I don't know, should you?" I think I was just as excited as he was. The box was beautiful too. I had bought this bright red foil paper, and I went to the fabric store and bought silver and red ribbon and made the most beautiful bow. This present was so pretty I could have been hired as a gift wrapper for the holidays. He gently untied the ribbon then removed the paper.

"What is this?" he said with excited anticipation.

"You'll see," I sang out. "Just open it, slowpoke."

See he had never won an Oscar before although, three years earlier he had been nominated for best supporting actor for his role in the hit movie, *"In an Instant."* It was the bomb too. My man knew he could act, but he just hadn't had his time yet was all. When he opened both sides of the tissue, there lay a gold velvet bag. He pulled out the treasure the bag contained. He was speechless. I had him. Go Anya, Go Anya, I sang to myself in my head. He held the fourteen-karat gold replica of an Oscar and read the inscription. His voice was a little shaky as he began to read, "Michael Harrison." He took a hard swallow as he fought back the tears. "For the role of best fiancé in *The Story of Anya.*"

"Wow." He leaned over and kissed my lips. "You always seem to amaze me. I didn't know what you had gotten, but I can tell you this, I never expected anything like this. This has got to be the best gift I've ever gotten, and I'm not just saying that. I really mean it. I don't even know what to say. This is just unbelievable." He stood, took a deep breath and reached for my hand. I grabbed it, and he pulled me up. We walked down to the game room, and I watched him place it in the spot that he had reserved for the Oscar he still hoped to one day get. Maybe he would, but until that great day, this was his Oscar, and I had a feeling this made him feel almost as good as receiving the real thing. We stood there for a few moments as he held me from behind and rocked me back and forth, looking at his little Anya Oscar.

"You really are amazing. You know that?"

"Yeah, I do," I laughed, "but nowhere near as amazing as you."

"Anya," he said, turning me around to face him, "do you really have to leave tomorrow? I need you here with me."

"Let's not start, okay? You know I have to go, and besides, after tomorrow you'll be back to work, and if I stayed I'd be here in this big house alone."

We walked back down the hall, and I waited at the bottom of the stairs while he turned out all the lights and put out the fire. I was tired, but I didn't want to go to sleep because I didn't know when I was going to see him again. We had had so much fun I kind of didn't want it to end myself. I watched him walk back toward me. He was so sexy I was getting a little warm just looking at him. That's why it was good we didn't see each other too often until the wedding. He grabbed my hand, and we continued up the stairs.

"Is it hard for you not having sex?" I blurted out.

"Where did that come from?" We stopped on the staircase.

"I don't know. I just wondered is all."

"I can't lie. It was real hard at first, but it helps that I've been so busy lately. Plus, it's not like I'm going without sex with no light at the end of the tunnel. I know May is just around the corner, and I'm marking down the days like a man in prison waiting for his release date. I'm going to be all over you. Why, you wanna give me some?" He laughed and leaned back against the stairway wall.

Even though he was laughing I could tell he was lightweight serious and was probably hoping I was going to say yes.

"Well just being honest, it did cross my mind . . . about oh seven hundred times since I saw you at the airport, but I'm trying to stay focused and be a good girl, but trust me, it's gonna be on in May. You can believe that."

"You know we could pretend it's May right now. I mean we are in California, there's no snow, and it's just a little chilly. That's how it will be in New York the beginning of May, right?" I didn't respond. "So I think if we psych ourselves up enough we can make ourselves believe it's May. I know I wouldn't have a problem doing that mentally. You know what I'm saying?" He grabbed the back of my neck and pulled my mouth to his. Umm my word he tasted so good. It was on, my body melted into him as he kissed my neck. "I love you, Anya," he whispered between his lips and my neck. He was breathing so hard he could hardly speak. He laid me back on the stairs, and I spread my legs and wrapped them around him. This wasn't sex, right? I didn't care how hard he was and how much bumping and grinding we did, we still had our clothes on so it wasn't sex, just a little something to get us through until the wedding. "Let's go upstairs, Anya please?" He rested his forehead on mine and kissed my lips. "I want you so bad. You can't leave here without giving me some." But that was just it, I could. I could leave without giving him some because we made an agreement.

"Anya, you're about to be my wife."

"I know," I said, kissing him back, "but about to be and being are two different things." I pushed him up a little so that I could slide from under him. I sat on the step above him.

"Man Anya, you make it so hard on me. What do you expect me to do with this?" He looked down at his pants as he sat there on his knees frustrated.

"Baby, I'm sorry. We just got carried away, but I feel the same way. I'm just as horny as you, but I just want to do it the right way this time around because I want God to bless our marriage, and I want it to last."

"Yeah, alright." He kissed me on my cheek and stood up. "Ay, I'm about to go take a shower and go to bed. I'll see you in the morning."

"Oh, it's like that?" I mumbled. "Cool."

"What is that suppose to mean? I mean dang, Anya, I'm still a man. You can't just rub all up on me and think it's not going to affect me. You had me thinking we were about to make love, and if you knew we weren't, you should have stopped it before it got this far. I'm not mad, but I'm about to go get in the shower and take care of this, then I'm going to bed and and get some sleep, and I'll see you in the morning when I'm feeling better. I'm still going to take you to the airport, and I'm still going to count down the days 'til May, because regardless of what just happened, I still love you, but at the same time I do want some."

Back At The Ranch

As I boarded the plane at 7:05A.M., still horny and definitely sleepy, I thought about Michael and wondered if maybe I should have given him some. After all, I was about to marry him, but I had to remind myself that I made the commitment to myself and God to not give it up anymore until I was married, so that was that. It didn't stop me from feeling bad though. Michael didn't really seem to still be tripping that morning, so I didn't know why I was.

I looked around and noticed the plane was pretty empty. There was only me and one other guy in first class. I guess people were already at their Christmas destinations. Who really wanted to travel on Christmas anyway? You should be home with your family, which is just where I was headed. The only problem was now I had two families, and it made me wonder how Christmas would be the following year. I know it was a long ways off, but that didn't stop me from thinking about it. I always thought like that. I worried in advance, I was cautious of everything since my divorce. I tried to avoid most problems, and I did pretty well at the big ones, but it seemed to be the no-brainers, the easy problems that common sense would tell me to avoid, that I just couldn't seem to do.

Julian, for example. See my point? Julian thought I was in California on business. He had called several times while I was there but I only answered once. That was only because he happened to call while I was in the dressing room trying on this cute suede patchwork skirt that of course I bought with the matching jacket and some burgandy suede boots, see no self-control. I had explained to him that I had really been busy shopping and stuff with the client that I had come out there to do work for and that I had early mornings and late nights because we were trying to cram as much in as possible before her and her family left to go to Switzerland for Christmas. Not to mention the time difference, which was really a lifesaver. I also told him that I was going to be doing two rooms in her house over the next month while they were gone so we had to get the major things picked out before she left and some of the minor stuff she was leaving to me. I figured this would give me an outlet if I needed to go see Michael about the wedding stuff during January, or if I just wanted to see him period. Although, I could imagine he wouldn't want me coming out much until he could get some. I knew this was a terrible thing I was doing, but I just didn't have the heart to tell Julian yet, but I was going to. I just didn't know when. I knew I was only making things worse, but I just didn't want to hurt him again. See another prime example of the common sense I sometimes failed to use.

I was taking out my phone to call Michael while walking to the baggage claim when I saw Julian. I didn't know what I was thinking. I should have called Michael when I first got off the plane. Now it would have to wait because I had already made eye contact with Julian. He walked over and greeted me with a huge kiss, which I tried to avoid, but simply could not, and a hug that could have very well crushed my lungs.

"Girl, you don't know how good it is to see you in the flesh."
To be truthful, it was good to see him, too, and if I'm being totally honest, I did enjoy the kiss. Not as much as Michael's but still, it was enjoyable, quite enjoyable, I might add.
"You lookin' good as usual," I said, peering at him from the corner of my eye, trying to keep an eye out for my bags. When I saw one of them come I motioned to it and Julian grabbed it.
"How many more bags you got?"
"Just one more." I had to buy another suitcase while I was there to put some of the stuff I had bought in. Some of the stuff I left there though, since it was my house too, right?
"Oh, that's not bad. I'm surprised. You know how y'all women always over packing."
"Whatever. Just get the bag." I pointed to the other bag.
"So did you miss me?" he questioned.
"A little somethin' like that." I smirked.
"Oh, I ain't trippin.' I know you did."

We walked to the car, and we bumped our shoulders against each other like we use to when we were younger. I just wondered what I was doing. Even though I knew I loved Michael, I loved Julian too. It was like the two of them together made the perfect man. Twisted, but true.

We got to the car, and he popped the trunk and put my bags in. I went ahead and walked to the passenger door and got in. Oh, you're still wondering why he's picking me up from the airport? Well, I told you we had been talking again regularly and I had seen him a time or two, but with our history, that's all it took. It's like we picked up where we should have never left off. And you know he was coming home to see his family for the holiday and that meant he was going to want to see me too, seeing as how we were picking up where we left off in his mind. So I told him it was okay for him to pick me up from the airport, and we agreed we would go by his parent's for a little while then we would go to Traci's since he had been with his parents all that morning, not to mention the last two days.

We didn't waste time dropping my luggage off at my house since it was already four o'clock, so we went straight to Julian's parents. It was a trip pulling up to this house that I had spent so many days at when we dated. Even when he wasn't even suppose to have girls over, he would sneak me in. As long as I was gone before his parents got home from work it was cool. Besides I could never stay late anyway, because I wasn't suppose to be over there anyway. I remember me and Kim would say we were going bike riding when we were like fourteen and I would end up right at Julian's and she would be right up the street at Eric's. Those were the days.

The house still looked exactly the same, white with brick-red shutters. We couldn't fit in the driveway with so many other cars there, so we had to park down the street a little. We walked passed the black-and-white house two doors down from his parent's. "Does Joe's parents still live there?" I asked.
"Yep, you know they ain't going nowhere. Joe came by the house earlier. That's his car right there." He pointed to a black Ford Expedition.
"He's still over there. You want go by and say hi?"
"Naw. I just wondered if they still owned that house."

We made are way through the snow up the driveway. It was so cold, all I could think about was that California sun. Even though the sun was out in Philly, it was only twenty-eight degrees.

We stopped at the back door and took off our boots. You know if it wasn't snowing, I would have had on the Guccis but I didn't want to mess them up in the snow. I wasn't worried about 'em keeping my feet warm because the cute Nine West boots I had on definitely weren't doing that. I remember back in the day we use to wear for-real snow boots with furry stuff all on the inside to keep our feet from freezing and falling off when we take our boots off. Not anymore. I don't know what happened. I guess we are to fashion conscious in the new millennium. This doorway brought back memories though. I remembered being pressed up against it many a summer day, knowing it was time for me to leave so I could get home before I got in trouble, but not wanting to, kiss after kiss, good-bye after good-bye. It seemed like just yesterday for real.

As soon as we walked up the three stairs that led from the back door to the kitchen I was greeted by warm hugs and smiles, and though it was good seeing everybody, I was really surprised that my reception was this warm seeing as how I had done this man in the past. I guess they chalked it up as me being young, and as long as Julian was happy, so were they. Little did they know, he wouldn't be happy for long, at least not with me.

His mom still looked the same, other than the fact she had put on a little weight, not much but enough to notice because she had always been so skinny when we were growing up. It felt like old times. One thing I always loved about dating Julian was his big family. Holidays at his house had always been a big production. Just in his immediate family, he had three brothers and one sister. So you can imagine combining aunts, uncles, wives, kids, cousins and family friends. It was chaotic, but it was always fun. When we first started dating, all his family would go to his grandmother's house, on his fathers side, but she passed after my senior year in college, and every since then, Christmas was always at his house, Easter was at his aunt Juanita's house, Thanksgiving was at his aunt Brenda's and Fourth of July and other holidays varied depending on the weather. All his mom's family lived in Alabama, and they would go to see them every summer.

Things had quieted down slightly because people were eating, but we just nibbled because we were going to sit down and eat at Traci's. I had told her that we would try to be there by six-thirty at the latest. She was not at all excited about me bringing Julian, but she promised to stay out of it. I told her that nothing was going on, that we were just two old friends hanging out. Of course she didn't believe it, how could she? But regardless, she decided to keep her opinion to herself after she voiced her initial disapproval.

I was sitting at the table between Julian and his sister when he got up and said he'd be right back. I sat there talking to his sister who was four months pregnant and wanted to know what was really going on with me and Julian. She said that she had heard about my miscarriage and that she was sorry. I told her it was for the best and that I was okay with it. She sympathized for a moment but then got back to her first agenda of business. She still wanted to know what was up with me and J as she had always called him. I told her it was too soon to tell and that we were just playing it by ear and enjoying getting to know each other again. I picked up my glass and took a sip of wine, but not even a whole bottle could have prepared me for what was to come.

Julian came back into the dining room where part of his family was seated. The rest were spread out between the kitchen table and the living room and family room. "Everybody, can I get your attention for a minute?" he said, standing between the living room and dining room. "It was good seeing everybody as usual. I'm getting ready to head out because we have to go to Anya's family's house, too, and I know most of you will be gone when I get back. So I love you all and will see you at the next function, but before I leave, there is something I would like to do." He began walking toward me, and suddenly I got this ache in the pit of my stomach. I began to panic. *Don't do it. Don't do what I think you are about to do*, I thought, but there was no point. He could not hear my thoughts, not that it would have deterred him if he could. He continued on his journey to me and got down on one knee. This could not possibly be happening, but it was, and maybe, just maybe, if this was happening and I hadn't already met Michael and hadn't already told him I would marry him, I might be a little excited about it, but the fact was, I had met Michael, he had asked me to marry him, and I had said yes so I thought it might be just a tad bit late for this proposal.

"Baby," he said, taking a deep breath and looking down at the floor then back up at me, "I have never in my short life loved anyone the way that I love you. Believe me when I say I've tried, but I just can't get you out of my system. I know a lot has happened between us, and I don't care about all that stuff in the past. That's history. All I care about is today and tomorrow, and all I know is that I want you to be a part of all my tomorrows. I let you get away once before, and I'm not about to let that happen again, so I'm just letting it be known how much I love you and how bad I wanna spend the rest of my life with you, and I hope you feelin' that too." He opened his hand and held up a diamond tennis bracelet. It was a relief. I thought I might be able to breathe. I thought this fool was about to propose.

"Do you remember that bracelet I made you that Valentine's Day when we didn't have money for gifts?" he asked.

"Forget? I still have it at home in my jewelry box," I said, smiling.

"Well, remember I promised you that one day it would be real?" I nodded. I couldn't talk. "Well, I didn't want to break my promise." He opened the clasp and put it on my wrist next to the tennis bracelet I was already wearing. "I can see you don't really need it, but I wanted you to know I never forgot. Besides, you may need it to go with this." He reached into his pocket and held up a ring with his thumb and index finger. "Anya, marry me man. Be my wife. I waited half my life for this moment. I have loved you since we were little. Even before I had the courage to tell you in junior high, I'd been in love with you since elementary school."

"Whoa." I choked out. "Umm, wow. I definitely wasn't expecting this, this Christmas." I didn't know what to say. How could he do this in front of everyone, especially his sister, I didn't even want to look over there at her because I already knew what she was thinking. I couldn't say no, not in front of his whole family, but shoot, I was already engaged. I know the ring was in my purse, but still, even if I wasn't sportin' it, it didn't erase the fact that I was just that, engaged. I felt dizzy.

"Anya, you okay?" his mom asked.

"Yes. I think I'm just feeling a little overwhelmed and shocked." I looked down at Julian with his eyes pleading with me for a yes. How could I say no?

"Yeah, I mean yes, I'll marry you boy. What you think?" Everyone clapped, and the claps made my ears ring. I stood as he did, and we kissed once again. Even though the kiss was good, it wasn't good enough to make me believe I could marry this man. I knew I couldn't. Yes, I loved him, but I couldn't marry him. I didn't care how much I loved him. I would just wait until after we went to Traci's to tell him. I didn't want to ruin the rest of the day, although at this point it was pretty much ruined and no Christmas for him would ever be the same. Me either for that matter.

I was bombarded by hugs and kisses from his family, until I just wanted to run and hide, but there was nowhere for me to run from myself, the two timing monster. Everyone seemed to be happy except Jillian, Julian's sister, and it was probably because she knew me. Jillian use to be my girl. She came up to me and hugged me, but before she let go, she said, "Anya, you my girl and I love you, but J is my brother and you already hurt him once. Don't do my brother again." She gave me a look of warning before turning to walk away. Wow, I would get mad if she didn't have reason to say it. How stupid could I be? Would I ever grow out of it was the question I most wanted to know. So came the age-old question, Can you be in love, I mean truly in love with two people? I know you can love a lot of people over the course of a lifetime, but could you be in love with more than one, and was there then a such thing as true love or a soul mate? And if so, how did you know when you'd found him?

I felt my phone vibrating, so I looked down. It was Michael. I had forgotten to sneak and call him when we got to Julian's parent's to let him know I had made it. My, my, how soon we forget our true love, right. I, of course, didn't answer it. I waited about ten minutes then I went into the bathroom to call him back. I explained that I didn't hear the phone ring and that I had just looked down and saw the missed call. I apologized for not calling him when I first got in, but I told him I was too busy telling Kim about my trip and his parents and the house and my shopping spree and everything else. I told him that I hadn't even taken my bags to the house, that I had gone straight to Traci's. He was okay with that. I also apologized for what had happened the night before. He said he was sorry too. We ended the call with the, I love you's that had become second nature, and I told him I would call him later before I went to bed. He was okay with that as well. He was so great, and I was so sorry. Not apologetic sorry but sorry as in no good.

I went ahead and used the bathroom while I was in there and washed my hands. I looked down at the ring on my finger and looked at my lying, deceiving face in the mirror and wondered how I even let this go this far. I gave a sigh of dread, placed my hand on the knob and put on a happy face before turning the knob to re-enter my life. When I came out and went back into the dining room, Julian had gotten my coat, and we said our farewells, and before I knew it, we were on our way down the highway to Traci's, the place I was really dreading going now. I would have to tell them Julian asked me to marry him, because if I didn't, he would think I wasn't happy about it or that I didn't want to be with him, which would have been accurate, but I didn't want him to feel like that.

"What's up?" He looked over at me. "You seem like you're a million miles away." I wasn't, but I sure wished I were.
"Oh, nothing. I'm just tired from working all week then flying in today, that's all. I didn't get much sleep because I had to be at the airport so early."
"Are you sure that's all it is?" I nodded. He reached over and held my hand. It almost felt like old times, but it wasn't. It was today, and I was engaged to two men at the same time. What was I thinking? Now what was I suppose to do?

We parked at Traci's and walked right in through the front door because it wasn't locked.
"Hey everybody," I said kind of nervously.
"Oh my word," my grandmother said. "Is that Julian? Now that's a face I haven't seen in a long time. How are you, sugar?" She walked over and hugged him, looking at me out the corner of her eye.
"I'm good, Grandma, never been better." He kissed her on the cheek.
"Stand back and let me get a look at you." She gave him the once-over. "Yes indeed, just as handsome as ever." It was no secret my grandmother had always favored Julian, and she was really upset when I broke up with him. She had always told me I wouldn't ever find anyone who was going to put up with me the way Julian did, and when I married John, she had no problem letting it be known how much he wasn't Julian. She had told me that you only find true love once and to make sure I knew what I was doing and at the time, I thought I did. Who knew? Plus, she knew I had lost my virginity to Julian so in her eyes that was who I should have been marrying.

Everyone there was happy to see Julian. It seemed as if I was the person they weren't too excited about. Of course no one was going to say anything except my grandmother, and it didn't take her long at all to start her line of questioning.

"So what are you doing here, Julian?" She smiled. "I didn't even know you and Anya were still in touch."

"We weren't," he replied, "until I ran into her this past summer when I was here for my brother Kenneth's wedding."

"Little Kenny?"

"Yeah, but he's not so little anymore. He just graduated from Michigan State, him and his wife."

"Well good for him. So you guys have been in touch since the summer?"

"Umm hmm. She tried to shake me for a minute, but she couldn't resist."

"Um, that's interesting." She looked over at me.

"But don't worry, Grandma, you'll be seeing a lot more of me soon." I began to sweat, literally, the heat ran throughout my body, and my scalp felt moist and warm, and my hands were clammy and moist.

"Is that so?" my grandmother replied curiously, constantly pumping him for information. "I thought you lived in Chicago now. Have you moved back or something?"

"No, but I intend to before I marry this beautiful young woman." He grabbed my hand and kissed my cheek. I was so hoping he would leave it at that, but life is never that good when you screw up as much as I had. I looked over at Traci who mouthed, "Married?" with a questionable face. She shook her head and continued to mouth phrases to me, unpleasant ones. Telling me I was trippin', asking me what I was doing, all kinds of stuff. I had to stop looking at her after mouthing for her to shut up.

"Who is that?" I saw Vic asking Kim. I didn't miss anything. I always knew what was going on around me and what people were thinking most of the time and at that point Vic was probably thinking I had broken up with Michael and how quick I bounced into the arms of another. If only he knew, it was so much worse than that. She obviously told him she would tell him later or either she briefly told him because I saw him lift one eyebrow and nod. I took Julian's coat and hung it up. He was way too happy to be there. He hadn't seen Kevin in a long time, so they took a few moments alone at the bar while I followed Kim into the kitchen. I wasn't worried leaving Julian with Kevin. I knew Kev wouldn't blab about anything that had been going on the past few months. We were followed into the kitchen by my grandmother who was followed a few seconds later by Traci. It was awful.

Before my grandmother could even say anything, I spoke first. "I know, Grandma, just let me handle this, okay? Please?"

"Fine," she sang and gave an arrogant smile. "If you think you can, I won't say a word, but you're playing with fire, and it's one thing if you don't mind getting burned but don't burn Julian and Michael's unsuspecting hearts."

"Well you may not say anything, but I will," Traci began.

"Let's just eat. It's getting late." Kim came to my rescue, cutting her off. "We been waiting all day to get some dressing and eat, so let's." She grabbed my arm and escorted me from one battlefield to the next, only to ask me what was going on.

"You know I can't fill you in now, but trust me, I will."

"Girl, this some straight soap opera mess you got going on. I ain't mad. Men been doin' this to us for years." But that was no excuse, and it definitely didn't make it right.

Kim told everyone to go wash up for dinner as we began to set the food on the table. My sister continued to talk to me with her eyes. In a minute I was about to put one of 'em on swoll if she kept on.

"Everything looks so good, Traci." My grandmother smiled. We all stood and held hands as Kevin blessed the food. Everything did look good. There's nothing like eating your own family's cooking, because that's what you're use to. Not that other people's food wasn't good, but there was nothing like what you grew up on. Traci had quite a spread too. The turkey was nice and golden, and as Kevin began to carve it, you could see the juice bursting forth. There was a bowl of macaroni and cheese, rice and gravy, yam soufflé with marshmallows, greens and green beans, why we needed both, I didn't know but I wasn't complaining. There was a pan of dressing in addition to the turkey, which was also full of dressing. There was also corn bread and rolls. The cranberry sauce was sliced perfectly and spread out on a dish. The ham was small and had pineapples and cherries pinned to it with toothpicks. Ooh, I could almost taste the glaze. Everyone began fixing their plates and picking at their food as if they were so hungry they couldn't wait two additional minutes for the plate to be complete so they could sit down and eat it all in harmony.

I thought we might be able to get through dinner with pleasant conversation, but halfway through, they had to start in.

"So Julian, you picked Anya up from the airport?" Kim asked, not even looking up from her plate, trying to act like she was just making conversation.

I thought. *Here we go.*

"Yes. I couldn't wait to get her. I hated she had to go to work so close to Christmas. I've been here for a few days, but it was good seeing my family. I'm going to head back Saturday so I can rest Sunday and be fresh for work Monday, so tomorrow will be the only day I get to spend some time with her."

"Well better one day than no day," she said.

"You right about that."

"So, Anya, how did the California trip go? Did you get everything accomplished you went out there for?" My sister glared at me like she was Sergeant Friday or something.

"As a matter of fact, I did," I said, rolling my eyes, "but I'm going to need to go back a few more times to complete the assignment." I glared back at her, unafraid of the consequences.

"Yes, I'm sure you will. Maybe next time you can take Julian with you so you don't have to go by yourself."

"Maybe. You never know. I would just hate to take him and not be able to spend any time with him. I'm working such long hours while I'm there, trying to squeeze all that I need to in on each trip."

"Um, I can only imagine having to put in those kind of hours. It's a good thing you love your job."

I could not believe this. Was she my sister or the enemy? Wasn't she supposed to be on my side, even when I was wrong? Dang, if my grandmother of all people who always had something to say could let it go, why couldn't she?

This continued along with other idle conversation throughout dinner. After everyone was full, Kevin jumped up and started clearing the table and asked if anyone wanted dessert. Julian leaned over and asked me what was up with me and Traci. I told him she was mad at me about something I had done, which was actually true, but that is was no big deal.

"Well, it seems like a big deal. I mean this is suppose to be Christmas and y'all feuding at the dinner table on the unda with fake smiles. What's happened since we been apart? I can't believe your grandmother even let y'all carry on like that. I remember back in the day she was liable to snatch anything off the table, including a pork chop, and slap y'all with it."

"Well you know, Julian, some things change. She'll get over it."

"Wait. Hold on. Don't take it out on me. It couldn't be that serious. What did you do?"

Of course I blew it off as nothing and refused to give any further information. "Nothing to be concerned about. Don't trip." I got up and began to clear the plates from the table.

Traci had gone into the kitchen with Kevin, and they both returned with a tray. One had German chocolate cake, apple pie and cheesecake. The other had coffee and more wine, which was definitely what I was in need of. Traci set her tray down in the family room on the end table next to the couch and went back into the kitchen. A few minutes later she returned with a tray full of cups, glasses and forks. Kevin went around the room serving everyone their requested dessert. He was so sweet.

It was now time to open the gifts.

"Okay hold up. I wanna be Santa this year," Kim said, handing her plate to Vic. She jumped up from her seat, walked over and sat next to the gifts under the tree. My grandmother was sitting on the couch next to my grandfather who was just trying to stay neutral, even though of course my grandmother kept trying to get him to say something about what I was doing. He was my grandpa, and that was one bond that could never be broken. I don't care how much wrong I did, my grandpa was always gonna be my grandpa and was always going to be in my corner. I was sitting on the floor next to him, and Julian was standing against the wall talking to Kevin.

I guess my grandmother must have gotten to him because my grandpa, the one who is always on my side leaned over and whispered, "I don't know what's going on here tonight, but we will definitely be talking about it later." He looked over the top of his glasses down into my face with a stern look. "I expect you over Sunday, straightaway from church."

There was nothing in the world I hated more than for my grandpa to be disappointed in me. "Yes, sir," I said, kind of motionless. I knew I had no business bringing Julian over or maybe I had no business marrying Mike. It was one of the two, but which?

Kim requested everyone's attention as she handed the first gift out. It was for Kevin from my grandparents. She continued on with this ritual until the last gift was passed out. I could tell my sister liked her and Kevin's gift, but she was so upset with me that she couldn't get all excited like she normally would have. She just put on a fake smile and said, "Thanks we can really use this."

Kevin, on the other hand, came over and hugged me, "This is right up our alley. We could use this fo' sho. I'm calling next week to see when we can get in. You always think of the gifts man. You good, I really wasn't expecting this."

"Well, you two deserve it, I just hope you guys enjoy it."

"Oh, we will." He walked back over to my sister and sat down. She gave him the evil eye and nudged his ribs, I guess for talking to me and being so appreciative when he knew she was mad at me. Traci and I had gone in and had my grandmother a mother's ring custom made with my birthstone, my sister's birth stone and my mother's birthstone set between ours. It was real nice. When she opened it, she began to cry through her smile, maybe it was a little too emotional for her with things being the way they were with my mom. I know she wished she was there, but we did too, and just because she wasn't, we didn't want to forget her.

It seemed as if time stopped and everyone watched as Julian opened his gift from me. I watched his face as he took the paper off his first gift. It was a pair of black silk pajamas and a black silk robe. I loved men's pajamas they reminded me of my dad, he always wore really nice pajamas, always a matching set, never just some raggedy shorts or pajama bottoms with an old T-shirt. I'm sure my mom probably always bought them, but still, he wore them faithfully, and he always smelled so good. I remember being little and going in their room after my dad would have just gotten out of the shower. The whole room would smell like him, and I would jump up on my parent's bed, lean on his shoulder and talk to him about whatever might have happened that day. Oh, that use to be so comforting. Why do things have to change?

Julian loved the pajamas. He leaned over and kissed me. "You know I don't need this much style to go to bed."
"Yes, you do."
"Well, whatever makes you happy. I'll wear 'em every day if I have to." He reached for his second box. I know I only got Michael one thing, but this was different, Michael had everything under the sun already. He began opening it. I looked up to see if everyone was still looking, and they were.

"Dang, why is Julian opening his stuff such an intense moment? Y'all wasn't all into it like this when everybody else opened their stuff." Man, I was so irritated. I wish I would have just waited to give him his stuff later.
"Aw man, no you didn't," he said, looking at me in amazement.
"Yes I did." I giggled and smiled at him.
"Well, what did you do?" Kim asked.
He opened the box all the way and took out the Movado watch I bought him and showed it to her. "Aw man, I love it. I needed a new watch too. My work watch is finished and I broke the band on my dress watch."
"Yes I know. I remember you telling me. See I do listen to you."

I knew he was in love with it. I wondered if it was too much though. I hadn't plan on spending quite that much on him, but he deserved it, all the turmoil

I had put him through over the years, and it was only about to get worse. He was going to deserve that and much more when it was all over with. He looked at me, and said, "I love you." At that moment, I could feel six pairs of eyes burning through me. I think they were waiting to see if I was going to say it back, but I fooled them all.

"I know. What's not to love?" I joked with him.
"You right. You are definitely right about that."

But would it have been so surprising if I did say it? I mean I did love him. We were friends, he was my first love and it's not like we broke up on bad terms or anything. So what would be so hard to believe about it?

"So, little sis, what did you get from your honey for Christmas?" I wanted to lunge across the room and attack Traci. Why was she doing this to me? She was being such a hater. I lifted my arm and showed off my tennis bracelet.

"You know you don't need no more jewelry, girl. Go on and pass that old one over to me." Kim came over and grabbed my arm for a closer inspection.

"I know she didn't need any more." Julian looked over at me. "It's sentimental. It was a promise I made a long time ago that I have been waiting for the opportunity to fulfill."

Traci started laughing. "I remember that. Are you talking about that bracelet you made for her a long time ago out of the string and the rhinestones?" He nodded. "That is so sweet," she exclaimed. "You are too good for her." I could not believe this girl. She said it jokingly, but I knew she meant it.

"Yeah, I know. I tell her that all the time," he joked, "but she finally wised up and realized what she's got. Besides, ain't nothing too good for the woman I plan on spending the rest of my life with. I want her to look well taken care of. Right, babe?" He looked at me.

"Right." What else was I going to say? Wrong. I don't think that would have gone over very well.

"Wait a minute." Kim didn't miss a beat. She's just like me. You can tell we've been friends way too long. "Where you get this from?" she said, referring to the one-carat ring sitting on my ring finger. I was really hoping she would adore the bracelet without noticing the ring. Not happening. "Well, I guess I might as well tell you all." I stood up and Julian stood next to me. I reached over, grabbed another glass of wine and took a big gulp. "Umm, Julian asked me to marry him today at his mom's." I tried to sound excited so as not to alarm Julian.

"And you said?" Kevin waited for a response.

"Man, what do you think she said?" Julian was all smiles.

"We don't know," my sister said, looking at me, "that's why he's asking." She continued to stare at me, still waiting to hear the words come from my mouth.

"What do you think I said?" I downed the rest of my wine. I couldn't get it out. I just held my hand up. "I'm wearing the ring, aren't I?"

"That you are," my grandmother said. "That you are." I could see her laughing to herself and probably thinking back to our conversation in the kitchen and wondering if this was my way of handling it.

"Congratulations, man." Kevin walked over and shook Julian's hand. "Well, I guess a toast is in order. Let me get the champagne."

"Let me help you." My sister got up and followed him.

"Wow, this is a trip. This has been one wild year. What a way to end it." Kim smiled and while hugging me, she whispered in my ear, "Do you know what the heck you're doing?" I just smiled and stepped back.

Kevin and Traci soon returned with champagne and glasses, and we toasted to my and Julian's fake future. Things were winding down, which was good because I was so ready to get out of there. I had never before felt like this about Christmas, and I hoped to God I never would again. I went and got our coats, and we hugged everyone and said our good-byes.

"Kim, you know I'll be calling you tonight, so just let Vic know he ain't getting none tonight." We both laughed.

"Wait. Excuse us for one minute, Julian." Kim pulled me to the side. "Let me just ask you one thing. Did you and Michael break up or something?"

"Girl, are you crazy? Naw."

"Okay you really are going to have to call me tonight as soon as you walk in the door." I headed back toward Julian. "Oh wait wait wait. What did he get you for Christmas?"

"Oh, it ain't what he got me. It's what his parents got me that's going to blow you away." "Come on. Tell me right quick. What they get you?" she said anxiously. I looked over to see if Julian was looking at us, but he was talking to Kevin.

"Okay. Okay. They got me a Rolex. It's bad too. Wait 'til you see it," I said excitedly.

"They got you what?" she said in disbelief. "Okay so what are you doing Anya?"

"Kim, I don't know. I just can't shake Julian. After all these years, there's still something there."

"One thing's for sure, it ain't no Rolex. But whatever it is, you better hurry up and find out so you can cure it and move on. But anyway, what did Mike get you? I know it was something good." I told her about the boots and the purse, and of course about the box with the keys and the alarm code.

"Girl, that rich man gave you keys and the alarm code to his house? That fool love you. Now if you don't marry him, he's going to have to have you killed because you have too much information." I laughed with her and pushed her shoulder advising her to be quiet.

"Yeah, I know, but Julian loves me too." I smiled and let out a fake cry of confusion. "Girl, I don't know what I'm going to do. I feel so bad and so confused."

"You can feel bad all you want, but the longer you wait to fix this mess, the harder it's going to be, and I know you're not seriously thinking about leaving Mike for no Julian. I don't care how much you think you love him."

"Why you say it like that? What if I was?"

"Well then I guess you just would be, but I just don't see it. Either way, I got you. I just want you to be happy, and I can't help but see how happy you've been since you met Mike. I really think y'all are good for each other. Don't get me wrong. I love Julian too. I do. He's like family, but I just have to be honest. It's time to let go."

"Yeah," I responded kind of lethargically and walked back over to Julian.

My Fault

Back at my house, Julian got my bags out of the car and brought them to the door, then waited for me to get my keys out and unlock the door so he could set the bags in the house. It was good to be home. Not that Michael's wasn't great, but there was no place like home when it was yours and everything was just like you liked it and just like you left it. I walked in and turned some lights on, then I watched Julian's sexy chocolate self place my bags down on the floor by the door. My, my, my, I had to get him out of this house quick, but was that even possible him being my fiancé and all? I continued to watch him as he closed the door and locked it. Whew, I felt a little quiver just looking at him. Remain calm, always remain calm in situations such as this, sometimes you have to talk some sense into yourself. You can do this.

"Julian, we really need to talk." He came in and followed me into the kitchen. This was his first time coming to my house, and it was probably going to be his last. "I was wondering if you were about to just kick me out or what." He looked around, stopping at a painting I had on the wall between the kitchen and the hallway. "This is nice. Your place is really nice, but I guess it should be, Little Miss Decorator." I thanked him as I poured yet another glass of wine. If I didn't know myself, I would begin to think I was an alcoholic. Good thing I knew myself, so I continued to not only pour, but take a few sips as well. I needed a little help to give this I-can't-marry-you speech. I tried to tell him that I couldn't marry him, I tried over and over and over again. I tried to tell him that the only reason I had said yes was because he asked me in front of his family and that really put me on the spot. Didn't he know you never ask someone to marry you in front of a lot of people unless you are like 99.9% sure they are going to say yes? Okay he obviously missed that class in family life study or something. I tried to tell him that I had no choice but to say yes because I didn't want to ruin the family moment and then have everyone talking about it feeling sorry for him after we left. Either he did not comprehend what I was telling him or none of it seemed to matter to him. He just sat there not saying a word as if he were watching a movie. Finally I broke out, "Julian, are you even listening to me?"

"Yes, I hear you, but you ain't saying nothing. Your mouth is just moving, but nothing of any relevance is coming from your lips." He walked over to where I had been pacing, sipping my wine and giving my speech. He took my glass from my hand and set it down on the counter. He wrapped me in his arms. "Why are you making this so hard? I love you and you love me. What else is there?"

I felt the tears coming, and I knew they were being influenced by the alcohol. I kind of wished I hadn't kept drinking all that wine. "I'm sorry, Julian. I am so sorry, but I can't marry you." I felt a tear getting ready to run out my left eye, and I tried to hold on to it, but when I closed my eyes, it escaped and went running down my face with several of its friends.

He talked softly in my ear. "You can't or you don't want to?"

It wasn't that I didn't want to, but it was illegal in the United States to have two husbands, and I couldn't go to jail. "I just can't." The tears continued to escape, one after the other. It was a conspiracy.

"Shhh. Why you crying man?" He wiped my face. "Anya, I'm trying my best to make you happy, but every time I'm with you, you end up in tears. What's up with that, man?" He sounded a little frustrated. "What is it that you're not telling me?" He didn't allow me a chance to respond before his lips were over mine. I closed my eyes and enjoyed that moment, which felt so good.

"Julian, you gotta stop." My eyes remained closed. I tried to open them but I couldn't.

"Naw, you don't want me to stop."

"Yes, yes, I do." That was so weak I didn't even believe it myself. "I'm not having sex again until I get married." I moaned.

"Well let's got to the justice of the peace in the morning, and we can have a wedding later if you want, cause I'm going to make love to my wife tonight. I missed you so much, Anya. I don't care how many women I date and how cool they turn out to be, I still don't want nobody but you."

His words were slurred with passion, not alcohol. He was almost drooling as he kissed the side of my face and tried to speak. I tried not to let myself get caught up in the moment, but I couldn't help it. I was gone. Gone to Julianland, and I wondered if I would be able to find my way back. I wanted him so bad I could already feel it. He picked me up and set me on the counter, then he crawled up over me and laid me down. He kissed me with such hunger. Hunger for me and only me. Nothing could fill him up at this point but me. I began to remember how good we were together with every kiss, every touch. I began to feel all the old feelings that I had buried so long ago.

"Let me have you, Anya. You know we belong together."

His breath was not in my ear, and I was almost there until the phone rang. It scared me. "Let me up," I said, jumping down. "Whoa." Thank God for the phone ringing before I did something I was going to regret.

"I don't believe this. Don't answer it."

"Let me just see who it is." I picked up the phone and looked at the caller ID. It was Kim's cell phone number. I didn't answer it. I put the phone back on the charger and turned back toward Julian. He was leaning against the island counter in the middle of the floor. "Come here." I walked back over and stood next to him, looking down at the floor. I leaned my head over on his shoulder and interlocked my fingers with his, then pulled his arm. "I want to show you something." I led him out of the kitchen through the entryway and up the stairs down the hall to my bedroom.

"Huh Yeah, that's what I'm talking about. I wanna show you something too."

"You so nasty." I looked back at him a little disgusted.

"Yeah, but you like it though." I knew I use to, but I wasn't so sure I still did.

We stepped into my room, and I walked over to my dresser and opened the bottom drawer of my jewelry box. He sat down on the bed with his legs hanging off the side and laid back. I went over and plopped down next to him. "Scoot over," I said. "Look." I opened my hand and showed him the rhinestone string bracelet that he had made me so many years ago. He sat up and held it. He couldn't believe I still had it after all this time. But I did, because it was special to me, whether it was the real thing or not. And even though I now had the real thing, I would still always keep the homemade one because it was part of who I was back then and even who I am today.

"Man, I can't believe you really still have this. That's a trip."

"Yeah, I know, but I told you I did."

"I know, but I thought you were just talking."

I got up and went into my closet, all the way in the back and pulled out a box. I came and sat down next to him and opened it. It was my Julian box. It contained every card and every letter he had ever written to me. Every little love note from when we were young right on up to the letters he had written me when we first broke up. I had pictures and postcards from when he use to go to Alabama with is family every summer. There were booksmarks, mirrors he had won me at carnivals and fairs . . . you name it, it was in there. I read some of the letters from junior high, and we cracked up. "Aw, man, I was whipped." He laughed.

"Was? You still are." It was great, until he had to go getting all serious on me again.

"I still feel that way. Ain't nothin' changed except our age. You should know that by now." And I did. I leaned over and kissed him.

"I do know it," I said, looking him in the eyes, "but I still can't marry you."

"We're going to see about that. I ain't going nowhere. I gave up like a punk the first time around, but not this time. You were mine then, you're mine now, and you're always gon' be mine." He was serious too. If only I could make that happen for him, but I couldn't.

He rolled me over on the bed, smashing and crinkling all of my letters, but I didn't care. It was just like old times. He tickled me until I almost peed on myself. I kept begging him to stop, and I told him I was about to pee on myself, but he thought it was just a ploy to get him to stop. It wasn't. Little squirts began to come out. I tried to hold it, but I couldn't. Now my panties were wet pee pee panties. I was so mad. "You play too much." I yelled. "I told you to stop. I hate being tickled." I knew he didn't mean to do it, but I was still mad. I took my pants off and walked into the bathroom to start some water. I poured just a drop of bubbles into the tub because I knew I wasn't going to be in there but a second, just long enough to get the ickies off me. I took of my things, put them in the sink, ran water over them and hung them up. I took off the rest of my clothes and grabbed my robe from the back of the door to put on while I waited for the water to run.

I came out of the bathroom to put my stuff in the hamper inside my closet.

"Sorry." He looked at me and began to laugh.

"You can laugh all you want the whole ride home. Come on let me walk you to the door before my water finishes."

"You can't be serious." He looked puzzled.

"I'm quite serious."

"All because of a little bodily fluid. Come on now, Anya. Quit trippin'." I stood there as if to say come on, let's go. He stood. "You a trip," he barked at me as he walked past on his way out the bedroom. We went downstairs, and he grabbed his coat and hat and began putting them on.

"I'll call you tomorrow," I said.

"Come on, Anya. Don't put me out, man. You know you want me to stay."

I kissed him softly at the door. He was begging so hard. Then I remembered my bath. "Oh shoot, my water." I made a mad dash for the stairs. I leaned into the tub and turned the water off, and when I turned around, I turned right into him. He kissed me one last time, and that was all it took. It all happened so fast. I know he was the one who initiated it by taking my robe belt a loose, but I guess I didn't have to reciprocate by undoing his belt and then his pants, then his coat and his sweater. His pants were down around his ankles, so he stepped out of his boots to step out of the pants. The movements were frantic. I snatched his hat from his head and I kissed him long and hard, until he lifted me up onto the sink and the begging ceased. After I finally let him have me, all over the bathroom, we ended up in the tub, relaxing. Well I imagine he was relaxing. I felt like crap, but fully and completely satisfied crap.

How could I let this happen? What was wrong with me? I had a man in Cali, a rich one at that who was in love with me, who treated me like a queen and there I was in Philly being a ho. Go figure. I played it back in my head as I lay there in the tub with Julian. I wanted to stop myself, but the moment was just too right, and it was too good, and I gave into every flesh-pleasing touch he gave. This could not continue. I was startled out of my thoughts of guilt by his words of pleasure. "That was even better than old times."

It's a trip that I could give a smile of total and complete pleasure and at the same time feel the guilt that filled my heart. No matter how I looked at the situation, there was nothing right about it other than the self-satisfying feeling of getting some.

I stood to get out of the tub. "Where you going?" He grabbed my hand.
"To dry off and go to bed." I pulled my towel from the rack. He followed suit short after I did. I was putting on my lotion when he came in the room wrapped in just a towel. He grabbed the lotion and began to rub my back. His touch felt so good. He kissed my neck before making it to my mouth. The kiss was still just as intense as it was before we did it. Now that was a problem. He pinned me down on the bed, I attempted to fight him off I my head, but that really did no good. A little naked kissing was one thing, not that it was right, but I couldn't do it again. This was really cheating. Not that kissing isn't, but this was cheating beyond control. That's exactly what it was, too, beyond my control. I continued to fight in my head, but no matter how much I did, my body just would not go along with it. It went until it was too late. Julian got up and went in the bathroom to get his pants, and I saw him pull another condom from them. That was the break I needed, the chance I needed to think straight, my moment to stop it before it happened again, but I didn't. I didn't have enough willpower. I just watched him and anticipated feeling his warmth again. I had lost from that moment forward until it was over, and I was filled once again with the guilty pleasure that I would hate myself for the next day. I should have just given Michael some the night before, then I probably would have been able to hold out and resist the sweet chocolate temptation that lay before me. It was

too late to dwell on the what-ifs. It was way too late for that. The only question left was what would happen? I pulled the covers back, and we slid into the bed and rested.

I woke up to a startling phone chiming in my ears, I jumped up, reached over Julian and grabbed it. I looked at the caller ID. It was my fiancé. Imagine that. You wouldn't know I had one the way I had carried on just a few hours ago. I whispered good morning as I quietly slid out of the bed, trying not to wake Julian. I went to the bathroom, grabbed my robe and put it on as I headed for the hallway.

"Good morning, beautiful. You sound tired. Were you still asleep?" I was but that didn't matter. "Why didn't I hear from you last night when you got in from Traci's? I fell asleep waiting for you to call or I would have called you."

Thankful that he had fallen asleep, I explained that I had had a little too much to drink and that when Kim dropped me off I came upstairs with every intention of calling him but I guess I laid across the bed and fell asleep and now it was 9:45 in the morning. I was turning into a big fat liar and boy, was it ugly, especially since I was becoming so good at it. This couldn't be a good sign.

The other line rang, I looked at the caller ID. It was Kim. I didn't click over and answer it because, "Lucy I got some splainin' to do." She called right back so I asked Michael to hold on so I could just tell her I would call her back. I clicked over.

"Kim let me call you right back."

"I don't think so. Open the door, tramp. What is Julian's car still doing parked in your driveway?"

Great, I thought, *that's all I need.* I looked out the window and there she was, sitting in her silver Infinity SUV on the phone with me. Dang I couldn't stand her. What was she doin' up this early anyway? We didn't even leave Traci's 'til after twelve. "Alright." I knew I appeared irritated, but that was only because I was. "I'm going to unlock the door but be quiet when you come in because I'm on the phone with Michael."

"You on the phone with Michael? Where's Julian?"

"He sleep!" I clicked back over and apologized to Michael and told him Kim was outside and wanted me to let her in.

"I guess she came to get all the info she can about your trip out here, huh?'

"What else would have her up and out this early on a day she's not working?" We continued to talk for a little while. The whole time Kim paced impatiently waiting for me to hang up. Finally, I did. I couldn't even wait for her to say anything. I just looked at her. "I feel so bad, Kim. What am I doing?"

"I been trying to figure that out all month. You should feel bad. What are you thinking?" Now that's not what a best friend is suppose to say, is it? She's suppose to be like, girl, don't trip. It happened. It's over. Men do it all the time. You cool." Or even a "just don't let it happen again" or anything other than what she had just said.

"You messin' up, Anya. I just have to be real. I love you like a sister, and you are my best friend on this whole earth, but you are about to end up with neither one of them playing this game you playing. 'Oh I don't know what to do. Oh I'm so confused," she mimicked me. "You know exactly what to do. Choose, make a choice and stick to it, and in the meantime, keep your legs closed and quit going around telling people you gon' marry 'em if you ain't.'"

How cold was that? I knew from that comment I had sunk to the lowest of lows. Kim usually always had my back, no matter what. In the past we had always been able to rationalize our screw-ups, but not this time. This time I could tell she was not happy with me and there would be no women's lib empowerment speech that day. It didn't matter because being truthful was part of really being a friend. A real friend can check you and y'all still best friends the next day.

"Anya, I could see if Michael was a dog and if you didn't really care about him, but if you do, you're about to blow it. I know you think you still in love with Julian, and I know you probably feel obligated because of what you did to him, but that's life. That kind of stuff happens, and you don't owe him anything, especially not your life. You only owe it to yourself to be happy. Y'all need to quit holding on to that teenage love and move on. You're both two different people now, very different. I'm not saying that there's anything wrong with Julian. You know he will always be like family, but can you honestly say you want to be married to him and spend the rest of your life with him? Anya. The rest is a long time."

It was, I agreed but it didn't make me any less confused. I was desperate for an answer. I just wanted to make sure I was doing the right thing. How do you know though? Everything always seems right while you're doing it. It's the aftermath that always comes back to bite you in the butt. I put on a pot of coffee and attempted to change the subject. "Hey, you want to see my boots and my purse Michael got me?"

She reluctantly agreed. I knew she wanted to see them but she wanted to talk about the mess I was in even more.

We were looking at my boots, and she was trying them on when Julian came down the stairs practically floating.

"I thought I heard another voice down here. What's up, girl?" He looked at Kim.

"Apparently you." She looked over at him then looked over at me.

"You ain't knowin'." He passed by us on his way to the kitchen.

"Naw you the one ain't knowin'," she said under her breath.

"Shut up before he hears you." I frowned at her. "And take off my boots while you getting all comfortable, because this is one pair that you will not be borrowing, I repeat will not, meaning no never." This day was already shaping up to be a long one.

"Are you going to cook something?" Julian called from the kitchen.

"I hadn't planned on it," I hollered back.

"I know you kiddin' after the performance I gave last night. I know you gon' feed me."

"Oh yeah, I can definitely see why you're having such a hard time making a decision." She rolled her eyes and shook her head. She sat on the floor and took off the boots. "Well, on that note, I'm out. Call you later, that is if your fiancé ain't givin' an encore performance."

Ooh, I couldn't stand her. I hated when she was right.

Before Julian left that weekend I explained to him that I had made a huge mistake and that I could not just be having sex with him.

"You didn't seem to have no problem last night." I gave him that. It was true, but I did have an inner struggle that he knew nothing about.

"Okay, what about phone sex? Does that count?" I could still hear the stupidity coming from his mouth and bombarding my head. Maybe Kim was right. I was about to blow the best adult relationship I had ever been in holding on to the past.

"No sex. Don't you get it? No sex at all." I wondered what was so hard to comprehend about that. Maybe I needed all this to happen to make me realize what I was almost thinking of giving up. I know that cheating on your fiancé, your real fiancé is not the ideal way to come to that realization, but better before the marriage than during right? So I kissed him good-bye that Saturday after we had come from the movies, I watched him get in his truck and drive off. At that point it was settled in my heart that he was not the man for me. I went into the house, got my real engagement ring and placed it back on my finger. I had tried to give Julian his ring back earlier that day, but he wouldn't accept it.

Moving On

That Monday I went straight to the storage closet when I got to work, before even going to my office. I got a Fed Ex envelope, some bubble wrap and a small box. I walked down to my office, making the morning greetings along the way with a "how was your holiday?" here and there. I got to my office and set my purse on my desk, then reached in and took out Julian's ring and bracelet and set them down. I cut the bubble wrap and placed the ring and the beautiful bracelet that I wanted so badly to keep in it, then I folded it up and taped it. I placed it in the box and taped that up then slid it into the envelope along with a little note: *the last few months have been great, but it's just not meant to be. I don't know any other way to say it for you to understand. I just can't be with you. It's time for us to let go of the past. Sorry. No regrets.* I made a little smiley face and signed my name. I sealed my fate and took it out to the front desk to be sent off.

The next few months leading up to the wedding were hectic to say the least, but I was glad because it made the time go faster. And after only about sixty-five dresses, I finally found the perfect one. The only problem was I was really pushing it waiting so late to order it. I almost got scared at first because no dress was the right one, no matter how much Kim and Traci tried to talk me into them. I thought maybe it was a sign, you know me and those signs, that maybe I shouldn't be getting married. But then finally this one bridal shop called me and told me they were more than positive they had the perfect dress. They knew how hard I had been looking and they assured me my search was over. Unfortunately, the shop was in New York, so I had to go up there one weekend to see it. So off we went, me Traci and Kim. We decided to make a girls' weekend out of it. You know shopping, spa, martinis, the whole nine. My treat. I was mere weeks away from being a millionaire. Of course I called Michael first to make sure it was okay for me to spend the money. I knew he wouldn't mind but still, I thought I should.

It was only right since I had been dragging Kim and Traci all over the east coast looking for dresses.

Monica, the girl who called from the bridal shop was right. The dress was gorgeous. It was so plain and so simple that it was amazing. When I slid my body into it, I knew it was the one. Of course it wasn't my exact size, but I could visualize it fitting my every curve, how it would wrap my body when made to my exact measurements. I had Monica to call the manufacturer to ensure that I would get it in time for the wedding and they assured her I would. You would think with me marrying Michael Harrison, I would have had something made by some fabulous famous designer, but I didn't think about it until Michael mentioned it after I told him that I finally found a dress. Men, they just don't think. I was happy though. May 5 was going to be a day to remember. It was going to be perfect. I couldn't wait until he saw me in my dress.

I was, for the first time, beginning to get a little excited. I had placed the order for the invitations through a printer friend of Asha's so I could get them back and get them out to everyone in time to get reasonable airfare and to lock in the rate on the block of rooms at the Waldorf. The Waldorf, I just loved saying that. It sounded so rich. So Saturday night, the three of us sat up and stuffed my invitations during our girls' weekend. I brought them with me because I wanted to be able to drop them off to the calligrapher for addressing when I got back.

As we were sitting at the table in the hotel suite, we laughed, joked and acted crazy like we did when we were younger. See, if I moved to California, these moments would be few and far between. I missed them already, and I wasn't even sure I was going anywhere. We talked about old boyfriends, high school, the up and downs of life and how no matter what we did, God always seemed to work things out in the end.

"So do you miss Julian?" my sister said without looking up from the invitation she was working on. I couldn't believe she even had the nerve to bring up his name after the way she acted with me during the whole Julian incident. It's funny how it had been reduced to just an incident. I looked off into nowhere and sighed. Or maybe I was looking back into somewhere, somewhere where my life once included him.

"Yes, I do, and I think I always will, but I knew it was time to finally let go so that I could move forward with my life. Some days are harder than others, and there are days I wonder if I'm doing the right thing, but this just seems to make the most sense, so I'm just going to do it and never look back."

"Never." Traci looked sad for me.

"Never." I felt sad for me.

Personally, I think that's best for everyone. I mean it's not like you can just be friends. Y'all have too much history. Your marriage to Mike will never work if you keep looking back at what could have been. I don't mean to sound harsh, but you know I'm telling the truth." Kim was right this time.

I still got letters from Julian. I had just gotten a card from him the day before we left for New York, and he continued to leave voicemails expressing his love for me. Sometimes, they actually scared me because he sounded so obsessed, but I kept tellin' him he was really going to have to let go because it just was not meant to be. I knew that I loved him too. I wasn't trying to make it sound one-sided, but I wasn't crazy in love. I wasn't sick in love. I wasn't I-can't-live-without-you in love. I didn't know if I ever really felt like that before. Even with John, I think it was more pride than anything else. Sometimes we would talk a little bit, but it would always end with him doing this whiny profession of love that kind of left me feeling that he was a little unbalanced. I felt so bad sometimes and so guilty, but I would have felt even more guilty messin over Michael. Eventually I had to stop taking Julian's calls. If I would see his number on caller ID, I dared not answer. He tricked me one day and blocked his number, and I answered. So I didn't even answer blocked or anonymous calls. I just couldn't take it.

"Sorry, Anya, I didn't mean to upset you, I just wondered how you were coming with the whole letting-go thing," my sister said.
"No, Traci, don't worry. I'm okay."
"Well, on a lighter note, since we're all here," she said with this goofy smirk on her face, "I guess I can tell y'all." Kim and I both looked at each other like what could this be about? Traci got up, got her purse, came back and sat at the table. She pulled out a little velvet bag and undid the drawstring. She turned the bag upside down, and a few seconds later, a ring dropped into her hand. She proceeded to put the ring on her finger and tell us that Kevin had proposed last Sunday when they had gone to dinner.

How she just gon' keep that from us all this time and we had been bonding in New York since the night before? What was this sistership coming to?
"Oh, man. I can't believe it, Traci." I jumped across the table to hug her, I was so happy. This had been a long time coming. I couldn't believe they were finally going to make it official. She had been waiting for a good time to tell me because she knew that I had been occupied with work and with planning my wedding. She just wanted the focus to remain on me. I was just in shock.

"Yeah." She giggled like a schoolgirl. "I talked to him about the blocked tube, and at first he was so mad, not mad at me because I couldn't have kids, but mad because I didn't think he loved me enough to stay with me in spite of it. He's okay now, apparently." She wiggled her finger in the air, allowing the light to bounce off her ring. We're not giving up on children though. We're going to try artificial insemination after the wedding, which by the way, we have decided to do in August. Nothing big, something real small and simple."

"Traci no, you have to have a wedding." I cried out. As long as they waited, everyone and their grandmother would wanna be there to witness it.

"Naw, Anya, we already talked about it. It's going to be real simple so that we can go ahead and do it. We don't want to wait another year just so we can have time to plan a wedding." I guess she was right. The important thing was that they were finally doing it.

"So he's cool with the artificial bit?" Kim looked a little puzzled. Traci nodded, and I believed this called for a celebration. I called room service to have some champagne sent up, then I called Kevin.

"Hey, what's up soon-to-be official brother?"

"Oh, she finally told y'all, huh?"

"Yes, she finally let the cat out the bag. I can't believe she waited a whole week before she told me. Kevin, I am so happy for you guys. This has been a long time coming."

"Way too long," Kim hollered in the background.

"I guess you heard Kim, right?"

"I know, but she was worth the wait, I guess." He laughed into the phone. "You know everybody can't be like you, saying yes to every proposal they get." He was now laughing hysterically into my ear. Me? I was not amused.

"Okay, your man is about to get hurt over here, Traci."

"Alright, alright, you know I'm just messin' with you, but for real though, you really going to marry Michael?"

"Yeah, far as I know, but you know me, you never can tell." I chuckled. "Okay, well I just wanted to say congrats and tell you that I love you. Talk to you later."

"Alright. Put my wife on the phone." I handed the phone to Traci, and they talked for a few minutes. She went off in the corner, all in love like they had not been together forever and a day. But that was good. I hoped after me and Mike were together that long we'd still be mushy in love.

We managed to finish every last envelope in spite of the champagne. I called Michael and told him we had done them. He was all excited. I could hear it in his voice. "Anya, I can't believe we're about to get married. I was in bed last night staring at the ceiling, wondering if I was ready for this." What? Wait a minute, he was what? "But I think it was just nerves, because I can't think of anything I've ever wanted more in my life, even that Oscar." He laughed. "Than to make you my wife." I was relieved. "I am so glad you called. I needed to hear your voice, but more than that, I need to see you. I can't wait for the premiere, but it seems so far away."

Oh, the premiere? Yes, the movie he shot in New York when we first met. Well the premiere was the first week in April. I still couldn't believe I was marrying a celebrity. I hoped I knew what I was getting myself into. I agreed though, I didn't want to wait that long either, but we did need to keep visits to a minimum because our flesh was weak, weak, weak. I still felt guilty about giving Julian some on Christmas. I got mad at myself every time I thought about it, but at the same time, it was so good that I thought about that too.

Everything was going so smooth, too smooth to be real life. My dress was finally ordered. The invitations were on their way to being completed. I ordered my headpiece and my shoes the same day and place I got my dress. I had pretty much already had in mind what I wanted but of course I had to wait until I found a dress to make sure it would all go. My girls' dresses were picked, but I still had to find their shoes and earrings, but that shouldn't be too hard. The cake and the menu had been decided, the hotel was booked for the reception, and the church was booked for the wedding. I had my toasting glasses and the cake cutter. The only major thing left was to decide on the favors and my bouquet. Like I said, everything was going smooth. We decided not to register because there was really nothing we needed and plus, with us getting married away from both our homes, it would be more hassle transporting the gifts to one place or the other. We thought about putting on the invitations *please no gifts, just the gift of your presence is enough,* but it sounded so over the top, so we just didn't include a registry card. I think that means people will give gift cards and money for the most part.

The Premiere

Michael's big day was at hand, and I had flown in the night before to be there with him. I had never gone to a real Hollywood premiere. I mean I had been to local premieres but never the ones that had the actual actors there live and in person, and I had definitely never been the guest of one of those live actors, let alone the fianceé. I was real nervous, but of course I tried not to let it show. I had a dress made for the premiere because I didn't want to make Michael look bad buying off the rack. I didn't think stars and their spouses bought clothing off the rack for this kind of stuff, and since I wasn't sure, I thought I'd better not. When you're famous and you have something made to wear to something special does that mean you can't wear it again? What if you really like it? I guess that doesn't matter much, huh? I couldn't get with that. If I was spending twenty-five hundred dollars on an outfit you can best believe you're going to see it again.

Okay, it was show time. We showered and got ready to go. I had Tamera, my stylist, do my hair Thursday before I left, and I was pretty good about keeping it up. I put on my lashes and eyeliner. I traced my lips and filled them in. I threw my mole over my left upper lip and coated my lips with lip glass. I took my shoes out of the box. They were kickin'. They had one really thin silver strap across my toes, that were lined with rhinestones, then there was another thin rhinestone strap around the ankle that buckled on the side, I fell in love with them at Nordstrom's when I saw them online. I put them on and admired them. The shoes were enough to make the dress, but I didn't rely on the shoes to pull the weight. I slid into my yellow sequined silk tie-dye backless dress. I didn't want it cut too low in the back though, because I didn't want to look like a slut. It had spaghetti straps made of rhinestones. It might not sound all that great to you, but you had to see me in it to fully appreciate it. I know Michael did. That would do it. I got my purse and put my necessities in it then I took one last look in the mirror and fixed a few curls that had fallen. My hair was really curly and all pinned up. I had found a pair of clear yellow chopsticks, and I glued rhinestones all the way down them on two sides, I stuck them through my hair and was completely satisfied with the results. If only I could have gotten my butterflies to go away, I would have been straight.

Michael came to the door. "You almost ready? The car is here." I added one more spray of perfume, walked over and opened the door. "Whoa. Girl, you look good."

"You're not looking too bad yourself." He had on a black Armani tux. How can you ever go wrong with that?

"I don't know if the world is ready for you in that dress." He spun me around, taking in the view from every angle. Suddenly, I felt self-conscious.

"What? Is it too much?" I looked at him like I was in high school, needing his approval. I was worried that maybe I had overdone it. I just wanted everything to be perfect for him. This was also going to be my intro to Hollywood, and I wanted to look as if I belonged, but not like I was trying too hard. I panicked.

"Calm down. You look great. I'm just saying you look so good I don't think they're ready for my fiancée. Come. We have a premiere to attend," he said very proper and stuck his arm out for me to slide mine through. We walked arm and arm right down the stairs out the front door and to the limo.

"Good evening, Miss Dennings. I think you might steal the old man's thunder tonight," our driver, Mr. Jon, said tipping his hat and opening the door. We got in, and off we went.

On the ride there, Hollywood looked so different at night. With all the lights, it was beautiful. Some of it was a little sad though. There were all these homeless people and you couldn't help but wonder, at least I in my ignorance couldn't help but wonder, what happened to them. I always thought of Hollywood as this glitzy, glamorous place, but some parts had no glitz and very little glamour, and it was sad. I almost felt guilty riding in a limo as we passed them by. They were probably the results of many broken dreams, and at that very moment there was nothing I could do.

"Anya. Anya."

"Oh, sorry, I didn't hear you."

"Are you okay?"

"Yes, I'm fine, just a little nervous."

"Not to worry. One thing you'll learn in Hollywood, you will never be able to please everybody, so just focus on pleasing yourself. If you like what you're wearing, never let anyone else make you question yourself, okay?"

"No, really, I'm okay. I don't believe you would let me go out here and make a fool of myself."

"Never." He squeezed my hand and smiled at me.

When we arrived, we had to sit in the limo for a minute and wait for our turn to make our way onto the red carpet. It was more overwhelming than I had anticipated. Everything was moving so fast. Reporters were asking questions and flashing pictures every step of the walk down. I would graciously stand aside when Michael would decide to stop and answer a reporter or reach over in the crowd and sign an autograph. I knew a lot of them were wondering who I was but no one had the nerve to ask until we were almost in and a reporter from E! asked, "So who is this stunning young woman here beside you, Michael?"

He smiled. I wondered what he was going to say, but not for long. "This beautiful young woman is my fiancée, Anya, whom you'll see by my side pretty much from this day forward." He lifted my hand, kissed it, said thank you to the reporters and then we went in to take our seats. There was a lot of handshaking and hugging along the way as he introduced me to his friends and coworkers, I guess they're still considered coworkers, even if they are these larger-than-life actors and actresses. Everyone was so nice to me, and Michael just kept introducing me as his fiancée and I was loving every minute of it. Everyone would hug me and tell me congratulations and I received so many compliments on my dress. By the end of the night, I was pooped from the premiere to the after party. But you know what? It was great. I had an absolute ball.

When we got back to the house, I wanted to call Kim and tell her all about it. About all the celebrities I had met, about the success of my dress, how good the movie was, everything. I even wanted to tell her that Hollywood had homeless people. I still couldn't get over that. I didn't call though because of the time difference. It would all have to wait until the next day. I sat on the edge of the bed unfastening my shoes. I felt Michael watching me as he leaned against the doorframe of the bedroom door. I could tell he was glad to be able to finally unveil me to his friends. He had been talking about me for months, but no one had ever seen me other than his parents. I think a lot of people were surprised. I guess Michael had been this hunky Hollywood bachelor for so long that no one ever thought of him as the settling-down type, but time changes even the baddest of habits.

When it was time to head back home, I really could honestly say that I didn't want to leave. I had enjoyed every moment I'd spent with Michael. This time we stayed in separate bedrooms so as to keep the naughtiness to a minimum, and it seemed to work out very well. I stared at him across the breakfast table the next morning and was glad that I had met my ex husband John and that he did me so cold that I warded off men and went through the liberating moment that drove me to go to New York by myself last year for New Year's Eve, because if all that hadn't happened, I might not have been sitting across from this fabulous man. I smiled at him as the thought went through my head. It really was all working together for my good, even when it didn't feel like it.

A few weeks later, Traci called me at work. "Anya, you have to go to the store and get the new *Entertainment* magazine." I instantly got scared. Why? Was something wrong? Was it something bad about Michael that was going to make me look stupid once again?

"Hurry up and call me back as soon as you get it." I hurried to finish up what I was doing. I rushed down to the newsstand in the lobby of our building. I grabbed a Snapple and a doughnut and scanned the magazines for the *Entertainment*. I couldn't believe my eyes. In the upper right corner there was a picture of me and Michael apparently taken at the premiere. There was a small caption below. "Engaged?" It was a picture of us holding hands as he waved to the crowd outside the premiere. I rushed and turned to page thirty-eight for the details as the cover had instructed. Yip, there it was, another picture, with us still holding hands and him kissing me on the cheek. I was smiling as if I was really enjoying it, which no doubt I was. The small paragraph talked about the big box office number the movie had done its first weekend and how Michael was working on a new picture blah blah blah. However, the caption under the picture read. *Michael Harrison pictured here with fiancé Anya Dennings.*

I made my way to the register to pay for my stuff. I was still tripping. This was really about to be my life in like two weeks. I rushed back upstairs to call my sister. "Girl, are you trippin' or what? Can you believe yo' butt is in *Entertainment* with Michael Harrison no less?" But I couldn't believe it. I could not believe it at all. I thought for sure one of these days I would wake up and my life would be back to normal. I wondered what this would mean for me. I liked being normal. I didn't want to be known as Michael Harrison's fiancée or wife. I just wanted to be plain ole Anya. At least my name was included I wasn't just labeled as one of his belongings.

When I got off the phone with Traci, I called Michael who of course didn't answer his phone because he had already begun rehearsals for his new picture. So I just left a message. I had to admit it was a little scary because I was a very private person. Us going out and him signing autographs and stuff didn't bother me, but I wasn't sure I liked the fact that people would take a picture of me and publish it and not even get my permission. I didn't know if I liked that at all. I guess entertainers were just used to it. I'm not sure I wanted to live my life in the public's eye.

Life just kept on getting better and better. That Thursday, I was sitting at my desk when I got a buzz on the intercom that I had a visitor who didn't want to give his name. I thought right away it was Michael surprising me. I opened my door excited beyond control and walked to the front only to find Julian standing there.

"Don't look so surprised, Anya."

"Hey," I kind of stuttered. "What are you doing here?"

"Naw the question is what are you doing here." He held the magazine up and pointed to the picture of me and Michael. There was rage in his face and his eyes were red, but I don't know if they were red from crying, or maybe driving, if he drove or plain old lack of sleep. But one thing for sure was that I wished I wasn't looking into them.

"So this is why you couldn't marry me," he yelled in disbelief. "Anya, you ain't nothing. How you just gon' be scandalous like that?" I was so embarrassed. How dare he come to my place of employment and act a fool? "What? You marrying this fool 'cause he got money or 'cause he famous or what? I know you can't possibly love this fool." I wanted to quiet him down, but I was just stuck, stuck on stupid as I stood there by the reception desk. Asha came out of her office, and no one would say anything. Everyone just held their peace and looked on in amazement, but I guess I asked for it.

"So what's up? Don't just stand there."

But stand there was all I could do, until finally I said, "Julian, just come into my office and let's talk about this."

"You know, Anya, I don't get you. Maybe you're right. Maybe we are two different people. I guess I just didn't realize what kind of person you had become."

"Julian, please." I turned and walked toward my office, motioning him to follow, but he wouldn't. "Naw, I'm cool. I don't need to come into your little office to hear more of your bull. You just don't want me out here because you don't want the people you work with to know how scandalous you are. How you said you would marry me then said you couldn't and told me you wasn't messin' with nobody else." I could tell he had definitely had a few drinks along the way. "Not this time, Anya. We're not going to do it your way this time. I will stand out here as long as I want until people know who you really are."

"You know, Julian, I really don't have to deal with this. I can call security and have you removed in the blink of an eye or you can come into my office and I can make you some coffee, and we can talk about the situation."

"Oh, I'm a situation now. Y'all hear that?" He looked around the office. "I'm a situation. I'm cool with that though. I don't need to come into your office, Ms. Dennings, to discuss anything else," he said mockingly. "To tell you the truth, there's nothing you could say at this point. I mean how can you explain a fiancé? Oh my fault, probably the same way you didn't explain me to him, right?" He threw the magazine at me as he turned and walked down the hall toward the elevators. I wanted to go after him because I didn't want him to hate me, but I guess you can't always have the best of both worlds. I looked over at my assistant and gave her the look, so she knew not to even ask, at least not that day, but that didn't stop Asha from coming into my office, slamming the door behind her and chewing me out. She told me that was her business and when I came there it was my business too, and to leave the personal mess at home where it belonged, or in the future I wouldn't be there to worry about it. The simple truth was I had made my bed, and I was now lying in it.

Asha suggested I go home early, to get this matter cleared up because she did not want to see Julian grace those halls again. It wasn't really a suggestion. I got in my car and put in the *Waiting to Exhale* soundtrack and made my way home. It was clearly one of those days. I entered the place I called home and went straight upstairs to take my clothes off even though it was only two o'clock. I got under the covers and turned on the TV. I tried not to think about what had just happened, but I couldn't stop seeing the look on Julian's face. How could I do this to him again.? First John, now Michael. I guess 'cause he let me. I know that's no excuse, but he did. I guess I really didn't love him the way he loved me. I thought it was a done deal, but this fool came all the way from Chicago for a ten-minute confrontation. Please. I never would. I don't think I'd ever be that in love. I guess that's obvious though. Well at least it was out in the open now, and it had been dealt with or so I thought.

Around seven o'clock my doorbell rang. I went over and looked out the window. It was Julian. I stood there for a minute debating if I should even answer. What could he want? To go off on me even more? Maybe he hadn't gotten it all out of his system yet. I did owe him that at least, so I opened the door and let him in. The first words out of his mouth were "You know I'm not about to let you marry him, right? You're my wife. Girl, I love you and ain't nothing ever going to change that. I don't know what it's going to take to make you understand that." But I did understand, but obviously he didn't realize that you can't make someone love you and I had moved on and wasn't coming back. How did he even know about the picture anyway? Somebody had to tell him. He didn't even read stuff like that. I looked at his little sad face, but I didn't feel bad enough to leave Michael.

"Julian, it's time to let go. I love you, too, and I probably always will, but if it's okay to say, I love Michael, too, and I'm happy, and if you really love me like you say you do then you'll love me enough to let me go and allow me to be happy. I wasn't trying to hide it from you. I just didn't have the heart to tell you, and when I ran into you last summer, it confused me and made me temporarily doubt my love for him because I still had such strong feelings for you. But I'm not confused anymore."

"How long you been with dude?

"A little over a year." I couldn't believe I was actually answering questions truthfully for a change.

"And you sure you love him?" I nodded. "Alright then. I don't ever want to lose our friendship, so if you say this is really want you want, I'm going to respect that. "I guess that's it then. I wish you luck. Maybe I should be wishing him luck. He's the one going to need it, dealing with you, Cybil." We both gave a weak chuckle. Closure is so sad sometimes, but I knew it was the only way I could have a healthy relationship with my husband. He walked over and wrapped his hand around mine. "Don't forget me man."

"How could I after your little display earlier?" I smiled.

"Oh yeah, sorry about that." I knew he was sorry and embarrassed he came to my office doin' the fool. He leaned in and kissed me on my mouth. My brain had a slight temporary meltdown because I didn't push him away. To be truthful I was enjoying it until he abruptly pulled away. I stood there with my mouth half open as he stepped back.

"You said you love him, right?"

"Um, Yeah." I tried to pull it back together.

"I can tell," he said sarcastically as he opened the door and walked out.

Why did he do that? That wasn't right, not at all. It might have been true, but it wasn't right. I couldn't believe I let him get me like that. Why didn't I stop him when he first attempted to kiss me? So there I was again, back in a state of confusion. If I wasn't doing the right thing, it was too late because in two weeks I was going to be Mrs. Michael Harrison whether I was suppose to be or not. There was absolutely no way I could back out of this wedding, even if I wanted to and not saying that I did, I'm just saying, if I did and *if* is a very big word. Who said I even wanted to back out? I mean it was just a kiss. I'd be fine as long as I didn't see Julian and that wouldn't be a problem. If I talked to him, I'd be okay, but if I saw him, my flesh would get weak, and I tried to control myself, at least I thought I did. But after what just happened, I doubted we'd even be talking. Besides, what would there be to talk about? All our past conversations had been about us building a life together, and that obviously wasn't going to happen. Whatever this thing was with Julian, it would be over once I got married. I wouldn't have to worry about seeing him or talking to him anymore. Therefore, I would be instantly cured. I tell you, this wedding couldn't come fast enough.

I went back upstairs in an effort to escape myself, but I was with me no matter where I went. I slid back into bed under the covers. This drama was even too much for the kind of comfort my Ralph Lauren down comforter normally offered. After several attempts to escape, I got out of bed and went downstairs to see what fatty substance I could find to fill my belly and my emotions. Nothing. Nothing would do it. Not ice cream, not cheesecake, not even the leftover pasta from Penne's. This definitely meant there was a problem. No matter, I was going to forge ahead and be happy no matter the cost.

I sat at the table stuffing my face with Mocha Almond Fudge ice cream, but still no gratification came. The more I thought about it, I was glad Julian finally knew the truth. I felt bad he was hurt, of course, but it's hard trying to be everything to two men at the same time. How do women do it? Please would somebody share the great mystic secret with me? Was there a class they all took that I along with several others missed? Why did it affect me this way? I guess it didn't make much difference now. I was a one-man woman, and that's how God designed it to be.

I really needed to be asleep though with this being my last week in the office until after Michael and I came back from Fiji, which was where we were going on our honeymoon. I was really excited about that. I couldn't wait. I just imagined it being all romantic and exotic. Hopefully it would be. I promised myself that I would not work right up until a day or two before the wedding. I wanted to be relaxed and stress free so I had to get as much done as possible by the end of the week. I was determined to have nothing on my mind other than getting through the ceremony without passing out. It seemed as if the closer I got to the wedding, the more unreal everything around me began to seem. People would talk to me, and I knew they were talking to me because they'd be looking directly at me and often they would even say my name, and most times, I would have some idea of what they were talking about, but the words would sound distant and faint and sort of distorted. It was a trip. Nevertheless, the show must go on.

Time Already

Time was in fact ready. The question was, was I? I was calm as I could be as I packed my bag. I was running around like a chicken with my head cut off. Kim was there with me, and we had made a checklist a few weeks prior, which stayed on the refrigerator so if I thought of things I wanted to add, I could just write them down. I think we had everything well covered and we were going to be in New York three days before the wedding so if by chance we forgot anything we could always buy it or I could send Kevin by the house on his way up Friday. We went over everything at least three times, and we were satisfied that we hadn't forgotten anything. I didn't feel excited or nervous or even anxious. The truth is I didn't feel anything at all. I wasn't even scared. I was just going with the flow as usual. Kim and I took all my stuff downstairs and set it next to hers because we were leaving at ten the next morning. She was staying over at my house and I was glad. My sister was riding up with us, too, but she was going to come the following morning.

I took two Tylenol PM because I wanted to make sure I slept through the night just in case I started thinking too much and began to get anxious. My alarm went off at six. I wasn't really going to get up until seven, but I figured it would take about an hour to wake myself up from those pills. I eventually got up and got into the shower around 6:45. I put on a sweat suit and went down the hall to wake Kim. To my surprise she was already up and in the shower. I couldn't believe it. That girl loved sleep more than me. I went downstairs to the kitchen and put a bagel in the toaster and took the crèam cheese out the fridge. About 8:15 my sister arrived. I went out to her car to help her bring her stuff in. We set it by the door with the rest of the stuff that had to go. You would think we were going to be gone for months not days. Even with my luggage for the honeymoon it still looked like we were going to be gone way longer than we really were.

Since I had a few minutes to spare, I called Michael. "Hey."

"Hey yourself. You alright?" he asked. I was fine. I just wanted to hear his voice. I actually couldn't wait to see him. I was more excited about seeing him than I was about getting married. I know that's awful, but it was true.

"Okay, get off the phone. The car is here." Kim and her big mouth came barging into my room. I told Michael that I would call him once we got settled in the car and got on the road.

"No you don't have to. I know y'all are about to have a girls' ride. Enjoy yourself. Besides, when I talk to you, it makes me miss you more and then I can't focus."

"Okay then I'll see you Friday at rehearsal."

"Now don't be ridiculous. I'll be talking to you before I see you."

"Yes, sir." I laughed "Well I'll call you tonight, but I'll see you Thursday."

"That you will, Mrs. Harrison. That you will. I love you."

"I know. I love you too."

"Oh Lord, let's go." Kim took the phone from my hand and hung it up.

The limo had arrived at 9:50. We had decided not to drive ourselves so we could just kick back and relax, and of course with Philly being so close to New York, it made no sense to fly even though I sometimes did. The driver began loading the car, and we helped because we had so much crap, we felt bad. I grabbed the bag I had packed with fruits, snacks and juice.

"Well, this is it, you guys," I said as I locked up the house and put on the alarm. Traci had my dress over her arm because we didn't want to put it in the trunk. She laid it across the side seat in the car, and Kim and I got in. We were all packed up and ready to go. And we were off, headed for the rest of my life. Kim couldn't wait to pop open the champagne, so we just mixed it with a little orange juice, you know that makes it legal to drink champagne that early. We hadn't even made it off my block before she got the glasses out.

"Well, girl, you ready for this?" Kim said as she handed me a glass. I turned and looked at her and lifted my glass to toast. "As ready as I'll ever be." I took a small sip of the mimosa she'd made. "Anya, I know you might be a little nervous, but I still think you made the right choice. No matter how you feel right now, you've got to start looking at the bigger picture. It's not always about how you feel at the very moment you are experiencing an emotion. It's about what God wants for your life. You must love Michael though because if you didn't, I don't seriously think you would be doing this, at least I hope you wouldn't. You guys have such chemistry when you're together, and I see how your face lights up when you talk about him, not the material things he does for you, but him." She was right. I did love Michael, and deep down I probably knew all along I was doing the right thing, but it was just that small ounce of doubt that said what if. What if I wasn't?

After the almost two-hour ride, we arrived in New York. I felt rich as we pulled up to the Waldorf in our limo. What am I saying? I was practically rich already, but it was a trip, because it was so hard to grasp. The bellman rushed out to the car and began unloading. The doorman opened the door and said good afternoon as we walked in heading for the front desk. He was kind of cute too. Good thing I was about to get married. I flirted with him just a little when I smiled and spoke, but not a for-real let's get it on later flirt, just a friendly flirt you know.

"Did you forget why you are here? You are getting married, right?" Traci pulled me by my arm through the door.

"Sorry, Traci. Everyone can't be as perfect as you."

"Don't worry, Anya. Leave that one to me." Kim said smiling as we gave each other a high-five.

"Ha ha nothing, did you forget Vic will be here Friday?"

"No, Traci, I haven't forgotten, but that's Friday and today is Wednesday. I don't see a problem, do you?" She waited for a response but my sister just shook her head in disgust. "Y'all the two about to get married, not me," Kim called out to Traci, but Traci just ignored her and forged on to the front desk extremely irritated with us both.

"Ooh I'm scared. Girl, you are so bad." I put my arm around her shoulder, and we both bent over laughing while making our way to the desk as well. Traci was trying to act like she didn't know us. Traci knew good and well Kim wasn't going to do nothing with that little college boy no more than I was. Although, it did bring back some memories.

We checked in, and although we all had separate suites, I knew Kim and Traci were going to spend the night in mine that night. They would probably stay in theirs the next day and for sure Friday when Vic and Kevin came. The bellman brought our stuff to our designated rooms, and we agreed to meet back in my room after we put our stuff away and got situated, so we could go eat. I watched as the bellman hung my gown along the wall. "So you're getting married? Congratulations." I thanked him and tipped him. "Let me know if there is anything else I can do for you. Good luck." He turned and walked out, closing the door behind him.

The fact of the matter is I was going to need more than luck. Why did people always say good luck? Where did that saying come from? What they really should be saying is don't forget to put in hard work and pray a lot or your marriage is doomed. Or how about, don't forget you're married and when you're married, you shouldn't cheat, or even marriage is a commitment and you can't just run out and get a new one when you don't like the way this one is going. I guess that would be too much like right.

Friday morning, we got up to get massages and get our nails done. While we were getting our nails done, my phone rang. I looked down. It was Julian. I tossed the phone to Traci. "Answer it. It's Julian." But she wouldn't. She just looked sternly at me.

"I'm not getting in the middle of that mess."

"Just tell him I can't get the phone because I'm getting my nails done."

"No," she said calmly and turned the other way.

The phone continued to ring until Kim jumped up. "I'll answer it. Give it here. Hello . . . Oh, what's up Julian? How are you? She's right here, but she's getting her nails done." She looked over at me and whispered, "He wants me to put the phone to your ear."

I nodded okay.

"Hello," I said nervously.

"You really gon' do this, huh?"

"Yes, Julian, I am."

"So y'all getting married in The Big Apple, huh? I saw it on the news last night. Why people think that fool getting married is news, I still don't know. Anyway, it ain't too late. You know you don't have to marry him."

"Yes, Julian, I do. It's not even that I have to. I want to."

"Man, whatever, you can save that for someone who don't know what's up." He hung up.

"You know you gon' need to cut all that after tomorrow. Shoot to be honest, it should have been cut by now. See, you be playin' but you gone learn eventually." I couldn't stand my sister. She was right though. She acted as if I didn't already know I had to cut Julian completely off. I didn't need her adding her dollar in. I sat back in my chair and took my Palm out and start playing Solitaire until we were done.

I had spoken to Michael since he had gotten to New York, but I hadn't actually seen him, so when we got to the church on Friday for the rehearsal, I was pleasantly surprised. He was so delicious, and he was all mine. Saturday couldn't come soon enough. I was getting all worked up just thinking about it. When he saw me come in, he stopped mid-sentence, ran over, grabbed me and picked me up. He hugged me for what seemed like a short eternity.

"Oh, it's good to see you. I missed you so much." We couldn't get a good kiss in because we were in church, so we just gave each other a little peck.

The rehearsal went well. I guess it helped that I only had four bridesmaids, or should I say three bridesmaids and Traci, my maid of honor. I was hoping that Kim wasn't too upset that Traci was my maid of honor. Even though Kim was my best friend, Traci was my best friend and my sister. Michael just had Mathew, who he said has been his best friend forever and their friend Jason who was one of their frat brothers from college and then his two cousins, Mark and Anthony. The ceremony was to be fairly simple, so I wasn't really worried about anything going wrong. Besides Mary, the coordinator had bossed everyone around enough that if they messed up, she was sure to pull out a gun and simply shoot them. The only thing that scared me was the fact that Michael wanted us to recite our own vows, which meant I needed to come up with something meaningful and loving, something to make people cry and say awww that was beautiful. The only problem was it was the night before the wedding and I still hadn't thought of anything. I thought I was just going to freestyle, I mean, I am a romantic person, so maybe it should be spontaneously from the heart and not premeditated and rehearsed from the head. At that point it really didn't matter because since I hadn't thought of anything that's how it was going to be.

We had rehearsal early so that we could go to dinner early and not be tired the next morning. At dinner, I could not even believe Kim, flirting with Jason, not that there was anything wrong with him, but she was acting as if Vic wasn't even there. I mean he probably didn't notice it, but I knew her well enough to know that's what she was doing. Jason was a cute little high-profile attorney in LA, but I mean he was white and since when was Kim attracted to white men? She knew she needed to cut it out, laughing that fake laugh at his corny jokes and trying to act all interested in what he was saying. She was trippin'. Vic was the best thing that had happened to that girl, and he put up with a lot of her crap and true enough he wasn't a lawyer, but he was in med school with only another year to go, so she'd better quit trippin'. Besides, he was good to her, and even though he was a medical student, he was just enough thug for her. I thought it might be time for a friend intervention when I got back. That girl was going to have to stop drinking. Maybe it was time we all did.

"Well, gentlemen," I said, standing, "I think we better call it a night. As you can see, some of us need to get back to the hotel." Traci agreed. Even she couldn't believe Kim was acting like that. We had never seen her throw herself at a man like that before. She never had to. They were usually busy enough trying to get on her. I hope Victor wasn't upset, and I surely hoped he wasn't embarrassed. He knew it was just the alcohol. I didn't know why she had been drinking so much lately anyway.

I tossed and turned all night. Even the Tylenol PM didn't help. I kept trying to sleep so I wouldn't look tired, but I couldn't. I kept running through the wedding in my mind over and over, and I kept seeing Julian's face. I wondered if he would ever forgive me. I wondered if I should even be caring. How could I cut all ties with him without seeming like a real butt hole? Well before I knew it, the telephone was ringing with my wake-up call at the other end. Too bad I was already awake. The room-darkening drapes had fooled me into believing it was still night. Oh no, I thought, *where did the night go, and can somebody please bring it back? I'm not ready to get up.* But I had to. I rolled out of bed and went into the bathroom to run some water. I stayed in the tub about twenty-five minutes trying to wake my already woke self up. It was already nine-thirty, and I new Tamera would be there at eleven to do my hair, but it was cool because there was nothing else I had to do that morning. Everything was already done.

It wasn't long before there were knocks at the door making sure I was up, as if the phone call wasn't sufficient. Suddenly I began to realize this was the day. It wasn't just words anymore, it was time to put the words in action. When Traci and Kim got there, we weren't running around frantic like you see in the movies. We were actually quite calm. We ordered breakfast, and when it came, we sat down and ate, and before long, there was another knock. Tamera was right on time. I looked over at the clock, which read 10:53 A.M. She came in with her hooded dryer and duffle bag full of curling irons, sprays, scissors . . . you name it and it was sure to be found in that bag. She shampooed my hair in the sink of the kitchenette portion of the suite. You know 'cause we can be ghetto like that should we need to be. I did hate to see that dryer come through the door though. I did not want to sit under no dang gone dryer, but I have to say I don't think she really cared. She had already seen my headpiece and my dress, and she said she knew exactly how she was going to do my hair. She never asked for any feedback. She just went to work, but I wasn't worried. I trusted her, and when she was done, I was pleased as usual.

The photographer came by the room because I wanted him to take pictures of us getting ready, so for the most part everyone got dressed in my room. I was really debating whether I was going to put my dress on at the hotel or if I was just going to wait and slide into it at the church. The church won. I didn't want to have any wrinkles from sitting down, so I did everything else that needed to be done except put on my dress. I had Tamera put my headpiece on before she left, and I put on my pearl earrings and my pearl necklace as well as my eyelashes and my make-up. I decided to wait and put on my lipstick at the church. I threw on a sweat suit and some flip flops, and I was ready. We carried my dress down, and I had my shoes still in the box in a duffle bag. This was it. I looked at my girls, especially my sister, and they looked good. They were working their dresses. They were fitted and Lavender, with one deep split up the left leg, and a plunging neckline held up by two-inch wide straps that criss-crossed in the back. We found the perfect lavender rhinestone earrings with matching necklaces to compliment them. Oh, they were sexy.

The photographer took several more shots of the girls in the lobby before we piled into the limo. The church was only about twenty minutes away, so that wasn't too bad, however, you know New York traffic. When we finally did arrive at the church, we went in through the back. I had planned on getting there no later than one-thirty because the wedding was suppose to start at two but that really means two-thirty because my grandmother said you were suppose to get married when the big hand was moving upward on the clock, never down. I didn't know why, but she said it so I adhered to her direction. Arriving at one-thirty, well that portion didn't quite go as planned because we didn't get there until a little after two, which was still okay because all I had to put on was the dress, shoes and lipstick.

Well, Here We Go

Now here we are today, with me locked in this dressing room and my sister trying to talk me out. I couldn't though. I couldn't face anyone at that point. I just wanted everyone to go away. I wanted this day to never have happened. What was I suppose to do? I could hear Michael making an announcement through the walls. He still wanted people to go over to the reception and help him eat all that food he had paid for. I heard him attempt to laugh but I could hear the embarrassment and disappointment in his voice. His voice wasn't shaky though. In fact it was quite loud and clear, but that's probably from all the acting. I guess he's use to the show going on in spite of whatever turmoil arises behind the scenes. How sad was that? I don't know what happened. Maybe he wasn't as strong as I thought. There was a brief silence, then I heard Matt, the best man, take over and basically say the same thing Michael had said. I guess people would go over to the reception, if for no other reason than the fact that they felt sorry for Michael. Plus, they were probably hungry, and on top of all that, ninety-eight percent of the people had come from out of town, so what else did they have planned? Not that there isn't a lot to do in New York on a Saturday night, but it's too chaotic when you haven't planned anything.

I sat there, no, actually, to be quite honest, I laid there on the floor staring up at the ceiling. I allowed my eyes to trace the crack that I found there, and I wondered if the owner knew it was there. I mean I didn't notice it until I was down there on the floor looking, actually staring up at it and I'm pretty confident the pastor didn't come in here on a regular maintenance check and lay on the floor and stare at the ceiling to check for cracks. Even if they did come in and get down on the floor like to pray for instance, this being a church and all, they would be facing down not up. But this is just my logic. My thoughts were interrupted by Traci tapping on the door again, which may have been a good thing because I don't know where I was going with all this.

"Anya, you can't stay in there forever." Maybe she was right, but let's just see how close to forever I could get. "It's going to be okay." How could she say that? It was not going to be okay, it was never going to be okay again. I was almost certain Michael would pretty much want to end the relationship, you know with me leaving him at the altar and all. The only problem is that I don't think I want him to break up with me. I think I really do want to be with him, and I think I might just want him to forgive me. The longer I sat on that floor, the more I saw me with him, and it dawned on me after an hour or so that I really did love him. I didn't just love him. I was in love with him. My heart began to beat as if it were going to blow right through my chest, and at that moment, I panicked. I panicked because I had lost something so great in a matter of moments. I had made a huge mistake, allowing Julian to get me off focus like that, allowing me to be distracted long enough to doubt what deep inside I already knew. Why is it that we can never see what we have until we almost lose it? Why can't we ever be content when it's there? I should have left Julian alone a long time ago. I knew I was wrong, but I thought there was a chance. A chance that I may have been missing out on what God really meant for me to have. I think I may have simply been in love with the thought of Julian loving me as much as he did, which was unfair to him too. However, after that little stunt today I was sure I didn't want to be loved that much. Not only did he make a fool out of himself. He made a fool out of me, and I in turn made a fool of Michael. It was a never-ending cycle.

I pulled myself up into the chair next to me, and I crossed my arms over my lap and leaned my head down on my arms. I was sick to my stomach, sick of myself. I took a deep breath, got up and walked over to the mirror. I wiped my face slowly, trying to figure out how God could even love me at this point, let alone Michael, but I knew that he did, God that is. I was just hoping Michael did too. I looked for my bag to try and salvage the look I had earlier in the day, but there was no use. My eyes were puffy as pillows and my nose was red and swollen from all the wiping. My eyelids and lashes were full of tissue particles, not to mention they were lifting and the glue had turned white from my tears. To put it simply, I was a mess, but that's when God works best. I felt an assurance that everything was going to be okay. The numbness I had been carrying around all week had even lifted, and I was no longer dazed nor was I confused. I knew exactly what I wanted, and it was Michael, and I wasn't just going to tuck my tail between my legs and run off and hide somewhere. Maybe it was too late. Maybe he wouldn't want to have anything to do with me, but maybe he would and that's the maybe I held on to.

I raced to the door and opened it, only to find Traci still sitting there on the floor in her dress, playing with the straps on her shoes. I thought she might have been gone because she hadn't said anything in over thirty minutes and that was a miracle for her. "'Bout time." She put her hand on the floor to balance herself as she stood. "Now you should know by now, I could always wait you out. Every since we were little." I was actually pretty happy to see her still there when I opened that door. I grabbed her and hugged her. "I'm so stupid, Traci. I know I messed up." She backed up and looked at me, not sure exactly which part I thought was a mess-up.

"Let me just clarify so that we're on the same page. Do you mean you messed up by letting Julian leave or do you mean you messed up like you let Michael, the best thing that has ever happened to you, go?"

I smiled a little. My face was too weak to give a full one. "The latter of the two. Do you think we can fix it?" I was so scared.

"Only one way to find out. Let's go." I was shaking as she grabbed my hand.

"Where we going?"

"Well for starters," she said reaching over and peeling one of my eyelashes off and dangling it in front of me, "we're going to get you fixed up." She pulled me into the dressing room and start going through my makeup bag. "Then" she paused and looked over at me, "Then we're going to get your man back." She said it very matter of fact, with not an ounce of doubt in her voice, and that gave me a shudder of confidence that surged through my body.

We fixed me up as she said, removing my tear-drenched, paper-filled eyelashes and cleaning my face. I couldn't go through all that again, so I just put on a little lip liner and some lip glass and my mole. We took all the stuff out of the room and put it into the trunk of the limo. To tell you the truth, I really wanted to take that dress off, but I thought I better leave it on, just in case it may have a little influence on Michael's decision. I was desperate and needed all the help I could get. After we piled everything into the limo, we were off. My stomach felt nervous the closer we got to the hotel. I had the driver stop at a flower stand so I could get some red and yellow roses. I explained to Traci how Michael had sent me those roses when we first met and what they meant. "Oh, 'cause I was going to say, you are really trippin', stopping a limo and getting out in a wedding gown to buy flowers from a stand on the corner of a New York City street, thinking that was going to get you your man back." She laughed.

"What if he's gone?"

"The last time I talked to Kim, he was still there walking around socializing, being consoled, you know."

I felt so bad. I really didn't think I could do this. What if he clowned me and just let me have it? I guess I was suppose to just suck it up after what I had done to him, but that wasn't me. I only wanted to act on sure things when my pride was at jeopardy.

Too late now, I thought as we turned onto Park Avenue and stopped. It took forever to get there, but we got there too fast. I wasn't ready, and I began to panic. *I can do this. I can do this,* I continued to repeat to myself. Even as the driver came around and opened the door, *I can do this* proceeded from my lips. Traci had the trunk unloaded and the things sent to her room. I stood on the sidewalk for about ten minutes before getting the nerve to go in. I was certain the staff knew what was going on by then so I tried to look as if nothing was wrong as I walked past the front desk to go to the elevators. I counted the floors on the way up to the eighteenth, which was where the ballroom was where the reception was being held. I could hear the music coming from the room, I took a nervous peek inside. I couldn't do it. I leaned against the wall and literally gasped for air. I don't think I've ever had a real panic attack until that moment. I could not get enough air to fill my lungs. I waited for Traci to come up to get her cell phone. I called Mathew and asked him to come meet me in the hall but he didn't answer. He probably couldn't hear it over the music. Why didn't he have it on vibrate like normal people. I was now going to have to send Traci in to get him.

"Anya, quit trippin' and go in."

"No, Traci." I pulled away. "Just please go in and get Matt for me. I need to talk to him first."

"Girl, you ain't worth the money I paid for you. When we get back to Philly, I'm going to get my receipt and get my money back, the whole ten cents I paid for your butt." She laughed, and I know she was just trying to loosen me up, but I was so focused on Michael and if he would forgive me, I didn't even get it at first.

She went in and after about oh an eternity she came back with Matt. "Over here," I whispered. I was standing behind a plant so no one would see me if they came out. "Yo, Anya man, what's up?"

"I needed you to come outside so I could talk to you." I looked at him. "Do you think he'll talk to me?"

"I don't know, Anya. I mean it's hard to call. He's pretty upset, not to mention hurt, embarrassed, and I could go on, but what would be the point? Besides, what could you really say now when you couldn't even say the one word that mattered just a couple of hours ago?"

Okay, he didn't know me like that.

"Alright, Matt, dang. Just help me okay?"

"Help you what? You're probably just here because you feel bad. He has enough sympathy in there with all the people he's still going to have to face in the future and try not to remember this day."

"Look I feel bad enough, but you have to trust me, Matt. I love him, and if it's not too late, I want to see if I can fix this mess I made."

"I don't really see how I can help with that. That's something you have to do on your own."

If he would just shut up and let me talk, maybe he could see how he could help. Lord! "All I need you to do is get him to hear me out if he tries to walk away when I come in. Can you at least do that for me, Matt? Please?"

He put his finger to his temple as if he were deep in thought. Why was he trying to torture me? Then finally he agreed. He began to mumble as he walked away. "I don't know why I'm doing this. I like you and all, Anya, but Mike is like a brother to me, and you're wrong." But I knew all this. I didn't need to hear it again. I really just wanted to say," Boy, if you don't get in there and do what I said . . . , but I couldn't. I was at his mercy for the moment.

Traci had called Pastor Blake's room while we were in the car and explained the situation, and I asked him if he would come up to the reception just in case Michael would be gracious enough to take me back. I was hoping he was already in there, but maybe I was getting a little ahead of myself. I still had to go win the man's heart back.

I mustered up all the strength I had left and walked in the reception, not like a punk, I walked with confidence ready to apologize to everyone, but most of all Michael. I could hear people whispering as I passed the first three tables on my way to the front, and I hated it. I didn't let it deter me though. I was on a mission, so I tuned them out and kept going. Shoot, if anything I should be the one talking about them, sitting up there eating, drinking and being merry when I just broke the heart of the man I loved. Now what kind of mess is that? They up there whispering about me. Any excuse for free food and a party I guess.

I walked over to the DJ booth and asked him for the microphone. I looked around for Michael's face, but I couldn't find it in the midst of all the turned-up noses and crossed eyes that were burning holes in my stomach. I had butterflies when I first got to the front, but I no longer felt them. I think they were dead from the same beams that burned the holes in my stomach. For a moment I wished I could hear what the people were saying, but I guess it really didn't matter. Why should I even care? It was extremely embarrassing, but I guess no more embarrassing than what Michael must have felt when I left him standing at that altar.

I cleared my throat and looked back at the bridal table, which was behind me. Kim mouthed to me, "What are you doing?" I began to speak, and I felt my mouth move, but no words came out, nothing but a faint cracked sound. I attempted to clear my throat again, this time loudly into the microphone. I had gone over what I was going to say many times in my mind on the ride over, so why couldn't I get the words to come out? Standing there didn't seem like such a good idea. This was not the way I had planned it in my head, and I was getting frustrated. I began to break out in a nervous sweat, and there was still no sign of Michael.

"Umm." I cleared my throat one last time. "First of all I would like to apologize to everyone here for inviting you to a wedding and then running out. How rude is that, right?"

Okay I guess this was not the time for humor. The room was at a quiet standstill, I swear you could probably hear me breathing. How stupid did I sound? Where were the carefully planned words from my head? This is exactly why you shouldn't plan things. They never turn out like the pretty picture you set up in your mind, never. "Okay, this is kind of hard, but I came over here because I messed up. I walked out on a man who has done nothing but love me from the beginning." Just then I saw Matt and Michael walking from the bar over in the back corner. When I saw him, I felt relieved. I smiled at him as the tears left my eyes and made their way down my face where they dangled until they dropped onto my dress.

"Michael." I said, taking an enormous deep breath, "I am so sorry. I was scared. I know that's no excuse, and I know you were probably scared, too, and I'm glad you didn't run out on me like I did you." I paused as I gripped the microphone tighter. "I had been numb all day and the only thing I could think about was if I was doing the right thing marrying you. Then when Julian burst in there like a crazy man, the fear became even greater, and I allowed it to overwhelm me. I couldn't think, and when I saw him, all these emotions began running through me. You know?" I paused again and wiped my face with the napkin Matt walked over and handed me. That assured me that he was on my side and that I was doing the right thing. "I thought things like maybe this is a sign that I was suppose to be with Julian. After all, who really breaks up a wedding for real? I had loved Julian since I was too little to remember and Lord knows I just didn't want to make the same mistake twice. *Wasn't one wrong man enough?* I said to myself while standing on that altar. But while I was laid out on that floor in the dressing room at the church, I missed you already. I missed your smile. I thought about your laugh. I thought about how I hurt you, and I began to ache all over. At that moment, I realized I had made a mistake, only this time instead of marrying the wrong man, I was letting the right man get away. I realized how much I love you. Everything about you, even that goofy dance you do when you get good news." I took another deep breath. My eyes were so full of tears I couldn't even see anymore. Everything was a big blur. "More than anything, I love the way you love me."

He just stood there staring at me. He didn't even seem to be fazed by anything I was saying. What could I say to get through to him, to make him believe me? My voice began to tremble a tremble of defeat. "I love getting lost in your kisses. I love the way your hugs warm me inside. I love the confidence in your voice when you assure me." I looked over at Traci, who was crying just as much as I was. Michael was really going to make me work for this, but I wasn't mad, who would blame him? This was becoming pure torture. "Michael, I can't imagine my life without you in it. I would be lying if I stood here and said I didn't have feelings for Julian, but I'm not choosing to spend the rest of my life with him. I want to spend the rest of my life with you and only you. Sometimes the heart can be very deceptive, and emotions are just that, emotions, which can be controlled. People always say you can't choose who you fall in love with, you can't control your heart, but I found out today, that you can choose. Michael, you can."

My voice began cracking as the lump in my throat made it hard for me to swallow. My heart was pounding, and I could feel it in my ears. I walked over to him. "I choose to be in love with you. I know it may take some time for you to forgive me, or even trust that what I'm telling you is real. That doesn't matter to me though. All that matters is when it's all said and done you choose me too. Whatever it takes, I'll do it to make you understand that you are the most important thing in my life." I stood there and waited for him to say something, anything so I could breathe, and though I waited, he failed to say anything. He stood there motionless.

Was it was really over? "DJ can you play something for me?" I walked over and asked him to play Jesse Powell's "You." Hold on," I said. "Traci, can you go get those things for me? They're outside in the hall on the small table against the wall." She walked out and returned a few minutes later. "Okay, DJ you can start it." As it played, I walked over to Michael and handed him the roses. "Yellow is for friendship and red is for love. I have loved becoming your friend, too, but I'm ready to become your wife, if you'll still have me."

I was trying not to cry again but I couldn't help it. I had never wanted anything more than this moment to pass and for him to say okay. I was scared that it was too late. Had I blown it for good? I continued to plead with my eyes for him to forgive me, to still want to love me. I was sure he still loved me. You can't just stop loving someone in a matter of hours just because they mess up. The true question was did he still want to love me. Then after what seemed like an eternity, the silence broke.

"You know what this means, right?" I shook my head no.

I didn't trust my voice to speak. He threw the roses down and grabbed me. He held on to me so tight I could have lost consciousness. "We're gonna live happily ever after." I let out an enormous sigh of relief, one that seemed to have been pent up inside of me all my life. I was so overjoyed that I felt weak. My legs almost gave out from under me when I heard those words. I smiled through my tears, and even though it had registered in my head, my body was still shaking.

"I wonder if we can get the pastor up here to marry us now. I'm not taking any chances." He laughed, but he was probably serious.

"Already a step ahead of you. I called him in the car and asked him to come up."

"I'm already here." He stood up. "And nothing would make me happier than to make this union official." He was pleased. I guess after all those counseling sessions if he didn't think we were ready, he would have never agreed to marry us in the first place. It's funny now. It all seems to be such a no brainer.

"How'd you know I would forgive you?" Michael smiled and swayed me back and forth in his arms. I just looked up at him. "Now you've been in enough movies to know that in the end, true love always conquers all." That smile came from deep in the depths of my heart. "No, I'm just kidding. I wasn't sure, but I was hoping for the best, and I wanted to be prepared. I wasn't going to take the chance of you coming to your senses later and deciding you don't forgive me after all." He laughed. "You're laughing, but I'm serious." And I was, very serious.

"Girl you are crazy. I just hope I know what I'm getting myself into."

Traci came over and hugged us both, for a really long time. I could tell she was glad I had woke up before it was too late, and she was even more glad that Michael loved me enough to see past my flaws. He was the bomb though, and this just proved it even more.

We quieted everyone down. My girls lined up on the left and Michael's men lined up on the right, and we stood right in the middle facing the pastor and thought we'd try this one last and final time. This was it, no more weddings, just love and babies. It was then I decided to move to California with him. How could I not after today's malfunction? Maybe I could just do some work here and there, or maybe even teach an interior design concepts class at one of the local colleges until we decided to start a family. I think I was finally ready to be a wife and a mom, and this was the first time I had a real desire to think about something other than my little world and how everything affected me.

"Let's pick up where we left off." Pastor Blake looked over at me so I could say my vows.

"Well, what can I say? I think I've said it all. One thing I do want to say though is that I love you, Michael, and I am going to spend my days with you trying to keep your days with me unbelievably happy. You are the best thing that has ever come into my life. I feel so blessed to be a part of your life and that's why I have decided to move to California with you. I don't want to live two separate lives. I don't think that's the way God intended for it to be. I think, no, as a matter of fact I know I need to be by your side and allow you to be the head of our house and trust your decisions are what's best for us."

"Amen," Pastor Blake said.

I leaned over and kissed Michael briefly and told him how much I loved him.

"See, it's not even time for that part yet." I could have just slapped Kim ruining my romantic moment.

The pastor then asked for the rings, which we exchanged, and he asked us to repeat after him. As we repeated after him, the words became more and more alive in my heart, and I made a vow to myself that I would do everything in my power to keep this union the continuous unbroken, endless circle that the rings represented.

"I now pronounce you husband and wife. Michael, you may kiss your bride." And that's exactly what he did. You would have thought this was the Super Bowl the way everyone was cheering and crying and carrying on, but it wasn't. It was just the first of many new good choices I hoped to make as my life moved forward.

"Let me please present to you Mr. and Mrs. Michael Harrison," Pastor exploded, and the cheers continued. It was a madhouse, and it was great.

Since everyone had already eaten, we went through the wedding rituals. We had our first dance, which was the best part to me. I felt so secure floating across the floor with Michael. The beauty of the ballroom made it so fairytale. The two-story windows dressed in silk that overlooked Park Avenue and the view from up there was gorgeous. I stared up at the twenty-four-foot ceiling and imagined being Cinderella for three seconds, then I realized I was trippin', and

I closed my eyes and thanked God for being Mrs. Michael Harrison, which was even better.

We tossed the bouquet and the garter and watched all the single women make their usual mad dash for the bouquet. I don't care how prim and proper they were when they got there, the bridal bouquet brought out the single woman's beast at every wedding. Then men of course are always cool about theirs and most of them aren't trying to catch the garter. What a difference a gender makes.

We, of course, cut the beautiful eight-tier cake. It was a little much but I went for it anyway. Two of the tiers had fountains that were flowing with a very faint light purple water. That was the closet they could get to lavender, but that was okay, I was just thankful for the way things turned out. I told Michael if he smashed that cake in my face he would be a dead man. Guess I'd have to kill him later, but he could do no wrong in my eyes that night. As we sliced into the cake and held it up to feed each other, I took a tiny bite and allowed the rest to be smushed into my mouth and cheeks. It wasn't so bad, but I didn't smash his into his face. I lovingly fed him and kissed him and sneakily rubbed my cake face all over his.

I was so glad the photographer and videographer were still there, but why wouldn't they be at Michael Harrison's wedding? They'd already been paid in full. Unless you were there no one would believe this day without proof anyway. I mean really, what are the odds of this happening in real life?

As things began to die down and the people began to leave, me and my girls and Michael and his guys and of course Vic and Kevin and a few of Michael's close friends sat around a few tables talking and laughing, and I felt great, exhausted, but great. Matt and them were crackin' on Michael about being left at the altar. I guess they really were close because I think this was just a little soon to be cappin' about that. It didn't seem to bother him though. He took it all in stride and laughed. They talked about some of their college days, and then of course everyone in the bridal party began swapping embarrassing stories about Mike and me, and that was our cue to go.

The place was just about empty when Mike gave me the, you know what time it is look, and I truly did know exactly what time it was. I had been looking forward to it for months. We were now in full compliance with the biblical laws. It was on.

"Did you just forgive me so you could get some tonight?" I leaned over and whispered.

"You know it." He smiled. I elbowed him in a playful way as we stood to bid our farewells.

Since we were leaving everyone decided to call it a night except two of Michael's old college buddies who were there. They and their girlfriends were going to hit a few clubs after all, the New York night life was a callin'.

"Traci, did you give the DJ his envelope?" I knew she had, but I wanted to make sure. He was the only person we didn't pay in full up front. We all walked out together heading for the elevators with bottles of champagne to set the night off in our rooms.

As we were walking out, Michael had his arm around my shoulder, and I had my arm around his waist. We were loud but we were trying to be quiet, as quiet as you can be when you just get married. This was a time for a celebration. The laughter filled the hall, and as we got closer to the elevator we seemed to get louder. I don't think I've ever been happier. I don't know why things turn out the way they do, but they do and that's why you have to enjoy life to the fullest, which is exactly what we were doing. We were singing, "Mr. Telephone Man" for some odd reason. We were jamming, too, dancing and everything, that is those of us who could dance. I thought I heard a voice call my name, but over the noise, I thought I was trippin'. I heard it again. It was soft and calm. "Anya." I quickly turned and looked in the direction it was coming from. It was Julian. He stepped from the wall he had been standing on the side of. "I've been waiting for you." Something looked different about him. I didn't know what it was, but it wasn't right. It didn't scare me. It just didn't feel right. Before I could respond Kevin stepped out from the group and began to walk over to him. Everyone else was quiet. I think they were in shock to see him show up again. I know I was. "Look, Julian man . . ." Kevin began to approach him, but it was too late. Before anyone, including me, knew what was happening, I saw the gun as Julian lifted his hand from the side of his leg, but I couldn't believe that he was actually standing there with a gun. Was he going to shoot Michael or himself? I really didn't get a chance to think it through. He was not playing. He wasted no time. He lifted his hand and pointed it at me and pulled the trigger. How could he shoot me? It happened so fast, I couldn't move, I couldn't run, I couldn't even scream. I don't even remember if I heard the shot. I think I was still living in the shock of him standing there with a gun period. Kevin lunged for his arm, causing him to fall and the second shot to hit the wall. I didn't feel anything until I looked down as my white fabric became saturated with my own maroon dye. I watched the stain on my dress become larger and larger before falling to the floor. It didn't hit me that he had shot me for a few seconds, but that few seconds was completely in slow motion.

I watched as Kevin and Vic got Julian under control and Matt got the gun away from him, but not before it went off one last time, shattering a vase sitting on the table, causing the water to drip onto the floor. I guess if Kevin hadn't jumped on him that would have been another bullet for me. I looked over and watched the water drip from the table. Wow, this man really shot me.

I heard Michael calling my name as he kneeled beside me and held my hand. I could see his lips moving, but I could hardly hear him. He sounded so faint, so distant. I began to feel my stomach burn, and I could hardly breathe. I don't know if I couldn't breathe because of the bullet in my chest or because I was panicking. My sister was calling 911 from her phone, and I could see the panic in everyone's face except Julian's. There was no panic there. I lay on that floor and watched his eyes. The same eyes that had promised me happiness stared at me and filled with tears.

"I love you. I always have, and I always will." He could hardly get the words out with Kevin's knee in his back. I couldn't hear him, but I understood. The tears were glassy over his eyeballs. Kevin turned him over and punched Julian in the mouth. He screamed at him, "Man, don't you ever say that again. You don't love her." He stood and I watched him kick Julian in the stomach as he lay there on the floor, and my heart fell.

"You just shot my little sister." He kicked him again. I couldn't let him do that. I wanted to help Julian, but I couldn't. "No, Kevin, stop," I tried to tell him, but my breaths were getting shorter and shorter. "Shhhh. Stop, Anya." Michael tried to calm me down. I guess so I wouldn't die, but I couldn't watch Kevin beat Julian like that. With every blow, my heart felt fainter and fainter, and I was helpless. There was nothing I could do to make this go away. I think the emotional pain my heart felt was worse than the pain caused by the bullet in my chest. My mind yelled "stop," but my lungs didn't have enough air to vocalize my feelings. So I lay there and cried as I watched Kevin beat the crap out of Julian.

I was so glad to see the elevator doors open with security. The two men quickly grabbed Kevin and pinned him to the wall. "No," my sister said, as she pointed down at Julian. "That man just shot my sister. My fiancé was just trying to stop him. Please, we need an ambulance now." He was more than trying to stop him. Did he deserve it? I don't know, but in some twisted way, I felt like this was my fault, but it didn't give him the right to shoot me. It doesn't work that way and it's not fair, that he thought it did, on what was suppose to be one of the happiest days of my life.

I watched as security cuffed Julian and frisked him, then pulled him up from the floor. He limped a little, but I guess if Kevin's big football-playing butt kicked me twice in the stomach, I'd be limping too.

"Hang in there sweetheart," Michael said to me, but I couldn't. I tried to take short breaths. I thought I could save the air if I did that, but that made my chest hurt. I was scared, there was no doubt about it. Not scared to die, just scared not to live out the rest of my life, but maybe God didn't intend for me to. That was obvious as I lay there bleeding to death. All I could see was Julian's face. He never took his eyes off my face, and it made my heart ache.

The elevator doors opened again, and there was a paramedic crew with a stretcher. They asked everyone to give them room to work and give me some air, but Michael wouldn't let my hand go. I could feel him there, but I was no longer there. How is that? I couldn't feel anything. I closed my eyes and I prayed and asked God to not let me die, to give me another chance. I was going in and out of consciousness and the paramedics slowly put me on the stretcher, but I felt like I floated up there. I know everything was probably moving at a hectic pace, but not to me. Everything was blurred and motionless. Things seemed to move in frames, flashing from one picture to the next.

I opened my eyes as my head was going into the elevator I glanced over at Julian struggling to get to me, but the police were restraining him.
"I love you, Anya. I love you."

Michael rested his face next to mine. "Please, Anya. Please don't give up on me." That was all I remember. The next frame was in the ambulance. "Michael?" I was calling him in my mind but I couldn't speak. I wanted him to know how much I loved him. I cried on the inside because I couldn't talk to him. This was probably going to be the last time I saw him, and I couldn't tell him that I loved him and that I was sorry and I hated that. I wanted to live just long enough to say it one last time. I felt bad that my last words were spent trying to tell Kevin to stop beating the crap out of Julian instead of turning to Michael and telling him I loved him. My eyes were full of tears for the words that I wanted so badly to express.

The sound of the ambulance siren became faint, or maybe I was just so out of it that I was becoming immune to the sound. I didn't feel as if anything was wrong, other than the fact that I was lying in an ambulance being rushed to the hospital due to a gunshot wound from my ex-boyfriend. But there was in fact something wrong, even though I felt no different.

"Do something!" Michael's voice instantly became loud and clear, and I could see him even though my eyes were still closed. In an instant all my pain was gone. "We're losing her," one of the paramedics said. But I wasn't lost, I was right there with them. I felt light and carefree, and Michael and the others began to quickly fade. There was nothing but blankness about me. I was standing in bleakness, but I wasn't afraid, I just stood there, and I was at peace, but I didn't know why I was there or where I was for that matter, and I didn't know how I'd gotten there. I don't know how long I was there in the midst of nothing but I was violently snatched away. My body felt jolted, as if a surge of power were infiltrating it and I felt like I was choking. I gasped for air, and there I was, staring up into faces I didn't know with bright lights blinding me.

"We got her. Call upstairs and let 'em know we're coming up." Where are we coming to? I wondered, still unable to speak. My body would not even react. I tried to sit up, but I felt like lead. There was nothing I could do but pray. I asked God to not let this be it for me. I still had so much life to live, and it was just the beginning. I didn't want to make a plea bargain with God for my life so I simply asked him to just spare me, in spite of all my mistakes and in spite of me being who I was. I felt the urgency in the air as we rushed through the hall into the elevator. As the doors opened, we continued our urgent life-threatening journey to the OR. It seemed pretty dark to be an operating room. Don't they need a lot of light? I saw a man coming toward me with a needle as he lifted the IV cord, and his smile was the last thing I remembered, and I said to myself, *this is probably it, unless God gives me a for-real miracle.* Did I deserve to die? I don't know, I just know I wasn't ready and that's all I know. I tried to think of Michael, but I couldn't keep my eyes opened as my lids fell like weights, and I was gone.

My life was playing over and over like a running picture while they operated. I knew I wasn't dead though, just in some kind of twilight sleep. I felt a hand on mine and I couldn't open my eyes, but I knew it was Michael's. I lay there and tried not to fight my body, but I was anxious to open my eyes, and I don't know how long the Lord made me lay there, because it felt like an eternity, but he eventually allowed me to open my eyes, and when I did, I saw the top of Michael's head. I could faintly hear him praying, and I squeezed his hand. He looked up in amazement. "Hey." He leaned over and kissed my cheek, his eyes filled with tears and happiness. "Well, one thing I can say, life with you won't be boring." He smiled. I wanted to smile, but I couldn't. I was in so much pain. My chest felt like someone was stepping on it, and my left side ached but I couldn't understand it because I was clearly high on something, something that wasn't doing the trick.

"I am so sorry," I attempted to whisper.
"Shhhh. Just be still and relax," Michael said. But I couldn't. I needed him to know how sorry I was about everything that had happened the day before

but I just didn't have the strength or the energy to fight him to listen to me. He stood and walked over to the curtains and opened them. The sun flooded the room. "You see that out there?" He looked over at me. "That's our future. I don't want to talk about yesterday because yesterday is gone. All that matters is today, right now, and I am so glad that you are alive that nothing else matters to me. Okay?" I nodded slowly. He came back over, sat on the edge of the bed and leaned over me. I thought he was going to kiss me, but he didn't. He just hovered there looking me in my eyes.

The nurse entered the room. "I see our little patient is awake. That's good news. How you feelin', honey?"
"Like crap." I smiled.
"Yeah," she said. "Figures." We both gave a little chuckle. She was cool.

When the doctor came in later that day, he explained that I had lost a lot of blood, but that they were able to remove the bullet that was lodged on my lungs. That explained the chest pains, I guess. He said they were not exactly sure how long they would keep me because there was some extensive tissue damage and I had some internal bleeding, which was probably from the body trauma but they wanted to monitor that to make sure they had gotten it completely under control when they closed me up.

I'm still trippin' that fool shot me.

After two weeks of that hospital smell, I was finally let out of hospital prison, and I was glad. I still had to take it easy, but at least I could take it easy out of New York and in my own home. I recovered fairly quickly and soon it was time to face the hassle of moving to California. The funny thing is, I was so looking forward to it. Of course we didn't go on our honeymoon then, because we had all the time in the world.

Happy Ending

Happy ending? Depends on who you ask. Kevin and Traci are doing well. She had just had a little girl, thanks to modern technology. They didn't waste anytime after the I do's last August. I went to stay with her for two weeks right after she had little Jade. She was so pretty. Kim's crazy butt sold her flower shop and opened a lingerie shop out here on Sunset. She's still my best friend, but we don't hang like we use to because moving here seemed to make her even wilder than she was, but I know eventually she'll come around and settle back into reality and realize that she is not twenty-one anymore. Her shop is doing well though. She's sellin' those overpriced thongs all day long.

As for Julian the love of my past life is still in prison serving a ten-year sentence for attempted murder. He probably would have gotten longer, but I refused to testify against him. Instead I forgave him. I couldn't go through the rest of my life with hatred and bitterness eating me alive. I remember before I moved, I would get so many letters from him trying to apologize, and I don't know how sorry you can be about intentionally shooting someone, but it wasn't for me to understand. I did, however, have to understand my role in how it all played out and accept partial responsibility for it, even though I didn't want to. He'll be eligible for parole in six years, and I will more than likely go to the hearing on his behalf because I don't want him wasting his life in prison when he can get out and hopefully move on.

I cried a lot at first when I would read his letters because in the back of my mind I felt like it really was my fault, but eventually I realized that it was a decision he made. I wrote one letter to him out of the hundreds he sent me, and it was simply to tell him that I forgave him and that I was sorry for my dishonesty. I also told him that he needed to forgive himself because if he didn't he would never be able to move forward. I told him that I would always love him, but just not the way he needed me to and to please let go so that I could move forward too. I asked him to stop writing and explained that this was the only letter he would get from me, and at first that didn't deter him, he still wrote, but I had to stop reading the letters so I wouldn't get sucked back in. I kept them in a box with the ones I had read as well as the ones I hadn't, and when I moved to Michael's I took them with me.

So as I sit here one year later by the pool in my big beautiful backyard wondering what type of mom I'll be when this little bundle I've been carrying around for almost four months finally arrives, I think to myself how God can turn things around for you even when you have messed up big time. I'm watching Michael showing off for me doing laps, and I know it's time to officially close the Julian chapter in my life, after all, why am I still holding on? The next day, I got the box out with all Julian's letters, which also contained the fake tennis bracelet and some pictures of us. I walked down the long hall and get into Michael's BMW and headed for the beach, you know, being dramatic and all. I planned on tossing the box into the ocean. However, when I got there, that seemed pretty stupid especially with all those people at the beach. So I sat in the car and figured I could just drop them off in the nearest dumpster or I could even go home and toss them into the fireplace.

I couldn't do it though. I could not get rid of my box full of my and Julian's memories. How sick was that? I stopped at the post office on the way back to the house and bought some paper and tape. I wrapped the box up and mailed it to Traci. I dropped a little note in to ask her to please get rid of these memories. As I stood at the counter paying to move forward, I felt sick, but it was too late, I had already handed over the hold on me, and now the clerk was waiting for me to pay him for taking this great burden of me, so I did. I handed over ten dollars and eighty-one cents to move forward. Pretty cheap compared to therapy at seventy-five bucks an hour and no progress.

I wanted to keep that box so bad, but I knew it was for the best, and that's what helped me to really begin to close that chapter of my life so that I could be completely dedicated to Michael and commit to the new life that the Lord had given us. So yes, I can say for the first time in my life, I am happy with the person I am.

So I will leave you with one piece of advice. Be careful, ladies, with these men's hearts. You never know who your Julian may be. Always be honest and upfront. Never settle for less than you really deserve but above all, love yourself enough to be happy and know that it is more than okay to be happy. Make sure you take time to find out what makes you happy before you involve someone else's feelings.

Printed in the United States
97277LV00005B/22-42/A

9 781425 785949